Summers

an FFSG novel

Bill Dughaille

Contents

Week One

Tuesday: Happy as Larry

Detective Sergeant Frank Summers was a happy man.

Once, as a ten-year-old schoolboy, he had been required to fill in a questionnaire, one of the questions being "What do you want to be when you grow up?". His answer had been "Happy". His careers advisor thought that Frank had misunderstood the question. Frank had assumed the same about the careers advisor.

He had never forgotten that day. It had been the day he had mislaid his newly-acquired pet frog, known as Phrog. Fortunately the screams of the careers advisor had alerted him to the frog's whereabouts. His effusive thanks to the careers advisor for locating Phrog, he remembered, had not, for some peculiar reason, been well received. Fortunately for the careers advisor Frank Summers had not then encountered the Greek philosophers, otherwise he might have had to suffer a philosophical dissertation on the benefits of a holistic approach to life including the acceptance of creatures such as Phrog.

But now, years later, Phrogless but imbued with the teachings of Epicurus, in an unusual moment when it seemed that he had achieved a unique combination of little work and the prospect of much play, he felt he had reached that fortunate state of contentment, not far off the hands-in-pockets-sauntering-down-the-road-while-whistling stage of his own personal nirvana. He might even be tempted to jump in puddles if he wasn't wearing his best, brightest, most highly polished shoes.

1

In his new posting to the genteel town of Wellbury, a place the steamroller of progress had overlooked, of tree-lined avenues and brightly filled window-boxes, basking quietly in its summer warmth and peaceful radiance, where even the criminals tended to take bank holidays off, he had met his salubrious ideal. He felt he had found his niche in life. In previous postings in some of the less salubrious parts of London, especially when still in uniform, he had been spat at, shot at, hit over the head with wooden stakes and other objects of less yielding material, had rocks and bottles thrown at him, been threatened with broken glasses and infected hypodermic needles and generally treated as someone whose presence was less than welcome — and, as he used to say, somewhere around the third pint, that was not only from his Chief Inspector, some members of the public were nearly as bad.

He felt, even though it did not appear so in the mirror, that he had more bumps on his head than the most enthusiastic phrenologist could cope with. He had a parallel scar on his inside left arm and the side of his left chest where a bullet had passed through, ruining his best jacket and not even earning him a single day's sick leave.

Wellbury was different, totally different. Wellburians had a powerfully ingrained belief in a sense of British politeness and good manners. There was a right way to do things and a wrong way to do things.

At least here they would say "Terribly sorry about this, old chap" before starting.

Frank Summers had developed a very positive philosophy of life. It was not a Panglossian "all's for the good in this best of all possible worlds". Rather he believed that, sooner or later, there would be another banana skin that he would not spot in time, and he was in no hurry to reach it.

It is also, unfortunately, a cosmic law that even banana skins come to those who wait.

These meanderings were the ones he made public. There were other, personal, reasons for which he was grateful for his posting to the quaint town. Reasons which would explain why he had developed his philosophy of this vale of tears. But also reasons which would forever remain solidly locked in the past. The past was not only a foreign country, he had no wish to learn their language nor apply for a visa.

Besides, you could never trust the drinking water. And the beer was bloody expensive.

No, this was a new start in his kind of town. He had made a firm decision. This time he was going to take no chances. Keep your head down and don't give superior officers any reason to question your hard work.

Oh, and make sure that the girl you're taking out on a first date isn't the Chief Constable's daughter before doing a highly amusing and comic impression of him. That sort of important detail training school had missed out, much the pity

That had been then.

Now, smartly suited, loudly coloured tie firmly in position, he was strolling down a sunlit corridor towards the pathology lab, located in the Old University. Why it was called the Old University no-one knew, since it was still a university, however small, and there was no New University. But that was probably the norm for Wellbury. His own police station, a solid and rather imposing Victorian structure, was located in an area known as the Old Town. There was, of course, no New Town, and the Old Town remained the centre of any social and commercial activity.

Wellbury even had its own Old Roman Ruins, so called just in case anyone might suspect them of being some gadfly, interloping Modern Roman Ruins, perhaps created after Emperor Honorius had decided that the cost of timeshare in the island had exceeded the benefit of the mild weather and had taken his legions and left.

Frank rather suspected that anything that might have the appellation "new" applied to it would not be welcome to the staid citizens of the area. He himself might take several years to be accepted by the local populace, but he was more than content to wait. It would be worth the wait.

He was humming a tune to himself as he walked along the corridor, a tune he thought came from the album Bat out of Hell, but was more like a cross between the 1812 Overture and Pink Floyd on speed, leaving any music fan he passed feeling completely disoriented.

Frank Summers had a passion for music. Whether that was reciprocated by music itself was another question. Frank, however, wasn't the type of person to ask music's permission before committing humming.

The reason for his early-morning cheerfulness was easily explained; Detective Inspector Frieda Garold – Frigid Frieda to the ranks – had yesterday given him until the following Monday morning to solve the "Dead Skeleton" case. Today, Tuesday, was the second day, and he had already done so. A small, metal, somewhat corroded but still legible identity disc had lain with the skeleton, a disk he had been given at what could be called the crime scene, before the pathologist and he felt he still had a few years of freedom before that happy event took place.

Doctor Susan Pleadle was sitting at her desk when he walked into her office. He gave her the full benefit of his twinkling eyes and charming little-boy grin and sat down nonchalantly.

'I'm feeling clairvoyant today,' he said happily.

'Oh? How so?' Her mouth turned up slightly as if amused by him. Most women had the same reaction. In her case he was not sure that she found him amusing company or just an amusement.

'I have this feeling, this intuition, that our skeleton is that of a nineteen year-old, named, strangely enough, Alfie Simmons, officially Alfred Reginald George Simmons.'

'Really? Do tell.'

He leaned forward conspiratorially.

'Just between us, he was a gunner on a Lancaster in 1945. The plane blew up short of its airfield. But keep it under your hat.'

'Otherwise your Inspector Frieda might give you some real work to do?'

He winked at her.

'Precisely. How do you fancy dinner sometime – over the weekend? Maybe a movie? If you're not otherwise engaged.'

Whoops, he thought, that had slipped out.

Damn.

'I'd love to, but I don't think you'll be able to make it.'

He smiled easily at the first rejection – there was always a first rejection. Most of the time it was the final one too, but these things are part of life.

Then his mind rewound and found out what she had said.

'What do you mean I won't be able to make it?'

She handed a file over. He flipped it open and read the first page quickly. And then groaned. The skeleton was that of a man in his late thirties or early forties. War might be hell, but it couldn't have aged Alfie Simmons that quickly.

Blast the Internet, he thought. The site he had found the information on had looked like a semi-official old-boys' organisation. It was probably something set up by a great-nephew with more interest in design than facts. No doubt when the Ministry of Defence received his letter asking them to confirm Alfie Simmons' date of demise they would think him incompetent.

Which he wasn't.

Well, not all the time.

Only when he actually tried to do some work, which is why he tended to hide from it as far as possible. Unfortunately it usually found him, despite his best efforts.

'Are you – '

He was about to ask if she were sure. One look at her face suggested it would be unwise. Frigid Frieda might be superb at sarcasm, Dr Susan Pleadle was lethal with a look. The one cut like a rapier, the other dissolved with death rays.

What exactly would happen if you stood between them while inspiring their respective ires was a scientific conundrum.

'So tell me why you thought it was a nineteen year-old,' she asked.

He explained about the identity disk, admitting his guilt, hoping she would forgive his boyish trick. She gave him a pitying smile.

'Poor Sergeant Summers, it rather looks like you are going to have a busy week.'

'Busy isn't the word. The press are going to town, the Chief Constable is insisting on results, The Inspector is giving me deadlines and demands for updates, and now I haven't a clue where to start. How do you trace the man behind a skeleton that's been buried for years?'

'About forty years in fact. I thought that's what police detectives were supposed to do.'

'No, we tend to prefer our crimes a little more fresh than that.' He looked back at the file. 'But he was definitely murdered, then?'

'Bullet hole in the back of the skull. Either he was murdered or it was an extremely acrobatic suicide, almost impossibly so. Oh, and he would have to have buried himself afterwards. So, yes, I would probably go out on a limb and suggest that it was unlawful killing. Unless ...'

'Unless?'

'Unless he was already dead when he was murdered. If you see what I mean.'

Frank rubbed his chin wearily. He had been night-duty officer the previous week up until Sunday morning, and everything had gone wrong. Frieda had had Words with him. He had played a silent part in that exercise. His earlier jauntiness this morning hid the fact that he still hadn't adjusted to daytime work.

For some strange reason Frigid expected the station to be clean and tidy first thing in the morning. Not an easy task if you spend most of the night playing office cricket with the night uniform constables.

'I don't suppose you have any good news for me? Distinctive features? An old tattoo? Multiple fractures which could be identified by medical records on the Internet?'

'You could try reading all of my report,' she suggested. 'However, today, Sergeant Summers, is your lucky day. You may know that my father was a dentist before he retired?'

'And it just so happens that he kept his clients' records? And this man's teeth are there?' he suggested, slightly sarcastically.

She smiled.

'Got it in one – almost. Not the skeleton's actual teeth, of course, but his records. My father collected all sorts of dental paraphernalia and records over the years. It's an obsession of his. He has this idea that one day he'll write the definitive dental history work. He spent the whole weekend sifting through the boxes in the lock-up garage he stores them in. Mum wasn't too pleased – that's an understatement, by the way, he brought a lot of the junk home, into the lounge, and it wasn't exactly in pristine condition – filthy might be a better word – but he found the right one in the end.'

Only in Wellbury could this happen, thought Frank.

But he was impressed with Dr Pleadle's devotion to duty.

He just hoped it wasn't catching.

'So at least we can put a name to the dead skeleton?' he asked.

'Indeed. Remember what you were saying about being clairvoyant?'

He looked at her. In his experience women only tended to repeat a man's words when the man had been wrong. He had yet to come across a woman who said something of the ilk,

"Yes, you were right you know, when you said Arsenal were going to win that game on penalties."

'Yes, okay, okay, I admit it,' he said. 'I wasn't being clairvoyant. So what is our skeleton's name?'

She paused before replying, another bad omen.

'Alfred Reginald George Simmons.'

Frank looked at her and said nothing.

'I think you might leave that identity disk with me, Sergeant, where it should have been in the first place,' she said, holding out her hand and smiling sweetly in the manner of someone thinking of the possible uses of scalpels. 'It's what we civilians like to think of as evidence. Those amongst us who believe in a professional approach to our work. Oh, and, if you ever, ever, even think of appropriating anything from one of my cases again, you will find yourself with a shortfall in the account of your testicular components. Understood?'

Not even the oldest, most weather-beaten, grizzled, veteran Sergeant with a homicidal look in his eyes and a raft of four-letter words to his tongue had made Frank understand something so quickly.

* * *

'Let me get this straight,' Frieda Garold said, sitting at her desk while Frank stared morosely out of the window, looking at the slowly fading light of the summer's day, and the inevitability of the cancellation of a dinner date.

'Mr Alfred Simmons disappears in 1945 when his bomber is blown up. Sometime in the mid-Sixties – during or after 1964, since he had a filling replaced in the summer of that year – he is murdered close to where the remains of the bomber were found. A week ago his skeleton is unexpectedly unearthed by

11

someone building a patio. That's the story as we know it, yes?'

'Presuming it's the same man, and it looks that way, yes,' Frank replied. He had been about to point out that the website had no doubt been incorrect, but a thought occurred to him, brightening his future prospects. With the media interest, and such an unusual case, topped off by the personal interest of the Chief Constable, it was bound to be handed over to a team headed by someone of higher rank. By the time the MOD announced that Alfie Simmons was not lost in an air accident it would be out of his hands. Then he could go back to giving talks on security to bored housewives and investigating nasty cases of graffiti. At least that meant he could leave the station on time each evening.

The thought improved his mood immeasurably. He was feeling much better.

There was one graffiti artist whose works he rather admired. He looked forward to nicking him and finding out exactly how he managed to make strange whirls which brought tears of confusion to the eyes.

'So what's our next move?' asked Frieda.

Next move? Frank thought quickly.

'Um, registry offices are an option.'

'Registry offices? In case our Alfie Simmons got married after his disappearance during the war – under his own name?'

'It's a long shot, but there might be something.'

And it's the only shot I could think of on the spur of the moment, he thought to himself.

'Go around to Doctor Pleadle's father's house,' Frieda said. 'Check out those dental records. See if he remembers anything. You should be able to fit that in this evening.' She rose, indicating that the meeting was over.

'Monday morning, Sergeant Summers, I want it concluded by next Monday morning. We have too much current work to waste time on something that happened forty years ago.'

He was about to make a grateful and gracious escape when she added:

'By the way, how's that flasher case going?'

The "flasher case" concerned the reports of one Miss Ingrid Hunley who had reported a man exposing himself at her kitchen window, something Frank guessed was more wish-fulfilment than reality.

'I'm working on it,' he said, meaning "I'm ignoring it as best I can."

He had paid one visit to Miss Hunley. She had turned out to be an attractive woman of about forty who reeked of gin. By the time they had reached her kitchen she had already undone two buttons on her blouse. He had managed to escape before anything came off. He had no urge to revisit her abode. And next time, if there had to be a next time, he would take a woman police officer with him.

'Don't spend too much time on it, Sergeant Summers. I get the impression that it's mostly her imagination.'

'Right, will do.'

Phew, he thought.

An idea occurred to him, and he smiled to himself. If, for some not unlikely reason, he should find himself driving Frigid somewhere, they would accidentally find themselves close to Miss Hunley's house. It would only be natural to pop in for a few minutes. Frigid could have Miss Hunley for breakfast. There would be no more calls about flashers.

The thought appealed to him. It showed that he had not lost that sense of self-preservation he was so proud of.

Before he left the station he made the phone call to Linda the Librarian, letting her know he could not make their date. She seemed unconcerned. The sound of a man's voice in the background suggested that the date would have been broken off anyway.

Unless she had the television on. And a man on the television was having a conversation with a woman on the telephone.

His romantic life was definitely not having a good week. But he resisted the thought that it could only get better. He knew very well from experience that, just when you thought things couldn't get worse, they did.

To his delight Susan was at her parents' house when he called. To his dismay her father seemed to think dental records were like holiday snaps to be shown to any and all visitors. The three of them sat at the dining-room table while Mr Pleadle enthused over long-discarded methods of tooth treatment. Mrs Pleadle sat in the lounge with the television volume turned up. High.

Listening to the sounds of the Eastenders' theme tune coming crashing into the dining room, Frank rather doubted whether she would now view with favour any romantic designs he might have on her daughter. For some reason she blamed the mess not on Susan, who had made the original request, but her husband and this young policeman.

It made a change. Normally it was the father giving him strange looks, and the mother wittering on about everything and nothing.

'I don't suppose you remember anything about this Alfie Simmons,' Frank asked desperately during a rare pause for breath Mr Pleadle made during meanderings about a particularly interesting molar. Susan gave him an enigmatic smile which suggested she was enjoying his discomfort enormously.

'My goodness, no. 1964? Those were the swinging Sixties young man. I was still single, only met Susan's mother in '69. Hardly likely to remember a client whom I saw – let me see, three times. Here we are, a filling, an extraction, and another filling. Not bad teeth for the times, you know. Of course in those days – '

'But you have an address?'

'An address. Of course. But client confidentiality, I don't know ...' Mr Pleadle frowned at the thought. 'Don't you need a search warrant or something like that?'

'Mr Pleadle, it was almost forty years ago. Client confidentiality only has a thirty year limit. For civilians, that is. Twenty years for serving military personnel.'

That was a complete invention. For all he knew there was no limit. Client confidentiality might well extend until the final judgement day and beyond. But there was a time and place for such things, and this wasn't either.

And by the final judgement day he would have been able to come up with an excuse for his actions. He had spent so much time and sweat in learning the art of making excuses to women, making excuses to the Archangel Gabriel or whoever would be waiting for him would be like an exercise for beginners.

'Well, I don't know, but if you say so ...' Mr Pleadle passed a dusty old folder over to Frank. Frank opened it and his eyebrows raised.

'It says here that he was a lorry driver.'

'Ah, yes, some old notes of mine. I was hoping to come up with a research paper concerning the different dental problems people face and how their occupation and status affected those problems. It could have been a major advance in those times, you know.' He sighed. 'Never came to anything in the end, I'm afraid.'

'You don't mind if I borrow this folder?'

'So long as you return it, my boy. I might still do that paper one day. And it's essential for my history book. You know I'm writing a – '

'Yes, yes,' Frank said hastily, standing up. 'Susan told me you're working very hard on it. So I mustn't take up any more of your valuable time.'

'Oh, and if you find Mr Simmons' relatives, could you tell them he still owes me a shilling and sixpence?' Mr Pleadle said, looking up at him.

A small twitch at the corner of his mouth told Frank that Mr Pleadle had Made a Joke. Frank gave a weak grin, made his thanks and then a quick exit. Susan escorted him to the front gate. It was now definitely night. The only socialising he would be doing in the hours remaining would be to go to the pub and discuss football with the landlord.

'So who did you have to disappoint tonight?' Susan asked as she closed the white picket gate between them.

'Disappoint?'

'Which breathless beauty were you due to escort to the delights of dinner – and possibly a movie if she's worth it?'

She was holding on to the gate, almost swinging on it. In her dainty summer frock she looked more like a schoolgirl rather than a thirty-year old doctor. He found the image disorienting.

'What makes you think I had to break a date tonight?'

'Disappointment Dan, that's your name around the police station, I hear. Or is that for some more intimate reason?'

He blushed, and was grateful that the streetlight did not reveal it.

'Anyway, I was thinking I might take you up on your offer,' she continued.

'Offer?'

'Dinner over the weekend. Have you forgotten so soon?'

'Dinner? Of course not. It's just that you said – '

'I said that you might not be able to make it. But if I say yes I am not going to be one of your disappointees. You will turn up.'

She looked at him.

'I organise myself into three compartments, Frank. Professional, social and personal. Only one person is ever going to share all three, and that will be a very, very special person. Understand?'

'Absolutely. I – '

'Sunday. You will pick me up on Sunday at six pm sharp. Okay?'

'Absolutely. Wild horses – '

'Six pm sharp, you can leave the wild horses at home,' she said, and skipped back towards her parents' front door. Frank watched her go, and then turned towards his parked car. He began whistling, a mixture of Beethoven and the Moody Blues. For some reason he felt like a very, very special person indeed.

As he reached his car he jumped and clicked his heels à la Chaplin mode.

He could do that so long as he didn't think about how he did it. If he stopped to think he invariably fell over.

Alfie Simmons, he thought, you will just have to be sorted by Sunday. Six. PM. Sharp. Okay?

If only he had relied on experience instead of hope he might have realised that things would turn the shape of a pear very, very soon. The philosophy of a cornucopia of hope included the fruits of Eden, and, by definition, things the shape of pears.

And bananas.

Had he been of the persuasion that sees shapes in clouds he might have looked up at a cloud scudding past the moon at that moment. It resembled, it could be argued, a grinning skull.

Alfie Simmons was not going to be sorted by Sunday at all.

Wednesday: Do you remember when …

'The house Simmons lived in was pulled down in the Eighties,' he reported to Frieda in her office the following lunchtime. 'It's now a new suburb, rows of red-brick terrace. Quite attractive architecture, from what I saw of them.'

'I shall note your approval of the architecture,' Frieda replied. 'However, it means we're no further forward, then?'

He liked that about Frieda. She almost always said "we", hardly ever "you" or "I". Say what they might, and sark as she would, Frieda Garold was very much a team player. She was also quite attractive, in a stern sort of way. Power-dressed in navy-blue jacket, silk blouse, navy-blue pencil-skirt. Raven hair, deep dark eyes with a hint of the Latin in them, lips that …

He hastily put that thought to the back of his mind. His last inspector had been an ageing, twenty-stone, coarse-mouthed brute. The word "inspector" still had those connotations for him. To combine that and "attractive" in the same thought made him feel ill. Images crossed over in his mind, ending with a twenty-stone unshaven brute wearing a navy-blue pencil-skirt.

'Not quite,' he said quickly, trying to suppress the image. 'The registry records have come through. Alfie Simmons did get married. In 1948. To one Gwendolyn Dunne.'

'Married? A neat trick when you're dead. Allegedly dead. What about records? Wouldn't someone have noticed that the man walking up the aisle was blown to smithereens three years before? You know that bit where they ask whether anyone knows any impediment to the lawful marriage etc. Being dead might fall under that heading.'

'Not necessarily. They don't normally ask for a death certificate when you get married. Not even in those days. And I'm not too au fait with wedding protocol, but I haven't heard any minister asking "Are you, or have you ever been, dead?".'

She gave him a look which indicated that he should work on his laughter lines.

She leaned back slightly in her chair, put a thoughtful hand to her cheek and regarded him carefully. He could just see, underneath her Inspector's desk, the leg she had crossed over the other. Beneath a navy blue pencil-skirt a slim calf swathed in nylon ended in a sharply pointed, shining black shoe with several inches of stiletto heel. He tried to keep his glance on her face. They were very nice legs.

Her face was pretty attractive too, if you discounted the stern look.

Her cool dark eyes returned a dispassionate energy.

He wished she wouldn't wear that red lipstick.

He wondered what it was called.

'Do we know for certain that this man – this skeleton – is that of the young Alfie Simmons of 1945? And the one who was married in 1948?' she asked.

'No, but all the wedding details match – date of birth, place of birth. Same middle names.'

'But it could be a case of identity theft. It was easy enough in those days.'

Frank resisted the urge to compliment her on her memory.

'It's possible. Someone could have adopted Simmons' identity sometime in the late Forties or even during the Fifties, without realising that he was dead – or even because they knew he was dead.'

'Okay. Say for argument's sake this is the real Alfie Simmons. Why – and how – did he disappear after his plane blew up? Accepting for the moment that his plane did blow up.'

Frank shrugged. He hated theorising at the best of times, and this was not the best of cases to do so. His preference was for hard facts, but, having seen what some humans can do to rock-hewn, steel-barred, concrete-cased facts he had early on realised how quickly they could dissolve in the oil of obfuscation and intrigue. Soft facts, on the other hand, never failed to convince.

He was beginning to regret not saying, after Susan's explanation, that he thought the website had been wrong. He hadn't bothered because it wasn't going to be his for long. At his previous station the case would have been assigned to someone more experienced in about three minutes.

No, not quite right.

At his previous station they wouldn't have given it to him in the first place.

'I don't know. Presumably he survived the explosion – let's say he was blown clear, and his parachute opened somehow, or he was still conscious and opened it himself – well, then, he lands safely, and ... I don't know. Amnesia? Decided to leave the air-force while he had a good excuse? Who knows?'

'And somehow retains his own name?'

She drummed her fingers on the navy-blue pencil-shirt just covering her knee. Below the desk Frank could sense the stockinged-calf and deadly shoe swinging slightly, backwards and forwards.

'So, what's our next move?'

It was like a fixed routine. "What's our next move" was the unignorable signal that the meeting was almost over, and it was time for him to be earning his salary.

'I'll check up on Mrs Alfie Simmons,' he said. 'See if she's still alive, if not, whether they had kids. Try to trace anyone who might have known him.'

'Good thinking. Just one thing, Frank.'

'Yes?'

'If you find her, don't let her know he was murdered. Not yet. Just in case she was the one who did it.'

'Right.'

'Good,' Frieda said, standing up. 'Update at six this evening.'

Frank almost sighed as he left the office. The date with widow Wendy would have to be postponed.

Didn't Frieda have a social life to go back to after work? A husband and family to organise? Kiddies to take care of? Dishes to wash? Navy-blue pencil-skirts to press? Various domestic staff and appliances to regiment?

Almost undoubtedly. She would have planned them, one husband, two children, supper at seven, children to be in bed at nine. Probably did a stock-take of them once a month to check everyone was in place and in order. Sex twice a week, Tuesdays and Thursdays at twenty-two-hundred hours, sleep at twenty-two-hundred-oh-five.

And a dishwasher.

* * *

'You're a bit late, aren't you?'

Frank hardly knew what to say. Mrs Alfie Simmons was very much alive and kicking, and despite being in her mid-seventies looked ready to kick something out of someone, the police preferably, and Frank was the nearest representative of that rabble. She lived in a small bungalow in the Grovelands, a suburb at the bottom of University Heights. It spoke of a dear little old lady enjoying the comfort of old age and looking after a small and well-kept garden, pottering amongst the petunias and pansies. Quite possibly that was what she normally looked like, until he had appeared on the scene asking about her husband.

'Alfie went missing in 1964,' continued the woman, standing in her kitchen. She had been about to make a cup of tea for the nice young Detective Sergeant sitting at the kitchen table when her husband's name had come up.'

'You lazy buggers did nothing about it. I remember one of you suggesting that Alfie had left me for another woman – that wasn't you, was it?'

'What wasn't me?'

'The one who thought that Alfie had been chasing some skirt.'

'Hardly, Mrs Simmons. I wasn't even born then.'

Her suspicious look lightened somewhat.

'I suppose you have a point there.' She turned to the kettle which had just boiled. 'Still, I suppose you young buggers are just as useless as the old lot.'

'Not quite, Mrs Simmons. We have computers these days. It means we can make mistakes twice as fast.'

The old woman laughed and put a cup in front of him. She sat down and regarded him out of shrewd eyes.

'So, why are you here then? The old man hasn't turned up

after all these years? Finally got tossed out of the pub after ignoring last orders for forty years or so?'

There was a softness behind the banter. Frank knew instinctively that Alfie and his wife had had a happy marriage. It must have taken her some years to get over his disappearance. Re-opening the wound was unlikely to be pleasant.

And he could hardly ask her to pop down to the lab to identify the skeleton. Recognise that skull, do we, Mrs Simmons? Any memories of the metacarpal? That tibia tell you something? You know, when he got his leg over, did you ... Perhaps not.

'There's not a lot I can tell you, I'm afraid. Just a very old case has come up for review, and your husband – or rather, a man with the name Alfie Simmons – is mentioned. It might well not even be your husband. There are quite a few people with the same name in the telephone directory alone.'

'Oh, aye?'

He was trying hard not to look at the copy of the local paper sitting on the table. Her eyes locked on his as her thin arm stretched slowly towards the paper, and then flipped the headline into view.

"Police Stumped In Dead Skeleton Mystery"

Police are pathetic, it might as well have said.

'Wouldn't be anything to do with that, by any chance, would it?'

'Why on earth would you think that, Mrs Simmons?' he asked, giving her his very best disarming smile. It worked about as well as it would have on an unexploded bomb. A not very happy unexploded bomb.

'Don't try to kid me, sonny. I'm old enough to be your grandmother. I've seen more of life than you ever will. And I can recognise when someone is trying to hide something from me.'

In that case, could you take over my job for me? thought Frank.

He raised a hand in surrender.

'Okay, Mrs Simmons, I'll tell you the truth. I was hoping not to upset you – ' A snort from a woman unlikely to have much left to upset her. 'There is a small chance, a very small chance, that the skeleton may be that of your husband. Unfortunately we have very little to go on.'

'What's the very little?'

He had retrieved the identity disk from Susan's office for this interview. Without her permission, though to be fair she hadn't been there to give it. He could only pray he would manage to return it without her knowing, and without him losing something of his own quite close to him. He took it from his pocket and handed it over. She looked at it carefully, rubbing it tenderly. There were tears in her eyes.

'Alfie, oh, Alfie,' she said softly.

He stayed silent as she sat there, looking down at the corroded little piece of metal. Finally she looked up, her face hard, trying to compose herself.

'It's Alfie's. Or was. He always used to wear it, even in bed. I liked playing with it afterwards.'

Now that's a little too much information, Frank thought.

She handed it back.

'I suppose you'll need it for your investigation.'

'Yes, I'm afraid so.'

'Can I have it back after you've done with it?'

'Of course, Mrs Simmons.'

She blew her nose on a delicate handkerchief.

'So what happened? How did he die? Fell into a ditch on the way back from the pub, I suppose.'

Not quite. Not unless helped there with a bullet, and then buried afterwards.

'I'm afraid we don't know, after all this time there's very little evidence to go on,' he lied fluently.

Apart from not welcoming the thought of having to tell her that her husband had been murdered, as Frieda had noted there was also the possibility that she was the one who had done the murdering. A sergeant told him in his rookie days that, once people had killed the first time, the second was so much easier. Especially if it was an unarmed policeman like himself. And there were some vicious-looking knives in that kitchen.

'Mrs Simmons, can you remember anything from the time your husband went missing?' he asked.

'I remember it as if it were yesterday,' she said with some feeling. 'Summer of '64, it was. Little Alfie – my son – he was, let me see, sixteen? And Edith, my daughter, she was fourteen going on fifty. You know, that age. Teenagers, only we didn't call them that in those days. Little Alfie was into motorbikes, wanted to become a mechanic, always pieces of engine dirtying the house out. So between them I had me hands full. Alf, my old man, he was always coming and going – he was a lorry driver, you know, he often did long trips, was away for days at a time, weeks sometimes. Course, nothing like the monsters you see on the road these days, but it took a strong man to drive a truck in them days, none of the electrics and pneumatics or whatever it is they have now.'

Frank was beginning to think he was in danger of being subjected to a sermon on the Sixties. Any minute now the Beatles would be back.

'But the day he disappeared,' she continued, 'or rather the night he didn't come home – he wasn't supposed to be back at work until the Monday. A Friday, it was. He'd got back that morning from somewhere, France I think, and he went out in the evening to the pub, the George it was then, before they pulled everything down. He promised he'd be back early, but you know what men are like.'

Frank decided it diplomatic not to agree or disagree with what men might be like.

'Anyway, around ten I go to bed, thinking if he gets back drunk and wants some he ain't getting any. He can sleep on the couch. But then he'd probably do that anyway, he was a very kind and gentle man in his way – and he was still knackered from a week of driving. Wasn't unusual for him to get back late and sleep in the lounge so as not to disturb me.'

She looked at the table in front of her with unseeing eyes. The furniture, Frank had noticed, was relatively modern, certainly nothing to hint of the garish Sixties. Almost as if she had, at some point, decided to invent a new home.

'Sorry,' she said, shaking her head, 'got a bit lost in me memories there. Anyway, not much more to tell. In the morning I wake up, go down the kitchen for a cup of tea, he's not there. Didn't worry about it at first, thought he must have stayed at a mates', hadn't done that before, but there's always a first time. Had to get breakfast for the kids anyway, loads of little things to do. It was only later, around lunchtime that I began to get worried. Phoned his mate Jack, he said Alf had left the pub at eight the evening before. So I phoned the police, they said not to worry love, he'll turn up sooner or later. Not in the cells. Not in the hospital. Just vanished. And he never turned up again.'

She used the handkerchief to dab at her eyes. Frank guessed at her emotions at the time. She must have wondered if her Alf had gone off with someone else. But he would have been back for his clothes and things, lorry drivers didn't earn enough in those days just to abandon everything – did they?.

So, what had happened to him? And when had she written him out of her life? Shortly afterwards, because she knew precisely what had happened to him, or some years later, when the chances of him turning up on the front step had gone for good?

'It must have been a tough time for you, Mrs Simmons, with two children,' he suggested softly.

'Aye, it were tough. But inside, not out. We didn't have a lot of money, but Alf had saved a little bit, and Little Alfie was already an apprentice, so he was bringing home a bob or two. We started working young in those days, not like now. And with Edith old enough to look after herself at home I could go out and work. Did quite well, really, opened the shop within two years, made a nice little profit.'

"The shop", Frank guessed, meant her own shop. A new undertaking presumably.

She was, he could see, extremely proud of her entrepreneurial success. No wilting flower this, succumbing to sadness after her husband's desertion, but a powerful woman determined to prove she could be a success on her own. Except that her husband hadn't deserted her.

And now he was back.

In a different way, though.

A lot thinner, for a start.

'What sort of shop?' he asked conversationally.

'A boutique,' she replied, and once again the self-pride came through. 'It was the Sixties, I was thirty-four, still had a good figure, good enough to pretend that I was young enough to be "with it", as they said in those days. Course, it was all tat – kitsch, as they call it nowadays, I think, something like that. No intelligent person would have bought the junk we sold, but youngsters will fall for anything. Still do, if you look at the junk they sell these days – same junk, different fashion.'

She nodded at Frank's gaudy tie.

'If we'd sold men's stuff it would have been that sort of stuff. Cheap, loud and nasty.'

Frank looked down at the offending item with surprise.

'Cheap?' he asked. 'This is pure silk.'

'Saw you coming, I reckon. Still, shows you're an honest man. No crook would ever wear that sort of thing. Not unless they were so crooked they ended up looking straight in the end.'

Frank smoothed down his tie and decided to abandon any sartorial defence.

'Did you have dealings with any crooks, Mrs Simmons? With running the shop? Almost every time I read about the Sixties the Kray twins seem to be everywhere, demanding protection money.'

29

'Nah, you don't want to believe anything you read, son. Firstly the Krays was London, East London, not here. Most we had was minor stuff, pilfering, shop lifting, wide boys trying to flog you something a mate of theirs had lifted from the factory they worked in. Funny thing is, some of our customers would pay extra if they thought they were buying something nicked. Made them feel – well, what's that phrase they use these days? Street credit?'

'Street cred. So what you're saying is, good girls wanting to look bad?'

'About the size of it. Never went through the war. Never knew rationing. Needed something to identify with, I reckon. You would have thought me accent would have put them off – I was a working class girl, after all. But not in them days. We were all classless, young and free and easy. Trouble was, I picked up some of their ways of talking, so my words sometimes go all over the place.'

Frank had noticed. Normally he could identify someone's class background, but her speech certainly did go all over the place and even took holidays in foreign parts. If he closed his eyes he could imagine a young women talking in Sixties' speak. Interrupted by various others.

'Made a pretty penny,' she continued, 'but I knew it weren't going to last. Edith came in with me. I taught her how to run the shop as a business. So when it became obvious that the Sixties were over we just shifted to the new fashion. Punk, Goth, Vandals, could hardly keep up some of the time. But Edith and me could smell which way things were going, she from her friends, me – well, I read a lot of magazines, if you knew what you were about you could tell what was going to sell.'

Why is she telling me this, Frank wondered. A warm memory of how she had beaten the odds? Or a diversion from 1964? Or did she just not want to remember that time?

Ever owned a revolver Mrs Simmons?

Perhaps not the question to ask at the moment.

'What about your parents, Mrs Simmons? Or Alfie's parents?'

'What about them?'

'Well, I was thinking as a source of support. When your husband went missing.'

And also as possible suspects, thought Frank.

'Oh, I see. Well, my parents were old, even then. They married late in life. As for Alfie's parents, they died in the Blitz, in London. He was all alone in the world, no brothers or sisters. He hardly ever spoke about it. But he never felt sorry for himself, just got on with life.'

No relatives. No history. No connections. Alfie the mystery man, a man without a past. Frank had a feeling that Alfie was probably not all he made out he was.

Or maybe not all he didn't make out he wasn't.

'Going back to that weekend your husband disappeared, Mrs Simmons, is there anything you can remember that was unusual? Was he in a strange mood? Did anything out of the ordinary happen?'

She gave him a fierce look.

'You lot asked me that forty years ago. And the answer's still the same. Bugger all. Bugger all unusual happened. It was so normal it was boring. Apart from my Alf not being there the following morning. And the ones after that. Do you know what it's like having your husband go missing? And then, day

31

after day, month after month, waiting to hear his footsteps, hoping you'll wake up and find it's been a nightmare? Not knowing whether you'd hug him first and belt him afterwards, or the other way round?'

Well, no, thought Frank, I don't know what it's like to have a husband go missing. Couple of girlfriends, yes, husband, no.

'I'm sorry, Mrs Simmons, I understand it must have been awful for you. Unfortunately I have to ask these questions. I'm afraid the officers you spoke to aren't around anymore.'

Her face softened slightly.

'Yes, lad, I know you have to. But it's too late for me now. I had to bury my husband years ago so I could get on with life. Only I hadn't a body to bury.'

She continued to look at him for a few seconds.

'I suppose I have one now. Will I be allowed to bury him? Give him a proper funeral?'

'Yes, Mrs Simmons, I'm sure we'll be able to release your husband's – your husband to you in a few days. If it is your husband, of course. I must stress that. It might not be.'

He was glad to get out of Mrs Simmons' house. Up until then the skeleton had been an object. Now it was becoming a person. Frank was a sociable man, a man who enjoyed company, having a drink and a laugh. His preference, however, was for the company to be alive at the time.

* * *

'We'll discuss it over a drink in the wine-bar,' Frigid Frieda said, buttoning her overcoat, the navy "it's not a raincoat but it will keep you dry in a monsoon" fashionable overcoat, light enough to wear on a summer's evening, tough enough to take on tiger-shoots.

Frank tried to imagine her wearing something that showed more than just her face and hands, possibly a thin-strapped top which left the arms and shoulders bare.

He didn't quite fail, but his mental self-defence mechanism kicked in before the image materialised. There are certain thoughts a detective-sergeant should not have about his Inspector, however attractive she might be.

Why a drink in the wine-bar, he asked himself as he followed her out. Not so much "why the wine-bar?" as "why a drink?". Even though he had no doubt the conversation would be entirely about the case, it was dangerously close to socialising with the underlings.

He had always kept away from senior officers. If they didn't know you, he maintained, they wouldn't know what mistakes you were making.

'So, what's the latest?' Frieda asked when their bottle of wine and two glasses had been served. White, a Riesling of some sort, suggested the label. His taste-buds' preference had not been enquired into. She was paying and she was ordering. And he was drinking.

The answer to her question could have been summarised as "pretty close to bugger all", but one thing he had picked up on very early about Frieda was her passionate hatred of anything suggestive of swearing, an unusual quirk. A "bugger" could earn a five-minute lecture on the correct use of the English language for modern police officers, and how careless talk at work led to careless results at work.

It had come in quite handy when he had been faced with a difficult question from her a few weeks before during a team meeting. He had "accidentally" stepped on the next person's foot, resulting in an imprecation from said individual. The imprecation earned the individual his own personal lecture. By the time Frieda had finished she had forgotten the question.

But there had been a look in her eyes which suggested that she realised why, and she was noting him down for further attention.

He took a sip of his wine found it rather tasty. She took a sip and shivered slightly, her eyes partially closing in enjoyment.

'Not much,' he said, trying to ignore the message his eyes were sending his brain. 'Mrs Simmons is pretty bright. She picked up that I was there about the dead skeleton case even though I tried to avoid the connection.'

'Did you tell her that it was her missing husband?'

'I told her that it might be. Unfortunately she believes quite firmly that it is. She even asked when she could bury him.'

Frieda sighed and shook her head.

'You shouldn't have allowed that to happen, Frank. What if it turns out to be someone completely different?'

It is him, Frank felt like replying, I know it is.

In a separate part of his brain one of his self-defence voices said, "She called you 'Frank', Frank. Bit personal, isn't it? An Inspector using your first name? Sounds well dodgy to me."

'Everything points to it being Alf Simmons,' he said defensively, ignoring the voice.

She sighed again, and took a deeper sip of wine.

'First of all we have to prove that,' she noted. 'Have a word with Dr Pleadle about a DNA test. I presume his children are still alive?'

'Yes. The son has a garage locally. The daughter still runs the shop her mother started. She's now Mrs Edith Finchley, with two daughters and a son.'

'A shop?'

'A boutique, Mrs Simmons said, started back in the Sixties. I don't think they call it that anymore.'

'What's the name?'

'Katrina's. It's in the shopping centre. Apparently they change the name every year, to stay in touch with the latest fashion.'

Frieda made scornful sound.

'I know it. Good for stuff you can wear once or twice and then throw away the next season. If you're willing to spend just a little more than common sense would suggest.'

A smile flitted across her face, her eyes going into memory-mode.

'Though I did once buy a rather nice boob-tube from a similar sort of shop when I had just left school. The shop was called Zaz, I think. It was a lovely coral-blue, tight and ... Well, this is no time for memory lane. Have you spoken to Dr Pleadle?'

'Not about a DNA test,' he managed to cough out.

He and Dr Pleadle had had words about another subject. About certain police officers who appropriate evidence from the office of a pathologist with neither request nor permission. About the concept of professionalism, and how said certain police officers might care to give it a try.

She had spoken very quietly, her words, like eternal justice, grinding slow but grinding exceedingly fine. Her blazing eyes made up for it, like the slow-burning, avenging flames of

35

some god's fury. Several gods, in fact, all at the same time, none of them happy.

She had caught him slipping in to replace the identity disk. He had handed it over meekly, and she had dropped it in a desk drawer, slamming it shut as if she wished his fingers were in the way.

Or some other part of his anatomy.

His contrite little-boy apologies had not worked. He had strangled the urge to ask her if this meant their date was off. She had finally slammed down a file in front of her and started reading. He had been dismissed without a word. A word wasn't needed. She had already used too many of the nastier ones.

'Do it first thing tomorrow then,' said Frieda, interrupting his awful memories. 'We can't begin to investigate anything until we know who it is with a bullet hole in their skull.'

'First thing,' he agreed.

Probably a phone call would suffice, he thought.

Maybe he could get a constable to make it. After all, Detective Sergeants needed to learn to delegate.

Frieda looked at her watch and then finished her drink.

'I'd better get a move on, much as I'd like to stay.' She cocked her head to one side. 'You know, Frank, I think maybe we should make that tie standard issue.' She put out a hand to straighten it. 'We wouldn't need to bother with flashing lights and sirens if everyone wore that sort of thing.'

Frank gave her what used to be called an old-fashioned look.

As they left he noticed a couple sitting towards the rear of the wine bar. The woman was staring at him with eyes that reminded him of Susan's that afternoon. She looked familiar. Very familiar. It was the widow Wendy. The one he had called this afternoon to postpone their dinner because he would be working late. He was about to go over and explain that the extremely attractive woman he was with just happened to be his boss. But you can hardly break into a couple's conversation to explain to the woman that the reason you broke their date was that you'd been ordered to have drinks with your boss.

The other bloke might take it the wrong way.

Wendy wouldn't be overly pleased either.

If she believed him in the first place.

What sort of a boss straightens their subordinate's tie for them?

As he drove home he reflected on the fact that he now had two women who wouldn't object to doing something rather nasty and vicious to him. Still, he thought, he'd been there before and got out of it. No reason why he couldn't do it again. He would be fine so long as one certain woman, the most important woman in his life, stayed with him.

He would be fine so long as Lady Luck did not desert him.

Unbeknownst to him Lady Luck had just popped out to do some shopping and have her hair done.

Thursday: Battles then and now

You want me to phone Dr Pleadle and ask her to arrange a DNA test?' asked Giggling Gertie.

Giggling Gertie – officially Woman Police Constable Samantha Gregson – was so known because of her propensity to break into giggles at any moment. She was also known for having a rather large bosom on her wasp-waisted, small frame, and for having some coloured belt in Aikido, something a number of unaware late-night revellers had discovered to their cost when they underestimated this smiling, pretty little uniformed police woman's capabilities. Frank had never underestimated her. Behind the giggling he had seen two very sharp eyes and a determined spirit. She had done him one or two favours over the past couple of months as he was settling in, and when he spotted her walking past his office he knew he could trust her to make the call without spreading the word.

The word that he was too terrified of Doctor Susan Pleadle to speak to her himself.

'Just try not to giggle while you're doing it,' Frank said, pushing the phone towards her, along with a slip of paper holding Susan's office number. Gertie giggled and dialled.

'Doctor Pleadle? Constable Gregson here. I've been asked by Detective Sergeant Summers to arrange DNA testing of the Simmons children to confirm the identify of the skeleton discovered last week.'

Her face was composed, the voice level and official, not a hint of a giggle as she listened to the reply. Then her face twitched. A smile crept onto her lips. Her chin quivered.

And she broke into a fit of giggling.

'Yes, Doctor, I'll tell him,' she said through her laughter.

She looked at Frank and covered the mouthpiece.

'She says that you're a no-good, useless coward, and a wimp. She knows that you're here listening and wants to speak to you personally.'

She held the phone out to Frank and he took it resignedly.

'Oh, and she seems to think that your father was probably a goat,' Gertie added helpfully. 'Not the best of breed, though. She used the word "mangy", in fact.'

Frank glared at her.

'Doctor Pleadle, how nice to hear your voice,' he said with as much enthusiasm as he could muster. Gertie giggled, waved her fingers at him, and left him to his fate.

'You haven't heard it yet,' Susan pointed out in a neutral tone.

'FF wants a DNA comparison between the skeleton and the Simmons children,' Frank said, deciding that the best way to cross a minefield was to sprint. If you were going to get blown up you might as well get it over and done with as fast as possible.

'Inspector Garold,' she replied, stressing the "Inspector", obviously not so appreciative of Frigid Frieda's nickname, 'and I think alike. The suggestion was on page fourteen of my report, if you ever bother to read it properly.'

Ouch. He had managed the first two pages. He had meant to finish it sometime.

That was one of his problems. He started out with the best of intentions, but they seemed to get bored and go away to do something else far more interesting.

'Can it be done?' he asked, hoping to get over the last yards of the minefield without injury.

'Of course it can be bloody done, Frank, I am capable of carrying out a DNA comparison, I did learn one of two things while I was studying, and I do happen to do quite a few of the things every month. Or maybe you think I sit here powdering my nose every day?'

'I'll have to get their permission first,' he said, pulling his tie loose. He was sweating. It must be a warmer summer day than he thought. 'I'll have a word with the daughter this morning. When can I bring her in if she agrees?'

'When you have her permission you may inform me and I will go to her to take the sample. Though I find it interesting that you choose the daughter rather than the son, who might be a better test case. Maybe it's something in your make-up.'

The sound of the phone crashing into its cradle almost burst his eardrum. It certainly confirmed that their discussion was over. Her telephone was the old fashioned type, he remembered, solid Bakelite from the Sixties. It would need to be to survive.

He realised that someone was watching him. Frieda was standing in the doorway.

'Problems?' she asked.

He wasn't sure what type of problem she was referring to. He was pretty sure, however, that she had deduced what kind.

He stood up and straightened his tie.

'I'm off to have a word with the daughter, get permission for a DNA sample.' He paused. 'And the son afterwards, of course.'

'Of course,' agreed Frieda.

41

She put her head on one side and inspected him, up and down.

'At least you dress smartly,' she said, and left.

He looked at the empty doorway, wondering what the "at least" meant, with the terrible thought that he knew exactly what it meant.

As he stood up to leave he noticed a buff-coloured envelope in his in-tray, the acronym "MOD" in one corner. He opened it quickly, not too interested in finding out from the Ministry of Defence when Alf Simmons had been demobbed. At least it would give him the chance of killing off the idea that Simmons had disappeared after his bomber had exploded.

After he had scanned it he sat down slowly and re-read it.

Alf Simmons had not died as a rear-gunner in an explosion in a Lancaster bomber returning from Germany in the early summer of 1945.

It had been the early summer of 1946.

* * *

'Ooh, I wish I could wear one of them,' Gertie said. They were in the shopping centre, outside Katrina's, and Gertie had stopped to window-shop. She had been ordered to accompany him. Why, Frank wasn't sure, but Frieda had so decided. The Detective Chief Inspector had gone off fishing. The Chief Inspector who should be in charge of the uniformed section was off sick. It had left a power vacuum, into which Frieda had smoothly stepped. Eric Johns, the duty Sergeant had been less than pleased. Displeased, but not stupid enough to complain to Inspector Garold.

'It's bad enough having to spare one of my uniforms,' he had complained instead to Frank, 'but when they tell you which one it's a bit much.'

'Hands-on policing, I suppose,' Frank had replied.

Eric Johns chuckled.

'I wouldn't try to get my hands on that one, son, you'd end up plastered against the wall.'

'Actually it was FF I was thinking about,' Frank said, missing the ambiguity.

Eric Johns' eyes opened wide, not having missed it.

'Blimey, now that's a thought. She's a fair looker when you think about it. I could have dreams about that, you know, in the – '

Fortunately Gertie had appeared. Her presence had stopped Eric Johns from going any deeper into what dreams he might have, saving both Frank and Freud from dangerous dallying. And now Frank and Gertie stood looking through the shop window at a boob-tube on a mannequin, a coral-blue boob-tube identical to that someone might have worn fifteen or so years before when, he presumed, they had last been in fashion, and that person had been a teenager with ...

He stifled the thought.

'Why can't you? Wear one of those, I mean,' he asked, not thinking which minefield this particular conversation might lead to.

Gertie grinned.

'Don't make them large enough, do they?' She giggled and swung her chest just sufficiently to prove the point.

'Time we were speaking to the proprietor,' he replied, swallowing dryly and hoping his face wasn't blushing as much as he knew it was. He walked to the shop entrance. She followed, giggling.

Just as parents often think of their children as youngsters even when grown up, for Frank Mrs Edith Finchley had, up until now, been a fourteen year-old teenager, rambunctious and complaining. Even her voice on the telephone had not dispelled that view. The Mrs Edith Finchley who received them in her small office was far from that image; well-built, dressed to kill, and eyes that suggested she was far from happy at the visit.

'You should have spoken to me first,' she said before Frank could get a word out, without inviting either of them to sit down. 'My mother's not a spring-chicken anymore, the news could easily have given a heart attack.'

Obviously Mrs Simmons had already spoken to her daughter. On the one hand that might be understandable. On the other maybe it had been a warning. What sort of fourteen year-old had Edith been? A slight waif of a child, or old enough and strong enough to handle a firearm? By the looks of her now, she would not have needed a firearm.

'I'm sorry, Mrs Finchley, but all we had to go on was the name of Alfred Simmons. Your mother was the only link that we knew of at the time. We did tell her that it was merely a routine call on an old case, but I'm afraid your mother isn't easily fooled.'

That was met with a 'Hmmph'.

'The problem is,' he continued, 'we don't know for certain that the – skeleton – that was discovered is that of your father.' He was trying to avoid using the phrase "the body". "The skeleton" sounded even more absurd.

'What? You told my mother that it was.'

'No, Mrs Finchley, I did explain to her that there was no conclusive proof, but I'm not sure whether she took that on board.'

'I see. Yes,' she said, grudgingly, 'I suppose Mum would like the idea that Dad didn't run away. Maybe enough to ignore other possibilities.'

'That's why we're here. I know this won't be easy, Mrs Finchley, but there is a way which might lend greater evidence to the theory.'

'And what would that be?'

'Um, it's called a DNA comparison. We can tell – '

'I know what a DNA comparison is, Sergeant,' she snapped. 'I sell skimpy clothing to teenagers about to go to a party. It isn't unusual afterwards for a DNA test to be needed to determine paternity. All I can say is that I'm glad my children are old enough to know better.'

He sensed that he was about to receive a lecture on the stupidity of modern teenagers. The same one her own mother would have given some years ago.

'So would it be acceptable for someone from our path lab to come around?' he asked quickly.

'Aye. I'll be here all day. What about Alfie?'

Up until that "Aye" her accent had been constant, a neutral, national standard undiluted with any local variations.

'Your brother? We'll be calling on him later with the same request.'

'Hold on.' She pulled the telephone towards her and dialled a number.

'Alfie? Edith. Listen, the police want you to give some DNA

to see if that skeleton really is Dad's. You going to be at the garage?'

There was a monosyllabic response.

'Right. I'll tell them.' Without a "Goodbye" of any sort she put the phone down.

'He'll be in. You have the address?'

'Yes, Mrs Finchley, we do.'

'Right, well I have paperwork to sort out. So if you'll excuse me?'

Frank and Gertie left the shop. Frank felt that he was getting used to being curtly dismissed by women.

'Strange woman,' Gertie commented as the walked back through the shopping centre.

'In what way?'

'Your father disappears when you're a kid. Forty years later it seems as if his body has been found. You'd think that she would show some emotion. Instead all she's interested in is her paperwork.'

And the brother had showed little interest either, just a brief word or a grunt in reply to his sister, thought Frank.

'Difficult to say,' he said, 'it must have taken them some time to write their father out of their lives. Now that it appears that he's back they might be desperate not to have old wounds re-opened.'

'Or maybe they knew where he was all along. Maybe the only surprise is that he's been discovered.'

Gertie might giggle, but she was perceptive.

'We still don't know if it really is the missing Alfie Simmons,' Frank pointed out.

'You going to give SS a call?'

'SS?'

'Sexy Susan, some call her,' Gertie said, 'Dr Pleadle. Otherwise known as Doctor Death.'

'When we get back to the office,' he replied.

"Sexy Susan", he thought. Indeed.

"Doctor Death" he ignored.

'You could use my mobile,' Gertie offered. 'Haven't you got one?'

'Nope. And I don't want one either.'

He hated mobile phones. People used them to call you at any time they felt. It made lying about where you were that much more difficult. Or, as a politician might put it, being economical with the actuality of your precise geographical location. Difficult to claim that you're stuck in a traffic jam when all around you were the sounds of people in a pub enjoying themselves.

'So what did you do to upset SS?' Gertie asked. She was remarkably lacking in tact.

'I borrowed the identity disk to show Mrs Simmons. Unfortunately Dr Pleadle wasn't around to give the okay.'

Gertie whistled.

'She must like you.'

'What makes you say that?'

'You're still alive. Old PP tried that sort of thing once. They say he was off sick for a week after she'd had a go at him. He's never been back to the path lab since then.'

PP was Percy the Pouffe, or, in another life, Inspector Percy

Hanson. In a police station where nicknames were almost de rigueur and often less than polite, he had made the mistake of, at the station, phoning a furniture company to complain that the lounge suite they had delivered was missing an item, a pouffe to be precise. Ever since he had been PP, or Percy the Pouffe.

Not to his face, of course.

'So who am I then?' Frank asked as they got into his car.

'How do you mean, Sarge? Philosophically speaking, or what?'

'You're GG, right? Then there's FF, SS and PP. So who am I?'

'Couldn't say, Sarge,' she replied giggling, transparently lying.

I can guess, he thought. DD. Disappointment Dan. No wonder none of the women police officers made any serious approaches. Not that he would have responded, relationships within a police station were notorious for their casualty rates, and he had vowed never to get entangled in one.

But he would have liked the option to say no.

'Anyway,' he said, 'my name starts with an F, not a D.'

Gertie giggled.

'Something Failure?' she asked with an innocent face.

* * *

An hour and a half later he was on his way to the path lab. At the station Gertie had gone back to her normal duties, and he had had lunch in the canteen. A rather enjoyable pie, gravy and chips had been interrupted by the appearance of a haggard looking Detective Sergeant Pete Phillips.

'You look awful,' Frank pointed out helpfully.

Pete grimaced, and then sighed deeply as he put his tray on

the table and sat down.

'Bloody PP. I wish I had that FF of yours as an inspector. Even better if I was her blue-eyed boy like you are.'

A forkful of pie paused on its way to Frank's mouth.

'Blue-eyed boy?' he asked in astonishment. 'You must be joking. If a day passes without a bollocking I get worried. And she doesn't give you the normal bollocking, it's much more subtle. Anyway, what's Percy done now?'

'It's these break-ins. He had this bright idea of predicting where the next one would be, so I was up half the night with him waiting for nothing to happen.'

Wellbury was in the grip of a spate of burglaries. Or, to be more accurate, the media were in the grip of a spate of lack of news, thus a few break-ins had been linked together to make headline news, and the local media were demanding that something be done about it. The Dead Skeleton case had provided a respite, but there was only so much time they could spend on it, and they were reluctantly returning to normal crime.

'Oh, well, think of the overtime,' encouraged Frank, who thought "overtime" a dirty word.

'It's all right for you,' Pete said through a mouthful of hamburger, 'you're happy to claim every minute you can. You don't have any ambition. Percy keeps dropping hints that excessive overtime claims might affect my promotion, and I want that promotion.'

Frank was happy enough to admit that he had little aim, hope or expectancy of making Inspector or any other further promotion. He had been amazed to have reached Sergeant rank. It had only sunk in when he had been transferred that the promotion had been to get him out of his previous station. His Inspector had been almost deliriously happy to see him go.

Understandably, considering the one or two gaffes he had committed. Or maybe it was three or four. Six at the most.

The prawn sandwich behind the radiator. That was a mistake anyone could make.

The piglet in the Inspector's office when the Chief Constable paid a surprise visit. Well, the Inspector had told him to leave the evidence in his office. He had tried to warn him, but he wouldn't listen.

The nude lap dancer. He preferred not to think about that one.

He tried telling himself that it was merely a case of getting off on the wrong foot, and ultimately a clash of personalities. He wasn't ever sure that he believed himself.

That, however, was not about to happen here. Wellbury was far too pleasant a posting to ruin it. He was going to keep out of trouble whatever it took.

'And I'm caught between Frigid Frieda and Percy the Pouffe,' Pete moaned through another mouthful.

'How do you mean? They haven't got a thing going, have they?'

'Don't be daft. Them two? You don't spot much, do you? They both want to be Chief Inspector, don't they?'

That was true, Frank conceded. He was vaguely aware of the race to become Chief Inspector, the current incumbent having announced his plan for early retirement, and immediately gone fishing somewhere along the river Wellbury or the Old Canal. But having little ambition in that regard within himself Frank rarely thought about it in others. In reality neither Percy nor Frigid stood much chance; no doubt someone from outside would be posted in. But they had to try their best; it would pay dividends in the future. The problem was that promotion to Chief Inspector relied on both public relations – or to be more accurate, networking and selling yourself – and results. The former was down to the Inspectors themselves. The latter relied on their subordinates. Promotion was a stick to beat Pete with.

Frank felt almost sorry for Frieda.

Possibly he would have been surprised to discover a comment made by Frieda when Percy had commiserated with her on having Frank as a Detective Sergeant.

'I believe in Napoleon's dictum, Percy,' she had said, smiling. 'Better to have lucky generals than good ones. Frank is one of the lucky ones.'

'Frank?' Percy had asked in surprise, noting the use of the Christian name.

Frieda hadn't expanded on her statement. But Percy had wondered whether this lucky Frank might be better than his own Detective Sergeant. Frank had the reputation of being an intelligent person, a university graduate, whereas Pete Phillips was pedestrian, though persistent. He also had a bad habit of breaking into places when he had no legal search warrant, and of being too physically aggressive with suspects. Frank, he presumed, would have a rather more sophisticated approach – or at least the nous to understand a situation, and luck to get away with doing anything he shouldn't be doing.

Or maybe, Percy had thought, Frieda was exaggerating

Frank's luck in order to pass him on to some unsuspecting Inspector, like himself.

Then again, Pete Phillips obviously wasn't lucky. Look at who he had got as a boss.

Percy's look could well have earned him a different name. Perplexed Percy. He was old school. He didn't like nuances. He didn't like anything that sounded French.

'How do you manage it?' asked Pete Phillips as he bulldozed his way through his hamburger.

'Manage what?'

'Manage to go through life without a worry in the world.'

'I consider myself, Phil, to be an Epicurean.'

'Yeah, well I'm a Pisces myself, but I don't see what difference that makes. Don't believe in that nonsense anyway.'

He nodded at the tie hanging below Frank's open mouth.

'Tell me something, why do you wear those crazy things?'

'Because they make me invisible.'

'Come off it Frank, a blind man would see one of those at forty paces.'

'Back at my previous posting I was wearing one of these one day. Some senior officer from the Met turned up and I managed to do something to upset him, can't remember what. Anyway, next thing he's charging down the corridor shouting, and I quote, "Where's that sonofabitch with the pink tie?". Three seconds later I'm wearing a boring old grey thing which matches my suit. He comes into our office, looks around, and goes on to the next one. He never did find the sonofabitch with the pink tie.'

Pete shook his head in disbelief.

'Only you, Frank, only you.'

'Well, no, Pete, it's logical if you think about it. Take suspect interviews. Someone guilty will be telling you porkies, right? So they've got to remember what porkies they've told, which ones they're going to tell, the ones they're not going to tell, the truth they're going to tell, and the truth they aren't going to tell. That's difficult at the best of times. When they're sitting opposite a tie that looks like it's radio-active, and the tie-owner has this huge grin on his face, well, that kind of undermines their concentration.'

Pete looked as if his concentration had been lost at the second mention of porkies.

'Actually, there was this time we had this bloke in, a bit of a hard nut to crack. I just happened to have a set of those joke spectacles, the ones with fake eyeballs hanging off the ends of springs. So I thought, why don't I do the whole interview wearing them? That'll put him way off his stride.'

'Yeah, let me guess, you broke him in under five minutes.'

Frank grimaced.

'Not quite, no. My Chief Inspector had decided to sit in on the interview without tell me. I breeze into the interview room wearing the specs and a huge smile. He looks up at me from where he's sitting for a few seconds, and then says, "Take those bloody stupid things off" – I paraphrase. Well, that was that. The suspect sat pissing himself laughing, the Chief Inspector didn't say another word, and the interview was effectively over.'

Pete laughed.

'That's your problem, Frank. Innovation. You should avoid it.

Old officers don't like new ideas.'

Frank made a face as if to suggest that Pete might be right but Frank was still going to try the odd experiment, if only for fun. And decided not to mention the interview he had carried out while doing a handstand against the wall. It hadn't worked as such, but the suspect and he had exchanged an interesting discussion of multitasking and how to combine staying fit with the demands of an office job.

Afterwards he went to his office to make the inevitable call to Susan. Much as he would have like to delay it, if he was going to have his ear chewed off it might as well be sooner rather than later. Then it might have healed sufficiently by the time it was Frieda's turn.

'You'll have to give me a lift,' Susan said on the phone, 'my car's packed up.'

He had been surprised. Susan drove an MGB, a sports convertible painted in British Racing Green. It was her pride and joy. Normally she called it "my baby"; "my car's packed up" sounded a little off-hand.

That aside, any number of ideas had popped into his mind. Such as the fact that Frieda would not look kindly on her people being used as taxi-drivers. Such as the fact that there would be official vehicles Susan could use.

Such as the fact that, were he to show the slightest reluctance, he would have another eardrum burst as the phone was slammed down.

He agreed immediately.

She was waiting outside the lab when he arrived, further surprising him. He had expected a period of being made to wait, a rather subtle lesson in what happened when ignorant police sergeants had the temerity to interfere with Dr Susan Pleadle's professionalism. But she made up for it with the silent treatment. They did not exchange a word until they were inside Katrina's.

'You wait here,' Susan said sharply, 'I doubt if Mrs Finchley wants you around while I take a sample.'

"Whatever you say, boss," he was tempted to reply, in the manner of the piano player Sam from Casablanca. He bit his tongue before it came out. He preferred to bite his own tongue than have Doctor Pleadle surgically remove it. Or possibly not so surgically.

So he stood in the shop, looking at the fashion on offer. Skimpy clothes for teenage girls. Bras, knickers and other assorted garments which, in some far-off good old days would never have been put on public display. Not, definitely, for display to males. He was, he admitted to himself, a little old-fashioned in that sense. The modern world had lost some of the intimacy and mystery of discovery.

He was not, however, he told himself, a romantic.

It was when he was wondering how on earth a girl of fifteen or older could fit into the ridiculously tiny top in front of him that he felt someone's eyes on him. A shop assistant, not much older than seventeen, was looking at him in some astonishment. He suddenly realised that he was a grown man, almost old enough to have teenage daughters himself, if only just, technically speaking, standing in a shop full of young girls' clothing, much of which was underwear.

He smiled weakly at the assistant.

'Can I help you, sir?' she asked, keeping her distance.

'Ah, no, thanks, I'm just, er, waiting.'

He had almost said "browsing".

'Waiting, sir?'

'Look, I'm a police officer,' he said, showing her his warrant card. 'I'm waiting for, um, a colleague who is currently with Mrs Finchley.'

She peered suspiciously at the card from a few feet away. He could have sworn that he heard the sound of laughter from the office where Susan was with Mrs Finchley.

'Anyone could make one of those,' the assistant said accusingly.

'You can – check with Mrs Finchley if you want,' he said. He had started to suggest she check with the station, but word would soon spread, and vivid imaginations could conjure up pictures of him covered in girls' underwear while being assaulted by a teenager. Eric Johns, desk sergeant and purveyor of the most unlikely gossip, would have a field-day.

'What, and leave the shop unattended?' demanded the teenage assistant.

And leave you to do something despicable? was the implied question.

'I think I'll phone the police station,' she decided.

She had just moved to the till when Susan and Mrs Finchley emerged, both looking as if they had shared a joke together.

'It's all right, Kylie,' Mrs Finchley said, smiling, 'he's a policeman. I'm sure we can trust him.'

'Shall we go?' asked Susan, hugely enjoying herself. He followed her out of the shop, gales of laughter coming from Mrs Finchley. He thought he could hear titters from the young assistant.

'That was deliberate, wasn't it?' he asked as he caught Susan up.

'What was?' she asked sweetly.

'Look, I said I was sorry. I said I would never do it again.'

He decided he had had enough. He would do a Percy. Get her back to the lab and never cross its darkened doors again. Take a week off sick. He felt he needed it.

'You can buy me a cup of coffee and we'll call it quits,' she said. 'How does that sound?'

It sounded like unconditional surrender.

'Mable's do a decent cup,' he said, surrendering unconditionally.

'Mable's it is then.'

She was checking her face in a compact mirror when he returned with two cups of coffee. It surprised him. He had never seen her wearing makeup before. Unlike Frieda, who wore it like a battle shield.

'I presume you still haven't finished reading my report,' Susan said, snapping the compact closed and dropping it into her handbag.

Oh shit! he thought. You think you've managed to dig yourself out of it, and then you're straight back into it.

'Damn!' he said. 'I took it home last night, but I was so completely knackered I decided to get up early this morning and read it while I was fresh. Then the alarm didn't work. Typical. Just when you need it most. And I was in such a hurry I forgot it at home.'

She smiled at him. She didn't believe a word of it. He hoped she didn't suggest a detour past his flat so that he could pick it up. It was still sitting safely in his in-tray.

And his alarm clock worked perfectly.

'I'll save you some time, then. It needs to be brought up to date anyway. Let's see,' she said, ticking the points off on her fingers, 'we know that it's a male of between thirty-five and forty-five. Death was almost definitely caused by a bullet entering the skull. We've identified the bullet, by the way.'

'Anything useful? Such as it was the only one of its kind? With only one revolver to match it up to? And we have the address of the owner?'

'Now, Frank, don't be silly. The bullet probably came from a Webley,' she said, resuming the ticking-off of points. 'Point 32 inch, probably the 218, also known as the Webley Pocket Revolver. The Mk VI was the last made, and that was declared obsolete in 1947. By 1964 there wouldn't have been many lying around.'

He was impressed. And to his surprise he was becoming intrigued. That was bad news. He might find himself doing some work by mistake.

'Not a modern gangland weapon, then?'

'Unlikely. Either a personal weapon someone had for years, or perhaps the only thing a minor crook could lay his hands on, possibly stolen.'

'Interesting,' Frank murmured. 'At least it's something to go on with.'

'Next point. The grave was dug with a shovel, or shovels. So it's unlikely to have been a chance place to put the body, like a naturally occurring ditch.'

'And then the soil was shovelled back in,' Frank suggested,

'which means that someone should have noticed it. It wouldn't have compacted for months.'

'Correct, Sherlock.'

'All I have to do is put up a couple of signs asking whether anyone was in the vicinity in 1964, and did they spot anything strange. Like a newly dug grave.'

'Yes, well, I doubt whether people would remember that sort of thing forty years later. Anyway, you said Frieda wants us to keep quiet about the murder bit, so I think it would be better not to mention anything about graves.' She finished off her coffee. 'Come on Sergeant Slowcoach. We've both got work to do.'

A good thing SS was already in use, Frank thought. Otherwise it might have referred to Sergeant Slowcoach.

And that combined with Disappointment Dan could raise all sorts of unfortunate comparisons.

Never mind about "Something Failure".

'You can drop me at my office,' Susan said. 'I'll pop over to see Alfie Simmons this afternoon.'

'I thought your car was out of action,' Frank replied, confused.

She paused only slightly before replying.

'I'm sure the garage will have fixed it by now,' she said, eyes down as she rummaged in her handbag.

'When will you know for certain?' he asked, standing up.' About the DNA, I mean.'

'Some time tomorrow. Who knows, maybe it will turn out not to be Alfie Simmons at all.'

'You do like looking on the bright side, don't you?'

* * *

'I've checked the ordinance survey maps for 1965,' Frank told Frieda that evening at his six o'clock debrief. This time he was sitting down and Frieda was slowly pacing up and down the carpet. In silk stockings, and stiletto heels. Or, at least, what looked like silk stockings. And the pencil-skirt which he now found out had a long slit at the back. And her wonderful legs went all the way up to ...

'Anything useful?' Frieda asked.

'Not such as you'd notice,' Frank said, trying to concentrate on the case in hand. 'The area where the skeleton was found was at the edge of a farm. Quite a way from any tracks or roads shown on the map. The farm was sold for property development in the Eighties. The farmer apparently retired to Spain. He passed on eight years ago.'

For some reason Frank found that, in relating the progress of the investigation, he suddenly appeared to have forgotten about the moving calves. Had he pursued this line of thought he might have wondered why the case had gripped him sufficiently for that to happen. But that was always the problem with curiosity. It killed cats. That was humane. It made humans commit overtime.

'And the farmer would be unlikely to bury a body at the edge of his farm,' Frieda noted. 'I would imagine there would be any number of better locations closer to home.' She stretched her neck and shoulders. 'Look, Frank, the Chief Constable is putting pressure on me to get this sorted.'

'I would have thought he would be well aware of how difficult it is.'

'Yes, but he's getting grief from the media. At the moment it's story of the month – or, as far as that lot go, story of the half-hour.'

'So why don't we let it lie until they forget?'

'I did suggest that. The Chief Constable said he agreed, though I suspect he wants a result. It's good for public relations, better than official statistics, anyway. The Dead Skeleton case will be remembered long after these burglaries are forgotten. But either way we've got to be seen to be doing something. Sooner or later the news about the bullet will leak out, and then we'll have reporters climbing all over us. Never mind the fact that he officially died in 1946. And that also tells us something.'

Frank had showed her the MOD letter. She had pursed the lips on her inscrutable face as she read. She used, he noticed, reading glasses. It had given her a sort of look he might have described as sexy, had it belonged to anyone other than his boss.

'Such as what?' he asked.

'How much do you know about World War II?' Frieda asked.

'About the usual, I suppose. Started Sunday the third of September 1939, ended 1945. Germany surrendered May 8th, Japan in August after the atomic bombs were dropped. Though you could be pedantic and argue that it started on the first of September with the invasion of Poland, or even that it wasn't a world war until the entry of Russia, or even Japan and the States.'

'You've missed out Italy, Bulgaria, Romania and a few others,' Frieda noted, the flicker of a smile on her face. 'You know a bit more than the usual, I would say. However, the main thing is that it was over in 1946. Alf Simmons was a gunner.'

Frank nodded, taking her point.

'Why take a gunner if a war is over?' he asked.

'Exactly. I'd like to know what was in that Lancaster, and why it blew up.'

'But surely – well, the military do things their way. Maybe they were just used to flying a full crew.'

'This is 1946 we're talking about, Frank. Petrol's rationed. Everything's rationed. Extra bodies mean extra petrol. Nothing would have been carried unless they thought it necessary. And why a Lancaster? The Dakota was far more efficient for transport. Maybe there was something special about that Lancaster. And that flight.'

'You know quite a bit about the war, Inspector.'

'I once had a boyfriend who was a nutter on the subject. I never thought it was any great problem until he asked me to dress up as an SS officer, including shiny boots. Men can have some strange fixations.'

I really, really did not need that image, Frank thought.

'Not much we can do until Dr Pleadle confirms that it is Alfie Simmons,' he said, quickly going back to the subject. 'It could turn out to be someone totally different.'

'You do like looking on the bright side, Frank, don't you? We'll have to presume for the moment that your original instinct was right. Get out the missing persons file tomorrow, there must be one in the archives if Mrs Simmons reported it. See if they recorded anything of any possible value.'

'Okay, Inspector, but I can't say I have a great deal of confidence in that. Grown man goes missing? Hardly likely to merit a lot of investigation. Especially if it was a busy year otherwise. Any idea what 1964 was like crime-wise?'

She gave him a Frieda look while putting on her coat.

'I hope you aren't suggesting that I was in the force in 1964, Sergeant. I wasn't even born then.'

'Of course not. But you hear stories. The older coppers are always saying that this year or that year was the worst ever.'

'Hmmmm.' It was a "you have just got out of that corner, Sonny, don't try it again" hmmmm.

Frank stood up and followed her out of her office.

'It's a hard day's night,' Frieda said as they walked out.

'You can say that again.'

'No, I was talking about the Beatles' album. It came out in 1964, I think.'

And that helps us how? Frank asked himself.

'Atmosphere, Frank, atmosphere,' Frieda answered his unspoken question. 'If a crime was committed in 1964 you look at it with the eyes of a copper in 1964, not that of the twenty-first century.'

'I'll buy some incense then, shall I?'

Frieda gave him a slightly different look.

'I'll bring some joss sticks in from home,' she said, and walked away.

He watched her go.

Even the stern-but-smart way she dressed could not disguise a very attractive figure. He hoped he wasn't about to have inappropriate feelings about her.

Nah, even he wasn't that stupid.

Friday: A hard day's day

'Bloody hell, Frank, what's that smell?' asked Eric Johns as he walked into Frank's office holding a stack of files. He gawped. 'Don't tell me that's what I think it is, Frank,' he pleaded, looking at a china holder containing three gently smoking joss sticks.

'Okay, Eric, that's not three sticks of incense.'

'Blimey, son, if FF sees that she'll think you've gone barmy.'

'You know the really, really big problem, Eric?'

'What's that?'

'I rather suspect it was our Inspector Garold who put them there.'

'You're joking!'

'I'm rather afraid it's FF who's having the joke. Put it this way, Eric, if it was her, and I throw them in the bin she might be somewhat displeased. If it wasn't her, and I don't throw them away, she might be somewhat displeased. Now I'm sure a conundrum like that appeals to someone of your experience.'

'Yes, especially when it's someone else's.'

'Tell me, Eric,' Frank said, opening the windows wide, 'what do you remember about the 1960s? 1964 to be specific.'

'Hard Day's Night,' Eric responded promptly.

'Oh, good. You bought the record I presume.'

'Don't be daft, Frank. I was only ten in '64. By the time I got into the music scene the Beatles were already ancient. Previous generation stuff. Now if you want to know about the Seventies – '

'No, thanks, Eric, but no. From what you say there aren't likely to be many coppers around still active from those days?'

'Not active, no. Think about it, son. If a copper was a twenty-year old beat-bobby in 64 he'd be at least sixty now. How many coppers below the rank of Chief Inspector are still in the Force at that age? Even Chief Constables, you'd be lucky to find one.'

Frank sighed and shook his head.

'I think we should hand this case over to Time Team.'

'Time Team?'

'That television programme. Archaeologists dig up and reconstruct the distant past in two days.'

'Ah, talking of the distant past, I've got those files for you, the ones you were asking about.'

He laid the stack in front of Frank.

'Files? I only wanted one.'

'Yes, but I decided to be a conscientious copper and tell young Bobby Stang to search the archives for all missing person cases from 1964.'

'What's he done wrong now?'

The archives were in the basement of the station, large, damp, dusty and dirty. They contained, it was rumoured, records going back to the late eighteen-hundreds. Sending someone to find old files was a minor form of punishment.

'Turned up late for his shift. His uniform will need cleaning. Maybe he might work out that it would be cheaper to buy a decent alarm clock.'

'Anything interesting in them?'

Eric's eyes opened in surprise.

'You think I'm going to look through that lot? I'd be sneezing for the rest of the day. Enjoy, Frank, enjoy.'

He disappeared quickly out of the office. Frank looked at the incense. At lest it offset the mildewy smell coming from the folders.

He sighed and sifted through them until he came to Alfie Simmons' file, and began reading. Paperwork was obviously as important in the Sixties as it was today. Without realising it he found himself immersed in the files.

About an hour later he was sitting with his heels on the windowsill, engrossed in thought. It was only at the second knock at the open door that he realised Frieda was standing in the doorway. He dropped his feet and swung around.

'Sorry, Inspector, lost in thought there.'

'Which is either a very good thing, or a very bad thing.' She glanced at the numerous folders scattered around his desk and on the floor. 'Been practising your speed-reading?'

'Oh, I've always read quickly. Comes of having a history professor as a father and a lecturer in English lit as a mother. I was always surrounded by books. I used to race through one in order to get on to the next.'

She raised her eyebrows as if impressed by this notable academic lineage, but also as if her next question was going to be, 'So where did you go wrong? Were you adopted?'

Instead she sat down on a chair in front of his desk, crossed her legs and said, 'Tell me about it. The files.'

'The coppers of '64 were very diligent in their paperwork,' he said. 'Did about as little or as much as we would do today when a forty-year old man with no previous convictions goes missing, but they recorded almost everything they did do. The description of the missing man, for instance. No photograph, unfortunately, but a good description.'

He opened Alfie Simmons' file and read.

'White male, forty years of age, light brown to blonde hair, blue eyes. Identifying marks: a small childhood scar which pulled the left side of his mouth up, giving him the look of someone always half-smiling, or about to smile.' He looked at Frieda. 'I'm guessing that description comes from Mrs Simmons. Sounds like our Alfie was quite attractive to women.'

'The point being?'

Frank put the folder down and picked up a second.

'A week after Alfie Simmons goes missing, another man disappears. A man married to one Elizabeth Simmons, nee Edwards, in 1960. Like to hear the description of our other missing man?'

'Quasimodo? Come on, Frank, I'm busy enough as it is without playing guessing games.'

'Age thirty-six. Light brown to blonde hair, blue eyes. Identifying marks: A small scar he had received while doing National Service in Korea. Pulled the left side of his mouth up, giving him the look of etc, etc. And his name? Alfred Simmons. Commonly known as Alf Simmons.'

He tossed the file back on to his desk. Frieda looked at him for a few seconds.

'You think they're one and the same man? Bit thin, isn't it? After all, there are plenty of Alfred Simmons in the telephone directory, you said so yourself.'

'Ah, but you haven't heard the other titbits. Our other Alf

was a lorry driver, away from home for long periods. What was Alfie Simmons number one? A lorry driver. And guess what our Alf wore around his neck?'

'A metal identity disk no doubt.'

'Spot on.'

'I don't see the connection.'

'It was the identity disk of another Alfie Simmons. According to his wife – Alf's wife, Mrs Simmons the Second – it was given to him by a friend of his uncle who died while bombing Berlin. How exactly the identity disk managed to return from that trip isn't mentioned.'

Frieda uncrossed her legs and leaned forward, her elbows on his desk. At another time Frank might have noticed that her blouse fell forward in a manner inviting further perusal. At that moment his thoughts were elsewhere.

'Alfie Simmons was also Alf Simmons? Married to another woman?' Frieda asked.

'His second wife was twenty-four. Maybe our Alf dropped four years off his age to sound like a better catch.'

Frieda shook her head.

'Frank, how much of this is you guessing? We have the skeleton of a man who was shot eighteen years after he died in a flying accident, something we have yet to tell the press. Now you're saying he was also a bigamist? We might as well invite national television and have a jamboree. International television. It would go down a storm in Japan. Wellbury would become a tourist attraction.'

Frank shrugged.

'I've told you what I know so far. Facts. The alternative

explanation is that there were two men with exactly the same description, exactly the same type of scar, who managed to go missing within a week of each other. Oh, and they both wore an identity disk saying "Alfred Simmons" on it. I don't buy it. It has to be the same man.'

Frieda tapped her fingernails on the desk.

They were painted scarlet.

'If that is the case, hopefully we'll find out that Alfie Simmons was shot by Alf Simmons for cheating on his wife,' she said.

'Eh?' asked Frank.

Frieda smiled.

'A joke, Frank. However, if Mrs Simmons – or even Mrs Simmons the Second – found out that Alfie was leading a double life, it could give us a motive for murder.'

Frank shook his head.

'You remember saying that we had to think about this case like coppers of the 1960s? Well, I agree with you, but there's something else. Every time I say 1964 everyone mentions It's a Hard Day's Night. But we're talking about a forty-year old man, not a music groupie. Mrs Simmons – the first – was in her thirties, also not a music groupie, not with two kids. Hardly the type likely to suddenly lose her cool and go around shooting someone for a bit of bigamy. They'd be aware of the consequences. The death penalty wasn't repealed until 1966.'

'It was suspended in 1965,' Frieda corrected. 'And Mrs Simmons the second was twenty-four in 1964. And the son Alfie was, what, late teens? So they were young enough to lose their cool, as you put it. And anyway, you might think of it just a spot of bigamy, other people might tend to take a stronger view of things.'

It was Frank's turn to drum his fingers on his desk.

'We're going to have to interview Mrs Simmons in more depth,' he said. 'The first, that is. And Edith and Little Alfie. And this other Mrs Simmons, if she's still around. If, of course, we can spare the manpower.'

It was a hint as subtle as throwing a brick through a bank window in a Western. Frieda pursed her jaw. Other people might purse their lips. Frieda was special.

'Womanpower,' she corrected. 'You can have Gertie when required so long as you clear it with me first. Even though Sergeant Johns might not like it when I specify which officer is to be used where.'

And why does it have to be Gertie? Frank asked himself as Frieda stood up. Answer came there none.

'Tell me something,' Frieda said as she smoothed her pencil-skirt down, looking out of the window, in a manner that stated an off-hand question was about to be asked, one that was extremely important, and his head was on the chopping block if he gave the wrong answer. 'Everyone in this station seems to have a nickname and initials. Like Gertie is GG for Giggling Gertie. I gather mine's FF. Any idea what that stands for?'

'I've heard it used,' confessed Frank in a half-truth, 'but nobody's told me what it stands for. I am rather new here.'

Their eyes met. Hers suggested she knew he was lying through his front teeth. His stated confidently that he was as innocent, nay, more innocent and pure, than any snow that had been driven, anywhere since creation. So innocent that the snow was not just driven but delivered in a chauffeured Rolls-Royce. A white one.

'But I would imagine the first letter can only be an abbreviation for "Fabulous",' he concluded.

She continued the eye-balling for five minutes, or more accurately, for five seconds, which was five minutes in Frieda staring time.

'Your spade work is exemplary, Sergeant,' she noted. She paused before continuing. 'It seems we have several summers here. There was the summer of '45, the summer of '46 and the summer of '64. And now we have the Summers of today.' She made no comment on what she thought of the various summers, or Summers. She nodded thoughtfully and walked towards the door. He noticed that the pencil-skirt definitely did something for her. From behind she looked like something from an erotic dream. Then she would turn around, and the eyes would tell you that, if you tried anything, you had just embarked on your worst nightmare.

'There was a film called Alfie in 1966,' she said, turning in the doorway. 'Michael Caine, playing a chauvinistic young Cockney who spent his life chasing what he called "the birds". He ended up with only a stray dog for company.'

She gave him a look to let him know she had just said Something Important.

His look suggested that he Didn't Get It.

Then she turned and her silk-clad calves were gone.

Gertie, thought Frank, turning back to the window and replacing his heels on the sill. He liked Gertie.

Alfie Simmons, he thought, if it were our Alfie, and our Alf, had also liked women. So much he had been married to two at the same time.

He thought of Susan and Gertie. And Fabulous Frieda.

And Widow Wendy, whom he had forgotten to call.

And Linda the Librarian, whom he should have called to arrange another date.

What if, forty years after his skeleton had been exhumed, Alfie's philandering spirit had been unleashed to continue some sort of strange mission to wreak havoc on men who played around?

Silly idea. Alfie's spirit would encourage men to play away.

Wouldn't it?

But Alfie hadn't actually played away, technically speaking. He had just established two home grounds, as it were.

The telephone rang to interrupt his thoughts. Or meanderings.

'Frank? Susan. Listen, we have some interesting results.'

He groaned. "Interesting" was a word people used when other people were about to have problems.

'Can we get together? I'll let you buy me lunch,' she offered.

'Best offer I've had since – well, ever, really. Where would you like to go?'

'Your canteen still do pie and chips? I'll be over in twenty minutes.'

The phone went dead.

He'd heard of kidnapping. Could you be lunchnapped?

He could see it right then. Susan and himself having a lunch-meeting while the rest of the station looked on and whispered, Oh, aye, what's going on there, then? Especially Eric Johns. Rumours would be more rife than the rifest thing ever.

Susan could be really naive at times, he thought.

* * *

The first thing Frank noticed when they stood at the canteen counter was that Susan seemed to be on first-name terms with the canteen staff. The second was that she got bigger portions than he did.

'Are you going to eat all that?' he asked as they sat down.

'Watch me,' she said, smiling. 'It's my once-a-month pig-out. I shall probably go home afterwards and have a siesta.'

'Nice work if you can get it. Wish I could take an afternoon off whenever I felt like it.'

'We have flexi-time. And I put in plenty of extra time, so my boss is happy for me to take some time off if I think I need it. He doesn't ask questions. Men don't tend to, not even if they have a medical degree.'

Frank decided that he would join the majority of men, and chewed on a chip instead of asking a question. He had opted for chips and omelette, having decided that pie and chips every lunchtime was not doing his weight any good. In his previous station he had worked out that sort of thing with regular games of squash with other officers, but so far he hadn't found any facilities or interest here.

'You should do some sport,' Susan suggested, as if reading his mind.

'Chance would be a fine thing. I used to play quite a bit of squash, but I haven't found any enthusiasm when I mention the subject. The uniformed lot either aren't interested, or have their own regular partners and times.'

'You can come and play badminton with my club. It's social, but you get a good workout.'

'Badminton?' he asked with undisguised dismay. If any of the others found out he was playing badminton he could end up with a different nickname, and it could involve the word "Nancy".

'You think it's a girlie sport, do you?'

"Yes" was the correct answer, but probably not the right one.

'Of course not,' he muttered, and quickly filled his mouth with omelette.

'I tell you what, I challenge you to the best of three. You win, I'll admit that it's a girlie sport.'

He considered this. Despite the deep enjoyment she was getting from the overloaded plate of pie, gravy, chips and peas she was shovelling down, she was not far off being of the petite class, hardly a challenge for someone of his strength and size.

'And I'll even throw in best of three at squash, how's that?' she added.

You must be joking, he thought. While he wasn't the world's best at squash, he could normally lose pretty impressively well against better men while putting up a good performance. He was sure he could outplay Susan quite easily. And what real man could say no to a challenge from this slip of a girl and hold his head high?

'You're on,' he said, smiling. She smiled back.

It was probably because she had a mouth full of pie that caused her smile to look rather evil.

'So, what is this amazing news you have?' he asked.

But she refused to say until she had finished eating. Instead he had to indulge in social chit-chat about his interests in television, film stars, theatre, what books he preferred reading and his star sign, the latter surprising him, coming from a doctor.

'There are more things in heaven and earth, Horatio, than are dreamt of in your philosophy,' she quoted, noticing the surprised look on his face. 'Anyway, it's just a bit of harmless fun.'

'In that case it definitely gets my vote,' he replied. 'I think there's far too little harmless fun in this world of ours.'

She gave him a quizzical look, and nodded slightly, as if he had confirmed some suspicion of hers.

'Right,' she said, sighing happily, after the last chip had been used to mop up the last dribble of gravy. She took a sip of coffee. 'DNA tests.'

'Yes, DNA tests. And?'

'Perfect match with Edith Finchley, nee Simmons. No doubt whatsoever. One in several million chance.'

'Brilliant. I like perfect matches.'

'So do I,' Susan said, in a way that suggested she was thinking of something else.

'But that suggests that there was a problem with young Alfie.'

'Got it in one, Sherlock,' Susan said. 'While Edith and Little Alfie are related, Alf Simmons pater was not pater to Alf Simmons fils.'

'Eh?'

'Alfie senior was not Alfie junior's father.'

Frank looked gobsmacked.

'But that's impossible. He can't be Edith's father but not Alfie's.'

Susan smiled coyly.

'You do know about the birds and the bees, don't you Frank? I could lend you a little book if you want. I could even try to find the one with pretty pictures in it.'

He looked at her.

'Let me get this straight. You're saying that Mrs Simmons was playing away when she had Alfie?'

'I'm saying Edith's father was not Little Alfie's father. As to playing away, well, that depends on whether Mr and Mrs Simmons were married, or engaged or whatever, when Little Alfie was conceived. You can only play away if you have already established a home ground.'

Frank considered this.

'Okay, I see your point,' he said finally. 'Maybe they weren't seriously involved, Mrs Simmons finds herself pregnant, lets Alfie senior seduce her, or maybe they already had a thing going. Maybe she was playing the field. Whatever. She convinces him he's the father because he's the best available prospect as a parent, they get married. Doesn't really help us either way, though.'

'Oh, I don't know. At least you have something to ask Mrs Simmons. She might be a little more forthcoming. And we can conclude, almost certainly, that the skeleton is that of Alfie Simmons.'

'Almost certainly?'

'Well, we still have a number of questions, one of which I would say is the most important.'

'And that is?'

'We know the skeleton is that of Alfie Simmons. But who is –

or was – Alfie Simmons?'

Their eyes met. Hers were twinkling. He nodded his head slowly. Alfie Simmons married in 1948. And again some years later he liked it so much he repeated the process as Alf Simmons. Sometime in 1964 he was murdered. Quite an impressive achievement for someone who died in 1946.

Or possibly 1945.

'Very curious,' she noted.

'Very,' he agreed.

* * *

That afternoon Frank was on his way to his office to write up the notes so far, official reports seeming to take up most of his time, when Pete Phillips hurried passed him in the corridor. Pete stopped suddenly.

'Here, I saw you and Doctor Pleadle in the canteen today,' he said.

'Yes?'

'She didn't challenge you to a game of badminton, did she? Or, more important, you didn't accept, did you?'

'As it happens, yes, on both accounts.'

Pete shook his head pityingly. There was a mocking grin on his face.

'You poor man. Still they say pain is good for the soul.'

'What do you mean?'

Pete Phillips was, Frank decided, the sort who liked to wind other people up.

'Look,' Pete said, 'you seem like a decent bloke, so let me give you some advice. Lose graciously and quickly. Very quickly.'

He could see Frank thought the idea ludicrous.

'Look, honest. She did the same with me when I got here. Here, you didn't suggest that badminton was a girlie sport, did you?'

'Not in so many words.'

'Oh dear. Oh dear.' Once again Pete shook his head sadly. 'So did I. I played a lot of squash then, still do when I can. So I refused to be beaten at a poncy game like badminton by a woman.' He sighed. 'You know, I could hardly walk the next day. Seriously. She's an evil woman, that one. She'll put that stupid bloody shuttlecock where you can just about reach it, even though you know she could place it well out of reach. So you feel you have to get there. And you find out that those courts aren't as small as they look.'

He shivered at the memory.

'Two hours, two long hours of humiliation and agony – well, two hours on the court, days of physical agony, and at least a month of being laughed at until someone else made an idiot of themselves. Don't do it, I tell you, don't do it.'

Frank felt that Pete was piling on the melodrama rather too heavily.

'I think I know how far I can push myself,' he replied confidently.

'Listen, Frank, you know in badminton, the rules mean that, if you're serving and you lose that point, the other side don't actually gain a point, it just means they get the serve. You'd be surprised how long you can play with no-one winning a point.'

'I have played before, Pete. A while ago, admittedly, but I think I can take care of myself on a badminton court.'

'Poor man,' Pete said, walking away, 'poor, poor deluded man.'

After a few steps he turned back.

'Set a date for the massacre?' he asked.

'Sunday, at the sports centre.'

'What time?'

'Four p.m. Why?'

Susan had suggested the time; an hour or two of badminton, a shower at the sports centre, and then their Sunday evening date, drinks followed by dinner.

'I know it's evil of me,' Pete said, 'but I'd like to be there. Nothing like a good bit of schadenfreude to end the weekend with. Such a pity I can't make it.'

He laughed and carried on walking.

Frank shook his head. Obviously some people thought he was still the new boy on the block.

Or maybe it was his degree. Somehow he had known it would be a problem. None of his fellow officers of his rank had been to university. They were not only much older than him, they had come up the long way through the ranks and hard work. They were automatically suspicious of this new man who, they presumed, would be some kind of intellectual, vaunting his superior knowledge. While he accepted that that sort of thing would happen, he felt it somewhat unfair: he had done his best to ensure failure, but had managed to scrape a pass somehow. It was hardly his fault.

* * *

Eric Johns caught him before he got to his office.

'FF wants to see you in her office. As of now. Immediately.

Do not pass Go, do not collect anything.'

'Sod it. Any idea why?'

'Not a clue. But that sort of invitation is rarely followed by a pleasant cup of tea and a choc digestive.'

'Don't I know it.'

'How do you mean?'

Frank sighed.

'Last time it happened, in my old station, it turned out the fifteen-year-old girl I had arrested and charged with shop-lifting was the Chief Constable's great-niece.'

Johns whistled.

'What happened?'

'Oh, a few words here, a few words there, director of the chain store was invited for drinkies with the Chief Constable, I was given the chance to change my report. Like a silly bugger I argued against it. Couldn't win in the end.'

'You argued against it?' asked Eric in surprise, stressing the "you". 'I thought you were dead against making trouble for yourself?'

'We all make mistakes, Eric, we all make mistakes.'

Eric nodded his head sagely, as one who remembers having made mistakes in his youth.

'You haven't arrested anyone lately, have you?' he asked.

'No, it must have something to do with ...' Frank's voice tailed off. He was about to say "to do with teenagers' knickers", but had realised that story would do him no good at all. And anyway, he hadn't done anything wrong as far as that was concerned. So long as no-one had reported some pervert browsing through teenagers' under-garments.

'Haven't a clue,' he ended lamely. 'Better get myself off there pronto.'

Quickly he left Eric Johns, whom he was sure was dying to prise something out of him, some juicy morsel for gossip. From his very first day in Wellbury he had noted Eric Johns down as a man who was entirely reliable and therefore also entirely never to be entrusted with delicate information.

When he reached Frieda's secretary's office he was instructed to enter the inner eyrie immediately. Inside Frieda's office he was introduced to a Mr Harley from the MOD, a grey-haired man wearing brown slacks, corduroy jacket and blue tie, who looked like a retired civil-servant more used to pottering in his garden than sitting supping tea in a police inspector's office. His first words confirmed the impression.

'I don't actually work for the ministry any longer – retired, now,' he explained in a soft, cultured voice. 'I'm researching the history of the post-war era, and I still see some people from the office from time to time. When I heard about your request I thought I might pop down, maybe make myself useful. Possibly find an anecdote or two. Very little available, compared to the war years.'

'It's very kind of you to offer, sir,' Frank replied. 'According to the letter Alfred Simmons died in 1946 – is that correct?'

'Yes, I spoke to the clerk who wrote the letter. Had a look at the records she used as reference. Looks like a rather tragic accident.'

'Why would a Lancaster be carrying a gunner in 1946?' asked Frieda.

'Oh, dear me, no, Inspector,' Harley replied, smiling. 'Aircraftman Simmons was a gunner during the war, that is true, but on the flight in question he was listed as a passenger – no doubt coming home for some well-earned leave. I wouldn't be surprised if he hadn't cadged a lift.'

'Is it possible he was listed as being on board but wasn't on the flight?' Frank asked.

Harley raised his eyebrows in surprise.

'Well, that is an interesting question,' he replied after several seconds thought. 'What you're asking is, is it possible he did not die in the explosion? That he was alive, and simply disappeared?'

'That's it in a nutshell, Mr Harley.'

'Well, well. My goodness, that is indeed an interesting question.' Harley appeared somewhat happily puzzled by the idea. 'The thought never occurred to me. Let me see.' He pondered for a few minutes, finally shaking his head.

'The answer to your original question, as to whether or not he was on the flight – well, certainly it is possible that he was not. Perhaps he was listed as being on that flight, but caught another. But he could hardly have turned up after having apparently been lost in the explosion without anyone noticing. After all, he would have to report on arrival – the military have always been fond of paperwork. Plus, if you're suggesting he returned to civilian life, he would need all sorts of things – demob papers, ration book, that sort of thing. So, highly unlikely, I would say.'

'Unlikely – but not impossible?' Frank asked.

Harley looked at him quizzically.

'You seem quite set on the idea, Sergeant. May I ask why?'

'I'm afraid not, sir. In fact it's probably totally irrelevant.

We're just trying to dot some i's and cross some t's. Curiosity more than anything, I suppose. But, to return to the question?'

Harley shrugged as if surrendering.

'Possible, yes. Unfortunately the war years resulted in a great deal of confusion. With rationing there was a large market for forged documents of all sorts. And the number of men who either failed to report for military service or went absent without leave is numbered in thousands – no doubt many relied on false identities to escape the attentions of the police. It is possible that Alfred Simmons bought fraudulent demob papers, though they would have been on the expensive side. He could have registered for a ration book – he would not be listed as AWOL, so no checks would show him as such. But, Sergeant, as I said, it's extremely unlikely. He would have been close to the end of his service in 1946 – why leave then?'

'What cargo was the plane carrying?' asked Frieda.

'Documents, mainly, Inspector,' Harley replied, transferring his attention to her.

'Mainly?'

'Documents and four passengers, four air-force personnel on their way back to Britain.'

'Nothing else?'

'Nothing official.'

'What about unofficial?'

Harley spread his hands.

'Who knows? Servicemen weren't allowed to transport certain things – most things, apart from their service-issue items. But I have no doubt that a great deal of minor loot travelled around Europe in those days. I can't imagine, however, that much of it was worth anything.'

'No gold bullion, then? Nothing worth staging an explosion in an aircraft?' asked Frank.

'No,' Harley smiled, 'no gold bullion, priceless emeralds or silver ingots I'm afraid.'

'What was the cause of the explosion?'

Harley shrugged.

'No definitive cause was found. The manifest did not show any explosive material, but there were suggestions that some of the servicemen were carrying – strictly against orders – military mementoes such as German grenades, firearms, bullets, possibly even a panzerfaust or two – the German equivalent of the American bazooka. Very efficient weapon in its time, but I wouldn't advise carrying an old one on board a Lancaster – or anywhere, for that matter. Old explosives deteriorate, become very unpredictable. Not that I've ever been overly fond of the fresh stuff, mind you.'

'Well, that's it, then,' Frieda said. 'Unfortunately, now that we know that Alfred Simmons died in 1946 he is no longer relevant to our investigation. But do let us know if you ever publish your research, I've always had an interest in that field.'

'Of course,' Harley said, putting down his cup and standing up. 'Silly of me, really, I should have guessed that your focus was on your investigation. One becomes a little too involved with one's own interests. Forgive me if I've taken up too much of your valuable time.'

'Not at all, Mr Harley, your offer of help is greatly appreciated,' said Frieda. 'Sergeant Summers will show you out.'

Sergeant Summers showed Mr Harley out the front door with effusions of gratitude, and then returned to Frieda's office. She was standing at the window, watching Harley walk towards a bus-stop.

'Very efficient subterfuge on your part,' she said as Frank walked back in. 'Your face didn't give a single thing away. I must remember that in future.'

'What do you think he was? An aged reporter?' asked Frank, something in his subconscious registering for future reference that she had been watching his reactions carefully.

He would have been well advised to continue his mental meanderings until he reached the all-important question: "Why?"

'No, he was from the MOD all right. I checked. Supposedly retired, writing about the post-war years.'

'You think he's what he says he is? A rather bemused old duffer, carried away with his pet project?'

She walked back to her desk and sat down.

'No, I don't buy that one. His eyes were too sharp.'

'Pretty strange co-incidence. Some lowly clerk in the MOD replies to a minor request for information from a police force, next thing our Mr Harley knows about it and hot-foots it here.'

'My thoughts exactly, Frank. Anyone would think he'd never heard of the telephone.'

Frank looked at her. She was tapping a pen against a folder, deep in thought.

'That flight that Alf Simmons made is sounding increasingly suspicious,' Frank offered.

'I know. I'd like to know what our Mr Harley actually did in the MOD before he retired.'

She looked at him.

'Frank, I don't want the Funnies involved. As far as we're concerned this looks like a domestic crime. I realise that the Monday morning deadline is no longer viable. But it has to be sorted soonest.'

Internally he gave a blessing of thanks.

'Friday, Frank, a week today. That's all I can give you,' she decided.

He nodded. Sooner or later decisions had to be made as to whether or not a case was sufficiently important to merit the resources required to continue investigations. Sometimes they had to admit defeat, or, officially, put the case to one side until new evidence became available or a regular review briefly re-opened it. This would be one of those.

And it would keep the Funnies quiet.

Though there was a part of him that didn't want the case left unresolved. A large part. He had become intrigued with Alfie Simmons.

'We have to have a solution in this one,' Frieda continued, surprising him.

'Why?'

'The Chief Constable has said we must release the fact that we believe it's a case of murder.'

'Oh, boy, that will be fun. Why on earth does he want to do that?'

'Because sooner or later it will come out. And because we can't put it to sleep before letting the press know. We might as well hand in our resignations if they found out. Besides which,' she continued, looking at him with a measure of anger in her eyes, 'I do not like suppressing facts. I believe it is our duty as police officers to be honest with the public – the people who pay our wages and expect us to act in an honourable way. We might have to hold back evidence during an inquiry, but eventually it has to become public knowledge. And I want a resolution in this case.'

Frank did not reply. He fully agreed. The difference was that Frieda would hold a press conference, while he would prefer to just hand out a release noting the salient facts. Some journalists might garble the written word, the spoken one they mutated into something entirely different. It was an art, beyond chemistry.

And he hated the concept of press conferences. Up to then he had managed to avoid every single one he had been invited to.

'However,' Frieda said in a sad voice, confirming his thoughts, 'unfortunately informing the press of facts does not normally result in their readers receiving those facts. What begins as our information often ends up being the tabloids' fiction.'

Frank let a few seconds go before speaking.

'And when they do find out, they'll be running around like a puppy with two tails,' he suggested.

'Precisely.' She paused for a few seconds and then looked up at him. 'That bit about forged paperwork – if Alfie Simmonds decided to buy a new identity he would no longer have been Alfie Simmonds, would he?'

'Unless the name on the forged paperwork was also Alfie

Simmonds.'

'You'd need to have a pretty simple or an extremely devious brain to think of that little trick.'

'Would you? It was the first thing I thought of.'

'Yes, you would. So did I. But then we're trained to think in devious ways. Or at least I was.'

Frank decided to deal with that insinuation by ignoring it.

'When were you thinking about letting them know? The press?'

'Tuesday or Wednesday next week. You're going to have to push the interviews before then. You can't let Mrs Simmons or the others know everything, not at first, but you're going to have to tell them before we tell the press.'

'And any interviews after that, since we've concealed the murder aspect, will be somewhat on the hostile side. To put it politely.'

'It can't be helped, I'm afraid. Get some good rest over the weekend, Frank, you're going to have a busy week ahead of you. Starting first thing Monday.' She smiled. 'There's a good French film on at the Arts Playhouse on Sunday, if you're interested.'

Frank contemplated this. It sounded like an invitation. Or possibly not. Fortunately he had an excuse. Or possibly not so fortunately, since going to see an artistic French film with Frieda sounded a rather appealing prospect. Ever since an ex-girlfriend had talked him into going to see a screening of a sub-titled *Un héro très discret* he had become hooked on that sort of French film. Filled with irony, parody, a good dose of noir and a mocking of the official government-sponsored view of France's past, he had found it hilarious. It was the sort of thing he could well imagine slipping into the video machine before sitting down next to Frieda on the couch to watch and enjoy. It would also fall under the 'trying to learn French properly yet again' ambition.

What am I thinking? he thought to himself.

'I'd love to,' he said rapidly. 'You know, it's been ages since I last saw anything decent. Unfortunately Sunday's already booked up.'

'So I'd heard,' she said, smiling ambiguously. 'Just don't overdo it, Frank. Some things aren't worth it.' As he wandered out of her office he wondered what, precisely, she was trying to tell him. Susan wasn't worth it?

He remembered Phil's warning. Whatever Pete might say, he couldn't have been lying about playing Susan at badminton. Did the delectable Doctor Pleadle pick up any new officers at Wellbury police station? Trifle with their emotions before disposing of them, a lover's litter in a well-worn charade of cheap sport?

No, surely Susan was not like that.

He had an image of Alf Simmons smiling down on him, shaking his head, a wry grin on his face.

Not me, Alfie my son, he thought to himself. You might have been suckered twice, but it is not going to happen to me.

Hubris is not the happiest of words.

But it was one Frank knew well.

His problem was that he always thought it applied to someone else.

Week Two

Monday: Meeting the missus

Frank was sitting at his desk at eight on the Monday morning, leaning forward while re-reading the 1964 reports. Eric Johns walked in and placed a mug of coffee in front of him.

'Special service for wheelchair cases,' he said, laughed and walked out.

Frank glared after him. He tried stretching his legs. They hurt like hell.

On Saturday he had bought himself a badminton racket, along with a new sports outfit, the smartest the little money he didn't have could buy. It had taken a lot longer than he expected. Squash rackets had evolved over the years into things which were as light as feathers, but they retained some bulk. The badminton rackets he had been shown wouldn't, he thought, had served as fly-swats. Still more reason to be confident that Dr Pleadle was in for a surprise.

But the surprise had been his own. Everything Pete Phillips had warned him of had come true. While he had been racing around the ridiculous court panting and sweating, Susan had hardly broken into a glow. With a flick of the wrist she could place that damn shuttlecock almost anywhere she wanted, while he charged around trying to control it like a squash ball. She could have polished him off in fifteen minutes. Instead she had kept three games going for two hours. And Pete had been especially right about the size of the courts. Theirs had been a lot larger than it had appeared when they first walked out.

Every so often she had sweetly enquired whether he wasn't

too tired to continue, which was like a red rag to a bull.

Admittedly a rather slow and very stupid bull.

The pain hadn't hit him then. He believed that, if you were fit, overdoing things would result in the pain coming in the second morning, if you weren't fit, it hit you the following morning.

On that morning he discovered that he had not been fit. His legs felt as stiff as concrete. He had to take a bath instead of his usual shower, in an attempt to unlock the muscles. It worked as long as he stayed in the bath.

The last time he had felt anything close to this was when one evening he and another constable, in his uniform days, had chased a suspect for almost three hours on foot. The bugger had been surprisingly nimble – and fit. Adrenalin had kept himself and the other constable going, that and the fact that the suspect had always appeared to be just within grasp. Afterwards he had sworn he would never do anything so silly again. Up until yesterday he had kept that promise.

He had been so exhausted and dehydrated after the badminton that he had only managed to have a couple of pints afterwards before going home and collapsing on his couch. Susan had been surprisingly sympathetic about foregoing dinner.

But then she had form. He wasn't her first victim. She had probably expected it.

She had certainly intended it.

She could have mentioned beforehand that the reason she only made county-level instead of trying for international competitions was her devotion to her career.

He wondered if he could do her for grievous bodily harm.

If the jury consisted of her previous victims, certainly. Otherwise ... otherwise.

He took a grateful sip of the coffee Eric had brought in. Walking the distance to the coffee machine without openly showing what everyone else would have guessed at, i.e. that he was almost crippled, would have been almost impossible.

'Oh, that this too, too solid flesh would melt, thaw, and resolve itself into a dew,' he groaned to himself, trying to shift into a more comfortable position in his chair.

He liked quoting Shakespeare. It gave him both the feeling that his education had not been entirely wasted, and also that this too would pass, namely that in a few days or centuries he might be able to walk normally again. Or at least walk.

'Morning, Sarge, good weekend?'

Gertie had walked in.

'So-so,' Frank replied off-handedly, trying not to move any muscles. 'Any news on our Mrs Simmons the second?'

Gertie handed him a print-out.

'Interesting,' he said, having skimmed it quickly. 'Re-married in 1971, name of Green. But had a son in 1968. Out of wedlock, or rather, without a husband around to do the necessary – a little naughty for those days, wasn't it?'

'I wouldn't know, Sarge. I thought that was the free-love and flowers decade. People didn't mind single woman having children.'

'People always mind single women having children. These days they just hide it better. And, in any case, our Elisabeth Green, nee Simmons, nee Edwards, was married at the time. Only her husband Alf, nee Alfie, had gone AWOL.

Permanently. But did she know that? Did she know about Alf's other wife? Or was it Mrs Simmons mark one who found out about Mrs Simmons mark two?'

Gertie rubbed her forehead and grimaced.

'I think I'm beginning to get a headache, Sarge,' she said. 'And I think you can only be nee once. It refers to your maiden name, not your later name.'

He grinned at her.

'I agree. Far too many nees about. Time we went asking some questions. Ready for the off?'

'Whenever you are, Sarge. Who's first?'

'I think the second Mrs Simmons, Mrs Green as she is now. Let's see what her memories of 1964 are.'

He stood up, normally to start off with, then very, very slowly.

'A bit stiff this morning, Sarge?' asked Gertie, her face distorted by a giggle she was trying to repress.

'Backache,' he replied, 'must had slept in the wrong position. I think maybe you should drive.'

He handed his car keys over, and they left the station as fast as he could shuffle. He hoped the stiffness would have gone before he next met Pete Phillips.

'Sarge, you don't think you're being a little – how can I put it?' Gertie asked as she drove and he tried to make himself vaguely comfortable in the bucket passenger seat.

'About what?' he asked.

'About the case.'

'Oh. You mean, "narrow minded", that sort of thing? Concentrating on the family alone? Not considering other possibilities'

'I suppose you could put it that way.'

'Yes, Gertie I have thought about it. Whole bloody weekend as it happened, almost.'

Once upon a time he had made a promise never to think about work while off duty. If you didn't leave the station behind, the station would leave you behind – burnt out, washed up, and the only hope a very early retirement. He had heard of too many detectives who ended up spending their evenings on their own with a bottle of whiskey, watching black and white reruns of old movies on television with the sound turned down. His own preference was to open a bottle of wine, sit down with his guitar, imagine he was Bob Dylan, and completely forget about the world outside. He found it a very soothing exercise, up until the neighbours started banging on the walls.

Which reminded him. He had yet to unpack the guitar. It was lying in a box somewhere in the so-called second bedroom in his flat, a bedroom large enough to sleep a very small midget. He made a mental note to retrieve it for a soothing session soon.

He might even get to meet the neighbours.

'What if it has nothing to do with the families?' he asked rhetorically. 'Our Alfie was a long-distance lorry driver with two marriages to support. How could he afford that? Did he have a lucrative little sideline, smuggling little packages, say. Diamonds, drugs, something like that. And one day he and his partners have a little falling out. Or a big one, as far as Alfie is concerned.'

'That was what I was thinking, Sarge.'

'Trouble is, Gertie, if that is the case, it rather reduces the almost non-existent probability of our finding any solution. At least if it's a family affair the family are still with us. Where on earth will we find evidence against unknown smugglers forty years ago?'

'True, Sarge, but surely we shouldn't forget that option?'

'I have no intention of forgetting it. But at the moment I intend to concentrate on what we do have.'

'I could do some digging,' Gertie offered. 'Trace the local lowlife of the period. See if anything comes up.'

He looked at her and smiled.

'Gertie, you are too good for me, you know that?'

She giggled.

'I was hoping to become a detective at some stage, Sarge. You won't forget that, will you?'

Everyone, it seemed, apart from him, was aiming at something. He knew that Gertie was studying with the Open University for a degree, distance learning, hard work and long hours. It made him feel embarrassed about his own lackadaisical studies. In a way he felt protective of the young woman. She deserved to go far.

'No, Gertie, I won't forget that.'

Maybe if she could control her giggling, he thought. But, no, then it wouldn't be Gertie.

He tried to imagine her as an inspector, himself reporting to her.

Strangely enough, he couldn't see a problem.

Except for one: by that time she would know his dodges better than he did.

* * *

The Green's home was a comfortable three-bed roomed semi-detached house in the suburb of the Old Village, a name that probably had a history, though no-one could remember what it was. The house had a cared-for front garden, packed with flower beds full of bright dancing flowers, of which Frank could have named about none. But they were pretty.

It was on his long list of things to do: find out the names of flowers. Unfortunately it was a long and ever-changing list.

Inside the Green's house was filled with memories of earlier years, including deep armchairs and a couch in the lounge. Frank found the armchair he had chosen too deep for comfort. His muscles had joined a militant protest group.

'It happened a long time ago,' Mr Albert Green said angrily from his own personal chair, a firm, upholstered leather one designed for people with back problems. Mrs Green was pouring tea into delicate china cups.

'Shush, now, Albert, the police have their duty,' she said to her irritated husband. 'And remember what the doctor said about your heart.'

'I'm afraid that is the case, Mrs Green, Mr Green,' Frank said, carefully accepting a cup of tea which he knew would end in his lap if he tried to drink it. 'We never close unsolved cases. Your first husband's has come up for review.'

'You got back problems?' asked Mr Green aggressively. 'I can see it, you know, the way you're trying to sit. Bloody uncomfortable those chairs, if you've got back trouble.'

He seemed to take great comfort from Frank's lack of it. No offer of alternative seating was made. Gertie smothered a smile. She had chosen to remain standing while taking notes.

'Just a slight twinge, Mr Green, nothing serious.'

'Probably a little arthritis, you can get it quite young these days, I'm told,' said Mrs Green.

'I can recognise back trouble a mile away,' said Mr Green. 'Had to go into hospital for a check-up last month, bloody porter reckoned he couldn't wheel me in 'cause of his trouble. Now the police send a semi-cripple. Shows what they think of us, eh Liz.'

'Arthritis, I think,' replied his wife.

'1964,' Frank said. 'Mrs Green, you reported your husband missing.'

'Yes. Yes, I did, Sergeant.'

'If they really meant business they wouldn't have sent a Sergeant, they would have sent a Chief Superintendent Inspector,' noted Mr Green.

'Hush, now Albert. I'm sure the Sergeant is more than capable. Where would you like me to begin, Sergeant?'

The capable Sergeant wished his muscles would go away and leave him in eternal peace. Mortality was a disposable option.

'Let's start with when you realised he was missing, Mrs Green.'

'I always said he was a good for nothing,' noted Mr Green sourly.

'Albert! Really, do you have to?'

'Sorry, love,' came the muted response as Mr Green developed an intense interest in his cup of tea.

'I apologise for my husband, Sergeant. He forgets himself from time to time.'

Her stern face softened as she watched her husband contritely try to sink into his chair.

'You see, Albert and I – well, we were almost childhood sweethearts, you know. We both grew up in Old Merrick – just beyond Lords' Acres, I don't know if you know it? Not a bad little place, but not as wealthy as Lords' Acres, of course.'

'I haven't had the chance to visit it yet, Mrs Green.'

'You must, when you get the chance, it's a lovely neighbourhood. Now, where was I? Alf, wasn't it?' She sighed. 'You see, I was two years older than Albert, so I knew we would never get married or anything – or at least I thought I knew, men very rarely married a woman older than themselves, not in those days. Then Alf came along, whisked me off my feet, and we were married within three months.'

'Your mother – ' began Mr Green.

'Yes, dear. So anyway, I was very happy being married to Alf, right up until he disappeared. My parents never thought much of him, I know, but I was young, and who listens to their parents at that age? He has no history, no family, they said. But I was too young to care about history or family.'

'You were twenty-four?' asked Frank.

'Yes, I know, these days a girl of twenty-four is street-wise, or whatever it's called. In those days – the permissive society passed us by, I'm afraid – a girl of twenty-four was still a girl. Yet at the same time, if she wasn't married she was almost a spinster.'

'I would have waited,' said Mr Green.

'You did, my darling, you did. And I do love you for it. Anyway, Sergeant, when Alf went missing everyone thought their worst predictions had come true. I had married a ne'er-do-well, and he had done a midnight flit, or something of the sort. I was determined to prove otherwise. The police then were hardly interested, so I went to the company he worked for. Inglebrookes, they were called. They said they too had no idea where he might be.' She paused, and looked out of the window. Frank shot a glance at Gertie to make sure she had noted the company name. Gertie nodded briefly.

'So it turned out that everyone had been right all along. The man I married was a fraud. A fake.'

Another pause, this time to take a genteel sip of tea.

'But you don't marry a fake, Sergeant. Maybe one day you will marry and understand what I mean. You marry a belief. Oh, I admit I made a mistake. But I would still make the same mistake if I had my time over again. I know I hurt Albert here. But I never realised at the time how much I hurt him. And when I was in the wilderness, as they say in the bible, Albert stayed with me.'

'Never did trust the bugger,' offered Mr Green.

'Yes, dear. Sergeant, have you ever loved someone? Truly, truly loved them?'

'I'm afraid that has never been considered part of police training, Mrs Green,' Frank replied.

He was thinking of Susan.

He was thinking he owed Susan one. Oh, yes, revenge would be sweet.

What it would consist of was a question for later.

He concentrated on what Mrs Green was saying.

'You can love in many ways, Sergeant. Women understand this, men apparently not. I loved Alf. I love Albert. Alf ran away. End of Alf. But not my love for what I believed he was.

You can love an image, you know.'

'I'm not a bloody image,' Mr Green interjected.

'Yes, you are, my sweet. Shush, now.'

'Mrs Green, did anything unusual happen when your husband – Mr Simmons – disappeared?' asked Frank. 'I have to be honest, we're clutching at straws, but – anything? Anything at all?'

Mrs Green shook her head.

'Don't think I haven't tried to remember, Sergeant. Alf was due back from a trip to France. He'd promised to bring back some French perfume. Personally I could never stand the stuff, but that was Alf trying to show how much he cared – or so I thought. He just never came back. That's all.'

'Muck, pure muck, that French stuff,' Mr Green offered.

Elisabeth Green's "that's all" was, Frank thought, her way of handling her husband's disappearance. Perhaps Mr Green felt the same way. Perhaps not.

'I know this is a delicate subject, Mrs Green,' said Gertie, 'but you had a son in 1968.'

Mrs Green wiped her eyes with a handkerchief.

'Yes, that's true. George. George, we called him. I wanted him to be named Albert, but Albert wouldn't agree.'

'Very well, Sergeant, now you know,' Mr Green said, defensively angry, 'we had a child out of wedlock. Liz couldn't get a divorce, nor a death certificate for seven years. We loved each other. Everyone else was doing it, the Sixties, everything goes, hah! Not in our case, though, we had to wait for the paperwork, didn't we! When we didn't the neighbours wouldn't talk to us. Hypocrites!'

'I'm sorry, Mr Green, I realise this is traumatic for you,' Frank said. 'And I realise we're digging up old ground, quite probably for no good reason. You will forgive us, I hope?' This last was addressed to Mrs Green. Mr Green did not sign peace-treaties.

She nodded.

'Can you remember where you were when Alfred Simmons disappeared, Mr Green?' Gertie asked of Albert.

'Who, me?'

'Yes, sir, you.'

'Are you accusing me of something?'

'No, sir, of course not. But you could be a material witness. Maybe you were the last one to see Mr Simmons before he – disappeared.'

Only by the slither of a minute hair had she avoided saying "before he was murdered".

'You see, Mr Green, we've been given an almost impossible task. Anything – even the slightest thing – could possibly help us. Though, to be honest, the chances are slim to non-existent.'

Frank was impressed. Gertie hadn't giggled once.

'Well,' said Mr Green, somewhat mollified, and, as Frank had noted from early on, somewhat in awe of Gertie's bosom – something he was sure Mrs Green had not missed – 'nothing I can tell you, really. I was in The Smoke – London – when Alf went missing. Good place for jobs, in those days, London. Walk out of one on Tuesday, start another on Wednesday.'

'What sort of work was that?' Frank asked.

'Any sort. Young lads today, useless. I worked as a building labourer. Learnt enough to start me own business. Came back to Wellbury and set up Green and Co – had me own office and shop works. You've heard of the name? Sold it when we decided to retire.'

'I'm afraid I'm new to the area,' Frank admitted. 'So you were in London when Alfred Simmons went missing. How long before you returned?'

'How long? I don't know. Weeks, probably. I didn't know the bugger had done a runner. No reason for me to come back here.'

'But Albert,' Mrs Green interrupted, 'you were back the following weekend. I remember seeing you, walking towards your parents' house.'

She turned to Frank and gave him a weak smile. 'I used to visit Albert's mother almost every week, I was on my way there when I saw Albert. I so terribly wanted to speak to him, you know. I called out, but he didn't hear me, and I thought he probably wouldn't want to speak to me, so I left it. It wasn't until a few months later that we met again.'

'Can you remember why you were back in Wellbury, Mr Green?' Frank asked.

'Why? My parents lived here. I used to come back every third or fourth weekend,' Albert said, apparently unaware that he had just contradicted himself. 'London was a fun place, Sergeant, but every so often you need to get away to somewhere more peaceful. If my wife says I was here, then I was here. I didn't keep a diary, you know. If I had known the police would turn up forty years later to interrogate me I would have done.'

Nothing, thought Frank. After forty years who would

remember where they were, unless something catastrophic or wonderful had happened? And if they said they were in London, or Timbucktoo, and someone else said, no, I saw you in Casablanca, whose memory could you trust? No doubt Mrs Green was right, but if Mr Green was here a week after Alfie Simmons stroke Alf Simmons had been shot, then it was unlikely that he, Mr Green, had been in town a week earlier – if what he said about returning every three or four weeks was true.

On the other hand maybe he was lying through his front teeth.

Frank tried not to think of that possibility. His head would begin to hurt as much as his metacarpals.

'Mrs Green, I don't suppose you have a photograph of your husband – of Alfred Simmons, I mean?' he asked.

Mrs Green glanced briefly but guiltily at her current husband.

'No, I'm afraid I destroyed everything of his. It was a very painful time, you know.'

Frank sighed internally and began the slow, painful process of leaning forward to place his still full cup of tea on the coffee table in front of him.

'Oh, dear, you are in pain,' Mrs Green said, standing up and taking the cup from him.

'No, that's okay, Mrs Green, just a little stiff from sitting down for too long,' Frank assured her, as every muscle he didn't know he had clamoured rudely and insistently for his attention.

'Mrs Green, I don't suppose I could use your little room?' asked Gertie, trying to appear slightly embarrassed while also trying not to giggle at the sight of Frank being aided by a little old woman.

'Of course, dear, let me show you where it is.'

'Nasty thing, backache,' Mr Green sympathised as the women left, his former aggression almost overcome by feeling for a fellow sufferer.

'Just a passing pain, it'll be gone in a day or so,' Frank assured him, stretching gently.

'Nah, son, it'll be with you for life. Gets worse every day.'

Cheerful bugger, thought Frank.

'Who does your garden?' he asked, looking out the window. 'It certainly looks very summery.'

'Liz, mainly. She's got a little arthritis, but nothing too bad. There's a young lad we pay to do the heavy work, when the little sod isn't too lazy. Just glad my days of digging trenches is over.'

Now was that a Freudian slip? Or even a sly dig, knowing that there was nothing the police could prove after such a long time?

'Of course these days they use mechanical diggers,' Mr Green continued, 'the youngsters nowadays half die if they have to do any real work.'

Mr Green, I hope someday a certain young Doctor challenges you to a game of badminton. You moaning old burke.

'Sorry about that,' Gertie said as she and Mrs Green came back into the lounge.

'I suppose you lot use these new-fangled computers instead of good old police work,' Albert Green continued, warming to his theme of a sadly forgotten past.

'They can be useful,' said Frank politely. 'Well – '

'Nothing like a good old, solid Remington,' Mr Green said.

'Remington?'

Frank wondered what revolvers had to do with computers.

'Typewriter. None of your plastic rubbish. Solid steel, that's what it is. Had it over thirty years now.'

'Albert has terrible handwriting,' Mrs Green said. 'No-one can read it, so he uses a typewriter when writing to people. It's his arthritis, you know.'

'I was typing a letter of complaint to the council only this morning,' Albert began.

'Right, thank you for your time, Mr and Mrs Green, we must be getting along,' Frank said, moving as fast as he could to the door, hoping to get out before Albert Green generously informed of the exact and comprehensive details of whatever his complaint was. It would probably come accompanied with the detailed description of the solid steel, key by key.

Mrs Green stood in the doorway, waving them goodbye as they drove off.

Gertie turned a corner and pulled into the side of the road. She took a photograph from her pocket.

'Alfred Simmons,' she said, handing it to Frank.

'Gertie, you are a treasure!' he exclaimed. 'How did you guess?'

'I saw that look on her face when you asked. No way a woman like that who has been in love would get rid of everything, not if she wasn't sure why her lover had left. Handsome young bloke, isn't he?'

Frank studied the black-and-white photograph. He supposed Alfie Simmons had been handsome. Much more slender than he had first presumed a lorry-driver would be. A half-grin, slightly foppish hair, bright, twinkling eyes. Tie and collar. Hat slightly to one side of the head. Scar as mentioned in the police report.

He would have arrested him on sight on suspicion of looking like he was about to commit some mischief. Or looking too self-confident and cocky.

'Pity they didn't spot the similarity back in 1964,' Gertie said. 'I mean the coppers who took down the details.'

'Probably too busy ironing their kaftans, I would imagine. Makes it more interesting for us, though.'

'Was that a hint of enthusiasm I just heard, Sarge? Interest in your work? Not at all like you.'

'Don't be silly, Gertie, you're letting your imagination run away with you.'

'Where to now, Sarge?' she grinned.

'Let's go see whether Mrs Simmons Senior has kept any photographs of her dearly departed husband,' Frank replied. 'And see if we can't have a game of snap.'

* * *

Mrs Simmons did not have a photograph.

She had photograph albums.

'This is Little Alfie when he was a month old,' she said, tenderly stroking the edge of a black-and-white picture of herself some fifty-odd years before, holding a little baby.

'Ooh, he's so sweet,' cooed Gertie.

For a moment Frank was afraid she would say 'Who's a little diddums then?' to the photograph.

They were sitting at Mrs Simmons' kitchen table, much to

Frank's relief. The hard wooden chairs gave him some relief from his physical agony. But even that had been banished from his mind the moment Mrs Simmons had shown them the first photograph in the first album, a pride-of-place faded sepia picture of a wedding couple. The bride was an eighteen-year-old Mrs Simmons, looking slim, pretty, and pleased as punch. The bridegroom was a younger version of the man in the photograph Frank now had in his pocket. Unless Alfie Simmons had a twin brother called Alf Simmons with an identical scar which pulled his mouth up slightly, then Gwendolyn Simmons and Elizabeth Green nee Simmons nee Edwards were in for a surprise.

'He was a sweet little baby,' Mrs Simmons was recalling. 'No bother at all. Unlike Edith, though.'

She turned a couple of pages.

'There's Edith, at the same age.'

'Oooh, such a cute little thing,' gasped Gertie.

What, wondered Frank, would the competent and forceful middle-aged Edith Finchley have thought had she known a twenty-two-year old female police officer with large bosom was drooling over a picture of her as an infant?

'She looked cute, but she was a right handful, unlike Little Alfie – more like her father, really, or at least how I imagined he would have been as a child. Little Alfie was, what's the word, stolid? Not at all like his father.'

Not like Alfie Simmons, certainly, but quite possibly like his father, whoever that was.

'Here you are,' Mrs Simmons said, finding another page, 'summer, 1960, Margate. Alfie was twelve, Edith ten. See how she makes a face at the camera? And poor little Alfie just stands there, waiting for it to be over so that he can go look at the cars and motorbikes. Such a darling boy.'

Margate, 20th July, 1960 was the written inscription. The colour photograph was faded. Standing either side of the two children, Edith in a bathing suit, Little Alfie in shorts and shirt, were their parents, Gwendolyn Simmons in a light blouse and knee-length skirt, Alfie wearing long slacks and an open shirt. They came across like an average happy family on holiday. Alfie senior looked as if he didn't have a care in the world.

'Did you go there often, Mrs Simmons? Margate?' Frank asked.

'Oh, no, my goodness, no,' she replied. If she was surprised at the interest of the two police officers she was not showing it. Rather she was intent on getting the most out of an extremely rare opportunity to show off her albums. 'Of course, you two wouldn't know, I suppose.'

'Know what?' asked Gertie.

'What it was like, my dear, in those days. We married in '48. Now there was still rationing then, even into the Fifties, some stuff. Sugar, if I remember correctly. Finding enough material for a decent dress was almost impossible. And hardly anyone owned a television, let alone a colour one, not like these days. Times were hard.'

She paused and smiled.

'Though we were lucky, really, we were young and in love, we could put up with a lot. Love does make such a difference. And of course we didn't know much better. I was born in 1930, so all I had known until then was the Depression and the war. Alfie's job brought in enough to live on, which was better than what we had before. That holiday in Margate was special, a big treat.'

'You never went there again?'

'Once. In the summer of 63.' She slowly turned the pages. 'There you are.'

Margate, another summer, 1st August, 1963. Thirteen-year old Edith was scowling, furious. Alfie Simmons' face was set angrily. Gwendolyn Simmons looked as if she was about to cry. Little Alfie looked embarrassed.

'I put this in two years after Alfie went missing. It was the last family photograph we had. Such a pity it was taken just after we had a row. The poor man we asked to take it was most embarrassed.' She laughed. 'He was about fortyish, had a young girl in tow, twenty, maybe twenty-five at the most. I thought they were having an affair at the time. Last thing he would have wanted was cameras all about the place. I've often wondered who they were, and what happened to them.'

'What was the row about?' Frank asked, drawing back to the point.

'Oh, usual silly thing, nothing much at all. Edith wanted a swimming costume, some skimpy thing – I can't remember whether it was a bikini or not – can't even remember whether we had bikinis then, wasn't that something to do with one of those James Bond films? Anyway, I just said no, but she argued and Alf became furious. Edith was at the stage where she was discovering boys, and Alf was dead set against that. Typical father, I suppose, determined that no dirty-minded young man was going to touch his angel.'

Frank studied the group. At thirteen Edith was as tall as her mother. In the shot she was wearing a frock at least a size too small – no money to buy a new one, or to show that she was definitely a young woman? Whichever, she was big enough to hold a revolver and pull the trigger. Probably not strong enough to dig a grave, though. But Little Alfie, at sixteen, shorter but stockier than his supposed father, looked strong enough.

'Little Alfie looked after Edith, did he?' he asked.

'Strange that you should say that, Sergeant, he did. How did you guess that?'

'That's the impression I get from the photograph.'

'Very perceptive of you, Sergeant, you obviously understand people. Yes, Edith was always getting them into scrapes. Little Alfie wasn't what you would call brainy, but he had brawn and something more important, common sense.' She sighed. 'Strange the way it turned out. Alfie turned into exactly the sort of person you'd expect, hard-working, gentle, a great catch for some young woman – and he married a lovely young girl called Beverly, and has a very happy family. Edith, on the other hand, I thought she'd be a trial until she found some poor man silly enough to marry her. She was too strong-willed, you see. And then she suddenly changed.'

'When was that, Mrs Simmons?'

'When I started the boutique. I made her give me a hand. It wasn't difficult, she was mad about fashion. But it was as if changing from being the buyer into the seller changed her also. It didn't take long before she was more my partner than my daughter, she had an excellent head for business.'

'When was that, just after your husband went missing?'

'Oh, goodness, no, a good few years after that.'

Damn, thought Frank. A psychological change at the right

time could have spoken volumes.

'How did your children react to their, er, father's disappearance.'

'Much as you would expect. He was often away for long periods, a whole month once. They were used to him not being there. It wasn't as if he had died or something. And they were young, with their own lives to get on with. It makes you sad, in a way. Your own children can't share your pain. Understandable. But still painful.'

'They didn't miss him?'

'Oh, I'm sure they did, in their own way. I think we all expected him to wander back through the doorway one day. I certainly did.' She gave another sigh. 'But – I don't know how to explain it, Sergeant. If you're a teenager with a father who disappears every so often, not having him there is, well, normal. I don't think they grasped the idea that he would never return. Not until they had become used to him not being there at all. And then it didn't make any difference. Not to them.'

'I understand, Mrs Simmons. Would you mind if we borrowed this album to take copies of one or two of the photographs? I promise to take good care of it.'

She looked puzzled.

'What on earth for, Sergeant?'

'We don't have the results of the DNA tests yet, Mrs Simmons. I don't like to have the grass growing under my feet; if the DNA tests aren't as positive as we'd like we might have to look at reconstructing the face. DNA comparisons aren't always as clear-cut as we'd like, I'm afraid.'

And the prize for number-one liar goes to? thought Frank

guiltily.

'My goodness, you are efficient, Sergeant,' she remarked. 'Such a pity they weren't more efficient in them days.'

Frank stood up, grimacing.

'Oh, do you have backache, Sergeant?' Mrs Simmons enquired sympathetically.

'Probably just slept the wrong way, Mrs Simmons.'

Gertie giggled. Gwendolyn Simmons turned to her.

'Now you take care of your Sergeant here. He's a very thoughtful young man.' Her eyes twinkled. 'And I dare say he'll make a good catch for some young lady one day.'

Gertie almost blushed.

'What makes you think I'm not already married?' asked Frank out of curiosity.

'You aren't wearing a wedding ring for a start,' she replied. 'And I rather think you would if you were married. And you don't look married, if I can put it that way.'

You mean I look too happy? Frank almost asked.

* * *

Back in the car he rubbed his jaw reflectively.

'Alfie Simmons was an incredibly lucky man, up to the end. Wellbury's not the size of town you'd expect to get away with bigamy for long. I'm surprised he even managed to get married a second time without being found out. From all accounts he wasn't the sort of person to blend into a crowd.'

'Being away a lot probably helped,' noted Gertie.

'True. But sooner or later Mrs Simmons would have found out. And Mrs Green, as she is now.'

'You think one of them did it after discovering he was a bigamist,' suggested Gertie, starting the engine. 'But then who helped her bury the body? The other wife? Alfie wasn't that big. They could have done it between them.'

'Doubtful.'

'The three of them, Mrs S and her kids?'

'Possible.'

'Or just Little Alfie and Little Edith? She shoots him in a fit of temper, he hides the body, to protect her.'

'That, I think, is the most possible scenario at the moment.'

Proving it was going to be the least possible scenario.

Gertie paused before asking him another question.

'Would you wear a wedding ring if you were married?' she asked.

Frank paused before answering, puzzled at the question.

'Of course,' he replied. 'Why not? Presuming that I did commit an act of marriage, of course.'

'Oh, just asking,' she replied off-handedly.

She waited for him to give her directions to their next port of call, but he seemed strangely engrossed in his own thoughts.

'Where to now, Sarge?' she asked. 'I'm starving.'

'Back to the station, Gertie my dear. You can fill your tummy-tum-tum in the canteen.'

She grinned. She had worked with a few newly-promoted detective sergeants before, and her experiences had not been positive. Mostly they had been desperate to impose their new authority on silly, empty-headed young women constables. Frank didn't seem to realise he was supposed to be a sergeant.

He was quite cute in a way.

A wedding ring, she thought.

She liked the sound of that.

Gertie knew exactly what she wanted from life. A career in the police force. A husband. Three children. She was working hard on the first. She hadn't found the right person for the second and third.

Or maybe she had.

Just maybe she had.

* * *

They went into the station via the back entrance. Gertie went off to the canteen while Frank satisfied himself with a cup of coffee in his office. For some reason he felt not at all hungry, which was surprising considering the energy he had expended the previous day. So long as he kept his limbs moving every so often the stiffness was not so agonising – or, at least, hari-kiri was no longer a major option.

He was performing a gentle leg stretch when Eric Johns walked in.

'You must have just missed your girlfriend,' he said to Frank, placing a carrier bag on his desk. 'She left you this.'

'Girlfriend? Which one would that be?'

'The delightful, delectable Doctor Pleadle, breaker of hearts and of muscle. Also known as Doctor Death for much the same reasons.'

'Droll, very droll, Eric. May you one day find yourself opposite her on a badminton court.'

'Unlikely, Frank, I saw what she did to Pete Phillips. Then again, in his case he deserved it. Cocky little shit he was when he joined. Learnt a lot since then, about being a human being, anyway.'

Frank considered this for a few moments.

'Tell me, Eric,' he asked, 'do you know any old coppers? Retired coppers. Ones who would have been around in the Sixties?'

'Back to the old coppers again? I might do, I suppose. Most don't stay in touch. I'll have a word with a few people, see what I can hunt down. What are you hoping for?'

'That they might recognise someone in a photograph. There's no record of our Alfie Simmons having been found guilty of anything, but that's maybe because he was too fly. They might have suspected him without being able to pin anything on him.'

Eric whistled.

'I've heard of long shots, but that's more like trying to jump a marathon in one go.'

'Please don't mention marathons, Eric. Or any form of physical exertion.'

Eric laughed and left.

Frank pulled the carrier bag towards himself. Inside was a folder, a small parcel, and a sealed letter. He opened the letter.

'Frank, the tube is for your body, the report for your brain. I've updated it. Try reading it this time. Susan xx'

He opened the little parcel. Inside was a tube of muscle rub. He smiled. Pity Susan hadn't offered to rub it on for him.

He put the thought very quickly to one side. He had just had the Susan Pleadle lesson on what happened to Sergeants who got above themselves. He didn't want the one on what happened to Sergeants who were too forward. He left the tube and opened the report.

Most of it he knew already. There was a section on analysis of the scraps of clothing found with the skeleton, minute fibres of socks, trousers, shirt, jacket, leather shoes. That was news to him. For some reason he had always assumed the body had not been clothed – or to be exact, he hadn't really considered the question. The clothing scraps had not revealed anything beyond corresponding to the right period.

Some coins which also matched the date; a couple of shillings, several penny pieces. Any paper money would have long decomposed. No wallet. Buttons, presumably from said clothing.

The subject had never suffered any broken bones. Was that unusual? Frank himself had never broken a bone. He tried to remember how many people he knew of who had done so. Three or four at school, couple at university. But then what was a broken bone? It didn't have to be the obvious ones in arm or leg; one girl at university had had her wrist in an elastic brace after punching her boyfriend during a philosophical argument. The relative positives between Kantian theory and Sartre's Existentialism, or something like that. Maybe CND versus Thatcherite economical policy.

Charlie Brown or Linus as a modern male role model, perhaps.

The girl had won, if he remembered correctly. She had had a very forceful argument.

No broken bones. Was that relevant? Not that Alfie Simmons sounded like the sort to end up in fisticuffs over philosophy, but his formative and later years were unlike the current time, with Health and Safety regulations now almost, allegedly, strangling business, and schools terrified to allow pupils to participate in any perilous – or perfectly safe – sports.

If you believed the newspapers, which he tended not to.

Height five foot seven inches, would most probably have been on the slim side. That was true enough, as he had seen in the photographs.

No signs of any serious illnesses.

A suggestion that the face could be reconstructed if necessary. Another suggestion that DNA comparison could identify the subject if potential relatives could be identified. That gave Frank a wry grimace. Susan was efficient. He was allergic to efficiency.

Confirmation that the bullet matched the calibre of a Webley Pocket Revolver. Soil analysis showed that the soil above and below the subject indicated that the subject had been buried rather than covered by the natural flow of nature.

The last section covered what had not been found. No trace of a hat. No spectacles. No weapon of any form. No belt buckle. No remains of braces. No case, brief or otherwise. No wallet. No watch. No form of identity, though that would probably have been paper and would have disintegrated.

Frank sighed. Susan was asking the right questions. Unfortunately there were too many of them, and the number of possible answers was even greater. He picked up the telephone and dialled her number. Not so much as to discuss the case, as to show he was not avoiding her. Beaten, not quite bloody, even though it felt he should be, but unbowed and still interested.

'Susan? Frank Summers here. Just called to say thanks for the report – and the muscle rub, I think I'll need it. Listen, what do you say to drinks after work tomorrow?'

'Drinks?' she asked, surprised.

'Yes, you know, the things they serve in pubs. Know of any good pubs around here? The ones I know normally have coppers in them.'

She laughed.

'There's the Hangman near Heading Square. Quite a nice atmosphere, and very few coppers.'

'What about six-thirty?' He thought he could probably make it if he kept his evening meet with FF short.

'Say six-forty five. You sound quite chipper today.'

'I've managed to survive the morning, and find that I'll probably live. Might not be able to walk properly for a few days though.'

She laughed again. He liked that laugh.

'Glad to see your male pride hasn't been too badly dented. See you tomorrow.'

He put the telephone down with a smile on his face and a happy heart in his chest. Maybe that's what Susan's previous boyfriends had failed to understand, that it doesn't matter if your girl could beat you at badminton.

Not, of course, that he was going to make any assumption about his being her boyfriend or any such rank at this stage. Oh, no. Oh, no, no, no. That would be like clearing the first jump at the Grand National and thinking you were home. The next twenty-odd or however many would be a fatal surprise.

Anyway, "girlfriend" carried a lot of emotional and other

baggage he didn't want to carry. At least, not yet.

Maybe one day, but not quite yet.

'My, we do have a happy face,' Gertie said, coming into his office while biting a chunk out of an apple.

'Life, my dear Gertie, is far too short to be unhappy. Enjoy it while you can, that's one of my mottoes.'

'Along with "do as little work as possible"?'

'Now, now, Gertie,' he remonstrated gently. 'I have a great deal of respect for hard work. But it's like religion – nice to have on the odd occasion, but not something to get too carried away with.'

She sighed.

'Wish I could have your attitude, Sarge.'

He smiled at her.

'When I was ten years old my parents sent me to boarding school for two years. I hated every single second of it. No pain, no gain was the general idea. I saw things somewhat differently. I never did see the point in pain when you could just as equally well be having a good time. There's plenty of pain and heartbreak in life. You don't have to go looking for it. It will find you, believe me. Epicurus understood that.'

She took another bite of her apple, as if it were the sole point of her thoughts.

She didn't want to know about his childhood. She had a career to follow. Getting mixed up emotionally with colleagues was not on the agenda. She had thought it over during lunch and so decided. Sergeant Frank Summers might be cute, but he was off the menu.

Changing the subject was.

She noticed the tube on his desk.

'Talking of pain, has someone offered to rub that in for you?' she asked with a twitching mouth. He quickly put the tube into a desk drawer and winced as his body reminded him of its parlous state.

'Tell me something, Gertie, supposing we were married.'

'That a proposition, Sarge? Are we allowed to?' she asked, a little too quickly.

'Frank proposing to you, Gertie?' asked Eric Johns, coming in with a slip of paper and dropping it in Frank's in-tray. 'I'd be careful of him, you know, they say he suffers from backache and is disappointing in some way or other. Not that I'd know, of course.'

'Been so long you can't remember,' Frank called after him as he left.

Gertie giggled and took another bite of apple.

'Now, where was I? Ah, yes, supposing we were married and you found out that I was already married – or later that I'd secretly married another woman. What would you do?'

She wrinkled her face in thought.

'Probably beat seven sorts of stuffing out of you then hand you over to the other woman to finish the job. Sarge.'

'Say you had a revolver handy. Would you use it?'

'Doubt it. Wouldn't be worth it.'

'Thank you very much, Constable Gregson, you are hereby nominated for the diplomacy of the year award. I "wouldn't be worth it"! Bloody hell, you know how to puncture a man's ego.'

'Sorry, Sarge.' Gertie looked almost contrite. She peered at him between the fringe of her hair and the apple in her mouth.

He sighed.

'Nope, that's the problem,' he said.

'What is?'

'As FF said, we have to look at this as if we were coppers of the Sixties. These days it seems that everyone is having a bit on the side, nothing to get excited about. I'm not convinced that was the case for most people back then, certainly not working class people of Wellbury. And, I rather suspect, Wellbury even these days has some pretty old-fashioned ideas. Of the better sort, of course. I think. I hope so, anyway.'

He stood up slowly, carefully testing his limbs for signs of overwhelming refusal, missing the look on her face.

'I don't know,' she said, 'people still murder people for the same reasons. Love can be a strange thing. So I'm told.'

He looked at her suspiciously, remembering something she had said, totally missing anything she might be trying to say.

'You weren't offering to rub that stuff in, were you?'

She paused for just a second.

'Sorry, Sarge, doing my hair tonight.'

'Ah, that's okay. Just worried I might have missed out on the offer of the century. Come on, time to have a chat with the one person we haven't yet spoken properly to. Little Alfie.'

* * *

"Little Alfie" had been given the title to distinguish him from his father. However, at five feet four inches the soubriquet had some force. On the other hand, his stocky set and firm jaw would make any man think twice before using it as a pejorative.

'Paperwork, mainly, these days,' he said, leading them into his office. It was both neat and sparse. Frank guessed that he approached paperwork with a grim implacability, as if it were a wild animal that needed constant beating back. 'Not like the old days,' he continued, sitting down while Frank took the other available seat, gingerly.

'Almost all electronics, these days, need a degree to understand them. Computers. When I started you needed brawn and a love of engines, also a good ear. Place was always filthy with grease and oil. These days you attach a machine to the engine, read a graph, and the place looks like a maternity hospital.'

'When did you open the garage?' Frank asked.

'Hmmm, would have been seventy-four, I think. Yes, that's right, I was twenty six. A mate and I went in together. Most people thought us daft, it was the oil crisis years, wasn't it? Though I don't expect you to remember that.'

'I vaguely remember something about 1978.'

'Aye, seventy-eight, but before then there was seventy-one and seventy-three. Bad years, those were. Seventy-three was the worst, just managed to keep going. And the unions. Mind you, we were lucky in a way. Because we were a small outfit we didn't have any bother. One youngster tried it on, seventy-nine, I think it was. Got a clip a round the ear and his papers. The others were wise enough to know that we couldn't afford that sort of nonsense, we'd go bust.'

'What about your partner? Is he still around?'

'Disappeared.'

'Disappeared? How do you mean?'

'Ran off with a sixteen year-old, let me see, late eighties that was. He was what, almost forty. Mid-life crisis, so I'm told. Stupid bugger didn't know when he was well off, what with a wife and three kids. He asked me for money, about two months later. I offered to buy his share. He agreed, now I own the lot. Soon I'll probably sell it and retire somewhere, Cornwall maybe. Spain's a possibility.'

Frank decided that they were concentrating on the wrong eras.

'Mr Simmons, I presume you know why we're here.'

'Aye. Edith and Mum told me. Don't think I'll be of much use to you.'

'Can you remember when your father disappeared?'

Little Alfie shrugged.

'Sort of. Not really, though, not anything you might be interested in.'

'In what way.'

'I remember what I was doing. I was an apprentice. I loved the work. Worked all the hours God sent. And then there was Speedway on Sundays. And the rest. Mum tried not to let on that Dad was missing, but it wouldn't have made a lot of difference. He was always going away.'

'You didn't have a good relationship with him?'

'Didn't have a relationship, really. He was Dad, just that. I suppose when I was a nipper I used to look forward to him coming home, always had a present or two. But come sixteen I had my own life. Kids these days, they think they don't need to start working until they've got a few degrees and – what do they call them? Vac years? Gap years? By the time I was sixteen I could lift almost any kind of standard car engine on my own, strip it to pieces and then put it back together again.'

Frank suspected that he was being a little imaginative, but he certainly looked powerful enough to lift a heavy weight.

Or dig a deep grave without breaking into too much of a sweat.

'What do you think happened to your father?'

Another shrug.

'If it's true that the skeleton is him, then most likely that he had a skinful, fell over and hurt himself somehow.'

'He used to drink a lot?'

Little Alfie frowned.

'Not as I recall, no. Once or twice he'd come home singing, but it wasn't very often. I think he liked the company, rather than the booze.'

'You know where the skeleton was found?'

'Aye.'

'Can you remember what that area was like when your father went missing.'

Another deep frown.

'Aye, more or less. I've been thinking that it was a strange place for Dad to end up. Not on the way to or from his regular pub. But then, if he was plastered he might have got lost.'

He looked at Frank squarely.

'Some strange questions you're asking,' he suggested.

'It's a strange case, Mr Simmons. There's a coroner's inquiry next week. We're trying to get together an understanding of what might have happened.'

Little Alfie nodded slowly, as if he didn't quite believe him.

'Mr Simmons, you say you've been thinking about it. Has anything, absolutely anything, come to mind? Any memories of strange people around? Something unusual happening around that time? Anything?'

Little Alfie shook his head.

'As I say, I was working almost every hour that God sent. Up at six, breakfast, then to work. Back at six, maybe seven or eight in the evening if there was a rush job, supper, and then bed. It was hard work. I was shattered most evenings. You could have had a party in the same room and I wouldn't have noticed.'

So, overhearing a gunshot was almost definitely out of the question.

Unless he was the one pulling the trigger.

'Well, thank you for your time, Mr Simmons,' Frank said, standing up carefully.

'You got backache?' asked Little Alfie sympathetically. 'It's the desk work that does it, you know. I never had a twinge until I started spending most of my time in this office.'

'I'm sure you're right, Mr Simmons,' Frank replied, noting that Gertie was keeping her mouth covered with her hand.

* * *

'What now, Sarge?' she asked as they drove back.

'I need to write up my notes for this evening's interrogation by FF. Your shift must be finishing soon.'

'I can work a little longer, Sarge.'

'No rampant boyfriend awaiting at your pied-a-terre?'

Gertie giggled.

'Sadly not. I share a flat with Allison – Allison Hardbury? She seems to get most of the action.'

'Constable Hardbury? The one with the, er, the ...'

'Flat chest and face like the back of a bus?' prompted Gertie. 'Okay, she isn't ugly, but she is plain. Yet she always has men floating around her. Most ones I get just want to talk to my chest.'

'Interesting.'

'What, my chest?'

'No, I was thinking of Alfie Simmons and his women. They weren't unattractive, from what you see in the photographs. So why did they fall for a two-timer like Alfie?'

'Charisma. You've either got it or you haven't.'

'Damn. That's me right out of the game then.'

'Oh, I don't know,' replied Gertie enigmatically, a reply that flew right over Frank's head.

Had Frank found himself in the Wild West with vultures circling overhead, he would probably have asked what those things like pretty parakeets really were.

What irked his worst friends from school and university was their belief that the vultures would, having heard Frank say hello, presume they must be parakeets after all, and so behave. Those friends had had their own nickname for him: Biscuit. Because he was such a Jammy Dodger.

* * *

'I suppose it's time to get them in for an official statement. Inform them that it is a case of murder,' Frank said to Frieda after he had finished his evening report. She had remained silent throughout, jaw set, a disapproving look in her eyes. He wasn't sure whether he had upset her, or whether it was someone else, but explosions often involved not their creator but innocent bystanders labelled "collateral damage". He decided the best thing was to say as little as possible as quickly as possible, and remove himself from the danger area as soon as possible.

'You think that will do any good?' she asked sharply.

'Unlikely. But, as you said yourself, it has to be done.'

Reminding your boss of their own words is a high-risk strategy. It was Frieda's attitude. He was rarely irritated by other people's moods, accepting them as inevitable human foibles, but this was a bit much. Whatever she was angry about was nothing to do with him.

'When?'

'Tomorrow. We'll have to try to get Edith Simmons in, and her mother straight afterwards, before they can exchange notes. Mobile phones make life difficult.'

'I don't know,' she replied tartly, 'some people seem to manage okay. What about Little Alfie?'

'I'll get someone to pick him up while we're interviewing Edith. I doubt he has a mobile.'

'Very well,' Frieda said, standing up to indicate the interrogation was over. 'By the way,' she added off-handedly, 'I hear congratulations are in order.'

Congratulations? He had done something right?

Not by the way she used the word "congratulations".

'Why's that?'

'Your engagement. I'm sure you'll both be very happy.'

Engagement?

'Engagement?'

Are you mad?

'To Gertie. I can't say I expected it, but she is a very young attractive woman, I suppose. If you like that sort of thing.'

'Um, Inspector, maybe you know something I don't, but I'm pretty sure Gertie and I aren't engaged. It's the sort of thing you notice, if it happens. Difficult to become engaged purely by accident, I would have thought. I – Oh, for Pete's sake! Or, in this case, for Eric's sake.'

Frieda looked at him in surprise.

'What on earth are you going on about?'

'How long do you think I would get for murdering a malicious police sergeant spreading slanderous rumours, Inspector?'

'You mean – Ah, I see. Sergeant Johns?'

'Exactly. I remember now. I was discussing the case with Gertie. I think I said something like, "Suppose you and I we're married and you found out I was already married". Eric came in as I was speaking, make a joke and left. No doubt he saw an ideal opportunity to spread some gossip.'

'He's not the sort to spread gossip, Frank. He must have thought you were proposing.'

There was a teasing smile on her face now. She was well aware of Eric's penchant for gossip. She slipped her coat on and picked up her briefcase.

'I'm sure you will make an excellent husband for someone,' she said, stroking his cheek as she walked past him towards the door. 'Just probably not for Gertie, she's ambitious.'

He looked incredulously at the empty doorway. Had his boss just flirted with him?

He shuddered and went to look for some strong coffee. His muscles reminded him of their pain. Good thing I didn't mention the muscle rub, he thought. I might have received an offer I couldn't refuse.

When he got home he took a cold shower and watched an Open University programme on some mathematical subject of which he understood about a tenth.

It didn't help much. When he fell asleep he dreamed he was on a desert island with Susan, Frieda and Gertie. They weren't wearing very much, Frieda especially. They approached him with offerings of trays of fruit.

As they reached him the trays of fruit turned into sharpened knives in their hands.

At that point he woke up, sweating.

He tried to remind himself that he did not believe in dreams. And especially not as portents of the future.

It didn't help an awful lot.

His dreams had a bad tendency to come true in most cases.

His nightmares always did.

Tuesday: Psycho Summers

Despite his interrupted slumbers Frank was in a good mood the following morning as he sat in his office, singing "I was born under a wandering star" to himself. Apart from the stiffness having largely left, a certain desk sergeant had turned up for his shift to find that the whole of his area in reception had been booby-trapped. Eric Johns had wondered why some of the leaving shift appeared to be hanging around instead of going home straight away as they normally did. When he opened a filing cabinet drawer he discovered the first reason: a small explosion left him covered in confetti. Sitting down to recover, his chair collapsed. So did a couple of idle constables hanging around in the hallway, only they were laughing.

It took Eric a few minutes, after he had recovered sufficiently to attend to someone reporting their car missing, to realise that the log-book he was trying to open was a dummy, glued solid.

The word spread quickly through the station. People made a special visit to see for themselves. The word was that Frank was exacting revenge on Eric for his gossip about Frank and Gertie being engaged. The general feeling, once they realised that that was all it had been, merely gossip, was that Eric Johns deserved it. After all, he had raised their hopes about an office romance and a forthcoming wedding: such things were not to be trifled with. Besides, a book had already been opened on how long the engagement would last, who would break it off, and, were that to be Frank, how many limbs he would retain. Now all bets were off. That cost money.

Frank was well aware that certain people – FF, for example – would be using words like "childish". But he rather thought she would be smiling when she said it. Police stations and, he presumed, other organisations, functioned far better when there was childishness and tomfoolery going on alongside the more onerous duties.

Anyway, Eric had it coming to him.

Although Frank would never know it, Frieda had happened to have occasion to pass through reception, had spotted a couple of errant pieces of confetti on Eric's uniform, and had enquired as to when the happy event had taken place and when Sergeant Johns intended to have his uniform cleaned properly. She hadn't paused for a reply, but after she left Eric could have sworn he had heard an impossible noise.

Frigid laughing in the corridor on her way to her office.

It had a result beyond dispelling the gossip about their engagement. Eric was subsequently sufficiently contrite – after he assured Frank that he would not re-offend, and would Frank mind disarming whatever other dangerous accidents his devious mind had thought up, please? – to assure Frank that the Simmons family members would be brought in by his uniforms in the correct order. He even made the telephone calls to ensure that said family members were available and willing to come in, though it had taken all his charm to achieve; people did not take naturally to visiting police stations.

Although Frank didn't realise it, he was gaining a reputation. Anyone who could make the old hand Eric Johns go out of his way to do something must have something special.

The law of unintended consequences, always busy around Frank, kicked in. Before long he was no longer "DD", but "Psycho".

Fortunately no-one mentioned this to Mrs Gwen Simmons before he walked into the interview room where an unsuspecting Mrs Simmons sat with a cup of tea a nice young constable had brought her.

He sat down opposite Mrs Simmons, with Gertie next to him. She switched the tape recorders on and intoned the incantations which informed the machines that an official interview had begun. Mrs Simmons blinked nervously, as if suddenly realising that more was afoot than simple statement gathering.

Frank suppressed the urge to assure her that this was just routine bureaucratic behaviour.

'Mrs Simmons, I must inform you that you have the right to have a lawyer or solicitor present.'

She gave him a look which mingled both surprise and outrage.

'Why would I need a lawyer?' she demanded.

'Because we have some bad news, Mrs Simmons.' He took a big mental breath. 'Your husband did not go missing. He was murdered.'

The confusion, followed by shock, on her face seemed genuine. Her mouth opened as if to say the word "murdered". There looked the real possibility that her teeth might fall out.

They sat in silence for seconds, many seconds, Frank determined to force her to speak first.

Her jaw quivered. She reached for her tea with a shaking hand, and then drew her hand back, as if she could not trust it.

'How do you know he was murdered?' she asked finally, her voice weak but determined.

It could be regarded as a strange question. It was the logical one for a something that had happened forty years before, but not quite the one you'd expect from someone who had just found out their dearly beloved and missing husband had been murdered.

'The pathology reports are quite definite. He was shot in the back of the head. We've recovered the bullet.'

Mrs Simmons said something they could not catch, and leaned forward, fainting. Gertie caught her before her face hit the table, and Frank jumped up, swung around the table, and held her shoulders.

'I'm alright,' she whispered, trying feebly to shake their hands off. Gertie lifted the tea to her lips, and she took a small sip, and then took the cup from her. She leaned back, trembling.

'Mrs Simmons?' asked Frank.' Are you okay? Do you need a doctor?'

She shook her head, took a gulp of tea, and put the cup down, A weak, bitter smile crossed her face.

'Lawyers, doctors. I'm being offered everything today. Oh, plus a murdered husband.'

Frank returned to his seat. She seemed to have recovered just enough to continue, and police comfort for a suspect could go only so far.

'I'm sorry, Mrs Simmons, but under the circumstances ...'

'How long have you known?' She gave a short, bitter laugh. 'Of course, silly me. You knew all along. Even while you were pretending it was an old missing person's case, nothing special. While I showed you the photographs. I wondered why you were so interested. Now I know.'

'It is a murder investigation, Mrs Simmons.' She looked into his eyes. He could see anger replacing the shock.

'I see. And I'm a suspect, I suppose.'

That was a pretty quick conclusion, Frank thought.

'We have no information to point to anyone at the moment. We're still trying to piece together what happened.'

'I'll tell you what happened, Sergeant,' she replied, her voice rising, the "Sergeant" spat out. 'Forty years ago my husband disappeared out of my life. I had to deal with that, that and raising two children, having to scrape money together, taking a risk on running a shop without anyone's help but my children. It took years to get over the idea that my husband – my HUSBAND, Sergeant – had walked out on me, his wife, and his children. But get over it we did, finally. And now you sit there and tell me he didn't leave me, someone murdered him. And you think that someone was me!'

By the final sentence she was shouting, standing up, pounding the table with her thin fist.

Frank and Gertie sat silent, waiting for the storm to pass. Eventually it did. Mrs Simmons sat down, eyes blazing, but regaining control.

'I don't know who did it,' Frank said softly. 'But I'm going to do my damndest to find out.'

She glared at him for a while, and then nodded her head slowly.

'I believe you, Sergeant. And I also want to find out. When I do you won't have to try him, because I will kill him.'

She spoke as if it were forty years ago, and the murderer still around to kill.

But, if it wasn't an act, if she were ignorant of the murder, why did she obstinately refer to a "him". Was it just an ingrained natural use of the male gender as a general reference to an unknown person, or did she know something that she wasn't telling?

'Or her,' Mrs Simmons added, blowing that theory away.

'Do you have any idea who might have wanted your husband dead?'

She shook her head slowly, still angry.

'Alfie didn't have enemies, Sergeant. Everyone liked him. He always said life was for the craic, not for fighting. He was too full of Irish blarney to get into arguments, even if it was invented blarney. He was no more Irish than I'm Peruvian.'

'Were women attracted to him?'

Another furious glare.

'Yes, Sergeant, they were. Did he take it seriously? No. Did I murder him in a fit of jealousy? No. He was a loving husband and adoring father, Sergeant.'

Such a loving husband he married twice.

'Could someone – another husband, say – have misconstrued any of his actions?'

She nodded slowly, as if the idea made sense.

'Yes, that's possible, I suppose. I didn't know his friends down the pub that well, but some men do get silly ideas into their heads. It's possible, especially after drinking, that they might get violent. Even if there was no cause. Yes, that would make sense.'

'Can you remember any names?'

She thought for a while, and then shook her head.

'It's too long ago. I seem to recall a Frankie, and maybe a Jim, or John, but as I've already said, I never knew any of them very well. Women – wives – were only allowed into a man's local on special occasions, and if you had children to look after you hardly ever got the chance anyway.'

'No surnames?'

A shake of the head.

'Can you remember the name of the pub?' asked Gertie.

'The George. But as I think I've told you, it's long gone now. It was pulled down for one of those high-rise flats, about ten years, maybe twelve, after Alfie went.'

She had two ways of measuring time. There was looking back, and there was after Alfie went.

'The area you lived in,' Frank asked, 'that was demolished as well? For the flats?'

A nod.

'Were the residents rehoused? In the flats?'

'Eventually.'

'So some might still live there.'

Another silence. Another nod.

'Possibly. But I'd say you're clutching at straws, Sergeant.'

She gave him a direct look.

'Still, it seems that straws are all you'll have after all this time. Well, I'm willing to clutch at them with you.'

'Going back to the time when your husband went missing. Can you remember what happened?'

'I've told you all that before.'

'I know, Mrs Simmons, but this is official. On the record. And you might have remembered something.'

But she hadn't. Her story was almost exactly the same, only minor changes in exact times – did she wake up at six that morning, or was it just before six? Did Little Alfie have porridge and toast, or was he in too much of a hurry to have the toast?

But nothing new.

Frank concluded the interview by thanking Mrs Simmons for her time, which earned him a dirty look. Gertie took her to the ladies' to freshen up. When they came back Mrs Simmons was almost smiling. You couldn't be down for too long with Gertie around.

'Sergeant,' Mrs Simmons said before she left, 'I understand that you have to do things that might not be pleasant, so I can't hold it against you. But, as I said, I want to find the person who did this as much – more – than you.'

She smiled a soft smile suddenly.

'It's a funny world, isn't it? For forty years I've hated Alfie for running out on me and the kids. Now I've got to get used to the idea that he never left us, that he always loved us.'

'Sometimes it's better to leave the past as it is,' suggested Frank.

Because, he wanted to add, you might be changing your mind again when you hear the other news we have waiting for you.

Unless you already know about that particular bit of other news.

'I won't make any hasty decisions, Sergeant. Don't go too

hard on Edith and Little Alfie, they were only children at the time.' She paused before leaving, turning to Gertie. 'I'd watch him if I were you, love, he can obviously be a right devious bastard when he wants to be. Still, I worked that out the first time I saw his tie.'

Gertie blushed and followed her out.

'She guessed that we'd pull them in,' she said on returning from escorting Mrs Simmons out. 'She asked me. I thought there was no harm in confirming it. Nothing she could do about it anyway.'

'True.' He paused. 'She didn't react as emotionally as I expected,' he said, 'or, more precisely, she recovered very quickly.'

Gertie considered this.

'Could be delayed shock. On the other hand, maybe she's just holding it in. She's what you could call a tough old woman, don't you think?'

'She's that alright.' He paused, thinking, and then shrugged his shoulders. 'We'll see. Our Edith awaiting?'

'Room number four, Sarge. Little Alfie's on his way in.'

'Might as well get this one over, then.'

* * *

Our Edith showed little reaction to the news that her father had been murdered. It was as if she had been told about a stranger's killing. Awful, but little other emotional comeback.

'You don't seem surprised,' Frank commented. She shrugged.

'As I've told you, he didn't figure that largely in our lives – Alfie's and mine. It's almost like hearing about a stranger. And it was forty years ago, a lot has happened since then.

God knows what he might have been up to.'

A young girl, furious with her father from a argument over a bikini, and the father did not feature largely in her life?

Still, she was fourteen. The following day she might have forgotten that she had wanted a bikini.

Probably not.

She gave her replies as quickly and spontaneously as she could. Every so often she looked at her watch. Eventually she said:

'Sergeant, I presume you've interviewed my mother? I heard her voice while I was waiting.'

'Yes, Mrs Finchley, we have.'

'My father might not have meant that much to myself and Alfie, but he was everything to Mum – apart from us. It took her a long time to get over Dad disappearing. I didn't realise that at the time. But I do now. And I'd like to make sure she's okay. She puts up a brave face, but it isn't easy for her, you know.'

Frank took the point and quickly tied up the interview. Edith had not remembered any further details, and if she knew anything about her father's murder she was plainly not going to mention it

* * *

Little Alfie was waiting in room number one, the room his mother had been in not too long before. He had finished his hospitality tea. Others might see it as a pawn in police psychological tactics – if I accept, am I accepting their control? – but he was the sort to look at cup of tea, say, aye, I'd like a cup, and finish it off.

'I'm afraid I have to inform you that your father was murdered,' Frank told him after the opening rites had been concluded.

'Aye, I know,' Little Alfie replied calmly.

Frank tried to keep a calm exterior. Inside he was jumping for joy. A confession! The only way he could see any conclusion to this case was with a confession. And now he had one! Next to him he could sense Gertie stiffen like a gun-dog scenting the prey.

'How do you know?' Frank asked.

'Mum texted me while I was waiting in here.'

For a moment Frank could not believe what he had heard. Next to him the gun-dog twitched, a danger-sign of imminent giggles.

He had blithely ignored the fact that Little Alfie might have a mobile phone, let alone even considered that his mother might spend her spare time texting across the universe. Not that it would have mattered.

These interview rooms should be screened to prevent mobiles being used, he decided.

'I see. Hum. How did you feel about the news?'

A shrug.

'Makes sense. In a way.'

'What way?'

'Mum loved Dad. I guess he also loved her. When he left we presumed that wasn't the case. If we'd thought about it we might have realised that he wasn't likely to run off with some other woman, as we did.'

You were right the first time. Only he didn't actually run off

141

with her, he married her.

'Did your dad have any dodgy dealings? Anything that might have got him into trouble?'

Another shrug.

'None as I knew of.'

'Who do you think might have wanted to murder him?'

'No-one that I can think of.'

'Did you ever go to the George with him?'

'Once, when I was ten or so. Mum had to take Edith to the doctor, and Dad said he'd look after me. Bought me a fizzy drink, and some comics to read while he had a pint and chatted to his mates.'

'Can you remember any of them?'

'I remember the landlord.' A sudden smile lit his face. 'He didn't like ten-year-old kids trying to take his pumps apart. I got bored with the comics, you see. Looked for something else to do. Landlord was sitting chatting with the others, so I thought I'd see how the pumps worked. I would have got a clip across the ear if Dad hadn't got there first, and before I'd had a chance to get the things apart. He told the landlord kids will be kids, not to worry, no damage done.'

'Your father didn't, er, chastise you?'

'Dad wasn't like that. He looked me in the eyes, said "You know that's wrong, don't you?", or something to that effect. Course I did, and had to admit it. Dad didn't need to use his hands, his tongue was more efficient. Wish I was more like him.'

'The landlord. Remember his name?'

'No. Wouldn't make any difference. He was old even then,

would hardly be likely to still be around.'

While Little Alfie might be a man of few words, he was a good listener. He understood why questions were being asked, and answered them the same way.

'Remember any of the others?'

'Big bloke, beard, patted my head. Kids don't like that, it's patronising. Young bloke, name of Albert, seemed pissed-off the whole time. The others I can't really say.'

'You remember Albert? Why?'

Shrug.

'Can't really say. I remember a place we stayed in Margate once, landlady's name was Rosemary. Course we didn't call her that – she was Mrs something or other to us. Can't say why I remember that either. Not even sure it's true. Maybe she was really called Cynthia. Who knows? Sometimes people remember things that didn't happen.'

Very true, thought Frank, having had the experience in interviews. Somehow it made his task almost impossible. If two people couldn't agree what happened a day before, how would they after forty years?

He took Little Alfie through his previous statement.

No change.

When the interview concluded Little Alfie gave him a straight stare.

'I used to think, sometimes, what I'd do if I met Dad in the street,' he said with the first hint of emotion he had shown. 'You know, maybe on holiday somewhere. I decided that I would punch him in the face for deserting Mum, and then walk off without a word. Now it seems he never left her and us in the first place. Makes me feel guilty.'

He paused.

'I hope you catch whoever it was. Not so much for Dad's sake. More for Mum.'

* * *

They watched as Little Alfie's solid shoulders exited into reception and then through the front doors.

'Are we watching the old guard, Gertie?' Frank asked, musing.

'How d'you mean, Sarge?'

'Stiff upper lip, that sort of thing. They hear that their father's been murdered. Mrs Simmons hears that her husband was murdered. Yet the only one to show any real reaction was Mrs Simmons, and she seemed to recover very quickly. Extremely quickly.'

'It was forty years ago, Sarge. And if he was away such a lot, well ... It does make sense in a way.'

'Hmmm. I suppose you might be right.'

He checked his watch.

'Damn, looks like we've missed lunch. Maybe the machine might have a sandwich or two,' he commented.

'You could ask the canteen staff if they have any leftovers, maybe they'd knock up something, Sarge – a small fried egg and bacon sarnie?' Gertie suggested.

'Don't be daft,' he replied, as if still thinking about the family Simmons. 'They'd probably go on strike at the thought. Didn't Pete Phillips try that once? I heard they told him where to stick his warrant card.'

'Yeah, but he demanded. You are much more diplomatic.'

Thanks for the vote of confidence, he thought, if that was what it was.

'Okay, let's try it. Might as well, I'm starving for a change.'

'Lucky you, I'm always starving.'

He would have been quite happy with a stale sandwich from the machine, tasteless cardboard with minimal filling of dubious material, but enough to keep the hunger pangs at bay – frighten them away, in fact. But now he was in that dreaded state he had always avoided, responsibility. Gertie's tum-tum-tum was his, as senior officer and the one who delayed her lunch-break, responsibility to fill-fill-fill. And he was well aware of the importance of the simple things in life, like a good meal. Had Napoleon not skipped breakfast, he might not have lost at Waterloo.

Frank approached the gleaming canteen counter with a certain dread. The canteen staff were notorious for their aggressive protection of their time, especially since cutbacks had resulted in the decision to strictly limit mealtimes. Frank empathised with their feelings, which added to the nervousness he felt.

The counter was gleaming because it had just been cleaned after the lunch period. To his dismay the only person there was Agnetha, a dour, ascetic looking woman who probably sold bibles to the needy in her spare time. If there was one woman you didn't want to cross it was Agnetha. In the Dark Ages she was the woman who would have been burnt at the stake as a witch by villagers terrified of her.

Though Agnetha would probably have turned them all into little frogs before they could get the stake and kindling anywhere near her.

'Hello, Agnetha,' Frank said meekly, hoping he'd pronounced it correctly, 'I suppose we're too late.'

She gave him a look which suggested that he was too late to save his immortal soul, let alone his mortal stomach.

'Not to worry,' he said hastily, 'the chicken place down the road will do fine.'

The chicken place down the road was famous for producing something almost food-like, and constipation or the runs – often both – for several days after.

He was about to turn and escape when Agnetha spoke.

'Do you an egg-and-bacon,' she offered.

Frank froze in his I'm-leaving posture.

'Or mushroom and cheese. Can't offer anything more. Means I've only got one or two pans to clean again.'

'Egg and bacon sounds delicious,' Gertie said with enthusiasm.

Agnetha's doom-laden eyes turned upon her.

'Thought you were going to marry him,' she said accusingly.

'I haven't crossed him off the list,' Gertie replied, smiling.

Agnetha considered this.

'Aye, well sit down and I'll bring them to you when they're ready.'

Frank and Gertie dutifully sat down, close enough to the canteen counter to limit the distance Agnetha would have to walk, far enough away to ensure they were not overheard.

'What was that all about?' Frank asked.

'Agnetha thinks all women should marry and have nice happy families. Her boyfriend died in Vietnam. She's never got over it. I think it's called substitution – she wants us little girls to have the life she was hoping for. She's very protective of what she thinks as her boys and girls. We're the family she never had.'

'But we weren't in Vietnam,' Frank pointed out.

'Thank god. Her boyfriend – fiancé – was an Australian. A great romance, from what I've heard. Love in England, letters from Australia, death certificate from Vietnam. Not much of a life.'

Before Frank could respond Agnetha appeared with two plates. Doorstoppers of toasted egg-and-bacon with mayonnaise and other delights Agnetha knew her boys and girls adored, plus crisp, newly fried chips, real thick chips, none of that fast-food French fries muck. Agnetha would never have even considered such heresy.

'The way to a man's heart is through his stomach,' she informed Gertie in tones of solemn admonition. 'Remember that.'

When she was out of hearing Gertie giggled as she took a chip and dunked it in tomato sauce.

'More often the same way to a girl's heart,' she said. 'Good thing our Agnetha isn't lesbian. She's frightening enough as she is.'

That image did his brain no good at all. Nor the association, however tenuous, of Gertie and the word "lesbian".

'So, what do you think?' he asked quickly.

'I think this mayonnaise is probably home made,' Gertie said, chewing happily. She looked at Frank. 'But I'd agree with you. If it is a – *crime passionel*, as they say – then we might solve it. Otherwise, not much chance. And if it is, will we want to prosecute after all this time? After all, he was a bigamist. Could well be considered extenuating circumstances if it was one of his wives.'

She spoiled this comment by adding, along with a chip to her mouth:

'Good looking bloke, though. Not surprised he was popular with women.'

Frank sighed.

* * *

That evening Frieda decided that the wine bar was again the place for him to deliver his end-of-day report. After he had brought her up to date he sat staring at his glass of wine moodily.

'You know,' he said, 'I've always thought of women as being loyal to their men,' he said, 'especially during that era. Must be all those terrible films I saw when I was growing up. But then Gertie comes along with comments ...'

There was a slight smile on Frieda's face as she watched him.

'She probably does it to shock you, Frank. You are very old-fashioned in many ways.'

'And naive,' Frank said with a trace of bitterness.

'And naive,' agreed Frieda. 'Maybe it has something to do with being an only child. You end up with a slightly utopian view of how the world should be.'

'Not necessarily a good thing in a copper,' Frank remarked, wondering how Frieda knew he had been an only child. It struck him that it must be on his personnel file – had she looked it up especially? Probably not. She was the efficient type who would make sure she knew the exact histories of all her staff.

'Oh, I don't know,' she said, smiling. 'I prefer it that way. I've known too many bitter coppers, too many who became cynical beyond their years. We see too much of the bad side of life in our job. I wouldn't like to see you turn out that way.'

'Were you an only child?' he asked suddenly. She hid her mouth behind her glass for a moment.

'Yes, I was, as it happens,' she said slowly. 'No siblings, but a father who was very ambitious for me.'

'He must be very proud of you.'

She paused before replying.

'I'm not sure of that. He died a few years ago. One of the last things he said to me was not to lose sight of the other things in life. What helpeth it a man if he gaineth the world yet loseth his soul, he said – though he wasn't talking about religion. Sometimes I wonder if he wasn't regretting ... ' She shivered. 'Anyway, this is becoming maudlin. Back to the real world. What next on the Alfie Simmons front?'

'Something I'm really not looking forward to,' Frank said, draining his glass. 'Bringing in Mr and Mrs Green. I think I'll start off with Mrs Green on her own.'

'Would you like me to sit in with you?' she offered.

The real answer was that he'd prefer someone else to do the entire thing, but that wasn't an option this time.

The real question was why Frieda was offering to baby-sit her Sergeant, but Frank tended to take such offers much like Little Alfie regarded cups of tea, nothing to be unexpected.

'No, thanks,' he said. 'Sooner or later I've got to earn the money I'm being paid. Funny, isn't it? Bad enough when you have to break the news to a young wife or husband that their loved one won't be coming back again, but this is worse. At least if they're young they've got a chance to recover.'

'And then there's Mrs Simmons to be told – about his extra marriage.'

'And then there's Mrs Simmons to be told,' he agreed, 'about his extra marriage. Both of them.'

* * *

'I'm not boring you, am I?' asked Susan in the Hangman an hour later.

'Hmmm? Oh, sorry, I was thinking about this case,' Frank said, realising that he'd been staring into space while she had been talking.

'I'm so sorry to interrupt,' she said with a bitter tone in her voice. 'Shall I leave you here to get on with it? I wouldn't like to think I was being a silly little woman getting in the way of a serious policeman's investigation.'

'Okay, okay, you're right,' Frank said, smiling. 'I'm doing the sort of thing I promised I'd never do, let work take over my social life. Here I am, sitting having a drink with a beautiful, intelligent young woman who's made a special effort with her hair and makeup. What more could any man want?'

'Don't try that flimflam on me,' Susan replied, her stern voice failing to cover the pleasured blush spreading across her face, 'I've heard it all before.'

'I'm not surprised, every word is true.' She slapped his arm gently.

'That's enough, Romeo. I'm beginning to wonder if you've discovered Alfie Simmons' book of chat-up lines. They don't work in the modern age, you know.'

'Don't they? Seems a pity. I'd rather like a world where romance wasn't dead.'

'Silly. You're far too young to be so old-fashioned.'

That was the second time in the one evening a woman had accused him of being old-fashioned. He wondered whether he was heading for a premature life of comfy slippers.

'Tell me something, you're a woman.'

'I'm glad you finally noticed. I was beginning to get a little worried.'

'No, seriously, looking at it from the woman's point of view. Firstly I don't understand how two women such as Gwen Simmons and Elisabeth Green could fall for Alfie – or at least in such a way that he could get away with marrying both of them. Secondly, what would they do if they found out? And thirdly, who was the father of young Alfie?'

'Different times,' commented Susan. 'I doubt whether women such as that had even heard of the word "liberation". Getting married wasn't part of life, it was life. Probably brought up dreaming of the ideal man, along comes Alfie with his smooth patter, his talk of visiting foreign countries, no doubt, and bang! Any common sense they had would have gone straight out the window.'

'No chance of that happening today.'

'I don't know. I'm sure there are just as many silly women in the world today, ready to fall for some stranger's sweet talk.'

'Let me try it on you, then.'

'You already have. It doesn't work.'

'Pizza.'

She looked at him.

'I take it back. You do know how to sweet-talk a girl. I'm starving.'

'Drink up then,' he said, draining his pint.

'I think it was rather romantic, actually,' she said, finishing her glass of wine.

'Romantic?'

'Alfie marrying two women. If he'd married one and fooled around with the other that would make him an adulterous little shit. Marrying both – well, it shows he loved them, doesn't it?'

'I'll have to see if I can sell that point of view to the ladies concerned when I tell them,' Frank said with a rueful smile. 'Unfortunately I think they might react the same way so many people do to the messenger of bad tidings.'

He paused as a thought popped into his brain, no doubt lobbed by one of the lesser responsible voices in his head.

'So would you say, that, purely hypothetically, a man who goes out with two women in equal relationships is being romantic? Presuming he doesn't let the one know about the other?' he asked.

She turned to look at him.

'If it was me, and I found out, I would skin him alive,' she replied with more than a hint of menace and promise in her voice.

'Fair enough,' Frank said quickly. 'Er, what sort of pizza do you prefer?'

Ah, but only if she found out, Frank, said one of his voices, only if she found out.

'It depends on my mood. If I'm angry I'll go for anything

with loads of sliced sausage,' Susan said.

Somehow Frank felt he had just received a metaphor. Not a very promising one. Alfie Simmons' wives looked as if they were going to be the least of his problems in the near future.

Wednesday: A complicated love life

Mrs Elisabeth Green was ushered into the interview room at eleven o'clock promptly, looking like a nervous hen in a plucking shed. She sat down and waited silently while Gertie went through the pre-interview routine.

'Mrs Green,' Frank said softly, 'I'm afraid we have some bad news. We believe we have found the remains of your ex-husband, Alfred Simmons.'

Elisabeth Green gasped and clutched her handbag in her lap.

'Is he ... is he dead?' she asked breathlessly.

Frank and Gertie exchanged glances. Quite how "the remains of your ex-husband" could refer to a living person was beyond their imaginations. Did she imagine they'd sewed him back together and he was currently dancing the last tango in Paris?

'I'm afraid so, Mrs Green,' Frank confirmed.

Mrs Green seemed to slump in her seat as if there had still been some hope in her, now gone forever.

'How did he die?' she asked listlessly.

'He was killed, Mrs Green. Shot, with a revolver.'

'Oh dear. Oh dear.' She looked around. 'Was he living with someone? Did they kill him?'

'I'm sorry, Mrs Green, I don't understand.'

'I just wondered whether it was personal, or maybe someone was trying to mug him. It's such a violent world we live in these days.'

Frank and Gertie exchanged another look.

'I suppose it will be in the newspapers,' Elisabeth Green

continued. 'I hope we won't have reporters at the door all hours of the night and day. It would upset Albert terribly. And it isn't good for his heart, you know.'

'Um, Mrs Green, when exactly do you think your ex-husband died?' asked Frank.

She looked at him in confusion.

'Well, I don't know. I think I presumed it must have been in the last few days. Is that why you came asking about him? I should have realised that something must have happened to make you come around. I can't think why I believed that story about it being routine. Oh dear, I am silly, aren't I?'

She rummaged in her handbag, brought out a tissue and blew her nose loudly.

'Excuse me,' she said, 'I didn't think I would get upset. It was so long ago.'

She wiped her nose and put the tissue back in her handbag.

'There, that's better. I'll be fine. You can tell me everything. Was he in good health when he died? I've often wondered whether he was taking care of himself. He really was a man who needed a woman to look after him, you know. I hope whoever he went to didn't leave him high and dry. After all he would have been getting on a bit. Like me, I suppose. Somehow I still think of him as he was then, silly, I know, but there you go.'

Frank and Gertie had remained in a stunned silence as she meandered on. It took a few seconds after she stopped for them to recover.

'Mrs Green, your ex-husband didn't die recently,' Frank said gently. 'He died in 1964, around the time you reported him missing.'

'But that can't be,' she replied.

'Why can't it be?' asked Gertie.

'Because he sent me a postcard last week. It arrived yesterday. They had to redirect it. I've got it here somewhere.'

Frank and Gertie looked at each other in amazement as Elisabeth Green began another rummage.

'Here we are,' she said finally, handing over a postcard. 'He used brown ink, difficult for me to read even with my glasses, but that was Alf, always doing things differently.'

They stared at the postcard in Frank's hands. On the front was a faded picture of the seaside, with "Greetings from Margate" printed at the bottom. On the reverse was a short message in faded ink.

"My Dearest Darling

I just want you to know that I have always loved you. Remember that, whatever happens.

Your loving A"

'He always signed himself that way,' explained Mrs Green. 'Just the initial A. He thought it had style.'

Frank guessed that the card and writing was forty years old. The stamp and postmark were recent. The stamped date was modern. The original address had been crossed out and overwritten in blue ink.

Too late he remembered to take out a handkerchief to hold the card.

'That slightly changes things,' he said, thinking what an understatement it was.

'So Alf might be still alive,' Mrs Green commented happily.

'Still alive?'

'Well, if this person you thought was Alf died so long ago, then it couldn't be Alf, could it? So he could be – probably is still alive, somewhere in Margate.'

'Mrs Green, why didn't you tell us about the postcard before?' asked Gertie. 'You knew we were looking into his disappearance, you could have given us a call.'

'Ah, well, I was going to. The problem was Albert.'

'Albert?'

'He doesn't know about the postcard, and I didn't want to tell him. It would have been very upsetting, you know, and his heart isn't as strong as it was. I was waiting for a chance to use the phone without his knowing, but I didn't get a chance. And then you asked me in, and that was my chance.'

'Mrs Green,' Frank said slowly, 'I don't want to upset you, but there is a strong possibility that your husband – your first husband, Alf – did die forty years ago. I know how upsetting – '

'Nonsense. How could he have sent a postcard last week if he died forty years ago?'

That one stumped Frank.

'I'm afraid we're going to have to hold on to the postcard for a short while, Mrs Green,' he said. 'We need to do some tests on it.'

'You won't lose it, will you? It means so much to me.'

'It means just as much to us, I can assure you, Mrs Green.'

'Can I go now? I have to get Albert's lunch ready. He hates it when his routine gets interrupted. And he has a weak heart, so I do try not to let him get excited.'

'Yes, Mrs Green,' Frank said, thinking that Albert Green's

weak heart was probably the Greens' main topic of conversation. Strangling him to get it over and done with could be regarded as a mercy-killing. 'But I'm afraid we're probably going to have to get in touch with you again in the near future.'

'Well, I'd prefer it if you could do it so that Albert didn't realise what was going on,' she said, standing up.

'That might be a little tricky,' Frank commented.

'But we'll try our best,' Gertie assured her.

'Funny, after all these years,' mused Mrs Green. She looked at Frank. 'Do you think there's any chance you could ask your colleagues in Margate to keep an eye out for him? I do worry so. I'd be much happier if I knew he was in a home, or looked after by someone who cares.'

'I shall see what I can do,' promised Frank hollowly.

It would have been the strangest request he would ever have sent. "Attached please find the photograph of a bloke who died forty years ago, and also a couple of years before that. If you see him, do me a favour and nick him for something. Try charging him with being an illegal alien or impersonating the living. P.S. Hope you're enjoying the seaside. Love to the seagulls."

He did at least remember to keep Mrs Green's teacup for comparison of fingerprints. Not quite the proper way of doing things, but he could always do things properly later on if necessary. At that moment he really did not wish to have to explain to Mrs Green why she was a potential suspect. She might well query why she would have wanted to kill her ex-husband after not having seen him for forty years.

* * *

'Greetings from Margate,' Frieda murmured sitting at her desk, holding the offending item in its newly-acquired official police transparent plastic evidence-folder.

'I thought we'd better let you know straight away,' said Frank, standing by the window. Gertie was by the door, practising the art of being as unobtrusive as possible.

'In a way I wish you hadn't,' Frieda replied. 'I'm meeting the Chief Constable for lunch. Somehow "No progress" would have sounded better than this. He's got a bee in his bonnet about the dead skeleton.'

'I don't know. It means that we've got something to go on. It also suggests that whoever killed Alfie Simmons is very much alive and very much aware of what's going on.'

'You think so?'

'Why else would they post that to Mrs Green?'

Frieda smiled at him.

'There is just a tiny possibility that the person who posted this to Mrs Green was Mrs Green, Frank. It would only have taken a day for it to arrive. She wouldn't be the first old woman to do a strange thing like that. Especially after we revive her memories of her long-lost love. I believe the non-technical term for it is going ga-ga.'

Frank swore internally. He hadn't even considered the possibility.

'Better get it down to the lab as soon as possible,' Frieda said. 'See if they can tell the difference between old fingerprints and new. If there are any old fingerprints from Mrs Green I think we can consider the matter decided.'

* * *

'Damn,' Frank said as he and Gertie went out to the car park. 'I should have thought of that straight away.'

'Never crossed my mind either, Sarge,' Gertie assured him. 'If it was her she's an incredible actress.'

'Deluding herself, more like it. People can trick themselves into believing anything if they're desperate enough. Let's get it down to the path lab.'

'Personal delivery, like, Sarge?' asked Gertie.

'No, I'm just in a hurry with this one.'

Like hell, thought Gertie. She was coming to some unpleasant conclusions about a certain Doctor Susan bloody Pleadle.

For a start that she was rapidly assuming the title of "competition". Even if there wasn't officially anything to compete about. Just because she wasn't going to go out with Frank didn't mean that Doctor Death could.

* * *

'I'll give it to Tracey to look at,' Susan said, holding the plastic folder while giving Gertie a disapproving look.

'Tracey?' asked Frank with mild interest.

'She's a bit young for you,' said Susan. 'And you aren't her type anyway.'

'I didn't mean it that way,' said Frank, 'I was just wondering who she was. I happen to like meeting people.'

'I'm sure you do, especially girls,' Susan replied.

'Any chance we can get some results today?' asked Frank to change the subject.

'Today? You lot always want the impossible, don't you? Do you think I sit around all day just waiting for you to turn up? With some work?'

'Sorry, sorry, I didn't mean it like that. Let me rephrase that. When can we expect – hope – to get the results?'

'I'll have to see how busy Tracey is. I think she's working on something for Inspector Hanson at the moment. I could ask her to put that to one side if this is urgent.'

'Very urgent,' Frank assured her. 'I'm reliably informed that the Chief Constable has a bee in his bonnet about it.'

'Very well, I'll let you know as soon as we have anything.'

Frank left with a smile on his face. Frieda would be more than happy to know that their investigation, which could hardly be termed urgent after forty years, had pushed out her rival's work. He wouldn't normally have agreed to something which could get him in hot water with an inspector, but somehow he was beginning to feel protective towards Frieda.

And anyway, the Chief Constable thought that it was an important case. So by definition it had to be.

'I can understand how she feels,' Gertie said, interrupting his thoughts as they walked back to the car.

'Who, Mrs Green?'

'No, Doctor Pleadle. Bitter and twisted.'

'Bitter and twisted?' It was not a thought that had occurred to Frank before. Though it was true that she hadn't seemed too pleased to see him. A tender but not overly aggressive good-night kiss the night before – probably just right for a man and a woman getting to know each other, especially as he had ordered extra garlic – and then treating him like something the cat had dragged in today. He had automatically ignored it, presuming she would get over whatever it was.

'She's getting on,' Gertie said. 'No husband, no kids. Spent her life on her career, now she regrets it. She goes out with every new officer at the station – goes through them, more like it. Dumps them as soon as she's had enough. Now she's worried about growing old alone.'

'What happened to sisterly solidarity?'

'Oh, I believe in women sticking together, just sometimes you have to accept facts.'

'Anyway, she's not that old,' Frank protested as they got into the car. 'Twenty-something? Thirty at most.'

'Thirty's old for a woman,' Gertie noted as they drove off. 'Men are lucky, they're not old until – well, never, some of them. Take yourself, you could marry now or in ten year's time, doesn't make any difference.' She looked at him. 'Ever thought of getting married?'

'Please watch the road, Gertie. If you don't look where you're going I won't live to think of getting married.'

Gertie giggled as she swerved to avoid an oncoming lamppost.

'It's okay, Sarge, I've done the advanced driving course. I know what I'm doing. But, seriously. I think you'd make a great dad.'

'Because I'm also childish?' Frank asked.

Gertie giggled again.

'Well, there is that,' she agreed. 'Sorry, I didn't mean it that way,' she apologised, again looking at him.

'The road, Gertie, the road. What's got into you all of a sudden?'

'Oh, I don't know. I don't want to end up like Doctor Death back there. I want a husband and kids, at least three, two boys and a girl, or a girl, a boy and another one of either. But I also want a career.'

'Sometimes you just have to accept reality,' Frank said. 'Kids need a lot of looking after.'

'That's a sexist comment. Why shouldn't a woman have a career and a family. I'm surprised at you, I never thought you were like that.'

When Gertie let slip the giggling mask, thought Frank, she really let rip.

'I never thought you were like that, Sarge,' he corrected her.

'Sorry, Sergeant,' she said with venom. He noticed that her eyes, now locked on the road, were moist.

'Now, Gertie, what's wrong? I've said something that upset you?'

'That's Constable Gregson, to you, Sergeant Summers,' Gertie said through clenched jaws.

'Jesus,' Frank said to no-one in particular, looking out the window, 'I don't think Alfie Simmons was murdered. I reckon having two wives drove him to suicide.'

Gertie tried not to smile, but failed.

'Sorry, Sarge, I lost it there. Won't happen again.'

'Why, though?'

'Some questions you shouldn't ask.'

Frank pondered this. That time of the month? Asking that was dangerous, a bit like asking a woman when the baby was due only to find out that she had merely been over-indulging in the cuisine department.

'But what about FF?' he asked, partially to change the subject. 'She's got a career. Is she bitter and twisted as well?'

'I think she's brilliant,' Gertie replied enthusiastically. 'She's so young, not even close to forty and she's already an inspector. Youngest ever, so they say. She's a real example to other women.'

'And happily married with two point four happy children, no doubt,' Frank replied, wondering how Susan at a maximum of thirty was old, bitter and twisted, yet Frieda, not even close to forty, was "so young".

'Didn't you know?' asked Gertie, throwing him a surprised look. 'She's divorced. Her husband was also a copper, a right bastard. He used to beat her up. That's one of the reasons she hates anyone swearing, apparently he had a hard mouth as well as hard fists. But she managed to come through. It must have cost her a lot, but she made it. And she's senior to him now. I reckon she's brilliant,' she repeated.

'And she manages two point four children on her own? She must be. Superwoman, I reckon.'

'She hasn't got kids. Not that it's too late, though. But she meets mainly coppers, and she wouldn't go out with another of them for all the love in the world. But I'm sure she wants kids. And I reckon what she wants she gets, eventually.'

Frank blinked. An idea walked over his grave. Had Frieda changed her mind about going out with a copper? A certain Detective Sergeant, to be precise?

Some things weren't actually making sense yet, but he could feel odd shapes moving into position.

What worried him is that the shapes, when they finally revealed themselves, could be a wonderful tableau. Or his worst nightmare.

They sure as hell weren't parakeets.

He put the idea well to the back of his mind. It was a ridiculous notion. Frieda was the epitome of a consummate professional police officer. There was no way she would ever even entertain such a thought.

The idea sat at the back of his mind chuckling quietly and throwing popcorn at him.

* * *

'The thing I like about Frank,' Gertie said to Eric Johns as they and Frank sat in the canteen having lunch, 'is that he never forgets a girl's stomach.'

'Sergeant Summers,' corrected Eric. 'I know it's a minor point, and I know you're planning to be Chief Inspector by the end of the year, but we've earned our stripes, so a little respect wouldn't go amiss. You wouldn't go calling FF Frieda, now would you?'

Unusually for Eric Johns, the fact that he had slaved for years to get his stripes, and Frank had more or less fallen – or been pushed – into his, appeared to make no difference.

'Sorry, Sarge,' Gertie apologised, unabashed. Eric's tone had been one of vague admonition, as if it were something he felt he had to say and would prefer to get it out of the way.

'You're looking a little lost in thought,' Eric said to Frank.

'Was I? Yes, I suppose I was,' Frank conceded. He had been eyeing his machine-produced sandwich with little enthusiasm, wondering whether his resolution to avoid Agnetha's cooking, in order to avoid ending up like Michelin Man, was worth the effort.

He had also been wondering what it would be like to call Frieda "Frieda".

'You okay?' asked Gertie with some concern, fortunately

interrupting his balancing of Agnetha and Frieda.

'Yes, yes, fine. Just thinking about the case.'

'No shop talk in the canteen,' Eric said, passing a chunk of bread through the gravy on his plate.

'I was thinking about it, not talking about it,' Frank pointed out.

Eric paused, bread halfway to his mouth.

'I reckon that qualifies,' he said. 'I'll have to check the Rules.'

The etiquette of station life was held in the Book of Rules. Anyone querying the existence of such a book was promised a sight of it. Actually reading the rules, however, was solely in the domain of the Keepers of the Book, otherwise known as Desk Sergeants. Sooner or later most people accepted this. It was difficult to keep beating your head against something which existed only in the erratic imagination of Eric Johns.

'What were you thinking, Sarge?' Gertie asked Frank.

'Now what did I just say about shop-talk?' asked Eric.

'You carry on,' Frank said to Gertie, 'I'm going to my office to go through some things. Give a shout when you're finished.'

'Poor lad,' Eric said mournfully, watching Frank leave.

'Why?'

'He's got it bad.'

'It? What, women problems? That Doctor Pleadle, I suppose.'

'Nah, lass. That's nothing. No, he's got the bug. He wants to solve a case. He's hooked. Women are easy compared to that. In fact I bet you he doesn't look at a woman until he's solved the case of the dead skeleton. You could dance naked in front of him and I bet he wouldn't notice.'

His eyes caught sight of her bosom and his nose twitched at the thought.

'You're happily married aren't you, Sarge?' she asked sweetly, noticing his glance.

'Aye, close to thirty years. Never regretted a moment.'

'What's the secret, Sarge?'

'Simple, love. I don't cheat on her, I do a decent day's graft, I earn the money. She looks after the kids, there's a hot meal waiting when I get home. She does her bit, I do mine.'

'And that's it?'

'What more do you want?'

'A career, perhaps? A little satisfaction in being able to do a decent job?'

Eric shrugged.

'If you manage it, good luck to you. Call me an old fool if you want, but I think you're being led on by this modern thinking. There's an old saying, you can't have your cake and eat it. You're trying to have two cakes and eat both. Come the end you might find yourself with neither.'

'I suppose you think it was okay for Alfie Simmons,' Gertie said with a hint of steam rising. 'He had two little cakes. One rule for men, another for woman. It's always the same.'

'From what I hear Alfie's wives were quite happy,' commented Eric mildly, unfazed by Gertie's outburst.

'Good little housewives. Deluded little fools, more like it.'

Gertie stood up abruptly and took her tray to the disposal point. She realised she had not eaten even half of her meal.

She went to the ladies' to wash her face. Her eyes were red. She was overweight. Big breasts were all very well, but they attracted the wrong type of man.

She was eating too much.

And it was that time of the month.

She needed to go to Aikido class more often.

She wondered if Frank would be interested.

She opened her handbag and began repairing her face. It wouldn't do her career options any good if her Sergeant thought she was the weepy sort.

She paused at the thought. "My Sergeant". She smiled for some reason unknown to her. But Frank was her Sergeant, wasn't he?

Frank was sitting with his heels on his desk, tapping a pencil against his knee while staring into space when she entered his office.

'Penny for them, Sarge,' she offered. 'Mind if I sit down?'

'Hmmm? No, go ahead,' he replied, quickly pulling his feet off the desk.

Gertie rather liked that. Frank was the sort who thought – probably unconsciously – that good manners applied to all, irrespective of rank or position.

'So?' she asked, sitting down, 'any great thoughts?'

'Nope. Not even any little ones, really. Not until we get some feedback on that postcard.'

'Come on, Sarge,' she said, leaning forward and putting her elbows on his desk, 'you can't have sat there all this time without anything coming to mind?'

Frank flung his pencil down on the desk in frustration. The point hit first, and a sliver shot off into Gertie's cheek.

'Aaah!' she cried, clasping her eye. 'Aaah! Aaah!'

'Oh, shit, Gertie, I'm sorry,' Frank cried as he leapt from his seat and rushed around to her.

'My eye!' she said, 'It's in my eye.'

'Look, just a second, I'll get the first-aid kit. I'll phone for an ambulance. I'll – '

'Could you take a look, Sarge,' she asked, offering her face. 'It might only be a little splinter. You could take it out.'

Frank took her face in his hands, looking carefully into her eyes, searching for a foreign body.

Which is when Frieda walked in.

'Not interrupting anything personal, am I?' she asked.

Gertie tried to shoot up, but Frank held her firmly in position.

'Just a tick, Gertie.' He looked at Frieda. 'I threw my pencil down and a bit of it went into Gertie's eye,' he explained.

Frieda's eyes opened wide. She leaned against the doorway and folded her arms.

'That's certainly one of the more novel explanations I've heard,' she said while Frank continued his explorations.

'I can't see anything,' he said. 'Probably best to get you to a doctor, though. Can't be too careful where eyes are concerned.'

'I'll be okay,' said Gertie, pulling herself from his hold, 'I'll just wash them out. Won't be a long.'

She shot out of his office. Frank watched in surprise. Frieda had a different look on her face.

'I came in to ask about Alfie Simmons, Frank,' she remarked, 'not to find his spiritual heir.'

Frank tried to work this one out.

'You've lost me,' he conceded finally.

'Unfortunately it appears, if physical appearances and my own optical functions can be relied on, that that is not the case.'

Frank thought about that one. He thought he had been able to interpret Frieda's convoluted messages, but this time he was flummoxed.

'I'm sorry, Inspector, I really do not know what you're talking about.'

'You and Gertie? I realise many men are transfixed by the sight of overlarge mammary glands, but I never thought you would fall into that category.'

It took a while for this to sink in.

'Inspector,' he said, taking a deep breath, 'all that happened was that I threw down my pencil, a piece shot off into her eye. I was just looking to see if I could take the piece out.'

'Really. Do show me.'

'What?'

'Sit down.'

He went reluctantly back to his seat and sat down. She sat in the seat recently vacated by Gertie.

'Now, throw down your pencil.'

'Sorry?'

She leaned forward and pushed the pencil towards him.

'Throw it. The same way as before.'

'But – '

'Do it.'

He picked up the pencil gingerly and gently dropped it onto

his desk.

Frieda reeled back, clutching her eye.

'Aaah!' she cried. 'Aaah! Aaah!'

'Oh, shit!' said Frank, rushing around his desk for the second time that afternoon. He put his hands over hers.

'Let me have a look,' he said breathlessly.

Frieda took his hands away from her face and looked up at him, still holding his hands. There was obviously nothing wrong with her eyes.

Nor her hands. They felt very nice indeed.

'Understand, Frank?' she asked. She stood up, patted his cheek, and walked to the door. 'I want you thinking about Alfie Simmons' death, not Gertie's bosom. Okay?'

I was, Frank thought to himself in a mood working up to unaccustomed rage, watching her svelte calves walk out the door. I was until you lot started playing silly buggers.

A little voice in his brain said 'Ah, Frank? Um Frank? Hello? You said – well, you said a naughty word there, and she didn't give you a lecture? Hello, Frank?'

Frank wasn't listening.

He opened a desk drawer and took out a photograph of Alfie Simmons. He stood up, walked to the wall, and pinned it on the notice-board. He looked at it for a while.

'You were lucky, Alfie,' he said in a voice of grim determination. 'At least you knew what you were doing. Maybe whoever shot you did you a favour. But I'm still going to find out who it was. Just this once I am going to make the effort. Maybe afterwards I can go back to what I know best. Or what I thought I knew best.'

He went back to his seat and sat down, looking intensely at the photograph of a happy-go-lucky bigamist, a slight scar pulling his mouth upwards in a way women found attractive.

I have to go back, he thought. I have to understand who Alfie Simmons was, who his wives were. What it was like in that supposedly glorious decade.

While people burned incense. Sang happy songs about letting the sunshine in. Made love. And murdered Alfie Simmons.

I will find out, he thought to himself. I will. Whatever happens, if it's the last thing I do, I will find out.

Several self-defence mechanisms got caught in the rush for the open door. They had no intention of being there when the   accident   happened.

Thursday: Early starts and surprise invitations

At eleven o'clock the following morning, having had no word from Frank, Frieda made her way to his office. Inside Gertie was listlessly reading a file.

'Where's Sergeant Summers?' Frieda snapped out the question.

'I don't know, ma'am,' Gertie replied unhappily. 'Sergeant Johns said he came in about just after seven this morning and went straight out. He said he should be back soon and I was to wait here for him.'

'Seven o'clock? Sergeant Summers? I think he was pulling your leg. I doubt whether our Sergeant Summers is awake before seven.'

'That's what Sergeant Johns said, ma'am.'

'Hmmm. Come on, let's go have a word with Eric Johns. His version of reality tends to be somewhat different to that of the rest of humanity.'

Gertie trailed after her as Frieda marched off to the front desk. Eric Johns' eyes lifted in surprise at the unusual and worry-inspiring sight of a clearly unhappy Inspector Garold being followed by a miserable Gertie into the reception area.

'Where's Sergeant Summers?' Frieda asked abruptly.

'I don't know, Inspector,' replied Johns nervously. 'Sergeant Bute was on duty this morning before my shift began. He said Frank – Sergeant Summers – came in about seven and left again a few minutes later. Said he was going to see his parents.'

'His parents?' asked Frieda in disbelief. 'They live two hundred miles away.'

Johns shrugged.

'I can only tell you what I was told, Inspector.'

'And did he say anything else? Such as why he had suddenly decided to disappear?'

'Said he could be contacted on his radio if he was needed.'

'And have you?'

'Have I what, Inspector?'

'Contacted him.'

'No. Nobody's asked for him.' A look came into his eye. 'He hasn't gone awol, has he?'

'Do people normally say they're contactable on their radios when they "go awol", Sergeant? In your world, at least.'

Johns was spared the need for a reply by the entrance of Susan Pleadle. She stopped just inside the reception area, looking at Frieda and Gertie in surprise.

'Good morning, Doctor Pleadle,' Frieda said coolly. 'Come to give us some good news?'

'Good morning, Inspector Garold,' Susan replied, recovering her composure. 'I thought I'd drop off the report on the postcard as I was passing by. Is Sergeant Summers available?' She held up a folder as evidence of her mission.

'He's usually more available than most,' Frieda said dryly.

Eric Johns' laugh turned abruptly into a nasty cough when Frieda's gaze turned towards him.

'Today he appears to have suffered some form of brainstorm. Come up to my office, Doctor. You too, Gertie, seeing as you're ... assisting Sergeant Summers.'

Susan was about to leave the report and claim a desperate

need to be somewhere else, but Frieda's swift about-turn gave her no choice. The three of them trooped up the stairs, Frieda irritated, Susan uncomfortable and Gertie miserable.

Behind them Eric Johns shook his head sadly.

'Frank, if those three ever get you alone in the same room together ...' he thought to himself.

* * *

'Take a seat,' Frieda offered, going around her desk. Susan sat while Gertie stayed standing, close to the door.

'The report?' asked Frieda, putting on her stern glasses. Susan passed it over. As Frieda took it Susan started, as if there was something she had just remembered. Too late. The folder was open.

Frieda held up a small page of light pink paper, scented, with little bunnies playing in the corner. She read it, frowned, and passed it to Susan.

'That seems to have slipped in by mistake,' she said. Susan took it back, blushing slightly.

Frieda read the two-page document quickly. Then she leaned back, taking her glasses off.

'One set of fresh fingerprints belonging to our clumsy Sergeant Summers,' she said. 'One fresh set belonging presumably to Mrs Green. Older prints too faded to identify, apart from one thumbprint. Postcard is of a sort commonly available between twenty and fifty years ago. Writing done by a fountain pen. Ink also twenty to fifty years old. Stamp could have been bought yesterday. New address written by a modern biro of the sort made in millions. That's the gist of it? Nothing conclusive apart from the age of the postcard and writing?'

177

Susan nodded.

'Tracey – the girl who carried out the checks – said there was a fingerprint partly on the stamp, Mrs Green's, but not the sort you get from sticking down a stamp. You would expect a thumbprint of some form. Probably made when she was holding it.'

'In other words, whoever put the stamp on was wearing gloves? Or somehow managed to avoid leaving a trail?'

Susan nodded again.

'It seems that way. But I wouldn't want to use that in a court of law. It's vaguely possible that whoever it was has a strange way of applying a stamp, but it seems unlikely to the point of exclusion.'

'And it's modern. Peel and paste, or whatever they call it. No licking. No saliva, no DNA.'

'Exactly.'

They sat in silence for a while. Susan coughed nervously.

'Um, Frank, Sergeant Summers – has he ... is he in some sort of bother?'

'Bother? I don't know. I will probably tear his ears off and do something unpleasant with them when he finally turns up, if that's what you call bother. Apparently he was up and out with the lark this morning, on his way to see his parents.'

'His parents?'

'While he was supposed to be on duty.'

There was a knock at the door. Frieda didn't have time to bid the knocker enter before he did. Frank walked breezily into the office.

She should have known it would be Frank. No-one else could

get past her secretary without prior warning like that.

'Morning,' he said, and then looked around in surprise. 'Not interrupting anything am I?'

He resisted the urge to use the word "coven" on the entirely reasonable grounds that he might be beaten to death for doing so.

'My goodness, no, Sergeant,' said Frieda sweetly. 'In fact it's rather good timing. We were just discussing you. And why you should suddenly decide to disappear to visit your parents while you should be doing what you are paid for.'

'My parents? Why would I go to see my parents? They live a hundred miles away.'

'Two hundred,' said Gertie helpfully.

Frieda glared her into silence.

'That, according to Sergeant Johns, was where you were.'

'Eric?' asked Frank in surprise, sitting down comfortably, 'I didn't even see Eric. His shift hadn't started when I left. Ah, wait a minute!' He snapped his fingers. 'Of course. I know what it is. Keith Bute was on the desk when I left. I told him I was going to see some old folks. Eric garbled the message, as usual. Good thing he never became a translator. He'd have countries at war with each other in seconds.'

'Frank,' Frieda said wearily, 'tell me, who are these old folk you went to see.'

'I thought I'd do the rounds of the old-age homes, see if I could pick up some information.'

'Information? Such as?'

'Well, I definitely learnt one thing.'

'Which was?'

'The Albany Home for the Retired do an excellent breakfast,' Frank said, grinning, 'but the coffee's absolutely dire at all the other places. Never accept a cup. It'll have you wanting to go for hours afterwards.'

This was met by a baffled silence.

'I'm sure we'll all find that information extremely useful, Sergeant Summers,' Frieda said through grinding teeth. 'Perhaps there was something apart from investigating the quality of breakfast at these establishments? Something to do with police work? Perhaps? If we're really, really lucky?'

Frank's grin was unruffled.

'Yes. But you're going to hate me for this.'

Frieda paused for a second.

'More, Frank,' she said 'we're going to hate you more. Get on with it.'

'Well, it struck me that we're too reliant on the memories of a small group of people, all of whom are directly involved. I wanted to see if there was anyone else who lived around here from that period who remembered something – at least get a flavour of what it was like then. Everybody talks of the Swinging Sixties, on television, anyway. But Little Alfie doesn't remember it that way, he was slaving away as a grease monkey.'

'Ah, ambience,' said Frieda with a strong hint of sarcasm. 'And did you find any old groovers? Perhaps even someone who said, "Cor, yes sir, I remember Alfie Simmons, I was there the night he was shot"?'

'No,' Frank said ruefully. 'No-one remembered anything special about the summer of 1964, apart from the Beatles and A Hard Day's Night – and even then most admitted that they had never bought the record or seen the film. Wrong age bracket, I'm afraid. Their main memories were about the war.'

'World War II, presumably, not the Napoleonic Wars. So, a bit of a waste of time. Try to let me know next time you have any more great ideas like that.'

'Ah, not entirely wasted, Inspector. You see, purely by chance I met someone who was on the same base as our Alfie.'

Frank paused to let this sink in. The other three looked at him in suspense.

'If you don't get on with it ...' threatened Frieda.

'He didn't remember Alfie,' Frank continued, a broad smile back on his face, 'though he pretended to after a while – wanted to keep chatting, I think, he was prepared to agree to almost anything to keep me there, probably bored out of his wits most days – but he did remember the Lancaster that exploded. It was a big event around here, apparently. Not surprising, I suppose. And then, when I mentioned it to others quite a few also remembered it. You see, there were quite a few rumours circulating about that at the time. Quite a few.'

He allowed another pause.

'The most extreme was that the Lancaster was filled with gold bullion from Hitler's Reichkanselrie in Berlin, or whatever it was called. Pretty much impossible, since the Russians were in control there, and they'd be unlikely to hand over gold bullion to the British, even if Hitler had bothered to keep a stash in his private office in the first place.'

'I'm impressed,' Frieda said. 'You actually do know a little history. Anyway, go on.'

'It was a colonel who told me that – well, he claimed to be a colonel, but probably wasn't – I don't even know if they have colonels in the air force. I think the Yanks do, not our lot. Anyway, the point, though, is that everyone believed that the Lancaster was carrying something important – gold, silver, precious paintings possibly, diamonds – apparently someone claimed that it was Hitler's body, brought back for scientific examination, but that wasn't popular. Especially as most of the population were scouring the countryside looking for this supposed valuable cargo – Hitler's body wouldn't have been worth much, hardly the sort of thing you could flog on the black market. And the army was out in force as well, which raised people's suspicions. It was quite likely the army were just giving the air force a hand in picking up the pieces, and that's what was said publicly at the time, but people don't want to believe such a boring idea.'

'But nothing was ever found?' asked Susan.

'Not officially – though of course there was nothing officially to be found. And if any civilian found anything they never mentioned it.'

'So, what you're saying,' Frieda said, 'is that there was a lot of rumour, all of it probably conspiracy theory. Nothing to go on whatsoever.'

'Ah,' said Frank, 'that's not the important thing.'

They waited for him to announce the important thing.

'Frank, your life is hanging by a thread,' Frieda growled. The other two women silently echoed the feeling.

'The important thing,' Frank continued slowly, 'is that they all agree about the year it happened. It was 1945. Not 1946.'

There was silence as they took this in.

'Why is that so important?' asked Susan.

Frank raised an eyebrow at Frieda. She nodded.

'Doctor Pleadle,' she said, 'what you hear in here is privileged information. It must not become public knowledge until we need it to be. Understood?'

Susan gave her a look bordering on contempt.

'I do know how to keep my mouth shut,' she said in an icy voice.

'The first thing you need to know,' Frank continued, apparently oblivious of the sparks flying between the two women, 'is that our Alfie Simmons was supposedly aboard that plane. He was listed as dying when it exploded a couple of thousand feet up. Remember what I first thought right at the beginning? There's a possibility that it was true.'

'You never told me that,' Susan said.

'It shows that Sergeant Summers knows how to keep his mouth shut,' said Frieda. 'Even during pillow talk.'

It was like lighting a match in a dynamite factory.

'I beg your pardon? What the hell is that supposed to mean?' Susan asked, lifting herself out of her chair.

'Do you two mind?' asked Frank mildly. 'If you're going to start World War Three let us know. Gertie and I can go carry on with our investigation while you're at it.'

Frieda raised a hand in surrender. Susan lowered herself back into the chair.

'I'm sorry, Doctor Pleadle,' Frieda said. 'That was totally uncalled for. I apologise.'

'The second thing you need to know,' Frank said, as if he was having a polite discussion in the pub rather than talking to people likely to kill each other in the very near future – or alternatively in the manner of someone who expects slaughter in the near future and is looking forward to enjoying the spectacle – 'is that we had a visit from a retired Ministry of Defence character who assured us that the explosion positively took place in the summer of 1946, there was nothing special about the cargo, and there was no doubt that Alfie Simmons did die in that accident.'

'Not strictly true, Frank,' Frieda said. 'He did say it was theoretically possible that Alfie survived.'

'Yes, but he said it in the same way that it's theoretically possible that I'm the Archangel Gabriel. He seemed very intent, in an understated fashion, on convincing us that Alfie was dead and there was nothing interesting about the explosion.'

'So we're back to the Funnies.'

Frank shrugged with a wry smile.

'It's possible,' he said. 'In fact we have a number of possibilities. That there was something on that plane, something Alfie managed to conceal until someone else caught up with him nearly twenty years later. Another is that he was killed because of a family dispute. Then there's the Greens; did they, one or both, discover Alfie's little bigamy on the side and do him in during a slight disagreement over the fact? Was it merely the result of a drunken argument after a night at the pub? Or was Alfie into smuggling, or some other criminal practice, and fell out with his colleagues? And no doubt others. He could have been mugged for all we know.'

Gertie coughed.

'There's something you would like to say, Gertie?' asked

Frieda.

'Um, there's also the possibility that the Alfie Simmons who was shot wasn't the Alfie Simmons in the plane,' she suggested. 'It could have been identity theft.'

'Very true, Gertie,' Frank said. 'Another option altogether.'

'A veritable plethora of choices,' commented Frieda.

'Precisely,' said Frank, standing up. 'However someone did send that postcard. If it wasn't Mrs Green in a fit of the wobblies, then who was it? And why?'

Frieda shook her head slowly. She sighed.

'Very well. What are you going to do now, with all these possibilities?'

'Check up on any friends of Alfie's. Anyone who knew him during the war. Anyone who knew him during the Sixties. Maybe I'll get lucky and find some old codger in a bath chair who's being waiting forty years for the coppers to turn up so they can confess.'

'Try not to beat a confession out of anyone, Frank,' Frieda said, smiling finally. 'You can see Doctor Pleadle out first. Gertie, I'd like a word before you go.'

As they walked down the stairs a smile played around Susan's lips.

'Frieda has the report on the postcard,' she said. 'In brief, it's right for the period, the Sixties. Including the writing. No identifiable fingerprints apart from yours, Mrs Green's and one thumbprint from an unknown. And no fingerprint on the stamp where you would expect to find one. Nothing conclusive, I'm afraid. A pity, really. Tracey worked late into the evening on it. She deserved to get some results.'

'Mrs Green didn't put the stamp on?' Frank asked, making a mental note to thank the anonymous Tracey at some stage.

'There's part of an index-finger print on it, but not the way it should be. But I'm not saying she didn't stamp it. Whoever did just made sure their prints weren't where they should be.'

'I can't say I can imagine Mrs Green being that devious.'

'You really should be more cynical about people, Frank,' Susan said as they reached the door to the reception area. She stopped, kissed him softly on the cheek, and handed him the note with the bunnies on the corner. 'Call me sometime,' she said.

He followed her wordlessly into reception and watched as she did her half-walk, half-skip, half-dance exit out of the front door.

'Wish I could make someone do that,' Eric said gloomily from the front desk. 'She's got a real nice little – '

He noticed Frank looking at him, his eyebrows raised.

'Figure,' he ended lamely.

Normally Frank would have given his "Don't know how I do it" shrug. Somehow he didn't quite feel like it at that moment. His mind was on different possibilities.

'Mind you,' Eric continued, 'it reminds me of me and the missus when we first went out. She was a stunner in those days. Stunned me, anyway.'

He patted his stomach.

'Seem to have put a bit of weight on since then.'

'You should get more exercise,' Frank suggested absentmindedly.

'Not me, son. Grow old gracefully, that's my approach. Eat

heartily, have a good night's sleep. Retirement in just over five years. I might even take up fishing, like the Chief Inspector. Or growing roses. Always wondered what the attraction was about growing roses.'

Frank shook his head in bewilderment and made his way back to his office. Gertie was waiting for him. She seemed a happy girl.

'Why the happy, smiley face?' he asked, sitting down.

'FF has said I can take my detective's exams at the next sitting, early next year,' she said.

'Next year? That's a bit quick, isn't it?'

'She said I'd earned it. I want to see Harry's face when I tell him. He'll be well p... unhappy.'

Harry Wheatley was a uniformed constable who had been trying for promotion for a long while.

'I don't blame him. He's got two years on you.'

'The old ways are out, Sarge. No more Buggins' turn. Merit for hard work these days. When you work for FF, anyway.'

'Merit? Hard work? Good thing they didn't have those silly notions when I was promoted.'

Gertie smiled. It contained a hint of self-interest. More than a hint.

'And there's even better news.'

'Go on, tell me.'

'FF said I was now Acting Detective Constable, assigned to you. I've got to change into civvies as soon as I get the chance. She said I was to keep on your tail every second, and make sure you don't disappear again.'

She giggled.

Frank raised his eyes to the ceiling. He was trying not to think of Gertie wearing civilian clothes. The uniform was bad enough.

'Right, time for lunch,' he said. 'After that we'll find that website again and see how we can get in touch with some of our Alfie's old comrades. If any of them are still around.'

* * *

After lunch Frank sat down at his computer thinking it would take him seconds to find the site as had happened the first time. The seconds turned into minutes as he tried various different searches, all of which failed.

'It can't have disappeared, surely?' he asked.

'Might have done, Sarge,' said Gertie, leaning over his shoulder. 'I hear a lot of these websites don't last very long.'

'Great.'

'You're quite a whiz with computers, Sarge,' Gertie complimented him.

'Aren't you? I thought everyone grew up with them these days.'

'Not me. Never did much like them. I just learnt enough for the job – wouldn't be able to earn much promotion if I didn't know how to use them. But apart from that, I don't see the point.'

'I don't know what the younger generation is coming to,' he mused.

'Come off it, Sarge, you're not that old.'

'Oh, thank you, Gertie, thank you,' he replied sarcastically. 'That really makes me feel better.'

'I didn't mean it that way,' she said in a little-girl-hurt voice which he totally missed.

'Got it!' he declared triumphantly as the screen finally filled with an image of a Lancaster. 'Now, let's see if they've provided some thing useful, like a telephone number. Or maybe even a list of the squadron members.'

He scrolled down the page, passing pictures of uniformed young servicemen, aircrew in front of their planes, drivers towing bomb-loads, a group in a pub, mechanics working on an engine. All seemed happy, smiling at the camera. At the end came modern-day photographs, the men looking old, but with a grim cheerfulness.

'Funny, that,' Gertie commented. 'Must have been awful to go through all that, but they're always reminiscing about it, as if it was the best time of their life.'

'Different days,' Frank said. 'They were fighting for something they believed in, something worth fighting for. Most of them, anyway. A massive shared experience.'

'Almost makes you wish you could go through something like that yourself.'

'No thanks,' Frank replied with a heavy sincerity, 'they had rationing and shortages, don't forget. The beer must have been awful. Here we go, a telephone number. Local, as well. That will save us a little wear on the tyres. Not that it's a good idea to leave your phone number on a website.'

He picked up the phone and dialled.

'Hello, this is Detective Sergeant Frank Summers of Wellbury police,' he began confidently, and then paused.

'No, madam, it isn't about the television licence. I'm sure your television licence is perfectly in order. In any case television licences don't fall under our jurisdiction.'

He was interrupted before he could continue.

'Yes, madam, if you say it's in the post, then I'm sure it's in the post. As I say, I'm not calling about your television licence. I'm calling about the website, the one about the bomber squadron based at Wellbury during the war.'

Another interruption.

'No, madam, as far as I'm aware it's not illegal. In fact I'm sure that it is perfectly legal. And very well laid out. Now – '

'Your great-nephew, yes, he obviously has a great deal of talent, and no, he hasn't broken any law in creating the website, and yes, I'm sure he hasn't ever been in trouble with the police if you say so. I'm more interested in the people who were on the base during the war. I – '

'No, madam, it isn't to do with anything that happened then, and I'm sure that your husband didn't steal any rations, and even if he had we wouldn't be investigating it sixty years later. What I – '

'Not so much as a parking ticket, that's very commendable. Mrs Jenkins, this is merely a routine inquiry about a missing person case, nothing to worry about. In fact I doubt that anything will come of it, but I do need to speak to any of the men who were on the base at the time who might still be around.'

'That's very kind, Mrs Jenkins. We'll pop along in about an hour or so. I promise we won't take up too much of your time.'

He put the phone down gently, with a sigh of relief.

'That was a Mrs Jenkins,' he said.

'So I gathered. She seemed worried about something.'

'I suppose having the police call out of the blue gets some people wondering whether they're about to be arrested, even if they've lived perfectly blameless lives all their life. Strange, that.' He paused at the thought, and then shrugged his shoulders. 'Anyway, the website was built by her great-nephew. Her husband was at the base. The nephew did it after discovering what his great-uncle had done during the war. Apparently a group of them who went through the war meet regularly every year to celebrate VE day. Which was very carefully designed to fall in early May.'

'Carefully designed?'

'Earliest time of the year you can have barbecues outside.'

Gertie gave him a look.

'And having helped defeat Fascism she's worried we're going to arrest them for having a website?'

'With this government you never know. Anyway,' he said standing up, 'she probably believes the rubbish she reads in the papers. The internet as a mixture of pornography and people luring young girls into slavery.'

'Isn't that what most people use it for? Pornography, I mean.'

'No it isn't. You should be ashamed of yourself, Gertie, you're supposed to know better. In fact it's more like having an entire reference library at your fingertips.' He sighed. 'Admittedly most of it's completely wrong in terms of facts, but there's no stopping people believing what they want to believe.'

'I'll have to investigate it. Just for you, Sarge.'

He glanced at her, surprised. She had a coy look on her face.

'No use buttering me up, Gertie, I'm not in a position to help

191

with your career. Now, to action. We have an appointment with Mr Jenkins. We'll stop at your place so that you can put some civilian clothes on. But try to remember you're a police officer on duty, not getting dressed for a night out.'

'You know, Sarge, you can be quite sexy when you become all stern.'

Frank closed his eyes for a moment. He had been so much happier as a detective constable.

* * *

He waited in the car when they arrived at her block of flats. To his surprise she came out wearing a navy-blue skirt-suit which spoke more of efficient business-woman than bosom.

'My smart suit,' she said, getting back into the driver's seat. 'I bought it on a whim a few months ago, just in case a day like this arrived.'

'Knowing that you'd become a detective constable sooner or later, you mean, and more like sooner than later. An unstoppable force moving irresistibly towards the height of police promotion.'

'It's not like that,' she said in a confessional manner. She paused. 'When I was young I was a bit of a Daddy's girl. There wasn't anything I wouldn't do to make him happy. I don't blame him, he was a great Dad, but it makes it difficult when you're trying to be independent, and build your own career.'

She looked at him before switching the ignition on.

'It's okay for you, you've got the confidence,' she added. 'I'm never sure I'm doing the right thing, or whether I'm just doing it to please someone.'

Frank absorbed this in silence. He had never thought of

Gertie, confident young woman, Aikido expert, and very clear on what she wanted from life, as a Daddy's girl. He didn't quite believe it now.

Pete Phillips envied him because he wasn't climbing the greasy pole. Gertie envied him because of his confidence.

He hadn't realised he had any.

Now if only he could suddenly discover he also had charisma that would really make his day.

And he could make a fortune out of the flying pigs.

* * *

The Jenkins' house was a modest-looking little bungalow with a well-tended and largish front garden. Only those aware of the high price of houses in England would realise that it would have cost a small fortune to purchase. Mrs Jenkins met them at the door and led them out into an even larger back garden which would have had an estate-agent calculating how much could be made by building a second house in it, and what percentage he could charge.

'It's Detective Sergeant Summers,' Mrs Jenkins said nervously to an old man reclining in a garden chair. Age might have wearied him somewhat, but powerful blue eyes looked out from a solid face which spoke of someone used to getting his own way.

'Take a seat,' he said, motioning to the chairs either side.

'I'll make some tea,' Mrs Jenkins said, moving quickly away.

'You've upset my wife,' Mr Jenkins noted. 'She doesn't like her routine being interrupted, especially not by the police.'

'I can only apologise, Mr Jenkins,' Frank said, taking the proffered chair. Gertie stayed standing.

'What's wrong with her?' asked Jenkins, gesturing towards Gertie with a thumb. 'Afraid of getting that suit dirty?'

'This is Detective Constable Gregson,' Frank introduced her. 'She'll take notes if any are required.'

'Ah, I get it, lower ranks, eh? Must know their place. Well, I tell you something, Detective Sergeant Summers,' Jenkins continued, leaning forward, 'I was only a corporal during the war. Not even aircrew, either. But I was the one who made it good afterwards. And I was the one who organised the get-togethers of the old squadron. The officers didn't like it much at first, seemed to think we weren't worthy or something. Aristocrats, they thought themselves. Didn't want women either, especially ones who hadn't been in uniform. It's called appropriating history, I read that phrase in a book. Bloody right, it is. If you weren't a hero you don't deserve a place. Well, sod that. We went through it all, and no-one is going to take our memories away.'

'You didn't get on with the aircrew?' Frank asked.

'Not like that at all,' Jenkins replied. 'It's the officers I have a problem with. The airmen and non-comms – gunners, bomb-aimers, that sort of thing – they don't have airs, didn't then, don't now. Back in '45 we put a Labour government in power, the aristocrats didn't like that, so they tried to steal our history. That's why I had Peter – my great-nephew – do that website like he did. Pilots couldn't have flown the planes without mechanics like me. And afterwards, what happened? I start my own business and do bloody well, thank you, even despite their attempts to nobble me.'

He glared at Gertie.

'You sit down, love, no ranks in this house. Take it or leave it.'

'Yes, please sit down, dear,' said Mrs Jenkins, returning with a tray of tea paraphernalia. Her accent suggested that Mr Jenkins had married into the "aristocratic" class he so despised.

Gertie sat down reluctantly. Frank guessed that standing was not for her a sign of respectful obedience, but rather her way of controlling a situation.

'Does the name Alfie Simmons ring a bell?' asked Frank as Mrs Jenkins placed the tea on a table and began pouring.

'Alfie Simmons?' Mr Jenkins asked, puzzled. Then his eyes opened wide as memories came flooding back. 'My god! You are going back, aren't you. Alfie Simmons, eh? He was a right character!' He looked at Frank suspiciously. 'Here, the wife said this was a missing person case. Alfie can't be missing. He died in '45. Plane exploded. I remember it well. What's going on? Why are you really here?'

Frank spread his hands, shrugging.

'I'm afraid the truth,' he replied, lying fluently, 'is that Constable Gregson and I have been given this as – how shall I put this? Not quite punishment, but a sort of rap on the knuckles, as it were. We've been given the job of investigating the case of a person who went missing back in the Sixties. It's routine to revisit old cases which haven't been closed, but this sort of thing is, to be quite honest, hopeless. But we have to do our best, and Alfie Simmons' name has cropped up from time to time. We haven't a clue why, though, so we're trying to find out.'

'Wasting the tax-payer's money, sounds like it,' Jenkins noted.

'It's one of those things we can't really win,' Frank said. 'If we said we weren't routinely re-investigating unsolved cases the newspapers would jump on us. When we do they have a go at us anyway.'

'Blasted newspapers,' Jenkins agreed. 'Can't believe a word you read. I see your point. Well, we'll do our best to help. I remember what it was like in the air force, officers giving you stupid things to do just because they don't like your attitude, only you haven't done anything wrong, so they can't punish you officially. Bastards all.'

'So what do you remember of Alfie Simons? Ah, thank you, Mrs Jenkins,' Frank said, accepting a cup of tea.

'Ladies' man,' Jenkins replied, taking a dainty cup from his wife. 'But also very – not clever, that's not the word. Oh, he was bright enough, but ... not cunning, that's not the word either, not underhand, as it were. Difficult to describe, really. He was always full of schemes, as if he couldn't live without having two or three things on the go. At the time most of us were thinking about what we'd do after the war. I knew exactly what I was going to do, and I remember thinking that Alfie would be a good partner if he wasn't so ... well, unfocused, I suppose they'd say nowadays. We all had plans for making money, but he was more interested in the plan than making the money. Eccentric, I suppose you could say. And women loved him for it. Evelyn married me for my money – '

'Really, Jack,' Evelyn Jenkins protested mildly.

'Oh, no, it's true, Evie, no use pretending.' He looked at Frank. 'I wouldn't have stood a chance if I'd been a mechanic on a few shillings a week, but Evie's dad could see I was going places. He swallowed his pride and let us marry, and very happy we've been. Hasn't been roses the whole way, mind you, but all in all I think we've had a pretty good life. What say, Evie?'

Evelyn Jenkins smiled at her husband in a way that did not need words to agree.

'Alfie Simmons,' said Frank, bringing the conversation back to where it should be. 'Was he a ladies' man or a womaniser?'

'Now there's an interesting distinction,' Jack Jenkins noted. He thought for a few seconds. 'A ladies' man, definitely. He never chased women, they chased him. Funny sort of a bloke. Most of us would have given our right b – er, arms, to be in his position. But he never took advantage, apart from the ones he was really interested in. And he was careful not to mix them up. Had something going with one of the clerks on the base at one time, and with a barmaid in a pub about ten miles away, but he made sure neither of them knew about each other.' Jenkins laughed and slapped his knee. 'I asked him once, what are you going to do, marry both of em? And you know, what he said, he said, "Why not?" Daft bugger.'

Eventually the daft bugger had done so, thought Frank, if to two other women.

He was beginning to heartily dislike this Alfie Simmons who had women chasing after him. Obviously in those days men had it easy.

'But he died in forty-five?' he asked. 'The explosion on board the Lancaster?'

'Aye. A lot of silly stories at the time, there were. Gold bullion, that sort of thing. Normal, law-abiding citizens going out into the fields – there were fields in those days – hunting for treasure. You wouldn't have believed it. Common sense went right out the window.'

197

'You never believed the stories?'

'Do you?' asked Jenkins quizzically.

'I don't know,' Frank replied slowly. 'Or, to put it another way, it isn't important whether or not the rumours were true, only whether people believed they were.'

'You've got it there in one, lad,' Jenkins said approvingly. 'That's what I realised very quickly in the air force. Reminds me of the time we were given punishment drill 'cause our cap badges weren't clean. Half an hour's drill, then five minutes to clean them properly, inspection afterwards. I didn't bother. Wasn't going to waste my time on that sort of nonsense. Just told the officer I had cleaned mine when we were back on the parade ground. He couldn't believe I wouldn't bother, so he left it – even though a fool could see it was in the same condition as before. Same in business, you can charge people a fortune for something shiny and useless, but they wouldn't give tuppence for decent workmanship. People didn't recognise class back then, they still don't. They see what they want to see – and don't see what they don't want to see.'

Frank put his cup down slowly.

'What if I were to suggest that Alfie Simmons did not die in that explosion?' he asked carefully. 'Any chance of that being the case.?'

Jenkins looked at him for a few seconds.

'Stone the crows!' he exploded finally. 'I'd believe you, that's what! That would have been typical of Alfie. I can see him now, coming down in a parachute, landing perfectly, and then scratching his head wondering what to do. And then deciding he'd had enough of the air-force and just leaving. Just like that!'

He leaned forward.

'Is that what happened?' he asked. 'Always thought it was a waste. Very unlike Alfie to die in such a stupid accident. After the war was over, and we'd managed to survive.'

'It's a possibility we're looking at,' Frank said. 'But it's so far-fetched we don't want the media knowing anything. You can imagine what they'd make of it.'

Jenkins nodded, leaning back in his chair.

'No worries on that score. Bloody newspapers. Ask me anything you want. Go ahead.'

Frank took a photograph from his pocket, a photograph from 1964.

'Is this Alfie Simmons, Mr Jenkins?'

Jenkins leaned forward and looked at the photograph. He rubbed his jaw.

'It could be, I suppose. I've never been good with faces. If it is, he's a lot older than I remember.'

'Did Alfie have any enemies?' asked Frank, putting the photograph back in his pocket.

'Course he did. A bloke takes a woman to the local pub, finds she's more interested in this gunner, even worse he doesn't take advantage, that would get to a lot of blokes. Course, those of us who knew him, didn't affect us. But there were others who didn't.'

'I was thinking of something more ... personal. Something that might make him decide to disappear.'

'Alfie? Can't see Alfie doing anything like that. We all got into scrapes. He always faced the music. Not because he thought it the right thing to do, I think he just didn't understand that he'd done anything wrong. Strange bugger, in many ways.'

'You don't think that perhaps there was something on board that aircraft – that it was one of Alfie's schemes?'

Jenkins looked at him through narrowed eyes for a few moments before replying.

'You're suggesting he planned it? Can't see it, myself. He would never hurt anyone – well, not in the way he understood hurting someone meant, and I think killing would include that. Some things he didn't understand, like the idea that going out with two women at the same time might be wrong. He understood they wouldn't like it, so he never told them – his idea of kindness, I suppose. But blowing up a planeload of people? Can't see it.'

'Were you living here during the Sixties, Mr Jenkins? In Wellbury?'

'The Sixties? No, lad, I was in London. That's where the money was. We weren't born here, you know. I was only here during the war. Met Evie in London. We worked our arses off for twenty years, got out just before '73 – the oil crash, you probably weren't born then. Decided Wellbury was the place to enjoy the fruits of our labours, I had fond memories of the place.' He gave Frank a suspicious look. 'But, hang about, what's this going from the war to the Sixties? You're not telling me something, lad.'

Frank coughed apologetically.

'I'm afraid we have to limit what we tell people, Mr Jenkins. The trouble is we don't have any hard evidence. And, as you said about the rumours flying around after the Lancaster exploded, well, people will believe anything. There is a vague possibility that Alfie Simmons survived, only to disappear in the Sixties – but if we suggested that the next thing we'd have is hordes of people suddenly imagining that they'd seen him in Kowloon in 1955, or Cairo in 1960. It makes an impossible job even more difficult.'

'I see your point,' Jenkins observed, and then burst into laughter. 'Aye, Kowloon in 1955, they would, the daft buggers. Amazing what people can convince themselves they've seen. Don't have the eyes they were born with, the poor fools.'

'And you definitely didn't see him again?'

'Definitely. If I had – I'd probably have gone for an eye-test. Tell you what, though,' he added as a thought struck him, an amused glimmer in his eyes. 'We're having a little get-together at the weekend. Was just going to be a few of us for a barbecue, but I can spread the word. That is, invite anyone I know who was around at the time, without telling them why. You can interrogate them to your heart's content.'

'Well, it's a very kind offer, Mr Jenkins, but I must point out that it will probably be a waste of time.'

'Not for us, lad. It will be great fun watching you – and them. But we can't tell them you're police, now can we? We'll have to invent a cover story, as they call it.'

Jenkins was warming to the idea. Frank wasn't. But he didn't have a chance to stop it from gathering pace.

'They could be graduate students doing a thesis of some kind,' suggested Evie enthusiastically, apparently having revised her view of policemen coming calling. 'Boyfriend and girlfriend, researching the Cold War years or something.'

'Excellent idea!' Jenkins said, rubbing his hands. 'They'd fall for that one. Can't walk down the street without tripping over someone researching something these days. You'd have to dress casually, mind you,' he added, looking at Gertie. 'Show a bit more of that impressive chest of yours.'

'Jack!' said Evie.

'Oh, don't mind me, girl,' Jenkins said to Gertie. 'Large bosoms don't do anything for me, but I know most men can't keep their eyes off them. Always employed secretaries with big boobs – the ones who took the money. Customer comes up to pay – always men, in those days – he intends to argue the toss, but then forgets all about it, pays as meekly as you like, eyes on stalks, on stalks, literally. More fool them, I say.'

'It's very kind, Mr Jenkins,' Frank said, standing up, thinking that it might turn out to be a very bad idea indeed.

'Come around at about eleven o'clock Sunday. A taxi would be a good idea. I stock a good bar. No sense in having money and not enjoying it. The drinks tend to flow a bit. Wouldn't want you nabbed by the coppers for drunken driving.'

'I'll bear that in mind.'

* * *

When they had returned to the car Gertie paused before switching on the ignition.

'Do you mind if I ask a personal question, Sarge?'

'Go ahead, Gertie. You might not get an answer, but ask away,' Frank answered, his mind on a bad idea and a Sunday barbecue.

'Well, what Mr Jenkins said ... Almost all the men I know do ... seem to find my chest fascinating. You don't. The only others like that I've met have been gay.'

She paused.

'You're not gay, are you, Sarge?'

'Course not, Gertie. But I am your senior officer. Wouldn't do for me to … well, you know.'

'But it'd be different if we're off duty, wouldn't it?'

'I'm never off duty,' Frank replied pompously, keeping his eyes fixed straight ahead.

Gertie giggled.

* * *

'Boyfriend and girlfriend?' asked Frieda incredulously.

'It's just a cover story for the afternoon,' Frank replied. He was sitting in one of the chairs in front of Frieda's desk feeling very uncomfortable. The more he thought of the idea the less it appealed. Gertie stood by the door, failing to suppress a grin.

She was looking forward to Sunday. Very much so.

'Let me get this straight,' Frieda said, closing her eyes. 'You're going undercover to a barbecue. This barbecue is going to be attended by what could be called war-heroes – old war-heroes, old-age pensioners to a person. And two officers of Wellbury Police Force are going to attend, undercover.' She sighed. 'I don't suppose you thought that that could be construed in certain quarters – the press, for example – as an example of the police state? Somewhat Orwellian? At the least of being somewhat underhanded?'

'It wasn't really my idea. Besides which, we're not going to interrogate them, we're just looking for unvarnished information. We don't want to put ideas in their heads. You know what it's like.'

'Indeed, I do know what it's like. It's like the press writing articles about undercover work against innocent pensioners, and then the Chief Constable asking me in for a quiet chat – which will be neither a chat nor quiet.'

She looked at him.

'Frank, this is Wellbury. We have a British sense of fair play. We are not some tin-pot South American police force. We have certain standards. We have certain ideals. And Wellbury Police Force is going to live up to those standards and ideals. Understand?'

Blimey, when did you become Chief Constable? he asked himself.

Though he had to admit that he fully agreed with the sentiments. Just, perhaps, not with the delivery.

'I agree. It was a silly idea in the first place. Okay, we'll tell Jenkins it's off.' He stood up, relieved at being relieved of the duty.

'Oh, no, no, no, Sergeant,' Frieda said in a sing-song voice which suggested that she was taking great amusement from Frank's discomfort. 'You've made the arrangement, so stick to it. Just make sure it doesn't blow up in our faces.'

'Yes, ma'am,' Frank said, heading for the door.

'And you can cut out the ma'am bit,' Frieda called after him as he and Gertie exited.

'Oh, no, no, no,' Gertie mimicked, laughing as they walked down the stairs.

'Be careful, Acting Detective Constable Gregson,' Frank replied. 'Be very, very careful.'

'Sorry, Sarge,' Gertie said meekly, but happily.

'Time to call it a day. You get off to your karate class.'

'Aikido, Sarge. It's non-aggressive.'

'Yes, I know. So long as no-one does anything dangerous like offering to shake hands they're okay.'

* * *

In his office he found an envelope on his desk. It was a note from Susan suggesting Sunday lunch.

He swore.

Then he wondered whether he could have lunch with Susan and a barbecue with Gertie at the same time.

Reluctantly he had to admit that that would probably be beyond even Alfie Simmons' impressive abilities, never mind his own more modest ones. He picked up the phone and dialled Susan's number.

'So, where are we going on Sunday?' she asked cheerfully straight after he had said hello.

'I can't make Sunday, I'm afraid,' he said. 'I have to work.'

'Work? On a Sunday? I thought you never worked out of normal hours if you could avoid it.'

'I don't. It's just this case – I don't seem to be able to spot them coming like I normally do.'

'So what will you be doing on Sunday then? Hiding in a deserted factory waiting for Mr X? Shivering in the cold, water dripping from a leaky roof, sacrificing yourself to a higher duty, keeping the civil population safe from the scourges of society? Maybe I could hide with you.'

'Um, no. Unfortunately I have to go to a barbecue with Gertie. As boyfriend and girlfriend, would you believe? Ridiculous, isn't it?'

There were two silences.

One was from Susan on the telephone.

The other was from Gertie standing in the doorway with a cup of coffee she had thought Frank would welcome, looking at Frank's back.

Susan slammed down the phone.

Gertie turned and marched off to the ladies'. She poured the coffee angrily down a washbasin, and then sat down and started crying.

Frank had totally missed Gertie's brief entrance and exit, but he couldn't have missed the sound of Susan's too, too solid telephone crashing down. He sat nursing his ear, debating whether to call her back. In the end he decided against it. He hadn't done anything wrong. The barbecue was business. It wasn't his fault that Gertie would be going – after all, they spent most of the working day together, and Susan hadn't mentioned a word about that.

He frowned, stood up, put his jacket on and left the office. If Susan was going to be like that maybe he should think of going out with someone like Gertie. Not, of course, Gertie herself, since, firstly, it was against his rule of not having office affairs, and, secondly, she didn't fancy him, and he never made the mistake of chasing after women who didn't fancy him.

Instead he went home and spent the evening with a bottle of wine and a good book.

Two bottles, and, instead of a book, he watched reruns of old black and white movies on the television with the sound turned down.

When he finally staggered off to bed he dreamt that he and Gertie were walking along a sunlit beach, hand in hand.

In his sleep his mind thought, Why not?

Why not, indeed?

Friday: A new partner

'Morning, Psycho,' Eric Johns said cheerfully as Frank entered reception. 'Frigid wants to see you as soon as you come in. Which is now, by my reckoning.'

'Any idea why?' asked Frank.

'Nope. She never tells me anything, you know that.'

'Right,' Frank replied, heading for the stairs. What Eric should have said was that Frieda never told him anything he could use as gossip. Otherwise she made sure he was as fully informed as he needed to be. Quite emphatically so when occasion required.

Frank knocked at Frieda's door and walked in. She looked up. Her face was impassive.

'Sit down, Frank,' she said. 'We have a little problem.'

'A little problem?' he echoed, taking a seat. he didn't like the sound of "we". It suggested that it included him. And a problem.

'Yes. Any idea of what you might have said to upset Gertie?'

'Upset Gertie?' Frank asked in astonishment. 'I haven't upset Gertie. She was happy enough when she left last night. Anyway, I doubt anything I could say would upset her. She'd just shrug it off.'

'Why, then, would she ask to be assigned to a different case?'

Frank considered this.

'Probably thinks Alfie Simmons isn't worth the bother, I suppose. Gertie is very ambitious, you know.'

'I know. And she knows that our Dead Skeleton is a high profile case, whatever you may think. And ambitious officers aren't almost in tears when they ask to be re-assigned.'

'In tears?' Frank's eyes opened wide in amazement. 'Gertie?'

'She said it was for personal reasons.'

'Personal reasons?'

'Frank, you're starting to sound like an echo. I want to know what's going on.'

'I wouldn't mind knowing that myself.'

'You and her haven't been ...'

Frank tried to work this out.

'We haven't been ... what?' he asked.

Frieda struggled to find words.

'Having a relationship,' she said finally.

'A relationship? Well, technically speaking, because we work together, we must have a relationship of some form.'

'You know what I mean, Frank.'

His first thought was "In my dreams", but that was a little too close to the truth.

'Yes,' he agreed. 'But I'm just trying to get my head around the idea. Firstly I have a rule of not getting involved with anyone at work. Secondly Gertie is far too career-minded to let anything like that happen. I just can't see it.'

'Stranger things happen, and rules do get broken,' Frieda noted enigmatically. 'She hasn't got a crush on you, has she?'

Frank laughed.

'The only crush she'd ever want to have on me would be a half-nelson. Purely for professional reasons.'

'Very funny, Frank,' Frieda said, unamused. 'Gertie's off today. She won't be back in until Monday. I want you to have a word with her when she gets back. Find out what the problem is and get it sorted.'

'Sorted? Why me?'

'Because you're a Sergeant, Frank. More or less her Sergeant right now. I haven't agreed to her being reassigned to a different case yet, and I'd prefer not to have to.'

He sighed.

'I knew that promotion was going to be a bad idea,' he said, standing up.

'Just one thing, though,' Frieda added.

'Oh? Just one?'

'The barbecue, Sunday. I've told Gertie it would be better for her not to go. Under the circumstances.'

Frank's brain worked furiously. If he was on his own he could make a token visit before shooting off to meet Susan. Or even take Susan with.

Now there was an idea.

'So I'll be coming with you,' Frieda continued. 'After all, they're expecting you to turn up with a girlfriend. But just remember we're going to pick up information – which there probably won't be any of.'

Frank's furious brain fused. Frieda looked up at him.

'Anything else?' she asked.

'No. Can't think of anything,' he replied, speaking the literal truth.

'Right. Get all your notes together. Ten o' clock We'll go through everything for the press conference this afternoon. I want you there. And I want to make sure we don't let anything slip out. The weekend newspapers are always looking for some rubbish to print. We aren't going to give them a free gift, you know what their imaginations are like.'

Frank left the office in a daze. Susan was angry with him for no real reason. Gertie – what was that all about? He was going to a barbecue on Sunday with his boss as his girlfriend. And now he was faced with something he had always managed to avoid: a press conference.

Maybe, just maybe, if his luck was in, there would be a major crisis just before two o' clock.

He wondered if he could arrange one with Eric.

* * *

'Sorry, Frank,' Eric said, sitting in the canteen with a cup of tea and a tabloid newspaper, 'much as I'd like to I can't organise a crisis just like that. Not one of the scale you'll need. To upset Frigid's plans I reckon would take a terrorist hijack – preferably of the prime minister – two rail accidents, half a dozen bank jobs and an invasion from Mars.'

'Just one burglary, Eric, that's all I'm asking for. Just by chance I'm walking past, there's no-one else around, you ask if I can take it, being such a helpful person and committed to my duty I say yes, totally forgetting about the press conference. Understandably, of course, my being so dedicated to duty.'

'Even if I could arrange a burglary at the right time, which certain senior officers might frown upon, I think Frigid knows all the tricks in the book. It's okay for you, Frank, she lets you get away with things like that. You'd get a bollocking. I'd be holding my pension and parts of my anatomy in my hands. I'm quite partial to those parts of my anatomy staying where they are, and I've worked hard for my pension.'

'There has to be a way.'

'If there is,' remarked Eric, turning a page casually, 'I'm sure you'll find it.'

* * *

'A thought struck me,' Frank said after he and Frieda had gone through the little evidence they had so far.

'Oh?' asked Frieda, only half concentrating. 'Did it hurt?'

'There'll be cameras, I presume.'

'I would expect so. Press conferences normally come with cameras attached. You're not camera shy, are you?'

'No more than the next man,' replied a man who had a phobia about having his picture taken. 'But if our pictures appear in the papers – and quite possibly on television – well, we can hardly turn up to a barbecue two days later pretending to be research students.'

Frieda smiled.

'Don't worry, Frank, We'll be so boring they'll prefer to write about little kittens stuck up trees. It's going to be a straight "sorry we have no new information" press conference. "Don't know why you bothered to turn up." That sort of thing. You can look bored, can't you? You manage it quite easily when I'm giving the monthly updates.'

Frank knew better than to reply to that.

Frieda slipped a piece of paper across her desk.

'Get half a dozen copies of that made. Make it look as if we didn't expect many people to turn up.'

Frank skimmed the sheet.

'These are the revised monthly crime figures for last month,' he pointed out.

'Yes. Terrible, isn't it? Modern communication. They think

they're coming to get some juicy morsels about a dead skeleton, we think it's just a standard briefing conference. These things happen.'

She gave Frank the most dishonest honest look he had seen in a long time. He smiled.

'You're enjoying this, aren't you?' he asked.

The sides of her mouth twitched.

'I've booked interview room nine for the conference. Should be just right for the two of us and three or four reporters.'

'At a pinch. Any more and they won't be able to move.'

'Getting a camera in could cause serious injury,' Frieda noted.

Frank left her office in a good mood. Frieda was much more subtle than he was. He made a note to pick up some tips from her.

It would save having to organise a burglary or an invasion of aliens.

* * *

Interview room nine was an anomaly. It should have been interview room five, there being only four others officially designated as such, but it had gained its name from an occasion when nine people had somehow managed to fit in; seven police officers, one elderly female suspect and her lawyer. The confession gained was later deemed to have been obtained "under duress", and the suspect never tried, a fortunate event as she later turned out to be innocent. The clinching factor had been that her lawyer had also signed the confession, apparently desperate to get out.

The press conference went almost as planned. A look of astonishment on Frank's face as he entered room nine was only slightly simulated. The room crowded with journalists and cameramen reminded him somewhat of a bagful of cats, except these were fighting to be inside rather than trying to get out. Frieda turned up carrying a mug of tea, dressed in a dowdy uniform, wearing thick, heavy glasses, hair in a bun, with no lipstick or makeup. She could have passed as some lowly inspector who was always given the dull, boring and simple work to do. Her performance emphasised this idea. Questions about the Dead Skeleton Case were met with baffled puzzlement. She spoke slowly, as if she wasn't quite the brightest police officer around, pointing out that there were more important, modern cases to pursue. She offered to list them, only she would have to get the facts from her office. That was the final straw. The press-pack, hot and frustrated in the tiny room, gave up and left.

Except for one who lagged behind the others, a quiet, smallish man in his mid-forties wearing a plain grey suit which had become rumpled in the crush. The plainness of the suit was offset by an extremely loud bow-tie and waistcoat.

'Quite the best performance I've seen in a long time,' he said in a low, cultured voice as Frank was about to pass him by.

'Performance?' asked Frank innocently, admiring the bow-tie and waistcoat.

'Phil Walthers,' the man introduced himself in a soft voice, 'Wellbury Herald. I've seen you around, but haven't had the chance to say hello.'

'Well, hello Mr Walthers. And goodbye, I'm afraid. Much as I'd like to chat I've got quite a bit of work to get through.'

'Alfred Simmons,' Walthers said softly. Frank stopped. Walthers smiled. 'Don't worry, I'm not about to blurt anything out so that that lot can hear. We have a shared interest, yourself and I. You want to keep things quiet, I want an exclusive that I can sell to the national papers. And I know how to keep my mouth shut. Eric Johns will vouch for me.'

'Sergeant Johns is hardly the best reference,' Frank noted. Walthers smiled again, sadly.

'No. Not unless you want something shouted from the rooftops. And even then he would get it wrong, he always does.'

'What is it you're looking for, Mr Walthers?'

'Co-operation, I suppose is the word. Wellbury isn't that large a town, we have to learn to, as I believe the phrase has it, rub together. I had a good relationship with your predecessor. And I have one with Inspector Hanson. I'm sure he will be a better reference than Sergeant Johns, though Eric tends to be easier to find. However, the crunch of the matter is that I have information that you know that the skeleton is that of one Alfred Simmons, that he allegedly disappeared in 1964, and that you now believe him to have been shot.'

'Interesting. I wish I had known that.'

'Now, Sergeant Summers, please be reasonable. You can't expect Mrs Simmons not to have mentioned it to anyone else, and, as a local reporter, for myself not to come across it sooner or later. In my job you get to establish many contacts who will gladly pass on information, if only for the pleasure of seeing their story in the local newspaper. Fortunately they don't trust strangers from the big, bad world outside. Though that, sadly, is changing.'

'You have a point you are getting to, Mr Walthers?' Frank asked.

'Oh, come, Sergeant Summers, no need to be unfriendly. But,' he sighed, 'if you so wish. My point, as you put it, is that sooner or later I have to publish what I know, or the national papers will beat me to it. My paper normally comes out on Thursdays, and that's my deadline – next Thursday. My editor won't hear of any other possibility. Unless – '

'Unless?'

'Unless we have an agreement – unofficial, of course – that we might have a little more access to certain information which, of course, we won't release until you're happy for us to do so.'

'I'll have a word with my Inspector,' Frank said.

As he was about to go he paused and turned back to Walthers.

'This editor of yours, what's he like?'

'Oh, terrible, Sergeant, a truly ruthless person, quite the philistine.'

'What's his name?'

'Phil Walthers,' replied Phil Walthers with a sad smile, and then began walking away.

'Tell me, Mr Walthers,' Frank called after him, 'where did you get the bow-tie and waistcoat?' Walthers turned and smiled.

'That could well be part of the information exchange, Sergeant. They also do ties. They could give yours a run for its money.'

* * *

Frieda seemed irritated rather than surprised by the news when he passed it on to her in her office.

'I suppose we were being a little naive not to have expected something like this,' she said. 'Hopefully this Walthers will keep his word. What did you make of him?'

'Effeminate sort of type,' Frank replied. 'Not camp, as such, more that he found his work rather distasteful, that he preferred more refined matters.'

'Mmmm. Sounds rather dangerous. Almost all reporters I've met have been pushy and macho – including the women. But that was in a big city. Wellbury appears to be rather different.'

'I quite like it here,' Frank admitted.

Frieda smiled at him.

'So do I, Frank, so do I,' she said. 'But this does mean that we're going to have to come up with something quickly. We can change our own deadlines, not the ones newspapers set.' She tapped her fingernails on her desk irritably. 'Somehow or other we're going to have to make things happen.'

'In more ways than one,' she added, softly and enigmatically.

Sunday: A very social investigation

Sunday dawned with hardly a cloud in the sky, a bright, warm, summer's day. Frank rose early, showered, and strolled down to the nearby newsagents for a copy of the Observer. He added a slightly out-of-date Thursday edition of the Wellbury Herald and strolled back. In the flat he dropped the Observer on the coffee table and flipped through the Herald. The front headline was "Burglaries Baffle Bobbies", followed by several paragraphs of how the police were no further in the investigation of the recent burglaries than before, written in more literary prose than might be expected of a local newspaper. Phil Walthers, Frank decided, was the Wellbury Herald, reporter, photographer, editor, typist and all, and a man who thought modern journalism somewhat lacking, if not indelicate.

Next to the article on the lack of police progress was a smaller one: "Dead Skeleton's Secrets". It promised that further revelations were imminent, hinted that they would be breathtaking, but failed to identify precisely what they would be. It brought a wry smile to Frank's face. Few people could resist a ghoulish story, and Phil Walthers was not one of them.

He dropped the Herald on top of the Observer and stood looking out of the window of his first-floor flat for some time. The streets were empty, all good citizens of Wellbury enjoying a Sunday lie-in. Despite what others might believe, he personally had always been an early riser, especially when he was alone. Normally he would spend a Sunday morning browsing through the overly-large newspaper for a couple of hours before meeting up with friends for Sunday relaxation, but he had yet to make any such social contacts. Such things took time in this slow-going town. Slow-going, apart from burglaries, of course – if you believed what you read in the newspapers.

He wondered what Susan was doing. And Gertie. And Frieda. Two were upset with him, the third was his boss, with whom he was due to attend a barbecue, as girlfriend and boyfriend. He shook his head at the thought, and went into the kitchen to make a cup of coffee.

What happened, Alfie? he thought to himself, as if he were talking to the murdered man's spirit. In his mind's eye he could picture Alfie's face, smiling, charming, so attractive to women, yet, and no doubt that was part of the attraction, somewhat of an enigma, as if there was something behind the face which could be sensed but not seen.

And of course there was. At least one secret.

Frank returned to the front window. He could not get rid of the feeling that Alfie's spirit really was watching him, not imploring him to find his murderer or murderers, but rather that he was mildly interested in seeing whether Frank would ever come up with the solution.

He shivered slightly, and told himself to stop being silly. Concentrate on the facts, he admonished himself.

Fact: Alfie Simmons was murdered with a bullet from a Webley revolver in 1964.

Fact: Alfie Simmons was a bigamist.

Fact: Little Alfie was not his son.

Fact: Elizabeth Green claimed to have received a postcard from him a few days ago.

Fact: Alfie Simmons died in an explosion on board a

Lancaster in 1946.

Fact: Alfie Simmons died in an explosion on board a Lancaster in 1945.

Fact: Frank Summers was going to a barbecue with his boss as his girlfriend, and he wasn't sure that he wasn't actually looking forward to it.

Fact: Frank Summers was getting a headache.

He decided to put some music on to divert his mind. He chose a CD at random and switched on the player. It turned out to be a compilation of film scores. The first was the theme from Dr Zhivago, Lara's Theme.

Good choice, he thought ironically. A song that starts "Somewhere my love".

On impulse he switched the CD player off, went to the spare room and hunted through the boxes he had yet to unpack until he found his guitar. It was some months since he had last used it, and he realised he had missed the soothing calm he gained from playing, however badly. His new flat in Wellbury was solidly constructed. The neighbours wouldn't be able to hear a thing.

He was standing with a foot on the low windowsill overlooking the street outside, strumming along to his personal interpretation of Ruby Tuesday when he saw Frieda's shining black Range Rover pulling up down below on the opposite side. As she got out he noted that she had her hair in a pony-tail, wore no makeup, had on large, thick glasses, and was wearing a loose-fitting top, all of which was designed to portray an earnest, mature post-graduate student, academically concentrated, oblivious to any pleasures other than the intellectual, and which also made her look some ten years younger.

It was thus, then, such a pity that she had chosen skin-tight jeans and pointed cowboy boots to complete the ensemble.

He hadn't wondered about Frieda's age. She was his boss, which made such a thought irrelevant. Now he suddenly realised that she must be about his own age, if not a little younger. Certainly not much older.

Now why did he find that thought a little worrying?

'Very nice,' she said, as she browsed through the books in the lounge after he had made coffee for them.

She stroked the back of one.

'Medea?' she asked in surprise. 'The ancient Greeks. Is that your cup of tea?'

'Not really,' Frank admitted. 'I could never get my mind around the idea of a woman killing her own children to spite her husband. I keep intending to re-read it, just in case there's something I missed.'

She smiled, and her finger ran along the shelf. She stopped and tutted.

'The Anarchist Reader,' she noted. 'Frank, if the Chief Constable knew that one of his officers was reading seditious literature he could well be concerned.'

'It depends on your definition of anarchist,' Frank replied. 'Originally the term merely meant free-thinker, someone willing to break rules if they considered the rules incorrect. The ruling elite transformed them into enemies of society and the word became a pejorative.'

'A little heavy for a Sunday morning, I think,' Frieda noted. She looked around the lounge. 'You're a very neat person,

Frank. No untidy piles of washing, no boys' magazines left lying around. Or are they hidden away?'

'I tidied up yesterday,' Frank admitted. 'Not much else to do.'

Frieda nodded as if she understood and empathised.

'And the guitar? Do you play?'

'Not very well. I prefer the piano, but I've never been able to afford one. Or somewhere big enough to hold one.'

'I'm sure you're being modest, Frank. You'll have to let me judge sometime.'

She hummed along to the theme tune from Cabaret. Frank felt uncomfortable. He wanted to be on the move. Frieda seemed happy enough to dawdle.

And he was finding it very difficult to keep his eyes from straying to those jeans and boots. Skin-tight jeans and boots did not suit all women. Some looked sexy in them, others merely silly. Frieda contrived to appear both erotic and elegant.

'Come to the cabaret,' she sang softly. She paused and looked at him. 'Are you an anarchist, Frank?' she asked.

The question stumped him.

'In a way I suppose we all are,' he replied eventually.

Frieda smiled at him.

'Our Alfie was definitely an anarchist,' she said. 'Time we were getting on and finding out more about him, don't you think? Time to go to the cabaret.'

Frank couldn't agree more.

He wasn't quite sure he was happy with the notion that it would be a cabaret, though. He had seen that film a couple of times. The good guy ended up having his face punched in.

'One thing, Frank,' Frieda added, just to make life really interesting, 'don't let me have too much to drink. I have a very low alcohol tolerance level.'

* * *

Their arrival seemed to separate the guests into two groups. Frank found himself sitting on a garden chair with a pint mug in his hand, surrounded by grey and white-haired women sitting in similar chairs. Frieda was amongst a group of men, like elderly bees swarming around a young honey pot.

'Of course things were different then,' a stout, bossy, white-haired woman was saying as if by rote. Frank took a sip of beer and wondered how to work the conversation around to Alfie Simmons. He rather suspected that these women had a fixed line of conversation with a new audience, honed down the years, which would run like a train on a track, without deviation, and, unlike modern British public transport, without unscheduled stops.

'I don't know,' said Mrs Jenkins, 'sometimes I think that human nature never really changes.'

'Youngsters will always be youngsters,' agreed a woman to her left.

'Well, that may be so,' replied the stout woman, 'though I'm not sure of that. What I am sure of is that we had it much harder than young people today. But we did have respect. We knew our obligations. These days it seems anything goes.'

'Funny you should say that,' Mrs Jenkins said, as if something had just occurred to her. 'Only the other day Jack was remembering someone he met during the war. Now, what was his name again? Alf something. Alf – I know, Alf Simmons. Apparently he was one of these people for whom rules never apply, you know the type of person.'

Thank you, Mrs Jenkins, thought Frank. About as subtle as dumping a barrel of bloodied chicken heads into a meeting of vegans.

'Alfie Simmons? That little rat!' exclaimed the stout one. She paused to take a brief sip of tea, oblivious to a sudden drop of temperature within the group. Frank noticed it immediately. Several surreptitious glances were directed at a little old woman in the middle of the group. Bodies were slightly moved, as if to distance themselves from her. She sat with her eyes cast down.

'In what way?' asked Frank conversationally.

'Womaniser,' said the stout woman who had missed the change in mood. 'Chased after anything in a skirt. Unfortunately there were some young floozies only too willing to oblige. Quite a few as I remember.'

Frank resisted the urge to remind her of the respect and obligations apparently so prevalent at the time.

'What happened to him?' he asked.

'Shot down over Germany,' the stout woman replied. 'Killed. Good riddance too.'

'I remember a Captain Hastings,' said a woman with permed hair, sitting next to the little old girl looking at the ground. 'Very handsome man. Or, at least I think his name was Hastings. Maybe I'm getting confused with the Captain Hastings in Agatha Christie's novels. Do you read Agatha Christie, Mr Summers?'

No, but I can recognise a sudden change in subject when I see one, thought Frank.

'I've read a few,' he said instead. 'I don't recall anyone called Alfie Simmons in them. So presumably that name is correct.' He smiled disarmingly. 'I'm afraid, when you're researching, you have to be completely accurate.'

'Hah!' said the stout one. 'If he was in a novel he'd be the prime suspect.'

'What is the title of this thesis you're doing?' asked permed hair. 'It must be fascinating to have to do all that research.'

'We haven't really thought of a title as yet,' Frank replied. 'We're really concentrating on the lives of people who lived through that period, the time during and just after the war, real lives, you could say, rather than most of the current work, which is more about the politicians and high ranking military officers. How people came to terms with a post-war world. This Alfie Simmons sounds like he would be an ideal candidate.'

'An ideal candidate as a rogue,' replied stout woman. 'No, if you want the story of how real people lived, we can tell you. Never mind the soldiers and the rest. I worked in a factory for over a year. So did a lot of us. But these programmes on the television, when they show what happened during the war, what do we get? Five seconds, if you're lucky, and then an hour on how the men won the war. They couldn't have won it without us, I tell you that.'

'Oh, that's a little unfair,' said Mrs Jenkins mildly. 'I saw a very good programme a few weeks ago, about factory workers and farm girls. Did you see that, Mr Summers? I would expect that would have been exactly the sort of thing you'd be interested in.'

'Unfortunately I missed it,' Frank replied, thinking that Mrs

Jenkins had promptly forgotten what he was interested in, to whit, one Alfie Simmons. From the look in her eyes he knew there was little hope of her remembering. He could hardly mention the name again without raising suspicions; there were some shrewd eyes amongst his audience. And it appeared that these women had little to offer – or, he rather suspected, that Alfie Simmons was a topic they preferred not to mention.

'Your glass is empty,' Mrs Jenkins noted. 'Let me get you another one.'

'No, please, Mrs Jenkins, I'll get it. I need to visit the little boys' room anyway. Too much coffee earlier this morning, I'm afraid.'

'Oh, dear, of course. The beers are in the fridge, Mr Summers, the, er, little boys' room is second on the left after you leave the kitchen.'

Frank muttered grateful thanks and left them to chat amongst themselves. He had been truthful when he said that he had drunk too much coffee, and now an early morning beer on an empty stomach was already making him feel light-headed. Unfortunately he knew from experience that the second would make him feel quite pleasant. By the third or fourth he would be droll and charming. Often he actually achieved charisma.

Well, that was the way it had always felt, anyway.

Until the following morning.

Unless Frieda had come up with something it was a bit of a washout, he concluded as he dried his hands on the guest towel in the downstairs bathroom.

He walked out into the passage deciding that an early exit with suitable thanks was called for. Maybe, if they got away early enough, he could call Susan, find out what the problem was, solve it, and meet her in time for dinner.

'Hello, Sergeant,' said a voice to his left.

He turned in surprise. There was a doorway to what he presumed was the lounge, the curtains of which were half-drawn, leaving it in semi-gloom. Half hidden in the shadow of the doorway was the little old girl who had looked so hard at the ground.

'Why don't you come in here where we can't be overheard, Sergeant?' she suggested.

He hesitated, and then moved carefully into the lounge, checking for any hidden assailant. Why, he didn't know. After all, it was just a little old woman.

She closed the door behind them.

'Shall we sit down?' she suggested. She sat in an armchair too large for her. He lowered himself gently onto one alongside, as if ready to spring up should the need arise, such as a little old woman pulling out a shotgun on him.

'You don't recognise me, do you Sergeant?' she asked. 'I saw you at the police station once, a couple of months ago.'

He remembered suddenly. It had been a brief passing. She was at the duty Sergeant's desk, reporting some crime, presumably. He had only noticed her because everything was new to him at the time.

'I do remember,' he said. 'You were talking to Sergeant Johns. I don't recall what it was about.'

'Of course not. But I am impressed by your memory.' She paused. 'Let me introduce myself. My name is Heather Ronan.'

'How do you do, Mrs Ronan,' he said awkwardly, and waited for her to continue.

'Miss Ronan,' she corrected him. 'You don't recognise the name?'

'No, I'm afraid not. You aren't a famous criminal, are you? A retired cat-burglar? A Wellbury legend?'

She laughed, a soft, mellifluous laugh, which spoke of an educated and wealthy background.

'Sadly not. It would have made my life so much more interesting.'

She paused again. He guessed that she was more used to listening than talking.

'I wondered why you were here, pretending to be a student doing – what was it, a post-graduate thesis? At first I thought that maybe you were really doing your doctorate, or whatever they're called these days, until I saw the Inspector.'

'You recognised Inspector Garold?'

'Oh, yes. She passed through while I was at the police station, just like yourself, only about half an hour later. I remember Sergeant Johns was very respectful. When you're a woman you notice these things, you see.'

'I suppose you must, thinking about it.'

'And you are quite a thinker yourself, I would say.'

'Well, Mrs Ronan, I wouldn't go that far, but right now I'm wondering why we're sitting here having this conversation.'

'Because of Alfie Simmons, Sergeant, because of Alfie Simmons. Why else?'

He rubbed his jaw slowly.

'I'll be honest with you, Mrs Ronan, I haven't got a clue what you're talking about.'

'Oh, you aren't going to deny that you're interested in Alfie Simmons, are you Sergeant?' she pleaded in an almost mocking voice. 'Though, if I didn't know who you were, I might have been quite taken in by your performance.'

'Oh, I am interested in Alfie Simmons, Mrs Ronan. What I don't understand is where you fit in.'

'Can you tell me why you're interested in him?'

'I'm afraid not, Mrs Ronan. Not at this stage. We might be on a wild goose chase. We prefer not to make fools of ourselves publicly. At least, not more often than necessary.'

She smiled.

'You remind me of Alfie, in a little way,' she said. 'That hint of self-deprecation. He had a very disarming manner. As if life was to be lived fully, but we should never take things too seriously. He had a lovely laugh, too. As, I'm sure, you do.'

Frank was not at all too sure that he welcomed the comparison.

'How did you know Alfie, Miss Ronan?' he asked.

'Oh, yes, I do apologise. You see, I thought, initially, that you knew. I thought that that was one of the reasons you were here. That you'd found out my guilty little secret.'

You bought a black-market tin of bully beef off him one Saturday night, thought Frank. Or, maybe, crime of the century, two tins, and it was Sunday morning.

'You see, Sergeant, Alfie and I were lovers.'

Right. Possibly more than two tins.

'Lovers?' he asked.

'You sound surprised, Sergeant. I understand. I wasn't always an old woman, you know.'

Frank coughed in embarrassment.

'I didn't mean it that way,' he said quickly. 'It's just – you sound as if you have quite an educated background. I wouldn't have thought you and Alf Simmons moved in the same circles.'

'Very perceptive of you, Sergeant. Yes, I was from a relatively wealthy family and Alfie was a mere gunner from nowhere, hardly in the same class.' She sighed. 'I'm sorry. It isn't a long story, but when I remember I always seem to start at the wrong point, and it becomes rather confused. Where would you like me to begin?'

'What about when you first met him?'

'Of course. Start at the beginning, as the Queen said to Alice.' She paused. 'Not quite the beginning, but as good as any. It was 1945, February 1945. I don't know if you know Harold Peters, Sergeant?'

'Er, no, I can't say I do.'

'He is standing out in the garden as we speak, no doubt entranced by your lovely Inspector.'

Another pause, as she turned to look out of the half-closed curtain at the blue skies above.

'Funny how you always remember them as young,' she murmured. After a few seconds of silence she turned back to him. 'Do forgive me, Sergeant, when one gets to my age memory can do strange things. Yet often it is all we have. Let me get back to my little story.' She took a breath. 'Harry and I were due to be married. I don't mean that we were engaged or anything like that, but it was more or less understood that that was what would happen. Harry's family were poor but landed

231

gentry, I suppose they would be called, mine were wealthy but untitled. We had more or less grown up together, and our parents made it quite clear – in a typically understated English way – that Harry and I were to be man and wife. We weren't rebellious in any way. Not at all worldly. We just accepted that that was what would happen. But it didn't, in the end.'

She looked out the window again, unfocusing.

'Alfie happened,' suggested Frank softly. She nodded.

'Alfie happened,' she agreed. She turned back to him. 'Harry brought him back one day.' She smiled. 'I'm afraid Harry was thinking of dabbling in some activities not quite on the right side of the law. The army had rejected him for health reasons. His family were in financial constraints. He felt he had to do something. I think he felt he was missing out on something, but wasn't quite sure what. In a way he was fortunate to fall in with Alfie, because Alfie was very good at not being caught, and he was, in his own way, very loyal. He would never have cheated Harry. Not in a way that he understood would be considered cheating.'

'But he did,' suggested Frank.' He took you away from Harry.'

She smiled.

'No, Sergeant, you don't understand. Harry and I never loved each other. We were fond of each other, more like brother and sister. No, I fell in love with Alfie, and Alfie fell in love with me. At any other time it could never have happened, but ... well, it was the war, you see. That, and the fact that I'd never been in love before. I knew my parents would disapprove, but I was sure they would come around in the end. Whatever happened, Alfie and I were going to get married.'

'He proposed to you?'

'Oh, yes. And I agreed, immediately. Which is when we became lovers. The war was over by that stage, we were out of danger, and we were going to get married.'

'And then he died when his aircraft exploded.'

Her eyes closed at the memory.

'And then I discovered that I was pregnant.' She re-opened her eyes and looked directly at him. 'Foolish of me, wasn't it?'

Frank returned the gaze.

'No. I don't think so. No, not foolish at all.'

'Ah, but it was, Sergeant. As Marjorie out there said, they were different days. Fortunately she doesn't know about Alfie and myself, though some of the others do. For a girl, unmarried, to be pregnant, was the end. For the daughter of wealthy parents, well educated, a prize catch ... it was also the end. If you were poor the option was prostitution, I believe. In my case the only option was embalmment.'

'Embalmment?'

'A quiet holiday with a so-called aunt, far away in Newcastle, so that people wouldn't notice the pregnancy. For appearances only, of course, almost everyone would guess what had happened. After the birth the child given away for adoption, or to an orphanage. And then a return in disgrace, because, though they were too polite to say so, as I said, everyone knew exactly what had happened. No-one spoke of it, but, as far as marriage was concerned, there was no hope. No man aware of the situation would humiliate himself by marrying damaged goods. All the joys of spinsterhood to look forward to.'

'The man in this case being Harry.'

'Exactly.'

A few hours of passion, thought Frank, the most natural thing on earth, followed by a lifetime's punishment purely because the individuals had followed nature's rules rather than society's. The woman ended up carrying the baby, literally.

But something niggled. Why had Miss Heather Ronan confessed her story? She could hardly believe the police would be interested in a love affair that took place all those years ago.

'Then what happened?' he asked on impulse.

'I became a teacher. Primary school, I loved children. I still do, if it comes to it. Everyone felt sorry for me, with no husband, nor family. They presumed it was the shortage of men, following the war. "A woman of a certain age". Do you know where that saying comes from, Sergeant?'

'I can't say I do.'

'Not surprising. You're too young. Some people say it came from the French, so I might be wrong, but for myself it always referred to the women who would have married during the Great War, but found themselves spinsters in their thirties. These days being unmarried and thirty, or even forty, doesn't mean very much. In those days it was a terrible humiliation. For the kind of society I lived in, anyway.'

There was something she was not saying, Frank thought. Something she wanted to say, but found it difficult to get out.

'And then?'

She smiled sadly.

'And then I discovered that Alfie had betrayed me.'

Frank almost groaned. Alfie "betraying" a woman wasn't news. Although "betrayal" wasn't the right word. After all, he had stayed loyal to two wives until he was murdered.

'You found out that he had been seeing other women?' he asked, hoping to end the conversation soon.

'Oh, no, Sergeant. Dear me, no. I could have happily lived with him seeing other women. Had he returned to me, had we married, I would have gone down on my knees every night to thank a merciful god, and may Alfie have as many mistresses as he wished. Naturally that was afterwards. At the time I dare say my feelings might have been otherwise.'

'So what was it you discovered?'

Her eyebrows raised in surprise.

'That he was alive, Sergeant, that he was alive. What else?'

Frank might have echoed that "What else" if his brain and tongue had been on speaking terms.

'When was this?' he asked finally.

'October the fifteenth, nineteen hundred and fifty-nine,' she replied slowly. For the first time there was real anger in her voice, anger and hatred.

'Do you know what it feels like to realise that you have given away your own child to strangers, never to see him again, when that child's father was – could have prevented that? Do you know – ' She choked and took out a handkerchief. Frank waited until she had composed herself.

'Are you sure it was him? That it was Alfie?' he asked gently.

'Yes. I am sure,' she said in a tear-clogged but firm voice. 'I knew him more intimately than I had ever known another man. I have always had good eyesight, and he had a very

235

recognisable face. He had a scar, you know. It pulled his mouth up slightly. It gave him a somewhat rakish effect.'

'But surely you could have been mistaken?'

She looked at him with all the imperiousness of a dowager being doubted by a recalcitrant peasant.

'I was less than fifteen feet away. He was talking with another man. He looked up, saw me, looked me directly in the eyes. Oh, yes, he knew me all right. And I knew him.' She blew her nose genteelly. 'As soon as he saw me he walked away as quickly as he could. I was too stunned to react until he was gone. And that was it. I never saw him again. For weeks I walked the streets hoping for another chance encounter. Months. I didn't eat. A nervous breakdown was the doctor's diagnosis. Three months in a sanatorium without the option, as I believe the phrase is. It didn't matter. I knew I would never see him again. I knew it. I just knew it. I felt that God was mocking me.'

Frank stayed silent for a while, giving her a chance to recover, and also absorbing the idea that, if Heather Ronan were correct, the Alfie Simmons of 1964 was also the Alfie Simmons who had supposedly died in the Lancaster.

Somehow he had never doubted it.

'Did you tell anyone else?' he asked when he judged the time was right.

'I told Harry. In a way I felt he deserved to know.'

'You were still in touch with Harry?'

'Oh, yes, Sergeant.' She looked at him. 'Do you have a name, Sergeant? A real name? A real name that makes you a human being instead of a police officer?'

Frank hesitated, and then smiled.

'Frank,' he said, 'Frank Summers at your service.'

He was rewarded with a watery smile.

'Tom, Dick and Harry,' she said. 'And Alfie. And now Frank. Well, Frank, I'll finish off my tawdry little tail. Harry stayed loyal to me. He could never marry me, so he never married anyone. It took me a long time to realise that he actually loved me. Really loved me. Loved me enough to forgive me. But his parents would never consider the idea that he could ever marry me after what I had done. And, like us all in those days, he obeyed his parents' wishes. God!' she suddenly shouted, 'I wish we had had more guts!'

Frank allowed her time to recover from this outburst.

'How did he react when you told him?' he asked when she had calmed down.

She gave him another weak smile.

'I'm afraid Harry is quite possibly the product of inbreeding, my dear Frank. He was never quite the brightest of the bunch. Rather like a well-bred gun-dog. Loyal, loyal, oh so loyal. But stupid as they come, poor thing. He declared – declared, mind you – that he would find the fellow and horse-whip him. Imagine that. Horse-whip him. As if, even if he found himself in a position to do so, Alfie would have ever understood a horse-whipping, let alone allow him to do so. It would only have puzzled him.' She sighed. 'Such different men, and I loved them both, in different ways.' She looked at him. 'Can you understand that, Frank?' she asked, pleading.

He returned her gaze, and then looked away. Finally he turned back to her beseeching eyes.

'I'm trying to,' he said. 'I can't honestly say I do at the

moment, but I'll get there in the end.'

She leaned over slowly and patted his hand.

'Frank by name and by nature, as the Americans might say. An awful phrase, very common. Will you do me a favour, Frank?'

'If I can, of course,' he replied, thinking that this old woman deserved quite a few favours in recompense for the way history had treated her.

'Tell those outside I'm indisposed.' She settled herself into the chair, a picture of weariness. 'Tell them,' she said in a whisper, 'I'm having one of my nervous turns. Now, leave me, go enjoy yourself. Jack Jenkins always provides the best of food.'

He hesitated before standing up. He wished there was a blanket he could put over her, to keep her warm, to comfort her. In the end he made his way as silently as he could to the door.

'Frank?' she called in a thin voice as he opened the door.

'Yes, Heather?'

He could feel her smiling at the use of her name.

'That Inspector of yours.'

'Yes?'

'She fancies you, as they say these days. I can see that. Have an affair with her, at least. You'll both enjoy it. It might not last. Live while you can, Frank.'

Frank stood contemplating the door frame for a while. It was possibly the strangest advice he had ever been given, including that by Sergeant Eric Johns.

Live while you can. Wasn't that supposed to be part of his own philosophy of life?

And why wasn't he following it?

And why did he have this awful feeling that he himself rather fancied the woman out in the garden wearing her hair in a pony tail, and tight jeans and cowboy boots?

He closed the door quietly behind him.

In the kitchen he stopped to refill his glass. It was a chance to think, if he could. Come out breezy, he said to himself, downing a quart of a pint.

Try not to look at Frieda any differently. We're two professional colleagues doing a job. That's all.

Miss Ronan's having a nervous turn, he told himself, downing the second quart.

Miss Ronan's either telling the truth, downing the third quart, or, downing the last, a bloody liar.

But why should she lie?

Same reason anyone ever lies. They're trying to hide something worse.

He looked at his empty pint mug. If he carried on pouring beer down his throat he'd end up feeling like an overfilled water bed. Instead he found a wine glass and filled it from a bottle that told him it was Chenin Blanc. He tasted it. Nice stuff. He downed that and poured himself another.

Then he breezed out into the garden.

'I'm afraid Mrs Ronan's not feeling too well,' he told the women in their deckchairs. 'She's having a little lie-down in the lounge.'

The woman with permed hair looked at her neighbour. They stood up.

'We'll look after her,' said permed-hair, giving Frank a

suspicious glance as they walked past him.

Frank nodded politely. His eyes were on the group of men around Frieda. She sat on a high stool someone had brought out for her, laughing, a glass of wine – champagne? – in her hand, the men laughing with her.

The pony-tail had gone, her raven hair fell down on her shoulders, her glasses had gone, and a little voice in his head told him, he would be gone shortly as well if he did not get out while ahead.

Jealous of the old men? asked one of his demons.

Of course not. It's just a bad idea to mix drinks. Wine and champagne probably didn't go together. It was up to him to look after her.

She fancies you, echoed Miss Heather Ronan.

As they say these days.

He downed his glass of wine preparatory to rescuing his boss from a bunch of old lechers.

'Oh, dear, Sergeant, you need a top-up,' said Mrs Jenkins, pouring fresh wine into his glass. 'The food is almost ready. Our butcher is really top-class, you know. So few left nowadays. It's all supermarkets these days, you know. Just not the same quality.'

Frank paused to take in the smell of smoke and cooking.

His stomach rumbled.

Very well, then, something to eat. And then they would eat. Leave. Then they would leave.

Frieda looked over to him and smiled. She took a sip of whatever it was she was drinking, and her deep dark eyes met his. They were bright, her cheeks slightly flushed.

It was the sultry look of the sirens. Suddenly Frank felt like a sailor caught in a whirlpool, oblivious to the many rocks before him.

Somewhere Frank could hear Alfie laughing.

It was the laugh of a man who had ended up paying for his infidelities.

* * *

'Weren't they lovely people?' Frieda enthused as their taxi left some hours later. 'A little too quick to refill glasses, but we might as well enjoy it while we can.'

Frank waved goodbye to their hosts. Frieda was slumped low in the back seat next to him, oblivious of hosts waving their guests goodbye. Her head fell against his chest. He put an arm around her shoulders.

Maybe they had enjoyed a little too much wine in the hot sun, he thought to himself. Yes, that was it, too much sun. It wasn't good for you.

'They asked what our thesis title was going to be, darling,' Frieda continued, slightly slurring the word "thesis". 'I told them we hadn't decided on one.'

Ah, thought Frank bemusedly, as usual FF is ahead by a straight. No confidential discussions while the taxi-driver is listening. Keep the disguise up. She had certainly played the role of girlfriend well during the barbecue, he thought, the occasional arm around his waist, the occasional squeeze. Apart from Mr and Mrs Jenkins and Heather Ronan no-one could have guessed that she was actually his boss.

'Absolutely, darling,' he replied enthusiastically.

Or it could have been "Absholutely, darling", if the taxi-driver's smug look in the rear-view mirror had anything to do with it.

He considered giving the driver a thump across the back of his head to encourage some respect.

Nah, he was far too comfortable where he was.

* * *

Back at his flat he opened a bottle of wine and they sat in the lounge exchanging results. Or rather he lolled in an armchair, while Frieda lay comfortably on his couch looking up at the ceiling.

'Harold Peters,' she said. 'Said he knew Alfie Simmons during the war. Said our Alfie was a little low-life, and it was just as well he died in the explosion, or he – Harry, that is – might well have done the job himself.'

'Did he say why?'

She smiled at the ceiling.

'I don't think our Harold is the sharpest chisel in the toolbox,' she said. 'Plus he had had a little to drink. Began muttering something about how Alfie had betrayed a friend of his, stolen his girlfriend, abused her and then dumped her. It was obvious he was talking about himself.'

'I know. I met his girlfriend.'

'Alfie's? Or Harold's?'

'Both, it seems.'

'Regular little charmer, our Alfie, wasn't he? Why do you suppose he dumped that particular girlfriend? After all, he married two others.'

'That is the question. It had something to do with the Lancaster exploding. That gave him an excuse to disappear. He could hardly turn up afterwards and marry her.'

He took a sip of his drink and slid down in his chair.

'But, I ask myself, would he have come back to her if he had known she was pregnant.'

Frieda considered this point.

'Will you do me a favour, Frank?' she asked slowly.

'A favour?' Frank asked, thinking an afternoon nap would be a nice idea. The food had been good, the wine had been good, the company excellent, and he himself had been rather droll and charming once the subject of Alfie Simmons had been dropped.

Jenkins really knew how to refill a glass. The others had probably been used to his tricks, and had the experience to avoid suddenly finding that their wine-glass was yet again mysteriously full.

'Take my boots off,' Frieda asked. 'They're killing me, and I just don't have the energy to do it myself.'

In his condition it seemed a perfectly normal request. He stood up slowly and staggered over to begin a tug of war between Frieda's boots and her legs.

She had lovely legs.

'She was pregnant, you say?' asked Frieda, continuing to look at the ceiling, almost oblivious of Frank's Herculean struggles.

'Ah, yes. Right, that's the first,' he replied, dropping a boot.

'What happened? To the baby?'

'The baby? I didn't ask. How do you manage to get these boots on in the first place?'

'With a great deal of difficulty. Women are martyrs to fashion. And I normally unzip them first. Why didn't you ask?'

He fell back with the second boot and sat on the carpet, back against the wall, looking at a zipped-up boot in his hand.

'She said something about it being given away to strangers or to an orphanage. I presumed she didn't know what happened to it.'

He left the boot and went back to his chair. Frieda turned onto her side and looked at him.

'It, Frank?' she asked. 'A little baby is an "it"? A woman gives birth to the child of her lover, and she doesn't know what sex it is, doesn't care what happens to her own baby?'

She turned and looked back up at the ceiling.

'Either Heather Ronan is an evil woman of the worst kind or you are an uncaring bastard, Frank Summers,' she said.

Frank considered this carefully. He had to. His normal quick thinking had slowed down into a pedestrian stumble.

Somewhere in the vast caverns of his mind someone tried pointing out that Frieda hated swearing, and would never, ever use the word "bastard". Eventually that someone gave up and went to find someone more appreciative and sober than Frank Summers.

'Different days,' he muttered. 'These days you might think of trying to find out what happened to your only child. Those days ... she probably blanked it out of her life.'

Frieda closed her eyes.

'The child would have been nineteen in 1964,' she murmured. 'Think about that, Frank.'

Frank thought about it. He thought about it as he watched Frieda's hand slip down, her wine-glass fall gently to the carpet, and her fall gently asleep, a strand of her hair across her face.

an the Inspector's. Which is unusual. Normally it's the
way around.'

aned forward, looked at her and tried his best, most
ningest smile.

on, Gertie, give us a hint,' he cajoled. 'Just a teensy-
sy hint. Just a leetle-leetle hint. I don't like to upset
le without knowing why. Especially people I happen to
– like quite a bit, as it happens.'

face coloured, but she remained silent.

ighed.

ay, then, bugger off. Get back into civilian clothes.'

es that mean I'm back on the case?' she asked, looking
n at him hopefully.

s. God knows why, but, yes. Just don't go funny on me
re than once a day. I think I could cope with that.'

anks, Sarge!' For a moment he thought she was about to
s him. Fortunately the desk was between them. Then she
pped out of the office.

nkers, absolutely bonkers,' he said to himself, pulling a file
m his in-tray.

ho is bonkers?' asked Frieda from the doorway.

e whole world,' Frank replied. 'I've come to the decision
t the whole world is stark-staring mad.'

nd you're the only sane one?' she asked, sitting down.

es, but I'm going to give it up. Only on public holidays and
wish festivals will I be sane.'

/hy Jewish festivals?'

/hy not? Maybe I'll change it each year. One year Jewish, the

He tried to keep thinking about it, but all he could see as he fell asleep himself was Frieda lying on the couch in front of him.

He had a vague feeling that the day had not quite conformed to standard police procedures.

Not even Wellbury's.

In his mind he remembered Frieda affectionately calling him darling. He had quite enjoyed holding her in the taxi.

Boy, are you going to be in for it tomorrow, a small voice in his brain told him.

Who cares what tomorrow may bring, he replied.

You will, Frank Summers, said the voice, you will.

He presumed the voice belonged to someone else. After all, he never worried about such things, did he?

Week Three

Monday: Gertie's back in the frame

'I apologise for my behaviour and reque
assigned to the case.'

Gertie stood in front of Frank's desk, uniform
He regarded her with some amazem
amusement. He had woken up late the prev
find a note on the coffee table:

"Frank, thanks for the day. Long time since I
thing. It was great fun. See you tomorrow. xx

He had taken two paracetamol along with two
and had woken up that morning feeling a lot
deserved to. He had a vague feeling that he sh
concerned about how Frieda would feel ab
happened the previous afternoon, but he brus
with the confident thought that Frieda would
little foolishness best forgotten.

In a way he actually regretted the fact tha
colleagues. It was a pity, really.

'Any chance of your telling me the reason?' h
Gertie. 'I mean the reason you asked to be taken
in the first place.'

'I think you know the reason, Sergeant,' she repli
the "Sergeant" as she looked above his head, di
wall behind him.

'Nope, Gertie, I haven't got a clue, though I can
very unusual. All I know is that you are upset w
some reason. So is Susan. In fact the only person
good books I seem to find myself at the moment is

I me
othe
He
cha
'Go
wee
peo
like
He
He
'O
'D
do
'Y
m
'T
kis
sk
'B
fr
'V
'I
th
'
J

next Catholic, then Hindu, Buddhist, American, whatever comes along.'

She smiled.

'Maybe being American is a religion, I suppose,' she said.

'Might as well be. However, closer to home, I was thinking of something you said yesterday.'

'And what was that?' she asked, in a tone he recognised, that of someone hoping they hadn't said or done something they might regret, but couldn't quite remember.

'Heather Ronan's child. Personally I doubt that the child found out who its father was and came back to kill him, but we might as well check. I'll get on to Newcastle and see what they can come up with, though I won't be holding my breath. But there's something else you said.'

'Yes?'

'You said that Harry Peters said that it was just as well Alfie died in the Lancaster. Except that Heather Ronan claimed she told Harry – and only Harry – that she had seen a live Alfie in 1959, and that Harry went out to find him and horse-whip him. So why didn't he mention that fact yesterday? Or at least say that he knew someone who claimed to have seen Alfie years after the accident?'

'Possibly he didn't believe Heather. After all, it was only her word that he had to rely on. And then she had a nervous breakdown. He probably thought that she had imagined it.'

He pondered this.

'I don't buy it,' he said finally. 'Heather said he wasn't the brightest boy on the block, and you came to the same conclusion. He doesn't sound like the type of person to have the nous to imagine that someone else might be telling tall tales. And he loved Heather. Would you disbelieve someone you loved?'

Frieda took a few moments to answer this question.

'Not if it were someone I really loved,' she replied in a soft voice which carried within it a suggestion of severe danger should anyone close by misconstrue her meaning.

'Well, there you go. So why did empty-headed Harry not mention that Alfie might still be alive? There you were yesterday, you've got ten blokes around you, all have had a couple of drinks, they're all trying to impress this extremely attractive young woman, surely they're all coming up with wilder and wilder stories just to get your attention?'

Frieda's face coloured just as Gertie's had a short while before.

'I agree that most men would,' she said, stressing the word "most". 'And, yes, they were doing their best to exaggerate whatever they had to say. Quite a few tall stories. Jack Jenkins was getting a good laugh out of it.'

'And yet Happy Harry stays stum.'

'What's your point, Frank?'

'Maybe he knew that our Alfie was alive in sixty-four – because he was the one that put a bullet into the back of his head. Maybe he finally found him again, five years after Heather Ronan came across him. Harry would be much happier if people thought Alfie had died in forty-five.'

Frieda considered this.

'I won't say it's clutching at straws, but we're going to have a problem proving it,' she noted, standing up and smoothing down her skirt.

'We would have a problem whatever conclusion we reach. If it were Alfie's wife, one or both of them, or his kids, or Harry the Empty-headed, or even Heather Ronan, who, to my mind has one of the best motives for revenge. We have hardly any evidence. I think our only hope is a signed confession.'

'And how will you get that? Beat it out of someone?'

Frank smiled.

'Not quite literally,' he replied. 'The vast majority of killers want to be caught – or, at least, they want to explain what they did and why, especially if this was something personal. We're dealing with people who are looking at the fact that they won't last many more years. I'm pretty sure that, if it is one of them, they'll be willing to confess. All I have to do is haunt them long enough and often enough.'

'Unless,' Frieda pointed out, 'it was one of Alfie's children who still have life in front of them and families to protect – or someone we haven't even come across. One of his partners in crime, if he was involved in some dubious cross-channel enterprise.'

'Thank you, Inspector, you always look on the bright side.'

Frieda smiled.

'I'm glad to see that you and Gertie have kissed and made up, anyway,' she said. 'Any idea what it was all about?'

'Absolutely none. Gertie won't say, and I intend to ignore it. Things you don't understand are best ignored, I always say. I don't bother quantum physics, and it doesn't bother me.'

She gave him a funny look.

'You are a strange man, Frank. I often wonder how you've

managed to remain single so long.'

'I run faster than most,' he said, a grin on his face.

'So, what's the next move?' Frieda asked as Gertie walked in. She was wearing a white T-shirt, cotton jacket and a wrap-around skirt which Frank suspected she had brought in with her, hoping – or maybe even confidently expecting – to regain her acting-detective role.

'Firstly we're going to find out why Heather Ronan was here at the police station. I doubt if it has a bearing on the case, but afterwards we'll pay her and Harry the bachelor a visit, and a little background information might be helpful. If nothing else I hope to find out what dodgy business he and Alfie were planning on getting involved in. It might give us a pointer to whatever it was that Alfie was up to on his trips to the continent.'

'Don't be too heavy on Harry, Frank,' Frieda said. 'He's dim, but he's not a bad old stick. Quite a pleasant person, actually.'

Frank resisted the urge to ask Frieda whether she fancied Harry.

It might turn out to be that she did.

Which made him feel strangely – jealous?

Nah.

'Right, Gertie,' he said after Frieda had left, hips swinging perhaps more than normal. 'Let's go have a word with Eric. Find out why our Heather popped in to speak to the plods.'

'Our Heather?' asked Gertie as she followed him. 'Someone you met recently? Some young beauty who attracted your attention? You seem to get more than your fair share.'

'Now there's a thought,' Frank said, stopping suddenly,

causing Gertie to walk into the back of him.

'What's a thought?' asked Gertie, realising that Frank hadn't even noticed that she had bounced off him.

'Heather Ronan was possibly a young beauty, but that would have been in the Forties – she must have been about eighteen in forty-five.'

'Oh,' Gertie said with a tinge of relief, 'so she's rather old now then.'

'Yes, and I saw an old woman. But what did she look like all those years ago? Good looking, sexy, slim and slender? Or plain-faced, a dull Jane?'

'Does it make any difference, Sarge?'

'Our Alfie proposed to her. They were going to get married. Why did he do that? She came from a wealthy family. Was he in it for the money, or did he really love her? And if he really loved her, why did he desert her?'

'Alfie wouldn't have done that,' Gertie said protectively. 'He wasn't that sort of a man.'

Frank's eyebrows raised. Forty years after he had been murdered Alfie was still attracting women. He wished he had met him.

'The trouble is,' he said, walking on, 'is that, according to Heather Ronan that's exactly what he did do – desert her.'

'He must have had good reason. She was probably a stuck-up cow.'

Frank shook his head sadly. He wished he could get the sort of forgiving attention Alfie was getting.

'Morning, Eric,' he said as they walked into reception. 'I need some information.'

'Wounded Lightning in the three-thirty,' Eric Johns replied, studying the racing form in a tabloid on the counter in front of him.

'Wounded Lightning? What sort of a name is that?'

'It's the name of a horse. They probably call him Joe or Nobbin or something like that when he's at home.'

'Glad to see you're working hard for the money the taxpayer's paying you,' Frank noted.

Eric shrugged.

'Not my fault crime's slow at the moment. Monday morning's are always like this, once you get rid of the drunks from Sunday night. What sort of information?'

'Heather Ronan. Ring a bell? Came into the station about two months ago. Must have been reporting something.'

Eric scratched his head

'Good looker?' he asked dubiously.

'You're the second person to ask. Why do we live in such a shallow world?' Frank asked. 'She's in her eighties, Eric.'

'Ah, in her eighties, eh?' He reached for the logbook and flipped through it. 'What day was it?'

'Late April. The second or third day after I got here.'

'And you've waited this long to chase her up? You youngsters, I don't know. She'll be gone before you have a chance. Here we go. Ronan, Heather. Ah, yes, I remember this. Two old coves, old friends, sharing the same house rather than going into an old-age home. She – Miss Ronan – wakes up one morning to find that the bloke hasn't come down for breakfast. Doesn't worry her, he has odd hours, sometimes up with the lark, sometimes lies in until nine or ten. Come

He tried to keep thinking about it, but all he could see as he fell asleep himself was Frieda lying on the couch in front of him.

He had a vague feeling that the day had not quite conformed to standard police procedures.

Not even Wellbury's.

In his mind he remembered Frieda affectionately calling him darling. He had quite enjoyed holding her in the taxi.

Boy, are you going to be in for it tomorrow, a small voice in his brain told him.

Who cares what tomorrow may bring, he replied.

You will, Frank Summers, said the voice, you will.

He presumed the voice belonged to someone else. After all, he never worried about such things, did he?

Week Three

Monday: Gertie's back in the frame

'I apologise for my behaviour and request that I be re-assigned to the case.'

Gertie stood in front of Frank's desk, uniformed, at attention. He regarded her with some amazement and some amusement. He had woken up late the previous evening to find a note on the coffee table:

"Frank, thanks for the day. Long time since I did that sort of thing. It was great fun. See you tomorrow. xx Frieda".

He had taken two paracetamol along with two pints of water, and had woken up that morning feeling a lot better than he deserved to. He had a vague feeling that he should be a little concerned about how Frieda would feel about what had happened the previous afternoon, but he brushed that aside with the confident thought that Frieda would regard it as a little foolishness best forgotten.

In a way he actually regretted the fact that they were colleagues. It was a pity, really.

'Any chance of your telling me the reason?' he now asked Gertie. 'I mean the reason you asked to be taken off the case in the first place.'

'I think you know the reason, Sergeant,' she replied, stressing the "Sergeant" as she looked above his head, directly at the wall behind him.

'Nope, Gertie, I haven't got a clue, though I can't say that's very unusual. All I know is that you are upset with me for some reason. So is Susan. In fact the only person in whose good books I seem to find myself at the moment is Frieda's –

I mean the Inspector's. Which is unusual. Normally it's the other way around.'

He leaned forward, looked at her and tried his best, most charmingest smile.

'Go on, Gertie, give us a hint,' he cajoled. 'Just a teensy-weensy hint. Just a leetle-leetle hint. I don't like to upset people without knowing why. Especially people I happen to like – like quite a bit, as it happens.'

Her face coloured, but she remained silent.

He sighed.

'Okay, then, bugger off. Get back into civilian clothes.'

'Does that mean I'm back on the case?' she asked, looking down at him hopefully.

'Yes. God knows why, but, yes. Just don't go funny on me more than once a day. I think I could cope with that.'

'Thanks, Sarge!' For a moment he thought she was about to kiss him. Fortunately the desk was between them. Then she skipped out of the office.

'Bonkers, absolutely bonkers,' he said to himself, pulling a file from his in-tray.

'Who is bonkers?' asked Frieda from the doorway.

'The whole world,' Frank replied. 'I've come to the decision that the whole world is stark-staring mad.'

'And you're the only sane one?' she asked, sitting down.

'Yes, but I'm going to give it up. Only on public holidays and Jewish festivals will I be sane.'

'Why Jewish festivals?'

'Why not? Maybe I'll change it each year. One year Jewish, the lunchtime she is worried, though. Checks his bedroom to find his bed hasn't been slept in. Phones around the hospitals, no joy, so she comes to report him as a missing person. Apparently he has these turns, she says. He could be out somewhere not knowing who he was.'

'Did they find him?'

'Oh, yes. Couple of lads in a patrol car see this old bloke walking along with a spade, leaning on it, using it as a walking stick. They think it looks a little strange and decide to investigate. Turns out the old boy had gone out for an early morning stroll, done his ankle in, and had borrowed the spade from somebody's garden to use as a crutch. Asked the lads if he could get a lift, and would they mind returning the spade with his apologies.'

'False alarm then,' Frank said, noting the address.

'Looks that way. Strange thing – well, probably not that strange, not for an old bloke who had strange turns – when the lads tried to return the spade no-one in the area was missing one. Old codger must have got muddled up about which garden he had nicked it from. It's in lost property if you need one.'

'No thanks, my flat doesn't extend to a garden. Where did they find him?'

'Not far from where the Dead Skeleton was found. Strange, that.'

Frank turned to go, and then paused.

'This friend, the old codger – he wouldn't be one Harold Peters by any chance?'

Eric checked the log.

'Indeed he was. How did you know that?'

'I'm clairvoyant,' Frank replied, walking out of the front door, Gertie in tow.

'Clair who?' called Eric. 'You want to be careful going around calling yourself girls' names.'

'Where to, Sarge?' asked Gertie as they got into the car, a smile on her face. Frank gave her the address.

On the way he told her about the Sunday barbecue, keeping back only non-salient details to protect the innocent parties involved.

* * *

Heather Ronan looked surprised and somewhat embarrassed to find them on her doorstep. She rallied herself, offered them tea, and took them to a table and seats in the well-kept back garden.

'Harry's still in bed,' she explained, 'I don't want to wake him up. I think he had a little too much to drink yesterday, not a wise thing at our age. Still, it doesn't happen often. Have to enjoy it when you get the chance. Did you get home safely, Sergeant?'

'Yes, Miss Ronan, perfectly safely,' he said.

'And the delightful Inspector?' she asked, a twinkling look in her eyes,

'She, er, didn't mention any problems when she came into work this morning,' Frank said neutrally, acutely aware that Gertie was listening. Gertie might not gossip, but a carelessly made comment to another girl in the ladies' could travel a long way, and if Eric Johns got his hands on it he would make it sound like a full-blown affair.

Which it wasn't.

And anyway, he had an instinctive feeling that it was best Gertie knew nothing about it.

Though he wasn't sure why.

'I'm sorry to have to trouble you, Miss Ronan,' he said quickly, 'but we were hoping to get some more information about Alfie Simmons.'

'I told you all I know yesterday, Sergeant. I haven't remembered anything else since then. And I'd prefer not to. I'd prefer to forget about it totally.'

'I understand, Miss Ronan. Unfortunately we have to ask these questions. I can't tell you why at the moment, but I'm afraid it will cause you a little more heartache when we do. So we want to make very sure of our facts before we do so.'

'It's all in the past, Sergeant, buried. Let it stay that way.'

It would have been, thought Frank, if someone hadn't accidentally dug it up again.

'Just a few questions, Miss Ronan,' he said soothingly. 'Firstly, is this Alfie Simmons?' He passed her one of the photographs Gwen Simmons had lent them.

Heather Ronan's angry face softened.

'Yes, Sergeant, that's Alfie. I'd recognise that smile anywhere.'

She looked up at him.

'Where did you get the photograph?' she asked.

'I'm afraid that's confidential at the moment,' he said, taking it back.

'When was it taken?'

'We believe the summer of 1948.' She looked down at her

257

hands.

'So I was right, then? He didn't die in that Lancaster?'

Frank was about to reply "I'm afraid not", but realised that that might not sound the way he meant it.

'You said he and Mr Peters had something going, something not quite legal. Can you remember what it was?'

She shook her head.

'I never knew what it was. But I'm sure it wasn't anything terribly bad. Everyone was doing things they would not normally have done in other times. A little bit of black market goods here, a few tins filched there, maybe a little cloth for a new dress. Sweet-talking the butcher into giving you a little more mince than he should. Not what you could call grand crimes, Sergeant.'

'Well, I never!' came a voice from the back door. Harry Peters stepped out, looking hale and hearty and unaffected by the previous day's indulgences, and also happy to see visitors. 'If it isn't the young Frank. Good to see you so soon again. How's the wonderful Frieda?'

He sat down next to Heather and continued before Frank could get a word in.

'Charming young woman, that. Damn fine body. I saw you two rushing off early. Eager to get home and engage in a bit of hows-your-father, eh?'

He turned to the sound of Gertie choking and offered her a glass of water. She waved the offer away with her one hand, the other covering her mouth.

'Harry, dear,' said Heather gently, 'I didn't get a chance to tell you. This is Detective Sergeant Summers, and the young lady is Constable Gregson. Frieda whom we met yesterday is Inspector Garold. They're police officers.'

Harry's face went white, and for a moment Frank was worried that he might pass out.

'I apologise for the subterfuge,' he said. 'We were looking for some information. We thought that, if people looked on us as researchers rather than police officers they would be more forthcoming, more unvarnished as far as the details go.'

'It's about Alfie Simmons,' Heather said. 'I've told Sergeant Summers what happened. All of it.'

'Alfie Simmons?' asked Harry, the colour coming back to his cheeks, turning from ashen pale to infuriated pink. 'I wondered why Frieda – the Inspector – was asking such strange questions. Don't tell me you finally arrested him?'

'Why would we want to arrest him?' asked Frank.

'Well, because, because – he was a bad lot. If Heather's told you how he ruined our lives, well, that's the sort of – I wouldn't call him a man, he was scum – that's the sort of thing he was. Sooner or later he'd find himself on the wrong side of the law.'

'You told Inspector Garold that he had died when a Lancaster exploded, in 1945.'

'Well, that's what we thought at the time. Heather said she saw him years later, I was never certain that she hadn't made a mistake. It didn't seem to make any difference anyway.'

'But you went out looking for him. To horse-whip him, I believe.'

'So I did. And if I had found him that's exactly what I would have done to him. Thrashed him to an inch of his life.'

'You didn't think of killing him?'

'Kill him? Most certainly not. We still had the death penalty in those days. I wasn't going to swing for him. And, had I got the chance of given him the beating he so richly deserved, any decent jury would have approved of my actions, I'm sure. We didn't have the soft notions they have these days.'

Frank paused.

'Tell me,' he asked quietly, 'what was the scam that you and Alfie Simmons were cooking up back in 1945?'

Harry's face turned infuriated red.

'Scam? What on earth are you suggesting? Scam, indeed. As if I would have anything to do with that little rat.'

'I've told them you and Alfie were up to something,' Heather said, putting a hand gently on his knee. 'Harry, it's a long time ago. I'm sure that whatever it was has passed the statute of limitations, or whatever it's called. Isn't that so, Sergeant?'

'I'm pretty sure we wouldn't prosecute anyone for any minor crimes they might have carried out in 1945,' Frank said.

What they did in 1964 was, however, a different kettle of fish.

'Well, if you must know, yes, we did have a little thing on the go, or we planned to have,' Harry admitted, embarrassed. 'Shotguns.'

'Shotguns?'

'They were in short supply. Plenty of the other sort of stuff, but not many shotguns. Most estates had handed theirs over to the Home Guard, who promptly lost them, or wouldn't return them. The end of the war was in sight, soon people would be getting back to normal – including hunting, shooting, and fishing. I had the contacts – that was when we still had the old house and the land, before death duties, inflation and taxation – bloody Socialists – took it all away.'

Only Harry could have believed that the end of the war would suddenly bring an overwhelming demand for shotguns which would make his fortune. Presumably Alfie, not being a member of the hunting, shooting and fishing set, had believed it at first. But that wouldn't have lasted long.

'Where was he going to get them?' Frank asked. Harry shrugged.

'I didn't enquire too deeply. He suggested that he had contacts in Europe who would have access to anything confiscated from the Germans. They were bound to confiscate all weaponry, including shotguns.'

'But it never happened?'

'Simmons, so we believed, died in the Lancaster accident. I often wondered whether he had found the shotguns, and somehow they caused the explosion. At the time I even felt sorry for him. Not any more, the two-faced little piece of rubbish.'

Frank turned to Heather.

'I know this is a long shot, Miss Ronan, but that's all we have at the moment. Can you remember the man you saw talking to Alfie Simmons? What he looked like, height, weight, that sort of thing?'

'Age, about twenty, early twenties maybe, stocky build, looked like a builder or a labourer,' she replied immediately. 'Dark brown hair, face quite stubby. I didn't see the colour of his eyes.'

'You remember that after all this time?'

'I've carried a mental photograph of that moment for a long time, Sergeant. When I rushed after Alfie, and found I'd lost him, I came back to see if the man was still there, but he had also disappeared. While I walked the streets looking for Alfie in the weeks after I was also looking for that man. But I never saw either ever again. I'm sorry.'

Frank stood up.

'Thank you for your time. We may have to return if anything new comes to light.'

Heather leaned forward and looked up at him.

'We've told you all we know. Can't you tell us why you're so interested in Alfie after all this time?'

Frank looked at her for a few moments before coming to a decision.

'It will be in the papers soon, so I might as well tell you now. But only on the understanding that, until it does appear in public, you must keep it to yourselves.'

'You have our word, Sergeant,' Heather assured him.

Frank paused for effect.

'We believe Alfie Simmons was murdered in the summer of 1964,' he said.

The other two looked at him in stupefaction.

'But how – ' began Harry.

'Of course,' said Heather quietly. 'The dead skeleton case. Not so?'

Frank nodded.

'How did you find out that it was Alfie?'

'We found his air force tags along with the skeleton. We

confirmed his identity via a number of ways which I can't reveal at the moment. There's still a lot we don't know at the moment, so some information needs to remain in our hands until we can put a fuller picture together.'

Heather stood up.

'If there's anything else we can help you with, we'd be glad to,' she said.' I'll walk you to the door.'

They left Harry sitting in his chair, apparently still trying to get to grips with the news.

'I suppose you're wondering whether or not to believe us,' Heather said softly as they walked. 'Maybe you think one of us – or both – came across Alfie in 1964 and murdered him. I can promise you that that did not happen. Do you believe me?'

'I believe you,' he replied.

For the moment, he added mentally. Until evidence proves otherwise.

'Thank you,' she said, as if it meant a good deal to her.

'Did you ever try to find your child, Miss Ronan? I don't think you mentioned – was it a girl or a boy?'

'A boy, Sergeant. And, no, though I thought about it often enough – every day, in fact, every single day – I decided it better not to try to find out who he was, who he had become. It was the most painful decision I had to take, but, in the end, I believed it better not to upset his life. It would only have been selfish.'

Frank nodded understandingly.

And that is definitely a lie, he thought. Heather Ronan had tried to find out who her only child was. Whether or not she was successful only she knew. At the moment he was hoping that Newcastle might come through with some interesting information.

But he didn't hold out many hopes of that happening.

* * *

'What was all that about?' asked Gertie as they drove away. 'You know, FF and all that?'

'I think our Frieda might need a new nickname soon,' said Frank, leaning back, closing his eyes and trying to think.

'Our Frieda?'

'Isn't that the expression around here? Someone is always "our" Alfie or whatever?'

'Only if you like them.'

'Right. I'll remember that.'

She tried to outlast his silence, but failed.

'So?' she demanded.

'So what?'

'So what about FF? Sounds like Harry Peters quite fancied her.'

'Promise me you won't pass that on,' he asked.

'Cross my heart and hope to die,' she assured him. 'You can cross it as well if you want,' she added suggestively.

Frank opened his eyes.

'Acting Detective Constable Gregson, watch your step. And keep your bloody eye on the road,' he said as a post-box looked at them with intent.

'Sorry, Sarge,' she said meekly.

He closed his eyes and composed himself once more to think.

Another silence ensued, but failed to defeat Gertie.

'Is it true what I've heard, Sarge?' she asked.

He considered the question.

'That depends on what you've heard, I would imagine.'

'That you never go out with other police officers. Absolutely never? Never, ever? Women, I mean.'

'I'm glad you qualified that statement, Gertie,' he noted. 'Personally I think it should be banned, totally. I've heard and seen too many cases of good people working together, trying to do their job and keep a relationship going, and failing. The odds are against you in the first place. I would imagine it's difficult in any job. In a police force it's nigh near impossible.'

For a moment Gertie wondered if he was speaking from experience. It certainly sounded that way. She could easily imagine having an intense affair with Frank Summers.

Someone having an intense affair with Frank Summers, she quickly qualified her thought.

'But it can happen, can't it?' she asked. 'It can succeed. People do fall in love and manage to continue working together.'

'More chance of winning the lottery, I would imagine. Let's concentrate on something more important. Like who murdered Alfie Simmons.'

Gertie pondered whether love was more important than who murdered Alfie Simmons. It was a close call.

'What if the woman gave up her career?' she asked. 'You know, as proof of her love.'

'None of Alfie's wives had a career,' he pointed out.

'No, Sarge, not Alfie. I meant, you know, if a male police officer and a female police officer fell in love. If she had the choice between him and her career, and she gave up her career for him, wouldn't that show she loved him? Like really, really loved him?'

He rubbed his eyes. This was getting all too much for him.

'I suppose so. Theoretically,' he said.

He wondered if she was talking about Frieda and himself. Had she spotted something, added two and two together and come up with five?

Well, it wasn't going to happen.

Definitely not.

'Sarge, you're good with the Internet and computers,' she said.

He sighed.

'Gertie, I know the basics. You really should study computers a little bit more. Especially if you want promotion, as I know you do. God knows why.'

'Will you teach me?' she asked.

'What, how to use the Internet? Gertie, you can suss that out yourself. After all, you're more than happy using your mobile phone.'

'That's different. That's talking to people.' She looked at him pleadingly. 'Will you teach me? I have to start somewhere.'

He sighed again.

'Okay, I'll show you the little I know. I don't understand why you're so shy of computers. They're only machines, you know.'

'Not flesh and blood,' agreed Gertie, happily, emphasising the word "flesh".

Frank opened his eyes and looked at the staid houses they were passing, tree-lined avenues, window boxes, immaculately tended gardens of bright summery colours. Innocent. Upright. The ordinary citizens of Wellbury living a blameless life behind net-curtains. Tea with the vicar. Making jam for the Women's Institute. What stories lay behind those blameless curtains?

'Why, that's what I can't understand. Why?' he asked.

'Why what, Sarge?'

'Why all these women fell for Alfie. By all accounts he was a right rogue. Or anarchist, or whatever you want to call him. He marries two women, but he runs from Heather Ronan. Why?'

'He didn't have a choice. The Lancaster exploding gave him a chance to do something. We don't know what. But when he sees Heather Ronan years later – what, fifteen years later? – he's caught on a dilemma. Does he lose all he's worked for by acknowledging the love of his life, or does he scarper, hoping to explain all later? I think he probably hoped to be able to come back to her when he'd made his fortune.'

'You are incurably romantic, Gertie,' observed Frank. 'When Heather Ronan saw him in 1959 he was already married. And he would become married again in a very short time. If he was to be a bigamist, why not a thrigamist, or whatever the word might be?'

'You don't understand love,' said Gertie disapprovingly.

'Then you will have to explain it to me some time.'

'I look forward to that,' Gertie replied, enigmatically.

* * *

When they walked into the station canteen for lunch Eric

Johns had a message for Frank.

'Ex-bobbies in Wellbury,' he said through a mouthful of treacle tart.

'Found some?' asked Frank. Eric nodded and swallowed. He took a piece of paper from his shirt-pocket and handed it over.

'Steve Handley, retired as a Detective Sergeant ten years ago. I gave him a call to make sure he was still alive and ticking. Then there's Mike Street, retired eleven years ago as a uniformed sergeant. I'm surprised he's still around. I remember him. He always looked like he was about to drop dead from overwork. Not that he ever worked very hard. Just looked that way.'

'Just these two?'

'Coppers don't tend to last long after they retire, it seems. There are a few others, but they've all buggered off to places like Devon, Cornwall, Scotland or Spain. Probably regret it now. There's no place like home.'

'Right, Gertie, after lunch we'll go look up our retirees. See if they remember anything about Alfie Simmons.'

'You can catch Steve Handley in the White Swan at three o'clock, Eric Johns said. 'Apparently he has a pint there regularly, on the dot. Then he goes fishing for two hours. Back to the Swan for another, and then home. Funny sort of a way to spend your retirement. I'd want a little more variety, myself.'

* * *

They found Steve Handley in the White Swan as predicted, a full pint in front of him at three o'clock exactly, browsing through the Racing Post. Frank introduced himself and Gertie and they sat down, declining the offer of a drink.

'Alfie Simmons,' said Frank. 'Does the name ring a bell?'

Steve Handley pulled an earlobe and looked at the ceiling.

'Simmons, Simmons,' he murmured. 'A vague, very vague tinkle. What period are we talking about?'

'Early nineteen-sixties,' Frank replied. Handley looked at him in surprise.

'Hell, you are talking ancient history. What's he done?'

'Got himself murdered. We'd like to arrest him for that, but since he's dead we're going for the next best thing, whoever murdered him.'

Handley chuckled.

'When was he murdered?' he asked, taking a pull from his pint.

'Nineteen sixty-four.'

Handley whistled.

'1964? A little ambitious, aren't you? Whoever did it is probably long gone.' He paused. 'Of course,' he said in surprise, 'this is the dead skeleton case.'

'Yes, but keep it under your hat. The media already smell a story.'

'Of course, of course.' Handley smiled. 'I feel sorry for you lot. In my day the newspapers were a lot more respectful. At the time we used to think they were nasty, lying little scroats, but compared to today ...'

Frank slid a photograph across the table.

'Recognise him?'

Handley took out a pair of reading glasses, slipped them on, and scrutinised the picture.

'Well, well,' he said. 'Come to papa.'

Frank waited. Finally Handley took off his glasses, pushed the photograph back, and looked at Frank.

'My goodness, the memories are flooding back. Alfie Simmons. I had high hopes of him.'

'You knew him? He doesn't appear to have any sort of record.'

'No, we never did nail him. But he was in to something, that I can guarantee you. So someone topped him. That makes sense.'

He took another sip of his ale and leaned forward.

'Yes, it must have been the early Sixties. I was a young beat-bobby then. I remember noticing Simmons' lorry one day. It looked suspicious, I can't remember why, quite possibly I was just imagining things. But I mentioned it to a detective I knew at the station, described Simmons to him. He took me to one side and told me to keep away from Simmons. Surprised me at the time. I wondered whether the detective was on the take. Then the Inspector calls me in and explains that they're keeping an eye on Simmons, they're pretty sure he's into some smuggling deal. Seeing as how I'd clocked Simmons, I was made acting detective for a week. Looked like my big chance. I was an ambitious lad in those days, that's why I remember it so well. Big thing in Wellbury then, would be even today. Then bloody Simmons disappeared, and I went back to the beat.'

'Nothing else happened? Nobody tried to find out where he'd disappeared to? After all, his wife reported him missing.'

Both of them, if the truth be known.

Handley shrugged.

'We didn't have anything on him, apart from a general suspicion. In those days uniform and plain-clothes didn't mix much, so I wouldn't be surprised if uniform filed a missing person's report and forgot about it. They weren't to know we were looking for the bugger.'

'So you never found out what he was up to?'

'Not so much as a twinkle. Could have been anything. Diamonds was the general theory, as I recall. But, you know something? When I look back ... Well, I was an impressionable young bobby, then. If a detective told me the moon was made of green cheese I'd have believed him. Thinking back I realise that they probably didn't have any evidence, that it was quite possible Simmons was totally innocent. From that point of view.'

'But you don't think so.'

Handley shook his head slowly.

'You get a feeling about some people,' he said. 'Right from the first time I laid eyes on Simmons and his lorry I knew he was as guilty as sin. What of, I never found out.'

He grinned.

'Maybe I blamed him for losing my first big chance of becoming a detective. If he hadn't disappeared I wouldn't have been sent back to the trenches.'

Frank stood, Gertie following suit.

'Well, thanks for that, Mr Handley,' he said.

'Steve's the name,' Handley said. 'Good luck. Can't see you getting anywhere, but good luck anyway. Let me know if you find anything.'

'Will do. Good luck with the fishing.'

Handley gave him a bitter smile.

'Never catch anything. If I do I throw it back. Know why I go fishing, lad?'

Frank paused.

'Because you enjoy it?' he suggested.

'To get away from the wife,' Handley replied, returning to the Racing Post. 'Take my advice, son, before you retire, get divorced. It's one thing when you've got the job to escape to, it's sheer bloody hell when you're stuck with a wife twenty four hours a day.'

* * *

'Miserable old git,' Gertie commented as they drove away.

'He's got a point,' Frank replied. 'If you come up to retirement without having planned for it, what do you do when you suddenly have nothing to do? I'd imagine his wife feels the same way. One day she's got the house to herself most of the time, next she's tripping over his feet every five seconds.'

'But surely if they've been married all that time – well, they can't hate each other, surely?'

'Damned if I know, Gertie. Maybe Alfie had the right idea. Have two wives. Split your time between them. That way nobody gets bored with each other.'

'That's a very sexist attitude, Sarge. Why can't the wife have two husbands?' She looked at him. 'Is that what you'd like, a woman in every port?'

'Gertie, if you don't keep your eye on the road I won't live to have one wife, let alone two.'

'Sorry, Sarge,' she said, paying more attention to her driving, a disapproving look on her face.

Frank leaned back and closed his eyes. How did Alfie do it, he wondered. He, Frank, couldn't even manage to have a constant relationship with one woman, namely Doctor Susan Pleadle. Were women more pliant back then, more trusting?

Possibly, he thought, but pretty irrelevant. He would give up the idea of Susan Pleadle. Join some clubs. Meet people. There had to be other women out there, ones that wouldn't slam the phone down on him just because he had to work on a Sunday.

He wondered what this Tracey, assistant to Susan, was like. Maybe he should pop into the path lab when Susan wasn't in and find out.

'Penny for them,' offered Gertie. He opened his eyes and looked at the road ahead.

'Oh, nothing much. Just wondering where I can find a girlfriend who doesn't lose her temper because I have to work on a Sunday. Your boyfriend doesn't lose his cool when you have to work odd hours, does he?'

Gertie considered this very carefully for some time. Possibly she was wondering how Frank could have forgotten so soon that she had mentioned she had no boyfriend at the moment. Perhaps "I don't have a boyfriend at the moment" had been too subtle for him. Maybe adding "But you'll do until something better comes along," while grabbing him by his flashy tie would have driven the point home. Maybe she should wait until an inappropriate moment, get him in an arm-lock and make sure he understood her feelings in a way even Frank Summers couldn't miss.

Perhaps not.

Not yet, anyway.

Not until she was more sure of what her own feelings were.

'I haven't quite got one of those things at the moment, not as such,' she said instead, slowly, as if she were choosing her words carefully, which she was. 'A boy-friend, that is. But if he did have to work odd hours, I certainly wouldn't get angry with him just for that. I think I'd be more grateful when he did get home. Especially if he was a copper. I'd be much more understanding. Yes, he would get a very warm welcome when he came home.'

Frank thought about that. It wasn't the answer to the question he had asked. What really surprised him was Gertie not having a boyfriend. She was young, attractive, sexy, bubbly, intelligent – and, possibly, secretly gay?

Which might explain what "not as such" meant.

He closed his eyes again. What he did know for certain was that he fancied an early night. The previous day's drink and sun was making itself felt. And he still had the evening debrief with Frieda to get through. He was not looking forward to it. Frieda, yes, the debriefing, no.

Back at the station Gertie disappeared to the ladies'. Inside his office Frank found two pleasant surprises. The first was a note from Frieda saying that she had to go out, and would speak to him the following morning. Great, no evening debrief. He could even get away early.

The second was a letter in his in-tray. Inside was scented pink writing paper with little bunnies at the bottom. It read:

"Frank

I suppose I have to eat humble pie. I thought you were going out on a date with Gertie and boasting about it to me. Now I'm told it was work, and that you ended up going with the Inspector. All I can say is I'm sorry about slamming the phone down on you, and I promise it won't happen again.

Give me a call sometime.

xx

Susan"

There was a broad grin on Frank's face when Gertie returned from the ladies.

'You suddenly look happy with life, Sarge,' she noted. 'Want some coffee?'

'I suddenly find life has improved greatly, my dear Gertie,' he replied, stuffing the letter into his pocket. 'FF can't make our evening session, so I think we can reasonably knock off early.' He checked his watch. 'Just short of five o'clock. Fancy a drink, Gertie? We can put it down to office time.'

'Best offer I've had for ages,' she said, smiling happily.

To her disappointment they only had the one drink. They spent it debating the merits of cricket as a sport. She was an avid fan, and tried persuading him to join the police team. She pointed out that the Chief Constable was also enthusiastic about the various police teams. He pointed out that, while he enjoyed a nice slow Saturday afternoon's cricket as much as the next man, the only thing he wanted from the Chief Constable was total ignorance of his existence, and joining the Wellbury Police Cricket Team was hardly likely to be helpful in that respect.

Neither noticed two young women entering the pub, one making a sudden change of decision, and forcefully dragging her surprised friend out.

Doctor Susan Pleadle had not looked too happy.

Tuesday: A meeting of wives

'What's the best time to tell someone that their husband was a bigamist?' Frank asked in Frieda's office the following morning.

'After lunch,' Frieda said.

'After lunch?'

'People tend not to eat when they receive bad news. Their appetite disappears. If they get the bad news in the afternoon after having had lunch they can miss dinner, and have a night to start recovering. By the following lunchtime they're usually hungry enough to eat something. Normality gradually returns.'

'Interesting,' Frank noted. 'I'd never thought of it like that.'

'That's because you've never had to cook for anyone.'

There wasn't much he could say to that. Not to someone who had probably cooked for a husband who had then beaten her up.

'I'll get them in this afternoon, then. Mrs Simmons and Mrs Green. Break the news as gently as possible.'

He stood up and looked out of the window.

'There are two options. Firstly that one or both discovered the fact of Alfie's bigamy back in 1964, and that led to Alfie's early demise. The second is that they're both blissfully unaware, and the news will come as the biggest shock in their lives. In which case their reactions might range from stunned silence to throwing things at me.'

'I don't think Mrs Green will believe you. Not after that postcard business.'

'If she sincerely believes the postcard came from Alfie,

possibly not. If she sent the postcard herself ... Now there's a thought.'

'A thought? I like the sound of that. What thought, exactly, Frank?'

'We presumed that the postcard was a blind, probably Mrs Green sending herself something she'd received years ago, the act of someone a little ga-ga. But there's something we completely overlooked.'

'Which is?'

'The postcard didn't have an original stamp on it, nor any post-office stamp – from the 1960s, I mean. So either it was somehow removed, or it was never posted in the first place. And if it wasn't posted in the first place, that means someone found it around the time Alfie was killed, because he never got the chance to post it, and that person kept it for forty years, for some reason. So even if Mrs Green sent herself the postcard, it still tells us something. Quite a lot, if you think about it.'

'Hold your horses, Frank. We don't even know if it was written by Alfie. It was signed with a single initial, just the letter A. It could have been a result of an affair someone had had. It could even have been written by a woman. We only have Mrs Green's word that Alfie wrote it.'

'I know, I know,' Frank said. 'But we do know that someone kept it for a very long time, and then chose to post it now. So it meant a good deal to them. And if it wasn't posted back in 1964, then either it was written by the person who kept it all this time, or that person found it and kept it.'

Frieda contemplated the idea.

'You may be right, Frank,' she said, 'but I can't see that it gets us any further. Not unless we can find out who posted it.'

'I'll have a word with Susan. Maybe there's something we missed. But, to my mind, it means that Alfie's murder was personal, not business. Which limits our suspects. His wife – both his wives – Heather Ronan, Harry Peters or Alfie's son and or daughter.'

Frieda looked dubious.

'I'm not sure that you aren't jumping to conclusions. But, even if you're right, there remains the problem we've faced all along. How will you prove it, short of a signed confession?'

Frank didn't answer the question. He didn't have an answer to the question.

Frieda looked at her watch and stood up.

'I'm seeing the Chief Constable this afternoon. I'm going to recommend that we give a press conference on Thursday, let them know what we've found out so far, admit that we're stuck, request information from the public, and then, if nothing comes to light after the media have their feast, put it in the unsolved pile.'

'But – '

Frank was about to protest. Frieda held up a hand.

'I know, Frank, you've put your heart and soul into it. I've also enjoyed – if that's the word – the case. The Chief Constable is fascinated by it. If we could come up with a result it would be gold stars and brownie points all round. Percy Hanson would turn green with envy, and probably stay that way for the rest of his life, an outcome I would dearly love to see. But we can't avoid the fact that there are more modern and pressing matters we should be dealing with. The taxpayer might enjoy reading about it, but they'd prefer us to concentrate on their stolen car or mugging or whatever.'

Frank grunted. Sod the gold stars and brownie points, he thought to himself, I want a result.

But, as much as he would like to deny it, he had to admit that Frieda was right.

He might have considered it interesting that he was personally happy, even obsessed enough, to continue, whereas Frieda, for whom a successful outcome would provide several feathers in her cap, and soften the way to promotion, was accepting the logical choice. The thought did not cross his mind. He wanted to know who killed Alfie Simmons.

He returned to his office in a less than happy mood. What really irritated was that he was again doing exactly what he had sworn never to do, getting overly involved in work.

'You look like your favourite puppy's been run over, Sarge,' Gertie commented as he walked into the office.

'That bad, eh?' he asked, sitting down. 'It's just that Frieda's decided the case gets canned if we don't come up with anything before the weekend. Press conference on Thursday, let the media have their fun, and then get back to real work.'

'Real work? I thought investigating murder was real work?' Gertie asked.

"Frieda"? she thought. He had said that far too cosily. Far, far, far too cosily. And she wasn't convinced that the barbeque had been the innocent excursion of two colleagues that Frank had portrayed it as.

'Not if it happened forty years ago. I'm afraid to say that Frieda has a point,' Frank continued, not realising that Gertie was now counting each occurrence of Frieda's name, and testing his use of it to see if it carried some hidden meaning.

'We probably have more chances of winning the lottery than finding out and proving who killed Alfie Simmons. And even then a good defence lawyer could come up with a story showing it was self-defence. And, should a miracle occur, and we get a conviction, whoever it is is so old now a prison sentence would only be a gesture, and not necessarily a good one. Count up the time and resources we'd be spending on it – us, the lawyers, judges, jury, Tom Cobbley and all – compare that to the result, and, as Frieda puts it, the taxpayer might not look upon us warmly. I'm afraid the dark face of that beast called pragmatism has reared its ugly head.'

Gertie sighed and made a face.

'First real case I get and it's a no-show,' she noted. Then she brightened up. 'Still, we've got a week together, Sarge, or a few days anyway.'

'Eminently true, my dear Gertie. This morning we have a word with our ex-Sergeant Mike Street. This afternoon we break the bad news to Mrs Simmons and Mrs Green. See how they react. But first, I must make a call to Doctor Pleadle.' He looked at Gertie. 'You wouldn't mind fetching some coffee for us, would you?'

'Okay, Sarge,' she said reluctantly, and left.

'Susan, Frank here,' he said when Susan answered.

'Yes, Sergeant Summers, and what can I do for you?' she said in a less than friendly tone. He looked at the receiver in surprise.

'Er, that postcard, the one that Mrs Green brought in. Can you remember whether there was anything to show that it had been posted back in 1964 or thereabouts?'

'I'll ask Tracey to have a look and let you know. Was there

anything else?'

Yes, he thought. What have I done wrong this time?

'Um, well, now you come to mention it, er, how can I put this? I had got the impression that I was no longer in your bad books, but you don't sound so, um, friendly this morning.'

'Why should you think that?'

Because ice is forming on this telephone, that's why. Either global warming has been completely reversed or I'm back on your list of the top ten slugs of all time, Frank thought.

'Okay, Susan, shoot me if you must, but at least tell me what I've done this time before you do it.'

'Why should you have done anything? After all, you're a free man, we aren't actually going out as such, are we? You're totally free to call me if you want, or, alternatively, to take your little girlfriend from work out for drinks!'

The last was said almost in a shout, and the sound of the phone crashing down almost burst his eardrum.

He replaced the receiver gently as Gertie came in with two cups of coffee.

'I think I'll become a monk,' he said, 'join one of those monasteries where they don't speak, the silent variety. Might as well, if Doctor Pleadle carries on her unique method of ending a telephone conversation I'll be deaf before too long.'

'She was angry with you?'

'She saw us having a drink last night. She seems to think there's something going on between us. Why does she insist on jumping to such silly conclusions?'

'I don't think it's that silly, Sarge,' Gertie protested.

'Don't you? If you were going out with someone, and saw them having a drink with a woman colleague after work, would you immediately presume he was having an affair with her?'

Gertie thought about this.

'Yes, I probably would,' she said. 'You know, I think you should find yourself someone who's more in tune with you. Someone who understands you.'

'A psychoanalyst, presumably. Do you know this girl Tracey who works at the lab? Maybe she's free and single.'

Gertie paused before replying.

'I've heard she's gay. Maybe you should look closer to home,' she said.

Frank sighed.

'Maybe I should just give up. Come on, shift yourself. Let's find out what Mike Street has to offer.'

* * *

Ex-Sergeant Mike Street was enjoying his retirement. Most of it he spent savouring fond memories of no longer having to be abused by the general public.

'Totally different when I started,' he said as they sat in the lounge of the Street's three-bedroomed detached house, the interior of which had not so much been bypassed by progress as avoided by it. 'People had respect for the law. Policing was an honourable job. By the time I left a police uniform was just a target, and it wasn't just kids, by then even grown-ups looked down on you. I don't envy you lot nowadays, I can tell you.'

'Ever come into contact with Alfie Simmons? Around the

early Sixties?' Frank asked, having immediately realised that this was likely to be a boring waste of time, and wanting to get it over with as soon as possible. He handed the photograph over. Street studied it for a while.

'Simmons,' he muttered to himself, 'Alfie Simmons. Now why does that name ring a bell?'

Finally he shook his head and handed back the photograph. Frank suspected that there were a lot of bells ringing in Mike Street's head, most of them imaginary, quite a few belonging to cuckoo clocks.

'No, there's something there, but it won't come. I seem to vaguely remember something about an accident. Lorry crashed into a car – or was it the other way round? Driver of the car was a young bloke, a member of a gang of some sort. Car was stolen. Driver was killed, two young thugs with him got away with minor injuries. Trouble is, I'm not sure the lorry driver was your Alfie Simmons. Probably not.'

'When was that?'

'Sixty-three. Same year as Kennedy got shot. I seem to recall it was before, but it could have been after.'

'Did the other members of the gang make any threats afterwards?' asked Gertie. 'Threaten the lorry driver, perhaps?'

Street looked at her as if surprised to find she could talk.

'They might have done. It was a long time ago. I don't even know why I remembered it, plenty of road accidents during my years on the force. Maybe it was because it was almost a case of just desserts. Young tearaway steals car, it kills him. Towards the end of my time there we would have celebrated. These days a kid wouldn't even get a ticking-off for nicking cars. Probably be rewarded, get sent on holiday to Florida. Bloody sociology mumbo-jumbo.'

'Well, thanks for your time,' Frank said, standing up, aiming to avoid having to listen to further ranting on modern youth.

'Not at all, lad. I'll let you know if I remember anything else, but I doubt it.'

* * *

'If that's what retirement does to you,' Gertie noted when they had left, 'I think I'll stay in the job until I die.'

'Do me a favour, Gertie.'

'What's that, Sarge?'

'If you ever, ever hear me refer to the good old days, slap me around the head with something heavy.'

Gertie giggled.

'You're too young to do that, aren't you?' she asked.

'I have a theory,' he said. 'That there's a certain point in everyone's life where they start looking backwards instead of forwards, and it happens so suddenly they don't notice. One second they're looking forward to the weekend, having some fun, the next they're talking about how things used to be in their day. The question is, how do you spot that moment and avoid it?'

'Can you?'

'Maybe Alfie found the way. Living a double life means you can't afford to stop and reminisce.'

'But he got himself murdered.'

'It's a conspiracy, then. Society can't handle the man who finds a way out, so he has to be done away with. It's not done consciously, just some natural force takes over.'

'You do have some strange ideas, Sarge.'

'I have an even stranger one. Going back through the records on traffic accidents in 1963.'

'You are joking, aren't you, Sarge? You don't think Alfie was murdered by a gang of teenagers because of an accident?'

'Of course I'm joking. I doubt if we even have traffic records going back that far.'

'I bet we do have. After all, Sergeant Johns found the missing persons files from then.'

'Point. Remind me to ask him exactly how far back we do have records for. Purely as a matter of interest.'

'Will do, Sarge. What do we do now?'

'Back to the office. Maybe our gay Tracey's got some information for us. And then I'd like to go back through what we have. Every single statement. Just for the hell of it. It shouldn't take us long.'

Tracey had indeed called while they were out. Frank returned the call, discovering that Tracey, whoever she was, had a very attractive, soft speaking voice, with just a hint of a lisp.

'No, Sergeant,' she said, 'there is nothing to suggest that the postcard was ever posted until recently. It was in surprisingly good condition considering its age. That suggests that it was put away somewhere, probably in a box in the dark. The fading is consistent with that theory.'

'Is there anything else you can tell me?' asked Frank. 'Even if it's just a guess.'

'There's nothing more I'd like to do than help you, Sergeant Summers, but I'm afraid everything I can tell you is in the report.'

'The writing. Was it done by a right or left-handed person?'

'Unofficially I'd say right-handed, but I couldn't swear to it.'

'Mmm,' said Frank thoughtfully. He was thinking how attractive Tracey's voice was, and wondered what other questions he could ask to keep her talking. That apart, there was a one in a million chance she might say something that could trigger his mind into understanding why he now thought the postcard of such importance.

'Er, was there anything else, Sergeant?' Tracey asked after a few seconds of silence. Frank sighed.

'No, no, I suppose not. Thanks for your help anyway, Tracey. I owe you a drink.'

'It's a pleasure, Sergeant. Any time I can help, just give a call. Or drop in if you wish.'

'Very kind of you. Oh, and call me Frank. Being called Sergeant all the time goes to my head, and we wouldn't want that, now would we?'

'I can't see that happening, Frank,' she said, chuckling.

As she put the phone down Tracey turned to a colleague.

'That Sergeant Summers has a very sexy voice,' she said. 'I'm not surprised Dr Pleadle fancies him. Wouldn't mind meeting him myself.'

'Word is he's gay, according to the doctor,' replied the colleague. 'Pity.'

'Damn,' said Tracey.

'Lovely voice,' said Frank to Gertie. 'Pity she's gay. Oh, well.'

He didn't notice Gertie's guilty look.

'Right,' he said, rubbing his hands. 'Let's get down to paperwork. Even if we don't find anything new, at least we'll have it ready to be filed away.'

After two hours they had found nothing new, but the paperwork was indeed ready for the archives.

* * *

'A chair at this end for whoever arrives first,' Frank said in the interview room after lunch, 'and a chair at the other end for whoever arrives last. Mrs Simmons in both cases. Marks one and two.'

'How are you planning to handle it?' asked Gertie, ripping cellophane off new recording cassettes.

'It's called the Summers' special interview technique. Go in with both boots, making sure your feet land in the right place to run like hell if it all turns pear-shaped. If you look around and I'm gone, then the wotsits has hit the fan and it's time to get out before the wotsits hits you.'

Gertie giggled.

'You wouldn't leave me in it, would you, Sarge?'

'Only if absolutely necessary. Like, for example, FF being after my blood.'

'That would be quite often, then.'

Frank paused.

'Funny that, she hasn't given me a good bollocking for a while. Why do you suppose that is?'

'Maybe she's got a soft spot for you,' Gertie replied off-handedly. Too off-handedly.

'Nah, FF hasn't a soft spot in the world.'

Gertie looked at him.

'You know, sometimes you can't see what's under your nose.'

'I'm sure you're right, Gertie my dear. I know I'm missing something obvious about the case, but what it is eludes me.'

'I wasn't speaking about the case,' Gertie said, ramming a cassette home forcefully.

'Oh?' He looked at her, puzzled. 'What, then?'

'Oh, bloody nothing! I'll see if your two dear old biddies have turned up.' She slammed her way out of the room. Frank watched her exit in bewilderment.

Let me see, he thought. Susan's mad at me. Again. Now Gertie's mad at me. Again. I'm just about to make two old ladies extremely unpleased. That leaves, from the front rank, only FF, and it shouldn't take much to get her going. After that I should probably have time left to sort out the remaining women officers, throwing in Tracey at the lab and Agnetha in the kitchen as a grand finale, somehow.

After all, everyone has to be good at something.

Mentally he cancelled Agnetha off the list. Some things you could take too far.

Gwen Simmons turned up five minutes early, and was installed at the far end of the table with customary cup of tea. Elizabeth Green arrived five minutes late. Frank preceded her by several seconds so that he could watch their faces when they first saw each other.

There was no reaction as Mrs Green sat down at the near end of the table, opposite Mrs Simmons, bar puzzled surprise.

'You'll have to bear with me for a short while,' Frank said. 'I'm going to show each of you a photograph. I want you to tell me if you know the person in it.'

He nodded at Gertie. She slid a photograph toward Mrs

Green, while Frank slid one toward Mrs Simmons.

'Of course I recognise him,' said Mrs Simmons.

'I've already told you who he is,' said Mrs Green.

'That's my Alfie,' said Mrs Simmons.

'That's my Alf,' said Mrs Green.

They looked at each other in surprise.

'Would you mind holding up your individual photographs so that the other can see them?' asked Frank.

It took them a few seconds to get it right, before they faced each other, each with a photograph of Alfie Simmons, otherwise known as Alf Simmons.

'Therein lies our problem,' Frank noted softly.

'I don't understand,' said Gwen Simmons.

'Mrs Simmons, you married Alfie Simmons in 1948. Unfortunately I have to tell you that Alfie Simmons married Mrs Green here, nee Simmons, in 1960. You have just, conclusively, I would say, identified the same man. I'm afraid, unless there were two identical twins, with identical scars, this has to be the case. And so far we haven't come across such twins.'

There was a long period of silence.

'He married me first. I'm still his legal wife,' Gwen Simmons noted.

'He's still alive,' Elizabeth Green declared. 'If we can find him he can choose.'

Frank had never attended the unmasking of a bigamist before, so, for all he knew, this was a perfectly normal reaction.

'Mrs Green, Alfie Simmons – or Alf Simmons, if you will – is dead,' Frank said calmly but forcefully. 'He died in 1964. I don't know where that postcard came from, but, take it from me, Alfie Simmons is dead. And he was murdered. He died from a gunshot to the head. The back of his head. It was, and is, a case of murder.'

Both women, he noticed had taken handkerchiefs from their handbags and were dabbing at their eyes.

'Poor Alfie,' whispered Gwen Simmons.

'Poor, poor Alf,' muttered Elizabeth Green.

Frank looked from one to the other in amazement. He had just revealed that Alfie Simmons had been a bigamist, and now they were saying 'Poor Alfie'?

'Now I intend to find out who murdered him,' he carried on, pushing the pace. 'And in my experience adultery is often a motive for murder. Bigamy would also fall under that heading,' he said.

'Bigamy?' asked Elizabeth Green in astonishment, as if she had only realised the significance of what she had been told.

'If you're suggesting what I think you're suggesting,' Gwen Simmons said, 'then you had better watch your step very, very carefully.'

Both boots in, thought Frank. He waited for a few seconds before continuing.

'You're a strong-willed woman, Mrs Simmons. How would you react if you found out Alfie was having an affair? Or how did you react when you found out Alfie was betraying you?'

She looked him directly in the eye to prove how strong-willed she was.

'So, he had affairs. So what? Men do, all the time, all of them.

But he only had one home, and he never brought any of it back with him. He was a loyal, dedicated father and husband.'

'So you knew he had affairs?'

'I presumed so. He was a man.'

Well, there's the entire male race disposed of in one sentence, thought Frank.

He turned to Elizabeth Green.

'And what about you, Mrs Green. Did you discover that postcard before he had a chance to send it? Did you realise he was about to leave you? Did you decide you'd rather have a dead Alf than let him desert you?'

'No! No! No!' she cried. 'I never saw that postcard until the day it arrived. I loved Alf,' she sobbed. 'I loved him, I loved him, I loved him. My poor, poor Alf,' she whispered.

Then a strange thing happened. Gwen Simmons stood up, walked around to Elizabeth Green, and put an arm around her shoulders.

'There, there, love,' she said. 'He's only trying to upset you. It's his job. Don't let him get at you.'

Frank and Gertie exchanged looks of amazement. Gwen Simmons noticed.

'You thought we'd be at each other's throats, didn't you?' she asked. 'I can't say that it hasn't been a shock. Alfie marrying someone else while he was married to me. But, once you think about it, that was Alfie. It was the kind of man he was. He probably loved both of us, and thought that was the best thing to do. Don't you reckon, love?'

This last to a weeping Elizabeth Green, who nodded her head.

'He was such a kind and gentle man,' she whispered.

Frank scratched his cheek. He had known he would only have one shot, and it had either missed its target, or the target had been too strong.

There was always the possibility that the two women were in collusion, and had prepared for this moment, knowing that it would come sooner or later.

'I suppose all this will come out in the newspapers,' he heard Gwen Simmons say.

He nodded.

'Newspapers. Television. Yes, I'm afraid they're going to have a field day.'

'You can't keep our names out of it?'

'It's a murder investigation, I'm afraid. Someone did kill Alfred Simmons. It was a long time ago, but it's still murder. There isn't a statute of limitation.'

'Remember what I said to you?' asked Gwen Simmons. 'In this very room, not so long ago? You want to find out who killed Alfie. So do I. And so does Liz here, I reckon.'

Elizabeth Green nodded weakly.

'I can understand why you think we're suspects, Sergeant,' Gwen Simmons continued, 'but I can tell you I had nothing to do with it, and so can Liz here, if I'm any judge of character. Which leaves the question of who actually murdered our Alfie.'

Frank returned her open look. He neither believed her nor disbelieved her. He knew how some people could lie as a way of life.

'You got anything more?' asked Gwen Simmons aggressively.

'Sorry?'

'I asked if you've got anything more. Or can we leave? After all, we've got a lot to discuss.'

Frank sighed and rubbed his eyes.

'No, Mrs Simmons, I have nothing more. You can go.'

'Don't take it too much to heart, lad,' he heard her say sympathetically. 'You've got a job to do. I'd imagine you're more used to hearing lies than the truth. Come on, Mrs Green, let's go indulge in a medical gin. I think we need it. And we have a lot of catching up to do.'

'Before you go,' Frank called as they headed for the door, Gwen Simmons supporting a weak Elizabeth Green. Gertie jumped up to escort them out.

'Aye?'

'We'll be letting the media know on Thursday,' he said, looking at the desk. 'Some of it might leak out before. You might want to think of taking a holiday somewhere anonymously for a few weeks. It would be good if you could let us know where, in case we need to contact you.'

She nodded.

'I know. Vultures. Had them round the shop a few times. Fifteen year-old gets pregnant – someone with important parents, of course – and they want to know what bra-size she was, what she had bought, what she had been wearing, sickening, it was.' A sudden grin lit her face. 'Know what? I've just thought. Normally it's the kids that give their parents grey hairs. Might be the other way round this time.'

Frank sat thinking for a while, as Gertie showed the two old ladies to the front door. He felt sorry for Elizabeth Green. At the same time he knew it could all have been an impressive act. But, if it wasn't, she would have to go home to Albert and reveal that she hadn't been married to Alfie aka Alf after all. The news itself was sufficient of a shock. Having to listen to Albert pontificating on how he had known, all along, that Alf aka Alfie was a bad 'un – that would surely be a reasonable motive for murder in anyone's books.

And it would be bad for his dicky heart.

'Well,' said Gertie, returning and closing the door behind her. She sat opposite Frank and looked at him.

'Well, indeed,' he echoed, still staring at the top of the desk.

'Kind of puts it into perspective, doesn't it?' asked Gertie.

'Does it? In what way?'

'Well, we fight over a man. He has to be ours, only ours. We'll scratch eyes out to keep him. Then you have these two old dears who shared Alfie without knowing it. Now that they've lost him, it unites them somehow. Maybe we women should learn how to share instead of fight each other. Better to love a bloke together. You don't know when he'll be gone.'

'Thank you for that insight, Gertie,' he said a touch acerbically. 'Let me know the next time the Martians are paying a visit. Or pigs learn to fly.'

'I'm serious, Sarge.'

'Well, hello, Serious.'

'You can be a right shit sometimes, you know.'

'Only sometimes? I must be losing my grip.' He looked at her. 'Any chance of your explaining what I've done to upset you?'

She blushed and looked down.

'No, I thought not,' he said.' Just call me Mushroom. Kept in the dark and fed wotsits. Which is what I wonder if was the case just now.'

'Just when, Sarge?'

'Just when two old biddies claimed to have absolutely no knowledge that they were sharing a husband.'

He stood and stretched.

'Did we learn anything, Gertie?' he asked.

'I believed them, Sarge,' she replied, looking at the floor. 'I thought Mrs Simmons was incredible. What a woman should be. Strong as – I dunno, an oak, I suppose. I've been thinking that, too often, we women try to be like men, which we aren't. Frieda – she's a strong woman, she's proved that.'

Gertie looked up at him under the fringe of her hair.

'I think she fancies you, you know,' she said softly.

'Jesus, Gertie, will you give your imagination a break?' he said, exhaling deeply. 'Whether or not Mrs Simmons fancies me – which is a ridiculous notion to start off with – it is hardly relevant to the case, is it?'

Gertie's jaw dropped, bounced along the floor a few times, and remained there until she stood up.

'I don't believe you,' she said angrily. 'I really do not believe you are for real. I'll bet a woman could dance naked in front of you and you wouldn't even notice.' She left the room, slamming the door.

Believe me, he said in silence, if Mrs Gwen Simmons danced naked in front of me I would notice.

What the hell was Gertie on about?

* * *

'So, we're no further on, then,' Frieda said that evening.

Frank, standing by the window, shook his head. Gertie stood by the door, tight-lipped.

'What was your impression, Gertie?' asked Frieda. Gertie started.

'Of what, ma'am?'

'Of our Mrs Simmons and Green, nee Simmons.'

Gertie shrugged.

'I quite liked Mrs Simmons,' she said. 'I don't think she would have shot Alfie. Beaten the merry hell out of him, yes, but not murdered him. And Mrs Green wouldn't have the bottle.'

'I see.' Frieda pondered this in silence.

'Okay, Gertie, get off with you,' she said finally.

'Ma'am?'

'Go home, the day is over. I want a quiet word with Sergeant Summers here.'

'Ma'am,' Gertie nodded, looking suspiciously at Frank's back. She closed the door behind her quietly.

'What's going on, Frank?' Frieda asked gently.

His eyebrows raised in puzzlement.

'I've told you. Maybe they were telling the truth, maybe it was a brilliant act. Either way there's no evidence. Nothing usable.'

'I wasn't talking about that, Frank. I meant, what's going on between you and Gertie?'

'Me and Gertie? How do you mean?'

'It's obvious she's not very happy. Somewhat like last Friday, if I recall correctly.'

Frank shrugged.

297

'I've done something to upset her, I know. Again. God knows what. She won't say. And if she won't say, how am I supposed to guess?'

She was about to say something when he continued.

'I seem to be good at that. Doctor Pleadle won't speak to me. Gertie, close to the same. I've just made two old women very, very unhappy with me. I was wondering whether I could go the whole hog. Get you upset, scandalise Agnetha, and then move on to Tracey.'

'Tracey?'

'Some girl in the path lab. She's gay, apparently, but I'm not prejudiced. I've never met her, only spoken to her on the telephone. It would be more efficient to upset people via telephone. I could start with the A's in the telephone book and go through until the Z's.'

'You sound like you're feeling sorry for yourself, Frank.' She stood up. 'Come on, I'll buy you a drink.'

'No, thanks. Was there anything else?'

'No, Frank, there wasn't. Just a little drink?'

He shook his head and left.

'Good thing Agnetha has left for the day,' Frieda said to herself. 'Maybe I should warn Tracey, whoever she is.'

Tracey, she thought as she wound her silk scarf around her neck. Young, obviously, with a name like Tracey. Undoubtedly not gay, as Frank might think. Slim, of course. With big boobs, naturally. Nineteen, maybe twenty. Good looking, no doubt, if you fancied that sort of young girl, which men, for some reason, did.

Including one bastard of an ex-husband.

She stopped, and flipped open a file on her desk. The photo-copied photograph of Alfie Simmons looked innocently back at her.

'It's all your fault, you son of a bitch,' she thought to herself. 'You handsome, charming, attractive son of a bitch.'

Frank would have to go, she decided..

He was a lovely man. He had a smile which could make a woman's heart stop momentarily. He had a wonderful sense of humour. At times he was like a little boy you just wanted to hug – or smack. He had absolutely no ambition other than to enjoy himself, possibly the most charming thing about him.

And his taste in ties was so bad it had gone around the corner and was coming back as good.

He also had the makings of a good detective. Once he got over his lack of confidence, stopped spending his energy on avoiding work, and used his brains as he should do rather than dreaming up ways of creating mischief, he would be a really good detective indeed.

But, there was no option, unfortunately. He would have to go, definitely. Plenty of stations around the country were pleading for extra staff. She had vowed to run the most efficient police station in the British Isles if not the Western world, even if other people had to die in doing so.

She couldn't have him upsetting Gertie, Doctor Death, and god-knows who else.

Including his own Inspector.

Including making his own Inspector think swearwords, even if she didn't say them out loud. Not often, anyway. Hardly ever.

Why was it, she asked herself, that she thought of herself as his Inspector, when, in reality, he was her Sergeant?

She closed the file on Alfie Simmons.

Tomorrow she would begin to close the file on Sergeant Frank bloody Summers. Get him posted. He could wreak his own personal brand of havoc on some other police station. All she needed was one more excuse. And he was bound to give her one sooner or later.

* * *

Frank sat sucking on a glass of wine in his flat, flicking between television channels. He knew his exit from Frieda's office had been less than diplomatic. Downright rude, if the honest truth were to be acknowledged. He tried to analyse the reasons, but it didn't take long. He had reached, as the saying goes, the level of his own incompetence. As a beat bobby he had managed people with charm and a joke. As a detective constable he had managed to hide his inadequacies. But, as a Detective Sergeant, these were all too clear. He couldn't solve an investigation, he couldn't even handle his own staff.

One. One member of staff. Gertie, who was reasonableness personified. Gertie, a girl he really liked as a person. A person ever eager to do the slightest thing for him. If he couldn't handle her, what would happen if he had two hundred to look after?

The first revolution since Cromwell's days, no doubt. With his own head on the chopping block.

The phone began to ring.

Piss off, he thought, I don't want any double-glazing.

Nor holiday-share apartments, he thought on the second ring.

Must be Jehovah's Witnesses. No more door-stepping. Call a

convert, these days.

Jehovah's Witnesses, he thought with a smile. Double-glazing salesmen. Any other salesmen. Who cared? It was a chance to vent his feelings on someone who deserved to be vented upon.

He stood up and picked up the phone.

'Yes?' he demanded, almost shouting.

There was a temporary silence.

'Frank?' asked a nervous voice.

'Which Frank are you looking for?' he asked roughly.

'Frank? Um, it's Susan here.'

He sat down clumsily.

'Yes?' he asked throatily.

'Are you okay, Frank?' A pleading voice.

'How do you expect me to be?'

'You're angry, aren't you? Look, Frank, I'm sorry. I really am. I shouldn't have lost my temper with you.'

'Why not? Everyone else does. Join the queue.'

'Please, Frank. I want to make it up to you. Look, what if I cook dinner for you tomorrow, my place, just the two of us?'

Frank considered this.

'What's on the menu?' he asked.

'Roast beef. Yorkshire pud. Roast spuds. A bit of broccoli with cheese sauce, and sweet carrots. Maybe something special for dessert. A surprise, perhaps.'

Stuff dessert, his stomach said. Roast beef and Yorkshire pud? With roast potatoes? Dessert could go jump in the lake.

'And gravy?' he asked, hopefully.

'Home-made. As much as you want.'

His stomach tried to elbow his brain from the telephone.

'What time?' either his brain or his stomach asked.

'You tell me.'

'Seven o' clock?'

'So You'll come?'

'Make it six-thirty. I'll be there at six-thirty on the dot. It's ages since I had a decent roast beef and Yorkshire pud.'

'Thanks, Frank. I love you.'

The line went dead.

It took a few seconds for him to cotton on why he hadn't recognised her voice straight away.

She had been drunk as a lark. Or judge. Or something.

Still, it meant that that particular cold war was temporarily over. If this was a portent, all things were possible. Maybe he could even, tomorrow, find out what it was that had so upset Gertie. Apologise to Frieda.

Well, one out of three was sufficient, he thought. Especially to a man who normally managed zero out of three.

That night he went to bed a happy man. He tried to dream of Susan. Unfortunately her face was displaced with another. A ghastly, laughing, psychotic Alfie Simmons.

Turn as he could, count sheep, think of good things, not bad, Alfie's face returned to haunt him, time and time again.

He finally gave up the attempt to sleep at four-thirty in the morning and got out of bed.

Alfie, if someone else hadn't got there first, I'd have shot you myself, he thought to himself.

He looked at the bleary-eyed person in the mirror as he shaved.

Might as well go in, he thought. The Dead Skeleton case was as dead as its object. Just get the day over. Tonight, you, my son, are having dinner with the delectable Doctor Susan Pleadle. And no-one, from Gertie to Agnetha to the omnipotent Inspector Garold, is going to stop me.

Omnipotent and sexy, he added as an afterthought.

And especially not Alfie-bloody-two-timing little sod Simmons, he added as a second afterthought.

The Caesars, if he recalled correctly, had employed a slave to stand behind them during their parades of triumph, whispering in their ears, "this too will pass". Frank would never have contemplated the idea of having a slave. He found it difficult enough trying to decide whether he should employ a cleaning lady.

But he did have his self-preservation voices.

Right at that moment one of them was looking at him, shaking its head sadly, and saying nothing.

After a while it packed its bags and walked away, shoulders hunched, dragging its feet..

Wednesday: Coming a cropper

Blimey, Frank, are you early, or has that clock stopped?' asked desk Sergeant Keith Bute as Frank walked into reception at five-thirty.

'I'm a little early, Keith. Couldn't sleep. Thought I might as well make an early start.'

'Early? It's damn near the middle of the night.'

'Have you got the keys to the archives? I want to go through some old case.'

'How old?' asked Keith, unhooking and handing over an ancient key.

'1964.'

'1964? The Dead Skeleton case? Rather you than me, Frank. But I tell you, if you can crack that one I reckon you'll be Chief Inspector within a year or two.'

'No thanks, Keith. Too much like hard work, all those meetings and socialising. Imagine, you'd even have to be polite to local councillors.'

'Point,' said Keith. 'I'll send young Wilkins down with a cup of tea when he gets back from his fag break. Good luck with your search.'

'Cheers, Keith.'

Frank walked down the corridor to the door concealing the steps down to the archives, switching lights on as he went. The further down, the thicker the air became, a musty smell of old paper, cardboard and dust. In the deep basement were long rows of green-painted steel shelving reaching to the high ceiling, stacked with boxes, files and heaps of paper threatening to cascade down, along with bags of various materials holding evidence from old to ancient cases. The 1960s began a third of the way down, towards the end of the rows.

Frank contemplated the task. 1964 spanned three crammed columns, from floor to ceiling. There was a wooden set of precarious stairs for access to the upper shelves. The probability that he would find anything was minimal. But if there was anything to find it would, by some law of nature, be wherever he chose to look last. So he might as well start at the bottom. If he were lucky he would get interrupted before the time came to start pushing rickety stairs around, trying not to fall from a height with the accumulated dust of years.

He picked up an armful of files and walked over to a table provided for such searches. He sat down on an iron chair and began to flip through their contents slowly, trying to get a feeling of how the paperwork was done so that he could move through later files with speed.

Missing people, lost pets, burglaries and neighbours' disputes.

Miss Agnes Hunley, spinster of 52 Hill Terrace, reported that her new neighbour, one Gerlad (should that have been Gerald?) Porter exposed himself to her on a daily basis, at his bedroom window. The constable dispatched to investigate had reported that, merely in order to see said window the spinster had to stand on a chair, open her own window, lean quite far out, and then strain her head several degrees. Even in this position the most that could be seen of Mr Porter's window rendered it unlikely that the reported exposure could have been more than that of Mr Porter's upper torso. Miss Hunley was advised to cease the practice of endangering herself by leaning out of her window.

Miss Hunley, eh? thought Frank. I think I might have met

one of your descendants recently.

Was Mr Porter ever informed of the incident, Frank wondered. Did Miss Hunley spread gossip about the man's "exposures", and then complain that the police refused to do anything about it?

Several university students cautioned after alcoholic exuberance had resulted in them painting the front of the library in psychedelic colours. The Technicolor Sixties had finally arrived in Wellbury.

Probably eminent bankers, politicians and lawyers by now, he guessed, maybe just on retirement age. A journalist with nothing better to do could make a story of that. A few careful questions, such as "Councillor Higgins, do you decry the lawless behaviour of students these days?", followed, if the honourable councillor swallowed the bait and responded with a rant, with the inevitable "Okay, mate, what do you have to say to your own lawless days then? Done any painting lately? I'll take that as a yes shall I? Mind posing for a photograph?"

Frank finished the first pile without discovering anything promising. He put that pile on the floor and fetched another armful.

Twelve-year old Teddy Foote caught red-handed breaking into a private home. Confesses to four other break-ins. Or maybe someone was tidying up the statistics.

Twelve-year old? Didn't they have more respect in those days?

Minor burglaries. Drunks causing weekend disturbances.

A Miss Hunley of 52 Hill Terrace reports that students recently moved into the street are having private orgies. No indication of what further action was taken, or what action would have been taken had the alleged orgies been public. Possibly Miss Hunley already had a reputation.

Reginald Smith charged with the offence of bigamy. Now that could have attracted Alfie Simmons' attention. Was that why he had written the postcard? Just before planning to disappear?

Had he written the postcard?

That pile of files went on the floor next to the first, and he retrieved another load. Another blank. Another pile on the floor, and another pile in front of him.

This time Miss Hunley had discovered that a young couple, newly moved in two doors down, were not actually married. The police, if the file was anything to go by, did not actually do anything about that.

Frank carried on reading.

'Blimey, Sarge, have you been coal-mining?' asked Gertie's voice. He looked up. She stood there with two cups of coffee, and a surprised look on her face.

'You're in early, Gertie,' he said, looking at his watch. 'Or maybe not.'

It was eight-thirty. Without natural light he had not noticed the time go by.

'Your suit's going to need a visit to the dry-cleaners,' she observed, putting a mug down in front of him.

He looked down at his clothes. His smart suit, tie and shirt were covered in dust streaks, plus a small splattering of grease which must have come from some part of the shelving.

'Nuisance,' he said mildly, taking a welcome sip of coffee. 'And I'm supposed to be seeing Frieda soon. She hasn't called yet, has she?'

'Not as far as I know.' She looked at the piles of files and folders. 'Anything specific you're looking for, Sarge?'

'Not specific, no. Just a long shot, the possibility that something happened in 1964 that caused our Alfie's murder. Or maybe complaints about domestic arguments between him and his wife – or wives. According to them all was peace and light and matrimonial harmony. Any indication that they are lying would be rather interesting.'

'Not asking for much, are you Sarge?'

'Only the moon. You can take a pile. Between us we might finish the lot sometime before next Christmas. Oh, and keep your eye out for anything from Hill Terrace. According to a Miss Hunley living there she was surrounded by men exposing themselves, students having orgies, and a young couple living in sin.'

'And that helps us how, Sarge?'

'It doesn't. Not at all. But it relieves the boredom somewhat.'

She sat down next to him, and they continued the attack on the files in silence. With two of them the remaining papers slowly but steadily diminished.

'Hullo, this time it's gypsies,' he noted at one point.

'Gypsies?'

'Our Miss Hunley. She was almost attacked and abducted by a group of gypsies to be sold into the slave trade.'

'Almost attacked?' Gertie echoed. 'Interesting concept.'

'The investigating officer notes that Miss Hunley is seventy-three years old. He doesn't seem to have drawn any conclusions from that. Or, rather, he doesn't seem to have felt the need to note them down.'

Gertie didn't reply, and Frank moved on to the next folder.

'Sarge,' she said after a few minutes, 'this might be interesting.' She handed over a large file. He flipped through the contents.

'You're right, it is, very interesting. Wellbury Revolver and Rifle Club broken into. What date is this?'

'May, 1964,' Gertie said.

Frank scanned the list of items stolen. Amongst them were three Webley revolvers. One owned by an Albert Green of seventy-three Wood Lane, Old Merrick.

'Now there is a coincidence,' he murmured.

'You think it's the same Albert Green?'

'Green lived in Old Merrick in those days, a couple of streets away from Elizabeth Simmons, nee Edwards. I think we might pop around and ask him a few questions.'

'But if the revolver was stolen before Alfie was killed – and we're pretty sure that was in June – surely, even if it was the revolver used, then Albert Green is in the clear?'

'If – and that's the operative word here, "if" – the revolver really was stolen. He wouldn't be the first to make a false claim to have an alibi against later measures. Come on, we can return to this lot later, if this turns out to be a false alarm.'

* * *

'Frank, have you looked in a mirror recently?' asked Frieda in amazement. She had encountered them on their way back to his office. 'You look like – like some strange soldier wearing night-camouflage. In a suit.'

'Dedication to work,' he grinned. He held up the folder.

'According to this, one Albert Green used to own a Webley Pocket Revolver which, strangely enough, was stolen from the Wellbury Revolver and Rifle Club in May of 1964. We're on our way to find out whether it's the same Albert Green who married Elizabeth Simmons. And, if we're really lucky, whether or not it was really stolen.'

'You think you can convince him to admitting he lied – if it is him, and he did?'

'It's called the subtle art of putting pressure on people. After all these years he won't have a pretty little story ready. It shouldn't be too difficult to work out whether he's telling the truth or not.'

'Be careful, Frank. I don't want any accusations of the police threatening little old folk.'

'Me? Threaten?' he asked disarmingly.

'The way you look at the moment any honest householder would lock the doors, bar the windows and call for the police if they saw you coming towards the front door.'

'Just a bit of dust,' he assured her. 'Come on, Gertie, let's hustle.'

'Your tie needs dry-cleaning,' she called after him.

Frieda watched them go with a strange look in her eyes. One of sorrow mixed with frustration tinged with exasperation. A complaint about heavy-handedness from the Greens would provide her with the excuse she needed, even though she knew Frank was anything but heavy-handed.

Normally she would have protected her officers like a lioness defending her cubs. But this was different.

This time she was protecting herself.

* * *

Elizabeth Green did not look too happy to see them, but invited them in anyway.

'I've told Albert the news,' she whispered in the passage. 'He hasn't taken it too well. His heart, you know.'

Albert Green looked even less happy than his wife. Sitting in his armchair, blanket across his knees, his face turned an angry red at the sight of them.

'What do you lot want now?' he demanded. 'Ruining innocent people's lives not enough for you? Come to hound us until we say whatever you want? Like bloody Chinese water torture, whenever we turn around you're there. You'll never bloody-well give up, will you?'

'Now, now, Albert,' Elizabeth said soothingly, tucking the blanket in around him, 'they have their job to do. I'll go make some tea. Please take a seat, Sergeant, Constable.'

Frank sat opposite Albert. Gertie stayed standing, taking out a notebook and pen. Albert eyed her suspiciously.

'Mr Green, did you ever belong to the Wellbury Revolver and Rifle Club?' asked Frank. Albert looked astonished.

'The Rifle Club closed years ago,' he said.

'Yes, but you were a member in 1964?'

'I joined in, when was it? 1963. Not that I went often. Wrong class. Not wealthy enough to rub shoulders with the other members.'

Elizabeth Green fluttered in with a tray holding teapot and teacups.

'Milk, one sugar, isn't it, Sergeant?' she asked.

'Er, yes, please. Now, Mr Green, you owned a Webley Pocket

Revolver, did you not?'

'Yes, and much amusement it caused the others. Kept making jokes about it.'

'Where did you get it?'

'An uncle gave it to me. I would never have bothered otherwise. In fact that was the only reason I joined the club, to please him.'

'And the revolver was stolen from the club?'

There was a sudden hooded look in his eyes.

'Aye, that's what happened,' he said cautiously.

'But, Albert, you said – ' began Elizabeth, and then stopped suddenly, looking embarrassed.

Albert glared at her briefly, and then turned back to Frank.

'Okay, the truth is I was never sure what had happened to it. I thought I had left it at my parents' house. Come the robbery I couldn't find it, so I presumed that somehow it must still have been at the club and got stolen. In a way I was glad to see the back of it. I never really enjoyed the whole business. Seemed a waste of time, shooting at paper targets. Only did it not to upset my uncle.'

'This was May of 1964?'

'Must have been about then, I suppose. Sometime around then.'

'When did you first realise it had gone missing?'

'I don't know. Probably when the club got broken into. They didn't keep records of which members had left their guns there. Part of the Hooray-Henry culture, thought being offhand about such things said something about them – which it did, though I doubt they realised it. Bunch of –

Anyway, they asked all members what they had left at the club, I couldn't find the revolver, so, as I say, I presumed it must have been there. What's all this in aid of, anyway?'

Frank paused before delivering the coup-de-grace.

'The bullet that killed Alfie Simmons came from a Webley Pocket Revolver.'

This was greeted with silence. As the meaning sank in Elizabeth covered her mouth with a hand, her eyes open wide. Albert's face turned slowly puce.

'What the hell are you trying to suggest?' he roared finally. 'You tell my wife that Alf Simmons was a bigamist, we're going to have to leave here to avoid being hounded by the press, and now you're suggesting that I killed him? This is bloody harassment, that's what it bloody well is. Bloody harassment.! I won't – '

'Calm down, Albert, calm down,' Elizabeth Green said, hurriedly getting a bottle of pills from the sideboard. 'Here, dear, take one of your tablets. Take a few of them.'

'I'm not suggesting anything, Mr Green,' Frank replied, unruffled. 'It's merely a coincidence we need to follow up on.'

Albert was too busy swallowing the tablet Elizabeth had forced into his mouth to reply.

'Did you know anyone else who had a similar revolver, Mr Green?' asked Gertie.

'No I bloody well did not. Only reason I knew what that one was was because my uncle told me. I really wasn't interested in the things.'

'Do you remember whether they caught the people who committed the break in?' asked Frank.

'I would have thought you'd be more likely to know that. Don't you have any records at your police station?'

Indeed Frank did. In fact the thick folder in the car showed that the thieves had never been caught. But he was interested in seeing what Albert would say.

'I have someone researching that right now,' he said. 'But I wondered if the revolver was ever returned to you.'

'No. I never saw it again. Good riddance, I thought at the time.'

'You didn't make a claim on the loss?'

'Waste of time. There were notices all over the club saying that people left their stuff there at their own risk. I didn't have any insurance, it wasn't like nowadays, most people I knew never had anything worth insuring.'

'But, surely a revolver must have been worth something?'

Albert glared at him before replying.

'Sergeant, let me make this quite clear, since you don't seem to be able to get it into your thick head. I didn't want the thing in the first place, everybody at the club thought it was a joke, I was spending most of my time in London working my guts out, and I could not give a tinker's cuss about the poxy thing. Understand? Even if you don't maybe your little girl here could explain it to you. Now it's time you left. Understand that?'

Frank nodded and stood up. Elizabeth escorted the two of them to the front door.

'And I'll be making a complaint about this, you see if I don't,' Albert Green's voice followed them on their way to the front door.

'You must forgive him,' Elizabeth Green whispered, 'he's taken everything really badly. And now, with everything coming out in the papers, well, we're going to move somewhere for a few weeks. But it's such a rush, such a rush. Fortunately Gwen has been a real help. She's such a strong woman. I don't know how she does it.'

* * *

'Gwen has been a real help?' echoed Gertie as they drove back to the station. 'They seem to have become pals very quickly.'

'They did, as you could say, have shared interests.'

'Not the sort women normally share,'

'Quite.'

'Did you buy his story, Sarge?'

Frank pondered this for a few moments.

'I don't know, to be honest. I wasn't sure whether he was genuinely and innocently angry, or whether it was bluster.'

'So, where to now?'

He checked his watch.

'Time for an early lunch. Then we'll carry on in the archives.'

'Ooh, Sarge, carry on in the archives? That sounds like it could be interesting. I could get to enjoy that.'

'Gertie my dear, I think you may have been watching too many reruns of certain films on television.'

* * *

'Here we go,' said Gertie, lifting up a slim folder. 'August 1964: Miss Hunley has spotted Soviet agents who have moved into Hill Terrace. She claims they're planning to kidnap her and brainwash her.'

'Soviet agents? She's moved a bit upmarket, hasn't she? Mixing with the Profumo lot was she?'

'Profumo lot, Sarge?'

'A sex and spy scandal in, let me see, 1963, I think it was.'

Gertie wrinkled her nose at the thought.

'Trouble is, Sarge,' she pointed out, 'if we're into August, haven't we gone past the period we're interested in? June, 1964?'

'Possibly. That presumes that this lot is in chronological order, and I wouldn't put any money on that notion.' He looked at his watch. 'We've got a couple of hours. Let's quickly skim through the rest and pack it all away. I doubt whether we're going to find anything of interest.'

He was wrong.

In November Miss Hunley discovered a coven of witches who were trying to turn her into a nymphomaniac.

But, of potential murderers of Alfie Simmons, there was no trace.

* * *

They returned to Frank's office, on the way exciting curious glances from other officers at their rumpled and dirt-stained appearance. Eric Johns' eyes opened wide at the sight.

'What on earth have you two been up to?' he asked.

'Don't even go there, Eric,' warned Frank. 'I might be tempted to dump 1963 in your lap. It's even older and dirtier than 1964.'

He sent Gertie off to organise some coffee while he slumped into his chair and stared at the ceiling. He was sure that Albert Green's revolver was the key to the case. He wondered whether he could get a search warrant for the Green's house. Even if he could – and that was pretty unlikely – what were the chances that Albert Green would have kept the weapon? About nil. Bunged it into a skip, threw it onto a rubbish dump somewhere.

It hadn't been buried with the body. Not surprising, had the body been discovered at the time it would have been a dead giveaway. Not even the coppers of 1964 would have swallowed Green's story of it having been stolen. So, what would he do with it? Chuck it in a rubbish bin along the way?

He stood up and pulled out the old survey map, laying it on his desk and scanning it for rubbish dumps. Gertie walked in with a tray containing two cups of coffee and a bowl of warm soapy water.

'Looking for something, Sarge?' she asked.

'Rubbish tips. If Albert killed Alfie, he would have dumped the gun somewhere. Somewhere where people don't go poking their noses around. Something like a normal domestic rubbish bin collected on a weekly basis.'

'Um, Sarge, I hate to mention this, but ... Do you really think there's much likelihood of finding a gun that was hidden in a rubbish pit forty years ago? Even if it really was dumped in one? There are so many other places it could have been hidden. Needles and haystacks come to mind.'

Frank sighed and stretched his back.

'No, I don't. I think I'm just trying to kick things around until a reasonable idea pops into my head. It happened once before. Well, almost.'

'So you think Albert Green is our man?'

'That's the strange thing. I don't. I don't know why, but I

can't help but feel that he isn't. Call it a hunch.'

'All good coppers have hunches.'

'The trouble with mine is that they're usually wrong. Which is fortunate, in a way. Hunches make you want to fit the evidence of your eyes to the theory of your thoughts. Not trusting hunches means that you learn to rely on evidence rather than your own feelings.' He noticed the bowl of water. 'What's that for?'

Gertie took a cloth and dipped it in the warm water.

'Your suit needs a little cleaning, Sarge. You can't go around looking like that.'

'Hang on, Gertie,' he protested as she began dabbing at his jacket. 'I can live with a few dust marks for a couple of hours.'

'Oh, dear,' she said, 'that doesn't appear to have worked.' She looked at her work. What had been dust had now taken the consistency of a streak of mud. 'Let's try a different spot.'

'Gertie ...' he tried protesting again. He looked up. Frieda was in the doorway, eyebrows raised, looking at Gertie bending over him in a pose that could be misconstrued.

'Inspector!' Frank said warmly. Gertie looked around and shot up. The bowl of water went flying.

Frank looked at it.

'You wouldn't mind mopping that up, would you, Gertie?' he asked pleasantly.

'Um, yes, Sarge, course, Sarge,' she said, retrieving the bowl and beginning the process of mopping up, keeping her head down.

'I won't ask what you two were doing,' Frieda said slowly, 'I'm not sure I'd like the explanation.'

'I was only trying to clean his jacket a bit,' Gertie said sulkily, on her hands and knees.

'I wasn't aware such were the duties of an acting detective constable,' Frieda observed. 'However, Frank can be unintentionally unorthodox at times.' She looked up at him as she sat down and crossed her legs. 'I have two pieces of news.'

'Two?' asked Frank in mock astonishment. 'Sounds like Christmas has come early.'

'Now, now, Frank. No need for sarcasm.'

Frank did not reply.

'Firstly,' Frieda continued, 'I had a call from our friend at the Ministry of Defence, Mr Harley, retired civil servant. He was most apologetic. It turns out that the Lancaster did indeed explode in 1945. Apparently the record was a bit smudged or something.'

Frank nodded.

'So we can probably rule out the Funnies, then,' he noted. 'I can't say I really believed there was anything strange about that explosion, apart from how it happened.'

Frieda didn't comment.

'So what's the second bit of news?' Frank asked.

Frieda paused before replying.

'We've just had a call. It appears that Albert Green has been taken to hospital with a heart attack. You weren't too heavy-handed with him, were you?'

'Not at all. We just asked him straight questions about his revolver.'

'Hmmm,' said Frieda slowly, wondering whether to believe

him, or even to appear as if she believed him. 'Well, apparently he's been asking for you. He has some information for you. Something he needs to get off his chest, I believe the phrase was.'

'How is he?'

'Not at all good, as far as I can tell. It doesn't sound as if he's going to last much longer.'

Frank stood up enthusiastically.

'Come on, Gertie,' he said. 'Confession time. I can feel it in my bones. Let's get to him before the old man with the scythe does.'

'I thought you didn't believe in hunches, Sarge.'

'When you have as many as me, one of them has to be right, sooner or later. Come on, you can even use that pretty flashing light they give us for when we want to break the speed limit.'

Gertie smiled. She liked using the pretty flashing light.

Frieda stepped out of the way, shaking her head in perplexity as she watched them race down the corridor. Watching Frank Summers in a hurry was a rare sight. His being dressed in a suit that looked like he'd slept rough in it for two weeks running was even rarer.

She could understand Gertie's trying to smarten him up. She had felt the same urge herself. She also felt like calling after him to tell him not to rush around like that, or he would hurt himself.

But it was too late.

* * *

Gertie brought the car to a halt outside the entrance to

Accident and Emergency with just a touch of screech of brakes to prove that she could. Frank hurtled out and she followed him. She followed him as he rushed through the automatically opening doors, racing toward the reception desk.

It wasn't quite a banana skin. It was an old porter with a bad back pushing an unoccupied wheelchair. What little training he had had did not include the expectation that a detective sergeant might suddenly appear out of nowhere coming towards him at full speed. He stopped, frozen.

Frank couldn't stop. He tried hurdling the wheelchair, and almost, almost made it. Just the tip of a dusty polished shoe caught one of the armrests and he spun over, flying for a few too brief seconds before hitting the polished floor, face down. He slid along the floor on his stomach scrabbling for hand-holds. A metal bucket, containing a mop and some liquid best not enquired into, slowed him down slightly. Finally a concrete pillar bounced off the side of his head, smashed into his shoulder, and stopped any further progress with agonising suddenness.

Two nurses on reception, a hall full of patients in various degrees of pain temporarily forgotten about, and an acting detective constable watched his acrobatics with fascination.

'I didn't know they were filming the Keystone cops here,' one nurse observed to the other.

Frank pulled himself up and hobbled over to the desk. Gertie joined him, a hand clamped over her mouth. He showed the nurses his warrant card.

'Detective Sergeant Summers. This is Detective Constable Gregson.'

'You were right, you know, it is the Keystone cops,' the second nurse said. Frank tried glaring at her. With his clothes now a complete mess, a wrist which felt like it contained at least two pulled muscles, a distinct feeling that something had hit him just above the eyebrow, and various other parts of his body lining up to complain, it wasn't an easy thing to do.

'Sergeant Summers,' said the other nurse, 'I know this is called Accident and Emergency, but that doesn't mean you actually have to have the accident here. I think it is the accepted norm of behaviour for people to have the accident elsewhere, and then we send one of our little ambulances out to collect them. It's all part of the service.'

She received her own glare. It came out as a grimace.

'Albert Green,' he said peremptorily. 'He was brought in a short while ago. Heart attack. Where can we find him?'

'If you don't calm down, Sergeant, you'll be having a heart attack all of your own. Now, let me see – second floor, ward D – '

'How do we get there?'

'Well, there's the lift, or, if you go through the doors there, the steps are on the left, go up to the second floor, turn right and – '

'Thanks. Come on Gertie.'

The nurses watched the two hurry towards the doors.

'I've seen it all before,' sighed the one. 'Ulcers before he's forty, dead from stress and overwork before he's fifty.'

'Pity, he looked sort of cute.'

'They normally do when they trip over wheelchairs and fall into buckets of cleaning fluid. He'll need stitches for that eye, though.'

'I think I'll pop up after them just to check.'

'No, you won't. It's my tea break.'

'During which you might just pop up to the second floor?'

'There is that possibility. In a purely professional capacity, of course.'

'Purely professional, my – '

'Yes, quite.'

* * *

Frank and Gertie found their way toward the room in which Albert Green lay, after having been further directed by a surprised doctor. As they got to the door a nurse and matron were coming out.

'You can't go in there,' the matron said sternly, closing the door firmly behind her.

'Detective Sergeant Summers,' Frank said, again producing his warrant card. 'And this is Detective Constable Gregson. We need to speak to Mr Green as a matter of urgency.'

She looked him up and down with a distinct look of distaste.

'You are a police officer?' she said in amazement, with great stress on the word "you".

'Look, I know I might be in somewhat of a state, nurse, but – '

'Matron. We still have them in Wellbury General.'

'Matron, yes, sorry. Look, Mr Green said he needed to speak to me. It's – '

'I would be extremely surprised if Mr Green said anything, Sergeant. He is certainly in no condition to.'

'How bad is it?'

Matron gave him a slow, appraising look.

'Is he a friend of yours?' she asked.

'That isn't quite the way I'd put it..'

'Well, in that case I shall speak frankly, Sergeant, but I don't want you passing this on to his wife.'

Frank looked through the observation porthole. In the room Elizabeth Green and Gwen Simmons sat looking at a bed, on which lay a body with tubes and wires coming out of it.

'Personally I doubt whether he'll see morning,' the Matron continued. 'In fact he could go at any minute. But the doctor has told Mrs Green that there is an outside chance of recovery. I disagree with letting them fool themselves, but, then, I am not a doctor.'

She looked at his face with a frown.

'I am a matron, however, and I will not let people walk around dripping blood all over my ward. It's extremely unhygienic. Nurse Proctor, take the Sergeant here and clean his face up. I think two stitches will do the trick. Three at the outside.'

'It's just a scratch,' Frank said, wiping his forehead. He looked down at his hand. It was covered in blood.

'Nasty things, cuts above the eye. They bleed like the devil. And you are not going to bleed around here. Take him away, nurse.'

'Look, Matron – '

'Sergeant Summers,' the Matron said softly but firmly, 'I meant what I said. Mr Green isn't going to be speaking to anybody soon. And it'll be a miracle if he ever speaks again.

You get along and get yourself seen to. There's nothing you can do here.'

Frank looked at her, recognising defeat when he saw it. He turned to Gertie.

'Stay here, Gertie,' he said. 'Just in case.'

The nurse took him to a small room at the end of the corridor. She sat him down and began cleaning his face gently. He winced. Apart from the cut above the eye, he could feel his cheekbone had collided with something solid.

'You police officers are so brave,' said the nurse. 'I've always admired the way you take risks for our sakes. To keep us – ' She blushed slightly. 'Well, safe and free, I suppose. I've often thought of writing a poem about that.'

Frank coughed in embarrassment. Not even Rupert Brooke could wipe away the reality.

'It wasn't quite like that,' he said, realising that the story would come out anyway. No doubt he would become known as the Flying Sergeant.

Flapper Frank of the Flying Squad.

Not so much The Eagle Has Landed as The Pigeon Has Plummeted.

He sighed.

'I tripped over a wheelchair, as it happens.'

'A wheelchair?'

'Then I slid along the floor until I hit a bucket and mop.'

'A bucket and mop?'

'And then a pillar stopped me. Concrete sort of thing. Not the sort of thing you want to have an argument with. They tend to win whatever you do.'

By this time she was laughing.

'I'm sure it was more heroic than that,' she said, clipping the ends off three stitches.

'I'm afraid not,' he replied, flexing his wrist and wincing.

'You've done something to your wrist?'

'Probably just pulled a muscle or two. Nothing serious. Should be okay within a day or two.'

'Let me have a look.' She pushed his sleeve back, prodding and manipulating, forcing him to gasp in pain.

'Mmm,' she said. 'Not too serious, but I think we'll put a wrist-brace on that. And you'll need to carry it in a sling for a few days.'

'Nurse, really, I don't – '

'If you don't believe me, I can get a doctor to have a look. Come to think of it, an X-ray might be in order.'

'A wrist-brace sounds just the thing,' he said weakly. Doctors would be the final straw. X-rays he could do without. He had no wish to sit in Accident and Emergency with total strangers for hours awaiting an appointment.

Only some of them wouldn't be strangers. He had already introduced himself, if somewhat informally.

He was sitting with his jacket off while the nurse tied an old-fashioned sling behind his neck when Gertie walked in.

'What are you doing here?' he asked abruptly. Gertie looked at the nurse, and then back at him. She shook her head.

'Matron was right, Sarge. Albert Green never made it.'

There followed a few seconds silence.

'Bugger,' he said. 'Bugger, bugger and bugger again.'

'He was a good friend of yours?' asked the nurse.

'He was my chief suspect.'

'Lucky for him then, in a way.'

Frank sighed again.

'That's one way of looking at it, I suppose.' He stood up slowly, feeling the weight of bruises and defeat. 'Come on, Gertie, nothing we can do around here. Let's get back to the station and call it a night.'

The nurse picked up his jacket and placed it around his shoulders.

'Take it easy for a few days,' she said.

'Don't worry, I will. It's one of my ambitions in life. Tell me, is there a way out of here without having to go back through Accident and Emergency? Just in case it's still packed with dangerous wheelchairs running around. Perilous pots and pails lurking in wait.'

She smiled.

'Go back down past where you found Matron and myself. There are some stairs just beyond there which will take you to the main entrance. And very few nasty wheelchairs. But be careful of the pots and pails, they get everywhere.'

They were just passing the room where Albert Green had recently passed away when Elizabeth Green and Gwen Simmons came out. Gwen was supporting a sobbing Elizabeth, oblivious to their presence. Frank and Gertie stopped in embarrassment. Gwen looked at Frank's appearance in astonishment.

'Um, we're very sorry to hear about your husband, Mrs Green,' Frank mumbled. She looked up.

'Oh, it's you Sergeant. I'm sorry you got here late. He did say he wanted to speak to you.'

'Though perhaps he might not have been here in the first place, if it wasn't for you,' said an angry Gwen Simmons.

'No, no, Gwen, dear,' Elizabeth Green said, patting her arm. She looked at Frank. 'His doctor warned him not to get excited. He said it was a miracle Albert had survived his first two attacks.' She sighed. 'It was only a matter of time. It wasn't your fault, Sergeant, it could have been anything.' She paused. 'That reminds me,' she said.

'Very kind of you to understand, Mrs Green,' Frank said as she searched for something in her handbag. He hoped he didn't sound as uncomfortable as he felt.

'Here we are, Sergeant, he asked me to give this to you if he didn't make it.' She handed him an envelope.

'What is it?'

'I don't know, Sergeant. And, quite frankly, I don't want to know. Oh.' She gave a weak smile. 'I suppose that was a pun of sorts, wasn't it? Your first name is Frank, isn't it?'

'It is,' he said, wondering if she had taken leave of her senses.

'Well, Sergeant, I'd like to go now, if I may. Gwen and I are going away for a few weeks. We don't want to be around when the news gets out. We'd just like to go somewhere and forget the whole business.'

'Of course, Mrs Green. Let us know if there's anything we can do to help.'

'Thank you, Sergeant. Come, Gwendolyn.'

Frank and Gertie watched the two women leave. Finally he looked at the envelope. He opened it, took out two sheets of typed A4 paper, and began to read.

'Anything interesting, Sarge?' asked Gertie. He shushed her until he finished. Then he looked at her, smiled, winced as his cheekbone said hello, and gave her a hug with his good arm.

'Gertie, my love, we've cracked it! We have our confession. Come, I'll tell you all about it on the way back. Our Frieda is going to be very pleased.' He looked at his watch. 'Seven thirty. Probably gone home. She'll have a surprise in the morning. A very pleasant surprise.'

* * *

'Blimey, Frank, looks like they got your already,' Eric Johns said as they walked into reception.

'You still on duty, Eric? Thought your shift ended ages ago.'

'Larry called in sick. I decided I could do with the overtime. Not much going on, anyway. So which one of them did the damage? Funny, that, I didn't see them leave. Must have gone out the back way.'

'They? Who would "they" be?'

The internal phone rang. Eric answered it.

'Yes, ma'am. Right away ma'am.' He put the phone down and looked at Frank. 'Frigid wants to see you immediately. She saw your car pull in just now. And I don't think she's very happy with you. In fact, I think it's reasonable to say that she is very, very unhappy with you. Furious, that's what I'd call it, furious.'

'What's she still doing here?'

'Ah, well, my son, now I could tell you a story.'

'Well, tell it, and hurry up before I do something you might regret.'

Eric Johns smiled and leaned forward, his elbows on the reception counter.

'Frigid was just about to leave, standing almost exactly where you are, just there, in that spot. And that's when your girlfriend turned up.'

'My girlfriend? Who would that be?' He paused as a thought struck home. 'Oh, shit! Oh bugger! Bugger! And triple bugger!'

'Yes, I thought you might feel that way. Something about a dinner? Someone had promised faithfully, word of honour, that he would be in place, all dressed up, bright and shiny and squeaky clean, at six-thirty on the dot? And here he is, looking like he's been through several bushes backwards, forwards and sideways, several times.'

'Well, okay, I messed up. I'll have to sort that out tomorrow. But what's it got to do with FF?'

'I don't think she's very happy about an officer's girlfriend turning up at the station to confess a murder she's about to commit. Takes a very dim view of that sort of thing.'

'Oh, well, another day, another bollocking. She'll get over it. Come on, Gertie, you can watch me being slaughtered.'

'Just one more thing, Frank,' Eric said with enjoyment that did not bode well for a certain Detective Sergeant. 'Frigid likes to take personal control. She invited Doctor Pleadle up to her office for a chat.'

'Wish I could have been a fly on the wall for that,' Frank said.

'Oh, I think you'll be something on the wall, my son,' Eric replied. 'You see, she's still up there.'

'Still up there?' Frank asked weakly. 'Both of them?'

'Both of them. Plus a large array of sharpened knives, I would imagine. Or possibly even blunt ones. Very, very blunt ones. Would you like me to order the ambulance now, or shall I wait until the extent of the injuries can be ascertained – just in case it's a hearse that's needed rather than an ambulance?'

Frank turned to Gertie.

'I don't suppose you'd go in first and ...'

'No chance, Sarge.'

'Oh, well,' he sighed, turning towards the path to execution, 'it is a far, far better thing I do now, etcetera.'

'You could play the wounded hero,' Gertie suggested, trailing after him.

'Falling over a wheelchair? Then sliding into a bucket, the contents of which I really don't want to know about? And finally crashing into a concrete pillar in front of a room full of the injured and dying – dying with laughter, that is?'

'They won't know that yet, Sarge.'

Frank paused in mid stride.

'Now there you have a point, Gertie my love. By the time they do find out I should have put some distance between us. Siberia sounds promising.'

'I'll come with you, Sarge,' Gertie promised.

He carried on, his spirits rising with every step. That tumble in the hospital was rather fortunate. In a strange way his luck was back in.

He walked into Frieda's office with a martyr's smile on his bruised and battered face. He was met by the looks of two women who have been sharpening scalpels in readiness for his arrival. Had they been the witches Macbeth had encountered, Duncan would still be alive. One look at those eyes and Macbeth would have left the country and gone to live as a hermit in a hole in the Holy Land.

The anger on their faces slowly turned to amazement as he greeted them breezily.

'Sorry I'm late,' he said, partly to both of them. 'A little accident. Nothing serious. Nothing that won't mend after a few days. Or a week or so. Doctor said I would be fine in a fortnight.'

'Frank, what on earth have you done to yourself?' asked Susan in a concerned voice.

'Call of duty, you know. Silly, really, just one of those things that happen.' He could hear Gertie stifling a giggle behind him.

Susan stepped up to him and checked the stitches above his eyebrow.

'You'll have a black eye tomorrow,' she noted. She felt his arm gently. 'Not broken, is it?'

'No, no, just a few pulled muscles. Honestly, it's nothing serious.'

'Now come here and sit down, Frank, you don't want to over-exert yourself. You can tell us all about it.'

'Well, there's something else you might be interested in,' he said, sitting down. He pulled the notes of A4 from his pocket with his good arm. 'Albert Green left this with his wife, to be passed on to us if he didn't make it.'

He looked at Susan and then at Frieda. He was tempted to ask if they were sitting comfortably before he began, but decided against it. He smoothed the sheets out on his leg and began to read.

'To Sergeant Summers, Wellbury Central Police Station

I have wanted to get this off my chest for a long time. Even though I thought I had got away with it all those years ago, it remained with me, every day. You see, I was the one who shot Alfie Simmons. You will not agree, but I still believe I was right to do so. I shall explain why. I hope you will understand.

Alfie and I were working a diamond racket, Holland to London. He would bring the stuff back to Wellbury, I would take it to London. Since he never went to London he wouldn't be a suspect if any of the stuff was discovered there, and if they did catch him in Wellbury, nobody would think of me, once they found out that Alfie had stolen my girlfriend. It wasn't easy for me, knowing that he was already married to Gwen when he married Elizabeth, but, in a way it made him more of a hero for me; he always took risks just for the sake of it – or, maybe he just didn't think the same way as normal people do. He was a strange character in many ways.

The trouble with Alfie is that he always had itchy feet. He would start a scam, then lose interest. Money never meant much to him, it was the scam itself. I never understood how he remained married to Gwen for so long, maybe that was the only stable thing in his life. Maybe he needed the one thing that never changed.

Or so I thought.

It was in May of 1964 that he told me he was giving it up. I thought he just meant the diamond smuggling, but it turned out he meant everything, Gwen, Elizabeth and his kids. I tried to argue him out of it, but Alfie never listened. Once he decided to do something he just did it, without further thought. I couldn't handle it. He had taken Elizabeth away from me, that was bad enough, but she seemed happy, and for that I was grateful. I used to see Gwen and the kids on the odd occasion, although they didn't know who I was. I always thought they seemed quite a happy family. Now he told me he was going to write them each a postcard and move on.

You see what I'm saying? He was going to ruin so many lives, just because he felt like something new, something different.

I met him coming back from the pub that night and convinced him to take a walk. I hadn't planned to shoot him, not as such. It was a total coincidence that I even had the revolver with me that night, I had just found it again at my parents' house. But when he absolutely refused to reconsider, I lost my temper.

I pulled out the revolver and shot him. It was the best way out, the only way out I could see. I couldn't let him do that to Elizabeth, nor Gwen. If his body were discovered the news of his bigamy would also. But if he simply disappeared, the police wouldn't put too much effort into it. Elizabeth and Gwen would presume he had run off. They would be hurt, but not as much as if they discovered what he had done.

I sent the postcard to Elizabeth myself last week. I don't know why. I panicked, I suppose. I realised afterwards that it was silly to hope that you might think the skeleton wasn't that of Alf Simmons just because a postcard arrived, seemingly from him. It was in his pocket the day I shot him. I had meant to post it then, but I had to go to London the following day, and forgot about it. By the time I remembered it was a year later, and Elizabeth was getting used to the idea that Alf had left for good, so it seemed best to forget it.

So, there you have it. It was the least worst thing to do. I hope that they will understand and forgive me. Please believe me that neither of them knew anything about it.

Yours Sincerely, Albert Green'

Frank finished reading, leaned forward and dropped the sheets onto Frieda's desk.

'So, there we have it,' he said.

Frieda picked up the two pages, put her glasses on, and scrutinised them.

'Not a very nice man,' commented Susan.

'Which one? Albert or Alfie?' asked Frank.

'Albert. Okay, Alfie was a bit of a rogue, but he did marry the women he loved. I've always thought that's the strongest expression of love a man can make.'

'What, getting married even when you're already married? If that's what women really want, I might try it sometime.'

She gave him a look.

'You watch your step, Frank Summers. You've managed to escape this time, but only just.'

Frieda stood up and came around to his side of her desk, leaned against it and looked down at him.

'Indeed, Frank, I think you can count yourself a lucky man. Just don't rely on it too much.' She smiled. 'The Chief Constable will be pleased. I think he might even attend the press conference tomorrow.'

'Er, I probably won't be able to make it,' Frank said, waving his injured arm slightly. 'Need to take it easy, as the doctor said.'

Frieda frowned at him, and then laughed, leaned forward and

ruffled his hair.

'Okay, Frank, just this once. I expect to see you first thing tomorrow to finalise details, but you can give the press conference a miss.'

'I suppose there's one thing we'll never know,' Frank mused.

'What's that?' asked Frieda.

'What really happened in 1945 – when that Lancaster blew up. Did Alfie survive the explosion, or was he not on board in the first place?'

They considered the idea for a few moments. Finally Gertie spoke up.

'I'd like to think that he managed to parachute down, and then decided he'd had enough, and just walked away from it all,' she said.

Frank smiled.

'Ever the romantic, Gertie,' he said, getting ready to stand up. 'I think he probably caught a different plane, and just took the chance to scarper when he found out everyone thought him dead. Seems he was that sort, from what we know. Still, the newspapers will make up their own stories, I suppose.'

'Come on, I'll take you home,' said Susan, giving him a hand. 'I think I'd better give you a check-over. That lot at A and E are too over-worked to do things properly.'

She noticed a look in his eyes.

'A medical check-over, Frank. I am a doctor, you know.'

Yes, Frank was tempted to say, but your patients are normally dead. He decided against it. It might give her ideas.

The other two watched them go, Gertie with a hangdog expression on her face.

'Don't worry, Gertie, it's not over until the fat lady sings,' Frieda said, putting on her coat.

'Ma'am?' asked Gertie listlessly.

'All's fair in love and war, Gertie, and the war's never over until the last battle. It's a great British tradition, losing most of the battles but winning the war.'

'If you say so, ma'am.'

'Oh, I do, I do indeed, Gertie. And in Frank's case I doubt if those two will get to his flat without war breaking out.'

Gertie brightened at the thought.

'Men may think they know what's best for them, Gertie,' Frieda continued, 'but they don't. It's up to us to change their minds. The time has come for a certain example of the species. And may the worst woman win.'

Gertie smiled at the thought. Frieda was right.

There was still a battle to be won.

Frank Summers was not yet done with.

Frank would not have liked that smile. Even less Frieda's.

Friday: A Summers storm looming

Frank sat in his chair, leaning back, heels on his desk, twirling a pencil through his fingers, singing softly to himself, 'oh the times, they are a-changing, it ain't me, my friend, I'm not the one you're looking for, the answer, babe, is blowing in the wind'.

Fortunately there were no Bob Dylan fans in earshot to be thoroughly discombobulated.

He was ready, at the slightest noise of anyone coming, to drop his arm back into its sling and adopt the pose of the injured hero. People had been amazingly considerate since his "terrible accident", especially the female officers. A few of the male officers weren't too happy at the attention he was getting, but he could handle that.

On the Wednesday evening Susan had driven him back to his flat. She had offered to come in to make sure that he was alright, but he had declined, having suddenly realised on the way back just how shattered he was. The lack of sleep the previous night combined with the excitement of the day, including assaulting a concrete pillar, had caught up with him. On the way he had hardly muttered more than a few words, and most of those were monosyllables. He had even been too tired to notice the anguished look on Susan's face as he trudged away from her car. After a long, hot bath he had collapsed into his bed and fallen asleep immediately.

On the Thursday morning the Chief Constable had been very appreciative of the result in the Dead Skeleton case, and the Chief Inspector had even given up some of his precious fishing time to attend the press conference. Frank had managed to slip Phil Walthers most of the results in time for the Herald's print run on the Friday – it turned out that Walther's fixed deadline was not as fixed as he had claimed – but it was a favour he thought could well bear fruit at some stage in the future. Certain facts not entirely relevant to the case had not been revealed, such as Little Alfie's questionable parentage and Heather Ronan's part in Alfie's history. Some things were best left alone.

Ironically the Herald's headline was to have been "Wellbury's Finest Bag Burglary Ring". At the very moment that he had been flying over a wheelchair Percy Hanson and Pete Phillips had been risking life and limb breaking into a house in University Heights following a lot of hard work and a tip-off about the burglaries they had been investigating. Finding incontrovertible evidence that the house was being used to store the proceeds of the burglaries they had called in reinforcements and then settled down to await anyone who should turn up. After a number of hours the gang had arrived, and, after a short but energetic refusal to come quietly, had been arrested. What should have been a page one triumph was quickly pushed onto page ten by the Dead Skeleton case. Frank felt almost guilty about it.

Even worse for Pete Phillips, he had taken a knee somewhere very painful, and could hardly walk. Such a wound was more likely to raise a snigger than sympathy; it was Frank, with his stitches, black eye and arm in a sling who was getting the attention.

Still, thought Frank, what can't be cured has to be endured.

Thursday afternoon he left work slightly early, claiming a desperate need for sleep, something not totally untrue, as the previous night's rest hadn't fully made up for Tuesday night, but also wanting to get away from the ministrations and sympathy. You really could have too much of a good thing, he had decided.

'Okay, Frank,' Frieda had said, 'I suppose one more day shouldn't make any difference.'

He hadn't quite understood that, but had gratefully disappeared before Gertie or anyone else could offer to drive him home and feed him chicken broth. Another long, hot bath, followed by a couple of cans of beer and the largest pizza the local pizzeria could offer and he fell into the sleep of the innocent. In the morning he had woken up feeling fully refreshed and confident that he could take on all that life and fate could throw at him.

After all, it was Friday, effectively the weekend already. What could possibly happen that he could not manage to avoid for the next few hours?

He heard Gertie's heels coming down the corridor. He considered slipping his arm back in its sling, but decided against it. Gertie wouldn't be fooled by the pose. She knew him too well.

She walked in carrying two mugs of tea.

'You should take more care of that arm, Sarge,' she said, 'you know what the doctor told you.'

'What is this?' he asked, dropping his feet and looking at the mug in front of him. 'Tea? Where's my coffee?'

'Too much coffee's bad for you. Tea's much more healthy.'

'You aren't trying to mother me, are you Gertie?'

'Someone has to,' she said, looking at him lounging in his chair. 'That chair okay, Sarge? Not giving you backache, is it? I could get you a cushion if you want.'

'Gertie, will you please stop it? I'm a big boy now. The only woman allowed to mother me is my mother, and the only reason she's allowed to do so is because I can't stop her.'

Gertie sat down and sucked her tea in wounded silence.

'I've been thinking,' he said.

'Painful, was it?'

'Very. Now that we've tied things up, the media are happy with their story, the Chief Constable thinks Wellbury can do no wrong, Frieda hasn't stopped smiling, well ...'

'Well what?'

'That confession was very convenient, wasn't it?'

'Convenient?'

'A typed confession. No handwriting to pick over, apart from a scrawled signature which could have been anybody's.'

'He said his handwriting was awful. His arthritis, remember?'

'Yes, but still. It's just too convenient.'

'Who else would have typed it out?'

'Only one person, isn't there? The same person who called the station to say Albert wanted to speak to me – though the Matron said he wouldn't have been able to speak to anybody.'

'He could have done it as he was having the attack, Sarge.'

'While he was having the attack? Pretty unlikely, I would have thought. And how convenient she has the letter on her when he dies. Why would she take the time to put it in her handbag while he's busy trying to breathe his last?'

'Could have had it there all along. Put it in there when he originally gave it to her, before his attack.'

'Gertie, would you mind not picking holes in my theories? Or, at least, not straight away. At least give them time to die of natural causes.'

'Sorry, Sarge, but they are full of holes, aren't they? I mean, you're suggesting that Mrs Green killed Alfie and used her husband's death to get him blamed for it?'

'Not just our Elizabeth Green. No, I've always been suspicious of the sudden friendship between her and Gwen Simmons. I think they knew each other all along. I'm convinced they were involved in Alfie Simmons' death.' He leaned forward. 'Albert Green claims he mislaid his revolver at his parents' house. Who used to visit his mother every other week or so? Elizabeth Green, or Simmons as she was then – it's quite possible that she already knew that her marriage to Alfie was illegal. That she had found out somehow.'

'She steals the revolver and uses it to shoot Alfie?'

'I think Gwen Simmons was the driving force. A very practical woman, our Gwen. She was also the one to suggest that lovely faked confession. I can see it now; "Look, Elizabeth, once Albert's popped his clogs, which he's going to do any day now, it won't do him any harm, he'll be dead". Elizabeth would have been in a tizzy, but finally agreed. Unless the tears were put on, and she was acting the whole time. Maybe she's a lot harder than we think.'

'I suppose Mrs Simmons could be capable of that,' agreed Gertie dubiously. She sighed. 'You can make it sound so plausible, Sarge. But I don't think FF is going to be happy. Here we've got the best result possible, and you're going to tell her, sorry, Frigid, you're going to have to tell the Chief Constable and the press that we've got it slightly wrong. Oh, and by the way, we have absolutely no evidence to prove it.'

'Do you have to call her Frigid? Not a very nice nickname. Anyway, I can think of a better one. Fatally Furious. Which is what, as you say, she would be if I did tell her what I think – or suggested that we should reopen the investigation. I'd probably find myself buried in a hole deep at night. Quite possibly the same one that Alfie found himself in. Frieda would re-open it specially for the occasion.'

'So you're not going to tell her? Thank heavens for that. I think you look much better in one piece.'

'Oh, I might tell her, but only as a possible theory. There's no way we're going to reopen the case. It wouldn't do any good to man nor beast.'

'Which one are you, Sarge?'

'Very funny. For that you can have the illuminating experience of taking Alfie Simmons' files to be archived.'

'Okay, Sarge,' she smiled. 'I'll do anything for you.'

'Buttering me up will do you no good, Acting Detective Constable Gregson.'

She made a face.

'Back to uniform on Monday. Pity, I've enjoyed working with you.'

'Files, Constable Gregson, files to archive. And take the butter with you.'

'Right, Sarge. Oh, there are some notes in your in-tray.' She picked up the files and left in a happy mood.

Notes? he thought. Dangerous things. They normally involved that four-letter word, work And look at where that had got him over the past couple of weeks, a member of the walking wounded.

Never look into your in-tray on a Friday. You might end up staying late, and quite possibly find yourself working the Saturday as well, as he knew from experience.

He took a peek at his in-tray. On top of files, memos and folders were three letters.

Letters. Letters weren't dangerous, were they? They were the sort of thing you could file and forget. Pass on to the relevant department, i.e. someone else.

The first one was unaddressed. He picked it up, sniffed it, put it down in front of him and watched it suspiciously for a while to see if it tried to move. Then he took the plunge and opened part of the flap to see if he could read it without opening it. Finally he went the whole hog and took a single sheet of paper out.

"Sarge

Just wondered if you fancied drinks tonight after work. You know, as a sort of celebration. And seeing as how I'm back in uniform on Monday. I'd really like it if you would.

xx

Gertie"

Well, well. He smiled to himself. Dear old Gertie, too shy to ask him straight out.

Funny girl.

Of course they could go out for drinks after work. She deserved a little celebration. So did he, come to it. Two colleagues toasting success. Very fitting.

He might even buy her some flowers to show his appreciation of her work.

He wondered if Gertie would like flowers.

He took the second envelope and opened it with much less concern. He decided he quite liked letters.

"Frank

I'd like to take you out for drinks after work to show how much I appreciate your hard work. And, seeing as it's your celebration, you can choose where. I'll even suffer one of those terrible pubs you prefer.

Yours

xx

Frieda"

Not so good. Not that he wouldn't have minded – in fact he would have rather looked forward to it. But it meant disappointing Gertie, and he didn't want to do that.

Perhaps the three of them could have drinks together?

Hmm, an Inspector, a Sergeant and an Acting Detective Constable. Gertie would feel obliged to call him Sarge and Frieda Ma'am, and he could hardly call Frieda "Frieda" in front of Gertie. Not the stuff of social success.

It was a dilemma.

He picked up the third envelope. Dilemmas normally resolved themselves if you ignored them long enough.

"Dearest Frank

I know I should have trusted you and not come charging around to the station on Wednesday evening, embarrassing both of us. I don't blame you for being angry with me when I drove you home on Wednesday. So I'm going to make up for it. We'll start with drinks after work, and then go on to dinner, my treat. Just to make sure you don't get lost again I'll meet you at the station, half-five, prompt.

See you then

xx

Susan"

He had been angry with Susan? He wondered when that had happened.

But the thing about being on the horns of a dilemma, Frank thought as he looked at the three sticks of dynamite the letters had turned into, is that there are only two of them.

Can you be on the horns of a trilemma?

He had to choose one.

But which one?

Who did he really fancy?

No, he decided, it would have to be Susan. He didn't want to upset Gertie, but ... he didn't want to upset Gertie.

And he didn't want to turn Frieda down. Drinks with Frieda rather appealed.

Could all four of them go for drinks?

Yes, but he'd probably have to pay for the damage and for the carpet to be cleaned afterwards. If he survived.

Glancing up he noticed the photograph of Alfie pinned to the board.

What would Alfie have done?

Definitely not accepted three invitations at once.

A light bulb glowed suddenly in his brain.

Of course.

Obvious, really.

A prior engagement.

That way he could apologise, be incredibly regretful, but sure that they understood, and why not organise another time? Susan on Saturday, Frieda, Sunday lunch, Gertie, Sunday dinner. None of them need know about the others.

But the prior engagement had to have two qualities.

Firstly one he could not plausibly break without being rude, an engagement with someone who had done him a favour recently, or something close to a favour.

Secondly with someone they wouldn't object to him having a few sociable drinks with, i.e. no competition. Either another bloke or something like a nun. Something like ...

He smiled to himself.

Frank, my son, if there is one thing you are really, really good at, he told himself, it's getting out of deep holes.

With an unerring skill he chose the worst possible option.

He picked up the phone and dialled a number.

'Hi, is that Tracey? About those drinks I mentioned ...'

After all, she was gay, wasn't she? Gertie had said so.

Other novels by Bill Dughaille:

The FFSG series (aka the Wellbury Chronics)

The Eighty-five-percenters

The second in the FFSG series.

Detective Sergeant Frank Summers is faced with an unexpected crisis as the staid citizens of the genteel town of Wellbury rapidly descend into disorganised anarchy after a sociology professor announces on radio that eighty-five percent of the population will die in a coming cull. The prediction appears to be coming true as apparently total strangers are felled one by one according to a list of the ten-most-disliked Wellburians, from nagging neighbours to estate agents ... and the police, at a poorly performing number ten. But Frank fails to realise that there is a graver danger closer to home. Three women have decided that he is their responsibility: his boss, his constable and the local pathologist have agreed to become best of enemies. Now they intend to re-arrange his fate the way it should be. And they aren't asking anyone's permission.

Fakes, Fraud and Deception

The third in the FFSG series.

Detective Sergeant Frank Summers is in the doghouse, despite having recently arrested an internationally sought con-artist. And since he is in the doghouse he has no intention of pointing out that there is something very strange about the attractive French police woman who has come to interview the arrested man, not to mention the two detectives claiming to be from Scotland Yard. Oh, no, he is going to stay well out of the way this time. Definitely.

Jokers

The fourth in the FFSG series.

The doctors have pronounced Detective Sergeant Frank Summers physically fit following recovery after his shooting, but his colleagues fear that his sense of humour was extracted along with the bullet. They are, as always, more than willing to interfere in his life in the pursuit of a good cause. If that wasn't enough, a bunch of criminals calling themselves the Joker Gang are laughing at him, the university students are creating mayhem during their rag week, and someone called The Shocker is trying to kill him. The only advantage is that it take his mind off of the ultimatum the three women in his life have given him, one that he has only until the Sunday to resolve. Or leave town.

Prophecies

The fifth in the FFSG series.

Detective Sergeant Summers is under a hex, otherwise known as his colleagues. First they don't want him to get married, then it is imperative it must happen. Then they decide that a prophecy has been made which threatens the wedding. They don't believe in prophecies, but aren't sure that prophecies understand that. So they'll have to Do Something About It. And if their bumbling efforts aren't enough to ensure he never makes it to the altar, he has to cope with visiting aliens and resident ghosts. He does have tiny Squishy to protect him, but what match can even this plucky little kitten be against a prospective mother-in-law?

Loonymoon

The sixth in the FFSG series.

The Inspectors Summers have tied the knot and embarked on their honeymoon in a small family-run hotel in Normandy. She has very definite ideas of what she wants out of a honeymoon: to set a seal on their love, and to form a foundation for life-long devotion. He just wants to nick a French police officer's kepi. He had a Bobby's helmet nicked from him once by a French girl while he was on crowd duty one New Year's Eve in London, and now he intends to return the favour. Neither is about to achieve their aim unless they can solve the mystery of the woman in the bath and the missing heroin. Which means pitting their minds against the French Inspectors Simenon. That's Mr and Mrs Simenon, whose marriage has gone beyond the rocks and is now beating itself to death against humdrum reality. One or either or both or neither could be the guilty crumpet. More importantly, is their marriage a portent of what could become of the Loonymooners? Ultimately the decisive question could well be: which side do the peas go?

Others:

The Window

Jim Allbright, ex-bobby and now easy-going window washer, innocently responds to an advert for window washing placed in the newspaper by the local council. The response is a torrent of paperwork, political correctness and a computer system doing exactly what it was told to do, but not quite what was intended. But if the system cannot be beaten, the interchange of letters can be used to have a little fun and get to know some of the people struggling behind it. There's Sandi, who signs herself as "(pp the Administrator)"; her four-year old little angel Helen; Graham, a shadowy computer programmer who definitely has too much time on his hands, and a slew of Project Managers and Senior Administrators eager to ensure standards are upheld no matter how many problems they create. Against a run of bad luck and circumstances Jim and Sandi aim to meet up one day, eventually. Hopefully. The window might even get washed. Maybe.

Diary of a Sane Man

In a cross between 'Last Of The Summer Wine' and 'One Flew Over The Cuckoo's Nest', set against a backdrop of the brave new world of New Labour's end of honeymoon, Fred is the Last Cynical Optimistic Realist.

Believing that he's found the perfect niche – three square meals a day plus all the newspapers he can read just for occasionally pretending to be mad – he's not going to be the one to rock the apple cart. Oh, no.

Safe from the wiles of women and the woes of the world, he's not going to rock the boat. Oh, no.

No, he's just going to sit and observe, and comment quietly on the insanity of life outside.

Well, maybe just little one tug of the loose strand of wool on life's jersey ...

Did you know they elected a monkey as mayor in Hartlepool?

The Weekend At Longwood

A whodunnit in the classic sense, set against the backdrop of World War II and the trials, tribulations and romances of nine suspects.

A group of friends get together during the last weekend of August 1939 at the rural retreat named Longwood, just a few miles from Portsmouth. They are there to celebrate the last time they will see Georgina Riley, famed American novelist and socialite, for some time, as she is scheduled to leave for her native New York in order to marry her childhood sweetheart. During the afternoon they good-humouredly assign to each other the most suitable names of the nine muses, the daughters of Zeus and Mnemosyne:

Calliope: the muse of epic poetry and rhetoric

Clio: history

Erato: love poems and mimicry

Euterpe: lyric poetry

Melpomene: tragedy

Polymnia: hymns to the gods and heroes

Terpsichore: dance

Thalia: comedy

Urania: astronomy, astrology and prophecy

The following morning Georgina is discovered in her bedroom covered in blood, her throat slit, barely alive. Her American maid is dead. A tiara Georgina had been flaunting the day before has disappeared.

Detective Inspector Rudman arrives to investigate. But with Georgina in a coma and no solid evidence there is little he can do apart from haunt their lives. With Germany's invasion of Poland a week later they disperse across the land, some to the air-force, some to the army, others to reserved civilian jobs.

But Rudman does not give up. Wherever they are he can be found. Whatever other duties he is tasked to, he will find time to keep tabs on them. Whatever the defeats and victories of the Allied cause, he has only one aim: to find the person responsible for the murder done that weekend in Longwood.

The war ends; some of the Muses have survived, some not. Some have prospered, some married, some matured, others have found despair. And then comes invitation to spend another weekend at Longwood. The message is that Rudman has found the evidence he has been looking for.

And so one of the surviving couples motor slowly down to Portsmouth, remembering the original weekend, the trials and the tribulations of the past years, and wonder: what will be revealed during the coming weekend at Longwood?

Firelight

A modern-day tale of an ordinary family gathering at Christmas; the good, the bad, the dysfunctional and the forgotten.

George Browne and his wife Winifred have retired to a large, run-down pile in the country. Rumour has it that it was once the abode of a mad aristocratic family with a penchant for Satanism, and that both they and their victims still haunt the corridors. Other rumours are that it was a lunatic asylum for much of the nineteenth and twentieth century, and bodies of the inhabitants are buried around the large gardens in unmarked graves.

The Brownes are an unremarkable retired couple who, depending on who you might ask, have bought it as an investment, or alternatively as somewhere with enough bedrooms to accommodate their children, grand-children, and the little baby great-grandchildren. Too often in the past excuses have been made at special times, the most common of which has been of the "I don't want to put you to any trouble" variety. That excuse can no longer hold water.

Now it is approaching Christmas. Winter has set in, but the house is snug with oil heaters and real fires. As the various relations arrive, or don't arrive, it becomes clearer why invitations might have been refused in the past. The men of the family believe in having their way. The women of the family are strong-willed in their own different ways, and have various means of getting what they want.

The guests of the family - friends, boyfriends, girlfriends, wives and husbands - discover that their partners have a totally different side to them as the explosive hatreds of long-nurtured fights and feuds simmer to the surface before quickly boiling over.

One evening Winifred Browne encourages them to each tell a story as they sit in the lounge with the large fire warming them, the television off, no access to broadband, computers or mobile connections. Reluctantly at first they begin. As each evening passes: with different members taking turns, they announce in stories the feelings and hopes they cannot voice in public.

Finally it's the turn of Winifred Browne. Her story will be the one that tells them who they are, where they come from, and maybe why they have turned out the way they have.

For further details on these visit:

www.dughaille.info